Sweet Reckoning

Eugenia Riley

WARNER BOOKS

A Warner Communications Company

WARNER BOOKS EDITION

Copyright © 1987 by Eugenia Riley
All rights reserved.

Cover illustration by Melissa Duillo Gallo

Warner Books, Inc.
666 Fifth Avenue
New York, N.Y. 10103

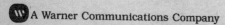 A Warner Communications Company

Printed in the United States of America

First Printing: December, 1987

10 9 8 7 6 5 4 3 2 1

In loving memory of my mother,
Elizabeth Gaines Riley.
She would have liked this one, I think.

The author extends special thanks to:

Charlou Dolan of Rolla, Missouri, for being the world's best instant, condensed research guide.

Professor Wayne Bledsoe, Rolla Archives, University of Missouri, for showing me *The Story of Rolla, Missouri*, by Dr. and Mrs. Clair V. Mann, which was most helpful to me in establishing the setting of this story.

Lonna Stephenson, Liz Denker, Linda Modesitt, and all the wonderful, friendly people of Rolla, Missouri.

Heartfelt appreciation to everyone at Warner Books for believing in my writing, and especially to my editors Claire Zion and Beth Lieberman, for so much enthusiastic help and support on this book!

BOOK

++

One

One

✦

Ayoung woman stood at the window of the modest St. Louis home, her bitter brown eyes fixed upon the deserted dirt street beyond, her fists clenched at her sides. Emptiness—no one in sight. Only a scant cloud of dust swirling down Twenty-fifth Street in the autumn breeze. Damn Lacy Garrett! He could not do this to her again, he simply couldn't! This was the third time the mercurial peddler had promised to come back and marry her, the third time he had made a fool of her—

"Amy Louise, where is my broth?" came an insistent, shrill voice from deep inside.

With a resigned sigh, Amy Harris turned from the parlor window and called toward the back of the tiny house, "In a moment, Ma." A wave of sadness swept her. Here it was midafternoon, and her mother was just now stirring. Esther Harris was having another bad day of it; no doubt following too much alcohol the night before. Amy wished she could ignore her mother's demand just this once, yet her sense of decency, as well as her religious convictions, forbade this. And she well knew her younger sister Hannah would suffer grievously for her own defiance if Amy disregarded the old woman's dictates.

Amy crossed the small parlor, her long gingham skirts

rustling on the threadbare rug, and entered the central hallway, heading for the kitchen behind the dining room. She found Hannah at the cast-iron kitchen sink rinsing the dinner dishes. Wearing a long gray housedress and a white apron, the little girl turned to smile at her sister as the older girl entered the room. Hannah, at ten, was a miniature version of Amy herself—both girls had long curling blond hair, deeply brown eyes, and pleasing, oval faces. But Hannah's young figure only hinted at the full womanly curves now so well defined in Amy.

"Is the chicken broth ready for Ma?" Amy asked her sister.

"Yes. On the stove." Hannah wiped her hands on her apron. "I'll take it to her."

"No, I will," Amy insisted firmly. More gently, she added, "You're busy, honey." Actually, whether Hannah was busy or not, Amy did her best to see that her sister was shielded from Esther Harris's volatile presence as much as possible.

Taking an earthenware bowl from a cabinet, Amy went to the iron stove, careful not to brush any part of her body against the burning-hot metal surface as she ladled chicken broth into the bowl. Hannah watched her. "Any sign of Lacy?" the young girl asked wistfully.

Amy turned to her sister, shaking her head, her jaw clenched. "I've been wondering all morning if he doesn't take a certain perverse pleasure in humiliating me."

Hannah's expression was crestfallen. "Amy! Why, Lacy's been your friend all your life and—I know he loves you so."

"Oh? Does he?" Amy returned irritably. "Is that why he has stood me up on three occasions now?" Then, noting her sister's wounded expression, she immediately added, "Hannah, I'm sorry. I know you like him."

"I do—and so do you, sister. You're just angry right now," Hannah asserted. The child came to her sister's side and placed a placating hand on the older girl's sleeve. "It must be so hard for Lacy to know when he'll be back to St.

Louis, his being a peddler and all. Maybe he just got caught up somewhere.''

"Hmmph!'' Amy finished ladling the soup and set the steaming bowl down on top of the nearby dry sink, turning again to her sister. "You mean he got caught up losing all his earnings in another poker game! That takes time and effort, I'll grant.'' Taking a spoon from one kitchen drawer, a linen napkin from another, she added, "Hannah, we may as well face it. He's three days late now. He's simply not coming.''

"Amy, I'm sure—''

"*Amy Louise!*''

Both girls half jumped as Esther Harris's annoyed voice again rang out from a rear bedroom. "I must see to Ma, before she does harm to herself,'' Amy told her sister tiredly.

Hannah nodded and returned to her chores at the sink. Amy remained behind a moment, feeling a stab of guilt as she watched her sister resume work, watched the thin young shoulders visibly sag. Hannah adored Lacy, and Amy knew her blunt words had disappointed the young girl. Yet she couldn't protect her sister from the truth forever. Lacy Garrett had deserted his fiancée. And that was that.

As their mother's harsh cry rang out for a third time, Amy took the bowl of broth, the spoon and napkin, and hurried from the room into the hallway.

The Harris home consisted of five cramped rooms—a parlor and dining room spanning the front of the house, with a kitchen and covered porch stretching behind on one side, two bedrooms on the other side. Although the more opulent homes in 1873 St. Louis boasted indoor plumbing, the Harris women had only the pump in their kitchen, the other "convenience'' being the small building in the yard behind the house.

Yet Esther Harris, with her supposedly chronic dyspepsia, seldom left the confines of her bedroom, and so, as Amy entered her mother's darkened room, her nostrils were immediately assailed by the foul odor of the chamber pot.

Amy steeled herself against a rising wave of nausea while her eyes struggled to adjust to the darkness. At last she spotted her mother, a huddled figure on the narrow iron bed.

Setting the soup down on the plain wooden dresser, Amy went to the window. She drew open the dusty drapes and raised the sash, letting in a crisp afternoon breeze. At once, her mother's tinny voice protested, "No, you fool, draw the drapes at once! The light is killing my eyes! And close that confounded window. Are you trying to give me my death of a chill?"

Struggling to hold on to her patience, Amy turned to face her mother. Esther Harris was partially upright now, shielding her eyes with a trembling, liver-spotted hand. In her soiled linen gown, she presented a totally unattractive figure—her stomach grotesquely large, her limbs gaunt, her once blond hair a filthy, gray-streaked rust. But her sallow, leathery skin was the most visible proof of her dissipation. The other proof was the empty bottle of Dr. Hammond's Stomach Bitters on the bedside table. Each day, come rain or shine, Esther sent Amy or Hannah to Ferguson's Apothecary on Cass Avenue for a new bottle of the patent medicine to which she had long ago become addicted. Both Amy and her sister had known for some time that any medicinal value in the tonic was lost on Esther; the old woman drank it for the alcohol alone.

Firmly Amy replied to her mother, "Ma, the room must be aired; the atmosphere in here is—er—stale. As for the fresh air, it will do you naught but good, I'm sure." With this pronouncement, she walked back to the dresser and picked up the bowl of soup. Crossing the room and sitting down on the straight chair next to Esther's bed, Amy handed her mother the napkin, bowl and spoon. Esther grunted without thanking her daughter, and began to feed herself the broth. But the older woman's hands trembled quite badly, and the bowl shook, spilling scalding soup on Esther's gown. She gasped in pain. Amy quickly took the bowl from her. "I'll hold this for you, Ma," she said dully, holding the bowl steady and within reach of her mother's spoon.

Depressing though it was to be in her mother's presence, Amy was glad she was ministering to the old woman's needs today, and not Hannah. Looking down at the steaming soup she held in her hands, Amy fought a welling sense of outrage as she recalled the last time her little sister had fed their mother. The old woman had gone into a fit and tossed a cup of tea in the child's face! Thank heaven the tea was not hot enough to do any real damage to Hannah. Amy had vowed nevertheless that that was one temper tantrum her mother would never be allowed to repeat!

Esther studied her daughter through narrowed green eyes. "So the ne'er-do-well Lacy Garrett has failed to come rescue you, eh, missy?" she asked.

Amy glanced sharply at her mother, stunned by the question. Finally, Amy managed to sputter, "I have no idea what you're talking about."

"Don't lie to me, missy," the old woman gritted. "Don't you think I hear you and your brat sister talking at night through these walls, that I don't know the horrible things you say about me?" The old woman laughed heartily. With sadistic relish, she went on, "I'm not surprised Garrett has sought his pleasures elsewhere—as I told you before, a man loses all respect for a whore."

Amy's high cheekbones flamed with color, and her eyes shot deep brown sparks at her mother's unjust accusation. Although Amy tried her best to employ Christian patience in ministering to her parent, she would not swallow her verbal abuse. With all the control she could muster, Amy told her mother, "Ma, if my presence makes you this unhappy, I'm afraid you'll have to feed yourself."

Amy moved to put the soup down on the nightstand, but Esther, evidently assuming her daughter sought to deprive her of needed nourishment, grabbed for the bowl. The action sent scalding soup splashing onto Esther's middle, and the old woman shrieked obscenities. With a maddened strength that amazed her daughter, Esther wrenched the sloshing bowl from Amy's hands and sent it flying across the room. It shattered explosively against the wall. Then the raving old woman drew back her hand and slapped Amy full across the face, something she had not dared to do in many months.

Reeling from the physical blow, Amy was at first too stunned to react. She stared blankly at the rabidly glowing eyes that raged back at her in triumph. Amy thought of striking her mother back, but realized that Esther would very likely vent her spleen on Hannah. So instead Amy turned to flee the room, her cheek throbbing. Esther's maniacal laughter followed her to the door, mixed with the hissed invective, "Whore!" At the portal, Amy turned as something snapped inside her at her mother's cruelty. "You're driving me away, Ma—and Hannah with me!" she warned the old woman in a voice trembling with anger. "And that's quite foolish of you, because you really need us. Is that what you did to Pa?"

"You little hussy!" the old woman shrieked back, shaking a fist at her daughter. "Need you? I don't need you or your leech of a sister! You can both rot in hell, for all I care! As for that bastard Abel Harris, he left because he was just like you, missy, weak and dissolute." Her eyes holding a bright gleam of lunacy, the old woman went on, "But no matter, I have the answer. I know what the Good Book says. 'If thine eye offends thee, pluck it out.' And both of mine eyes offend me!"

Now Amy could only shake her head in horror. She had no idea how to respond to her mother's bizarre outburst, so she hurried out of the room, the sickening echo of Esther's crazed laughter in her ears. She closed the door behind her and leaned against the panel to catch a deep breath. Amy had a sinking feeling. She well knew she could defend herself against her mother now, if necessary, but she never completely lost her worries for Hannah.

Amy headed back for the parlor, unable as yet to face cleaning up her mother's mess. Rubbing her throbbing cheek with her fingertips, she desolately wondered what she and Hannah were to do. The two girls were at Esther Harris's mercy for a roof over their heads. Amy knew now, unequivocally, that she could not count on Lacy Garrett to rescue her and her sister; and Amy's father, Abel Harris, had not been home since his first leave during the Civil War—eleven years before. The only alternative for Amy was to leave and take Hannah with her. But how could she support the two of them? Here at the Harris home, the three women managed to eke out a living by taking in laundry and sewing. Yet if Amy left with Hannah, she would have to start afresh, which meant she would have to have money. She had no funds of her own, nor any real skills, either. Her education had been catch as catch can, adding up to a few years in the St. Louis public schools. For a young woman in her position, the only viable alternative was marriage. And Lacy Garrett had turned that option into an impossibility.

Walking to the front of the house, Amy again stared out at Twenty-fifth Street through one of the narrow windows that flanked either side of the front door. Yet this time, her heart lurched with wild longing as she caught sight of a distant buggy starting down the dirt street. At the front of the conveyance sat a man wearing a wide-brimmed hat. Could it be. . . ?

Yet her expectations were dashed as the rig grew closer, and she realized that the long-legged, broad-shouldered man in the buggy could not possibly be Lacy Garrett. No, this stranger was much more muscular than Lacy, and surely taller by at least several inches.

Nonetheless, Amy watched the approaching newcomer with a fascination born of forlorn hope. As the little brown horse drew the rattling carriage closer, she caught a hint of his features beneath the brim of his hat—a tanned, handsome face, with a strong square jaw, long straight nose and deeply set eyes that she couldn't, under the shadow of his hat, see well enough. It struck her that there was something vaguely familiar about him. He wasn't Lacy, yet his presence did produce a spark of recognition in her mind. Who was he? Where had she seen him before? And could this stranger actually be coming to the Harris home?

* * *

The man in the buggy was, indeed, coming to the Harris house, though for reasons Amy Harris might never guess. Matt Kendall was on his way east to Virginia to meet an eager, "marriageable" young woman his sister had recently written him about. The young bachelor now owned a prosperous farm near Rolla, Missouri, ninety miles southwest of St. Louis, and he had recently decided it was high time for him to seek a bride to help him with his land, with whom to start a family. Thus, Matt Kendall had boarded the Atlantic and Pacific Railroad in Rolla this morning to begin his journey east. But at the St. Louis station, he had disembarked and rented a carriage, heading for a familiar neighborhood. Painful as it was, he knew he had a matter of conscience he must face up to here in this city.

As Matt directed the horse down the bumpy street with its scattering of trees, studying dismal row houses crunched together like so many wooden crates, he thought of why he was returning to this St. Louis neighborhood, which held many bitter memories for him. Twelve years before, he had been a carefree seventeen-year-old, living in a house with his parents and sister in a more fashionable area just a few blocks from here. That house was gone now, but the memories would always haunt him, the searing recollection of how the War Between the States had changed his life tragically and irrevocably.

Matt thought back to those painful days. In Missouri, the news of war had pitted citizen against citizen, and bitterness ran particularly high in the St. Louis area. Matt's family had favored slavery, even though the bulk of the St. Louis citizenry did not. A clash between warring factions in the city became inevitable; and, disastrously, both Matt's father and uncle were killed in a skirmish with Pro-Unionists during the early days of the war. And as Matt and his younger sister reeled from the loss, Matt's mother became ill with pneumonia, succumbing ultimately not to the malaise, but, Matt was sure, to a broken heart.

Of course, neighbors had tried to help the young man and his sister, and none was more compassionate or caring than

Abel Harris, whom the Kendalls knew from church. With Abel's help, Matt sold his father's business and home, placed his sister with a trustworthy maiden aunt in Virginia, and later enlisted, along with Harris, in the Confederate cause.

But early in the war Abel and Matt, along with another member of the St. Louis brigade, Lacy Garrett, had hooked up with Quantrill's faction and begun raiding towns and homesteads sympathetic to the North in the Kansas-Missouri border region. At first, the taste of revenge had been sweet in Matt's mouth, his only worry the deadly animosity that was developing between him and Lacy Garrett. Yet that day in Lawrence, Kansas, when Quantrill's band suddenly emerged as little more than a gang of cutthroats, it was again Abel Harris who came to Matt's rescue, saving the eighteen-year-old from making what could have been a fatal choice in life. . . . Even now, Matt shuddered at violent memories that frightened and shamed him. He well knew that he owed Abel Harris a huge debt of gratitude, and he had never really thanked the older man for his caring and guidance during those years. Today he would own up to that responsibility. . . .

Leaving his sad recollections, the young farmer drew his horse to a halt in front of the graying picket fence and climbed out of the buggy. He opened the ancient, creaky gate. The yard was full of frail, shedding trees and scatterings of unraked leaves, and the small house, he noted, had grown quite gray and ramshackle over the years. The cracked wooden steps leading to the porch groaned beneath the pressure of his boots. Matt crossed the weathered planks of the gallery and knocked on the wooden door. Waiting for an answer, he removed his hat, drawing a hand through his thick blond hair.

After a moment, the door opened, and a beautiful young woman appeared before him. Matt swallowed hard, and for a moment all he could do was stare at her.

Her housedress was of faded blue gingham, old and patched, yet she would have been stunningly beautiful in the most tattered rags. She was fairly tall with a pleasing, willowy figure, a lovely oval face, straight, delicate nose and wide mouth. Her hair absolutely amazed him—long, well past her shoulders, and beautifully curling in layer after layer of thick, golden waves. A distant memory of a six-year-old child with similar hair leapt into his mind. Could he be looking at Abel Harris's young daughter, now twelve years older?

All these images and thoughts crowded Matt's mind in a mere fraction of a second. And in that same electric moment, Amy's eyes locked with his, their brown orbs slamming him with a sensation he'd never known before. Her eyes were simply incredible—deeply set, vibrantly, gorgeously deep brown, shaded by long, dark lashes and surprisingly dark, yet delicate, eyebrows. As much as the beauty of her eyes amazed him, the expression they reflected was soul-searing, for he saw there many powerful, unaccountable emotions—anger, hurt, vulnerability, and pride, all of which made him strangely long to take her in his arms. She stepped forward slightly now, inclining her face inquisitively toward the light, and he was amazed at the silken glow of her youthful skin. Yet, studying her illuminated visage, he also now noted the fading shadow of a welt across her lovely cheek, as if a hand had been viciously applied to her tender young face. Outrage rose up in him like bile. Who had dared to strike her? The question filled him with an anger so vivid it hit him like a physical blow, even as he wondered at the intensity of it. . . .

As Matt studied the young woman, Amy, in turn, appraised him. Whoever this man was, he was tall and magnificently handsome, and despite the fact that Amy knew her behavior was unseemly, she found herself staring at him quite boldly. He looked about six feet tall, very muscular and tan. Everything about him was quite male and appealing, from his beautiful strong hands with their long, tanned fingers, to his superbly sensuous mouth. The cut of his brown suit accentuated his sinewy frame, and his handsomely tooled boots, gold satin vest and black wool cravat bespoke his refinement. And the gentle strength in his deep-set brown eyes hinted to Amy that he was responsible, even trustworthy. Just by looking at this stranger, Amy instinctively knew that here was a man who would stand by his promises. The realization fascinated her, and she found herself trembling slightly from just being in his presence. She was no doubt gaping at him like a fool, she thought, yet she couldn't take her eyes off him.

Finally, the man cleared his throat, ending the charged moment. Nodding at Amy with a smile, he said in a deep, if strained, voice, "Afternoon, ma'am."

"Afternoon," she murmured back. Breaking out of the spell, she stammered, "May—may I help you, sir?"

"Why, yes, ma'am," he returned politely, shifting his stylish felt hat from one hand to the other. "Can you tell me if this here is Abel Harris's house?"

A chill fell over Amy at the stranger's words. So that was why this man looked so familiar! She clutched at a distant memory of herself at six, watching her father in the parlor talking calmly to an embittered seventeen-year-old boy who had just lost his parents at the start of the Civil War. The memory was vague and fleeting, and she couldn't even recollect the reason the young man's parents had died. Could that boy be the man who stood before her now?

"Ma'am?" the stranger now prodded, noting her preoccupied expression. "I mean, if I'm at the wrong house . . ." His words trailed off lamely.

Amy quickly pulled herself from her swirling thoughts. "No, you're not at the wrong house. This is Abel Harris's home, all right. In fact, I'm Amy Harris, Mr. Harris's daughter. And you're . . . ?"

"Matt Kendall, ma'am."

She offered the stranger a sad smile. "Well, Mr. Kendall, I wish I had better news for you. I'm afraid my father has not lived with us for eleven years. I have no idea of his whereabouts."

The man sighed, his features sagging. "Oh, I see. Well, then, I'm sorry to bother you, Miss Harris. I guess in that case . . ." Again, his words trailed off as he shifted his weight, the worn boards of the porch creaking beneath his boots.

Amy didn't know what prompted her to make the next move. Perhaps it was the disappointment in his eyes, the fact that he looked weary, almost sad. She somehow sensed his reasons for wanting to see her father were quite important, and she reached out and touched the sleeve of his brown frock coat. "I think you'd better come in," she told Matt Kendall.

Two

‥

A my ushered Matt into the small, ragtag parlor of the
Harris home. She gestured at a threadbare wing chair
for him to sit in, then seated herself across from him,
on the ratty, uncomfortable horsehair settee.

Amy studied the handsome newcomer who eyed her so
expectantly, and found his deep brown eyes intense and
searching, treacherously unnerving. Finally, she managed to
say softly, "My father hasn't been home since the first time
he came here on leave from the Civil War. He simply left
and never returned. We didn't receive a report of his being
killed—so we've assumed he's still alive." She shook her
head ruefully. "Actually, it's all a very sore subject with my
mother."

"I see," the stranger replied, frowning thoughtfully.
Placing his hat on a nearby tea table, he leaned forward and
asked, "Tell me, Miss Harris, has there been no word
whatever—no letters, nothing?"

At the newcomer's question, a distant, painful memory
clutched at Amy's heart. As much as she felt compelled by
the man's frank query, she knew she couldn't be totally
honest with him. Forcing the images to recede, she said
rather breathlessly, "Nothing."

Matt Kendall shook his head, leaning back in his chair. "That's odd. It just doesn't sound like Abel Harris to me."

Amy bit her lip. She was tempted to blurt out, *You don't know my mother, sir*, but caught herself in the nick of time, instead asking, "Do you mind if I ask what business you have with my father?"

The man was silent for a moment, then said carefully, "Your father was a friend of mine. You see, my family used to live in this very neighborhood."

"Yes, I thought you looked familiar," Amy ventured.

The man looked intrigued by her remark, staring at her in a direct, almost amused way. "You remember me? Why, you couldn't have been more than six years old at the time."

"Yes, I remember you, and . . . it seems you remember me, too," Amy murmured, blushing beneath the scrutiny of the stranger's dark eyes. Finally, she managed to stammer, "You—you and my father went off to the war together, didn't you?"

"Yes, that's right."

"Then—then you may know more about him than we do," Amy pointed out eagerly. "We haven't seen him since 'sixty-two."

The stranger gave Amy a compassionate smile and shook his head. "I'm afraid I can't help you much there, Miss Harris. I last saw your father briefly at the end of the war, back in 'sixty-five. Abel was fine then, but I'm afraid I've had no contact with him since."

"I see," Amy murmured, frowning pensively. It was good to know, at any rate, that her father had survived the conflict. "Then your visit today is a social call?" she asked.

"More or less," he agreed, leaning back farther in his chair, a glint of thoughtful amusement in his fine eyes.

Amy twisted her fingers self-consciously. "I suppose under the circumstances that my father wouldn't want me to send you on your way without the courtesy of at least offering you a cup of tea or something."

"Probably not," he agreed solemnly.

She stared at him miserably, starting to feel quite foolish, especially at the glint of humor in his eyes. She had only known this stranger for a few moments, and it was already obvious that he was a man of few words. She didn't know if his laconic attitude were an attribute of his nature, or if he were deliberately baiting her. Somehow, she strongly suspected the latter. He doubtless thought her forward and foolish, perhaps even of questionable moral fiber, for ever asking him in. Why had she done so in the first place?

Fortunately at this point, Hannah saved Amy from further discomfort by bursting into the room with a half-finished baby dress in one hand, a needle and thread in the other, saying, "Amy, you must help me with the smocking on this—" Then, spotting Matt, Hannah froze, blushing shyly as she stared at the stranger.

Matt stood, smiling at the child. The little girl was precious, he thought to himself, a miniature version of her older sister, with her curling long hair and angelic face. Like Amy, Matt had been sitting there wondering what he was doing in the Harris parlor, especially with Abel Harris obviously so far removed from his family. But he realized as he stared at the younger girl that both sisters intrigued him mightily.

Amy also now stood. "Hannah, we'll work on Mrs. Simpson's layette later. Right now we have a guest. This is Mr. Matt Kendall."

As Hannah turned to stare at the newcomer, he explained, "I'm a friend of your pa's."

Amy hastily added, "I told Mr. Kendall that Pa—Pa has not been home for some time. But I do think we owe the gentleman the courtesy of some refreshment before he goes on his way, don't you agree, Hannah?"

Now the little girl brightened, happiness dancing in her brown eyes. To Hannah, actually having a guest in their home other than the Methodist minister was a rare, rare treat. "Of course!" she agreed gleefully. "I'll fetch tea, sister."

Matt chuckled as the little girl bounded out of the room, her blond curls dancing behind her. As he and Amy sat back down, she asked, "So, Mr. Kendall, is seeing my father the only reason you're in St. Louis?"

He shook his head. "Actually, I'm on my way east to Virginia. You see, I'm—" All at once, he paused, at a loss for what to say next to the beautiful young woman sitting across from him. It had been on the tip of his tongue to tell Miss Harris that he was going to Virginia to meet a young lady with a mind toward matrimony, yet he couldn't quite bring himself to say this. After all, he reasoned, he had made no commitment to the girl in Virginia. Hell, he hadn't even met her yet . . .

"Yes?" Amy prompted, still waiting for the man to finish his sentence. Why did she have the feeling that he was enmeshed in some private struggle?

At last, he smiled. "I'm on my way east to visit my married sister."

"Oh, how nice," Amy murmured, wondering why she felt unaccountably relieved by his answer. "And where do you make your home these days, Mr. Kendall?"

"Rolla. It's a small town southwest of here, in the foothills of the Ozarks."

"I've heard of it," Amy murmured.

"Have you?" With obvious pride, he went on, "Just bought me a spread down there, 'bout ten months ago. A hundred acres—right nice little farm."

"It sounds lovely," Amy agreed wistfully. It did sound wonderful, the thought of a prosperous farm, a tidy, spacious home, a smokehouse crammed with succulent meats and a garden bursting with vegetables. . . . Not to mention a man like this handsome stranger to provide for a wife and family—

Amy stopped herself in the nick of time, stunned by her runaway thoughts. Whatever was she thinking? She practically had herself married to this man she had met only minutes before, and here she was, supposedly engaged to another! Anyway, for all she knew, Matt Kendall might already have a wife . . .

No, a voice in her mind swiftly amended, this stranger had no wife. If he had a missus, he was hardly the type to go traipsing off visiting family without her. And what woman in her right mind would let *him* out the door for a jaunt by himself?

"Here we are," came Hannah's gleeful voice as the ten-year-old padded back into the parlor with a rattan tray bearing a chipped china teapot, three mismatched cups with cracked saucers and a few stale cookies. The little girl placed the tray on the coffee table in front of the settee and glanced across at Matt, the vulnerability apparent in her bright young eyes. Both girls knew the tea wasn't much of a repast, but it was the best the Harris home could offer.

"Looks good enough to eat," Matt Kendall told the child with a wide grin, and Hannah beamed. Amy watched the exchange with a feeling of tenderness in her heart, touched by the stranger's sensitivity toward her sister.

As Amy began to pour tea, Hannah seated beside her, Esther Harris slowly entered the room. Matt Kendall's abruptly getting to his feet was the first sign Amy noted that the atmosphere had changed. Looking up, she gasped, "Ma!"

Supported by a gnarled walking stick, Esther Harris crept into the room with the painful gait of dissipation and progressing arthritis. The old woman wore one of her better dresses, a shabby affair at best, of faded brown muslin. Her greasy hair was pinned back haphazardly in an attempt at a bun, which came across instead as slovenly and pathetic. Pausing a few feet beyond the portal, Esther stared at the newcomer in keen appraisal, her yellow-green eyes then darting to her two daughters suspiciously.

Amy struggled to her feet. "Ma, we have a guest."

"So I see," came Esther's carping voice.

"This is Mr. Matt Kendall," Amy went on miserably. "He's here..." She struggled momentarily, fearing her mother's reaction when Esther learned the truth regarding Kendall's visit. Yet the woman would have to be told; if Amy didn't tell her, surely the stranger would. Taking a deep breath, Amy blurted, "He came here looking for Pa. Mr. Kendall and Pa were soldiers together during the war."

With the words out at last, Amy held her breath. She feared a harsh stream of invective would come spewing from her mother's mouth with enough force to propel the man straight out the parlor door. Yet curiously, Esther did not react as Amy expected. The old woman's face did become gripped in a fierce struggle, and the trembling hand clutching the walking stick tightened until the knotty knuckles turned white. Yet Esther Harris miraculously kept her peace.

"Pleased to meet you again, Mrs. Harris," Matt said, breaking the strained silence. "It's been some time since—"

"Of course, I told Mr. Kendall that Pa hasn't been home in many years," Amy put in, struggling not to twist her fingers together in betrayal of her nervousness. "Anyway, I thought we should offer him the courtesy of—"

"Sit down, sit down, all of you," Esther suddenly interrupted, with a weary, irritable sigh. Peevishly, she asked Amy, "Why didn't you tell me we had company?"

Amy's brown eyes widened in amazement at her mother's question. "Why—why Mr. Kendall only just now arrived—"

"Hmmph!" Esther snorted, lumbering farther into the room. "He's obviously been here long enough for you to fetch tea—and not a cup for me either, I see."

"I'll get another cup, Ma!" Hannah put in fretfully. Eyes wild with apprehension, the child bolted to her feet and dashed out of the room as Matt Kendall watched, looking perturbed. Still, no one followed the old woman's directive to sit down until she plopped herself down with a painful sigh into a creaky old rocking chair flanking the settee. Amy and Matt then followed suit.

In the strained silence that ensued, Esther Harris studied their visitor with a ruthless eye. The man looked vaguely familiar to her, too; but like Amy, Esther couldn't quite place his family from before. Obviously, though, the boy knew her bastard of a husband, she thought irritably. Well, she'd set that aside for now. She knew she couldn't afford to alienate their guest, for as soon as Esther saw Matt Kendall, she realized that he might well serve a purpose for her. This man was obviously no low-life scum, no Lacy Garrett. On the contrary, the stylish cut of the stranger's brown frock coat and dark trousers, the fine tooling on his black dress boots, bespoke a man of respectable means.

"Mr. Kendall is a farmer from Rolla," Amy now explained to her mother, embarrassed that Esther was staring at their guest so brazenly. "He's on his way east to Virginia, to visit his sister."

"How interesting," the mother muttered, her calculating mind spinning. As had her daughter, Esther surmised that Kendall was not married; yet the old woman's devious mind seized this fact with a greedy purpose that defiled the honest, innocent rush of attraction Amy felt for the handsome newcomer. In a deliberately syrupy voice, the old woman coaxed their guest, "You must tell us about this farm of yours, Mr. Kendall."

Matt Kendall frowned hesitantly. Much as he feared the old woman had a scheming purpose in mind, Matt found the two girls had touched something in the softer side of his nature. And ultimately, he couldn't help but warm to the subject of his farm, since his new spread in Rolla was his pride and joy. "Well, ma'am," he began to Esther, abruptly shifting his earnest gaze to pretty Amy, "I hope you won't think I'm braggin' if I say that I have a hundred acres of the richest bottomland in the Ozarks. . . ."

While Matt continued with glowing descriptions of his property, Hannah silently reentered the room and handed Amy another chipped cup and saucer. Amy served everyone tea, placing a stale cookie in each saucer as Matt continued to talk, Esther prodding him with endless questions that would have mortified Amy had not Matt seemed so eager to talk. As he spoke, he continued to stare at Amy—covertly when her mother was questioning him, more openly as he furnished the answers—and she found his heated perusal quite stirring. It also warmed her to see this quiet man so animated and proud. His love for his land touched something elemental in her, made her realize he was a man who wanted to put down roots, who would be staid and responsible; exactly the opposite of that wanderer who had so many times let her down . . .

"And when is it you'll be journeying on to Virginia, then,

Mr. Kendall?'' Esther now asked their guest, raising a stale cookie to cracked lips.

Matt looked somewhat flustered as he set his cup and saucer down on the small table flanking his chair. ''Actually, ma'am, I haven't bought my train ticket yet. You see, I didn't know how long I'd be—er—''

''It's settled, then,'' Esther interrupted firmly. ''You must stay to have supper with us, young man, and for the night, too.'' The crafty gleam in Esther's eyes now rested pointedly on Amy, charging her daughter not to reveal anything, upon pain of direst consequences, as she added, ''After all, it's only what your pa would want, is it not, missy?''

With great effort, Amy managed not to choke on her tea. ''Yes, Ma.'' Esther Harris's invitation to the handsome stranger shocked Amy beyond belief.

What shocked her even more was the fact that Matt Kendall immediately and graciously accepted!

Three

✤

"Ladies, that was excellent," Matt said as he leaned back in his chair contentedly.

It was three hours later; they had all just finished supper in the dining room. Meager by most standards, the meal was the best the Harris kitchen could offer—fresh pea soup, shortcake biscuits and an apple cobbler for dessert.

"Thank you, Mr. Kendall," Esther now said. "My daughter Amy Louise is the finest cook in these parts."

Sitting next to Matt on one side of the plain old wooden table, Amy resisted an urge to stare dumbfounded at her mother. For the past two hours, Esther had been brazenly talking up Amy's charms to the stranger from Rolla. Amy listened, amazed, as her mother listed for Matt's benefit an endless parade of assets Amy never knew she possessed. "My Amy Louise is the smartest, the thriftiest, the most sweet-natured and obedient..." It could not have been more obvious that Esther had matchmaking on her devious mind. Amy wasn't completely sure why, although she strongly suspected that her mother was implementing some scheme in order to dip her hands into this prosperous stranger's pockets. The thought was absurd, Amy realized—why should this gentleman want her, Amy, who was penniless, with no dowry even? Nevertheless, he had been staring at her quite oddly throughout the meal. . . .

"Well, Mr. Kendall, would you care for some after-dinner entertainment now?" Esther went on. "My Amy Louise plays the piano like an angel, you know."

Amy swallowed a mouthful of apple cobbler with a painful gulp, and this time she did stare at her mother in disbelief. For the beautiful old cabinet grand piano in the parlor, the one luxurious piece of furniture the Harrises owned, was a sore subject between Amy and her mother. Amy's father had bought the musical instrument for his first child's fifth birthday, over Esther's vehement protests at his extravagance. Had it not been for the fact that the piano had been, over the years, used by church ladies during occasional meetings held in the Harris home, Amy was sure that her mother would have long ago sold the instrument. To hear her mother speak with pride of her musical ability was wonderfully absurd!

Matt Kendall had a curious grin on his face. "I'd love to hear your daughter play," he replied graciously to Esther, giving Amy a sideways wink. Amy blushed in resigned misery, knowing it would do no good to protest.

The four gathered in the parlor, and Amy sat down at the piano and dutifully drew out the Methodist hymnal. She was opening the book to "Rock of Ages" when Esther's voice firmly directed, "No, play something pretty for our guest, Amy Louise."

Amy whirled on the swivel piano stool, struggling to hide her incredulity. Esther had always termed all nonreligious music "licentious"; in fact, Amy could safely practice her favorites by popular composers only when she was sure Esther was passed out cold in the bedroom. Now her mother was requesting that she play "something pretty"?

"Chopin?" she finally ventured to her parent.

"Yes, Chopin will be fine," came Esther's prompt reply.

Carefully, Amy replaced the hymnal on top of the piano and drew out her favorite Chopin piece. Though largely self-taught, Amy was quite advanced as a pianist. The music that flowed out from her hands was hauntingly beautiful. The nocturne she had chosen started out with a sad, sweet melody, contrasted by passages of crashing power and passion. Though she hadn't intended to, Amy found herself pouring out her feelings in the song—her need, her pain. As she so often did when she played Chopin, she began to feel a sense of transport, of oneness with the music itself. As the piece concluded in dramatic runs followed by rolling chords of exquisite poignance, Amy's breath came quickly and her eyes stung with tears, her fingers trembling on the final notes. . . .

Amy finished the song to the sound of clapping behind her. She turned, blushing, to find Matt Kendall staring at her as he applauded her performance, his face a touching mixture of astonishment and reverence. "Lovely," he murmured. "Quite lovely."

Amy's heart pounded. Meanwhile, Esther Harris addressed her daughter in a none too patient tone. "Amy Louise, can't you tell that our guest is enjoying your music? Play something else, pray."

"Yes, Ma," Amy murmured.

Turning back to the piano, Amy played for her audience the other few songs she had sheet music to—two other Chopin selections, a Stephen Foster melody and a minuet by Bach. Matt applauded each piece and complimented Amy lavishly for her talent, until her cheeks bloomed with becoming color.

Following Amy's fifth selection, Esther Harris cleared her throat and informed their guest with a self-satisfied smile, "Now, if you'll excuse me, Mr. Kendall, I must put my child to bed."

At this, Amy fought not to laugh. Hannah had been putting herself to bed for some time now, and even before that, Esther had never showed the slightest motherly concern for the little girl. Amy had practically raised the girl alone.

Matt got to his feet as the old woman stood, and Esther added, "I'm sure my Amy Louise will keep you entertained with more of her music, Mr. Kendall."

"That would be right fine, ma'am," Matt told his hostess.

Amy wanted to tell her mother that she had exhausted her repertoire already, but she thought better of the idea.

Esther hobbled for the door, but Hannah didn't immediately follow. The old woman turned to half snap at her younger daughter, "Well, missy?"

"Oh!" Hannah exclaimed, flustered as she hopped to her feet. She curtsied to Matt, and with an embarrassed "Good night, sir!" followed the older woman out of the room.

Now Amy had to lower her eyes, feeling the sudden burning of tears. The exit scene of Hannah and Amy's mother would have been amusing had it not been so pathetic. Knowing that the stranger had glimpsed such an intimate look at the dynamics of the Harris household, that he knew that poor, unwanted Hannah had not even initially identified herself as the "child" her mother spoke of, somehow humiliated Amy. The fact that Esther had deliberately left her alone with this man she hardly knew, and the obvious, mercenary nature of her mother's intrigues, made things so much worse.

The silence lengthened, and Amy began to feel the heat of the stranger's gaze focused on her. At last, she gathered the strength to look up at him. He was leaning back against the settee, appraising her. The same smoldering intensity that had unsettled her before now made her heart beat wildly, erratically.

At last he spoke, stretching forward and lacing his fingers together. "Is something wrong?" The words were soft, concerned.

Amy bit her lip and smiled shyly. Even the slight movement on Matt Kendall's part had made powerful muscles ripple in his arms and legs, reminding her of what a strong—and surely virile—man he was. At last she said apologetically, "I've no more pieces to play for you."

The stranger laughed, a deep, melodic sound. "Is that all? Why, your music was so fine, Miss Amy, I'd love to hear every one of them pretty songs ten times more." His grin deepened, and he winked at her again. "Actually, I was afraid your ma's leaving you all by your lonesome with me had you feeling forlorn enough to start cryin'."

Now Amy smiled, too. Despite herself, she was being charmed. "No, it's not that, it's . . ." Her voice trailed off miserably as she realized she couldn't reveal to the visitor the dark truth of what was really going on in this house. That was a Pandora's box she didn't dare open.

"Yes?" He looked intrigued.

Amy gestured helplessly. "Look, I'm really sorry about what happened just now. My mother—I'm so embarrassed, Mr. Kendall. I'm sure you must see right through what she's doing, and you mustn't . . . I mean, you mustn't feel . . ." She twisted her fingers, feeling wretched as he studied her with amusement.

"I mustn't feel what?" he asked softly.

The stranger wasn't helping matters any, and again Amy had the distinct feeling that he was baiting her as she looked up and saw the laughter in those dark eyes. Feeling as if she were plunging off a treacherous cliff, she nonetheless forged on. "Well—surely Mr. Kendall, you noticed what my ma was trying to do."

He chuckled again. "Yes, ma'am, I did notice." He was silent for a moment, then asked thoughtfully, "But your ma didn't exactly hogtie me into staying, now did she?"

Amy stared back at the stranger, and their eyes locked for an electric moment, a moment of discovery, of realization, for them both. Her heart seemed to pound in her ears, and she couldn't force herself to speak . . .

After a moment, Matt said gently, "Girl, come sit by me a moment." The words were tender, husky, and he patted the empty seat beside him in welcome.

Giddy as she felt in his presence, Amy did instinctively trust the newcomer. She got to her feet, crossing the parlor on unsteady legs. At last she arrived at his side, looking down at him expectantly. He reached out and took her hand and drew her down beside him. The heat of his strong fingers on her wrist was so stirring she was sure he must feel her pulses surging wildly against his fingertips. It was all she could do not to gasp for air, sitting there so close to him, studying the appealing shadow of whiskers on his face, inhaling the aroma of the bay rum in his hair. As he continued to hold her hand, his dark eyes smiled at her, drawing her treacherously into his spell. She stared back at him and wondered at the strange light-headedness she was feeling. She had never felt this way with Lacy, not even when he kissed her. She had known Lacy all her life, and she supposed being around him was, in a sense, almost like being around a brother. This man, on the other hand, was so male and commanding, so intriguing. He seemed to ooze excitement, stimulating her virgin senses in a new, enervating way.

They continued to study each other in passionate silence, until Amy thought she would die if one of them did not speak. At last, she stammered, "I—I did wonder why you agreed to stay here, Mr. Kendall. I mean—it does seem odd, with my father not being here and all. . . ."

Again, he chuckled. "Well, lady, it doesn't seem odd to me. What man in his right mind could resist having three women fuss over him?" More seriously, he added, "I live by myself, and it does get right lonely, you know."

"Oh—I see," Amy muttered, removing her hand from his to smooth her skirts, studying the faded gingham as if the dress were an object of sheer fascination to her. After a moment, she glanced up at him and ventured, "You lost your folks when you lived here before, didn't you?"

His expression abruptly became guarded. "Yes."

"It was . . . at the start of the war, wasn't it?"

"Yes."

"I don't remember the circumstances very well," Amy went on in a rush. "I mean, I was quite young and—"

"It's best not spoken of," Matt Kendall said gruffly, staring off at an étagère in the corner of the room.

Amy bit her lip, feeling she had put him off somehow. After a moment, she said simply, "I just wanted to tell you I'm sorry."

Now he turned back to her and smiled. His eyes appeared strangely glazed, but in every other respect he seemed in command of himself. "Do you? You know, that's right fine of you, Miss Amy, to be thinking of others that way,

considering what you're up against yourself in this house."
A meaningful silence settled between them. Then he glanced
about the room and asked softly, "Life is hard for you here,
isn't it?"

She nodded, realizing a denial would be both foolish and
futile. "Yes."

His hypnotic gaze now fixed upon her, urging her to
confide in him, to seek her comfort there. "Tell me about
it, why don't you."

Amy swallowed hard. "I'm sure you don't want me to
bore you with—"

"I won't be bored. Now, tell me," he scolded. More
gently, he reasoned, "You see, Miss Amy, Abel, your
father, was my friend. He . . . when it happened with my
folks, Abel helped me more than I can say. And I think he'd
want me to inquire after the welfare of his daughters now."

Amy couldn't deny his logic; nor could she tear herself
from the compelling question in his eyes. With a bracing
breath, she confided, "Well—after Pa left, things did get
rough. Ma turned to bitterness—and to . . ."

"Drinking?" he supplied.

"Yes."

He looked perturbed now, angry. "Did she strike you
earlier today?"

Amy turned away in acute mortification. He had noticed
the welt! This was too much; she could not share these
shameful matters with a stranger—friend of her father's or
not! Instinctively, she tried to slide away from him, but he
stopped her, his hand gripping her sleeve. "Did she hit
you?"

"Yes," Amy whispered miserably.

He released her, cursing under his breath. "Why? Not
that hitting you would be excusable under any circumstances!"

Amy was both amazed and warmed by Matt's sudden,
explosive protectiveness. "Well . . . we argued. Ma threw a
bowl across the room, and afterward . . . she hit me."

Outrage smoldered in his eyes. "That must never happen
again."

She stared back at him blankly, her heart pounding. What did he mean?

The charged silence between them grew until it seemed to scream with its own intensity, even as their eyes remained locked, anguished and searching. Then he reached out, took her hand and coaxed, "Tell me something."

"If—if I can," she stammered back, drowning in the unexpected emotions he aroused in her, the heat of his touch.

"How old are you, Miss Amy?"

"Eighteen," she whispered.

He smiled. "That's about what I thought. Why isn't a pretty thing like you married off yet?"

Amy's cheeks stung with the blush that remark stirred. Finally, she said in a small voice, "I suppose Ma scares a lot of folks off."

"Yes, I reckon she would." He hadn't released her hand, and when his thumb boldly stroked the inner, sensitive palm, she thought she would go insane. "If that's the case, then, in a way I'm thankful."

"Thankful?" Her ears smarted now.

His dark eyes glowed with debilitating fervor as he murmured, "That your ma scared the other men off."

Amy's heart lunged into a frantic tempo at his words, and she instinctively withdrew her hand from his burning touch. He didn't seem offended, and after a moment continued thoughtfully, "You know, you're quite something, Amy Harris. You're obviously strong, to be raised without a pa, to deal with that ma of yours and bring up baby sister, too. Yet you haven't let what happened to you harden you. You're soft and feminine, too. I like that—I really do." He was staring at her so directly and sincerely now that she thought he would burn holes in her very heart as he added, almost as if to himself, "I think Abel would want this too."

"Want what?" She could hardly breathe, let alone talk.

"I think he'd want me to take care of you," Matt Kendall said.

Amy was drowning, fighting tears at the stranger's tender

words. "Take . . . care of me?" she repeated. It was a novel idea. Whoever had wanted to take care of her?

Determinedly, Matt went on, "This may seem brash, but—"

"Yes?" Amy queried in a frail, rising voice.

"Girl, how would you like to come home with me?"

For a long moment, Matt's words reverberated through her mind: *Girl, how would you like to come home with me?* He simply couldn't be saying this to her, she thought, not mere hours after they'd met! And what, precisely, did his words mean?

Before Amy could really ponder this question, Matt Kendall answered it for her. "Amy, I know this seems rash, but I'm asking you to be my wife." In a rush, he added, "I'm a man who knows his own mind, and ever since I laid eyes on you this afternoon"—here he smiled broadly—"well, what can I say?"

Amy herself could say nothing at all, still astonished by Matt's unexpected proposal. Marriages of convenience were not unheard of in Amy's realm of experience, but for a gentleman to propose to a young lady mere hours after he'd met her . . . well, that was unusual, to say the least!

As Amy continued to stare at Matt in shock, he went on, "You know, I have a right nice spread down at Rolla. I can provide for you well."

At last, Amy found her voice. "Yes. Yes I know that. But—but why should you want me?"

As soon as she said the words, she blushed, as she realized their unintentional double meaning. Before he could comment, she blurted out, "I mean, I've nothing to bring to a marriage, Mr. Kendall. I've no dowry."

At this, Matt threw back his head and laughed. "No dowry? Is that all that's fretting you? You think I give a good rip about a dowry when I can have a pretty thing like you?"

Again, Amy lowered her eyes. This was too much, too soon. She was simply overwhelmed.

Matt seemed to sense her teeming state of mind, for he gave her a moment to collect herself. Finally, he said softly,

"Miss Amy, believe me, I mean what I'm saying. I'm asking you to be my bride, and I assure you, my intentions are strictly honorable."

"Oh, I know that," Amy replied sincerely. "It's just that this is so sudden." Insane, she added to herself. To Matt, she explained carefully, "Mr. Kendall, it seems to me that you've made a very important decision regarding your life in a very short period of time. Don't you think you might just as quickly—"

"Oh, no ma'am, no ma'am," he interrupted adamantly. "Like I told you, when my mind's set, that's it. Dynamite can't budge me."

Amy smiled again at his zealous ardor, but managed to ask, "But how can you decide so quickly on—on the woman you'll be having to spend the rest of your life with?"

A tenderness approaching reverence lit his eyes then. "When I laid eyes on you, I just knew it. There was something between us, girl, even then. You felt it, too, didn't you?"

"Y-yes," Amy admitted querulously, even as that same rush of excitement made her cheeks burn once more.

"And I may as well admit to you that there's a practical side to this, too," Matt continued frankly. "I need a wife. I'm ready to settle down and rear a family." He glanced around the parlor, then added gravely, "And you need to get out of here, Miss Amy. You don't belong here."

Amy nodded, knowing Matt had spoken the truth. She respected him for that. Nonetheless, his speaking of starting a family prompted her to ask shyly, "If I did accept your suit, sir, what would you expect of—I mean, when . . ."

As her voice trailed off in acute misery, he seemed to sense what she wanted to know. He took her hand again, squeezing the soft flesh with a gentle but persistent pressure that compelled her to look up at him once more. His eyes seemed to burn with an inner fire as he said sincerely, "I know you're young and modest. I'll try to be patient in asserting my husbandly rights. But I have to tell you I'm a man of strong urges. With you, ma'am—well, I reckon they'll be even stronger. So I must make it clear to you that I'm talking about weeks, not months.''

At this, Amy felt her entire body burning, inside and out. As he released her hand, she tore her gaze from his. She felt an odd yet pleasurable aching deep in the pit of her stomach at the stranger's bold words. He was not a man to mince words, this Matt Kendall! Now it was perfectly clear what he would expect of her as his wife—and when.

After a small eternity, Amy recovered her composure, noting that Matt was again looking at her with some amusement. He had been honest with her, she decided, and she owed him honesty, too. Staring at him with her chin firmly set, she said, ''You must know, Mr. Kendall, that I'm not nearly as meek and self-sacrificing as Ma makes me out.''

His response was totally unexpected. Amy watched, stunned, as Matt laughed until tears sprang to his dark eyes. She studied him with a mixture of confusion and delight, for he looked utterly enchanting—his eyes glowing, his straight white teeth gleaming, the lines about his mouth so compelling. Why on earth had he perceived her remark as so amusing? she wondered.

Finally, controlling his mirth, Matt said, ''Oh, girl, I knew from the first moment I saw you that you weren't some earthly saint. I'm not looking for a noble wife. That would be right dull, don't you think?''

Amy continued to stare at him, flabbergasted. He was the most amazing man she'd ever met! Everything she said to him seemed to encourage him more, not dissuade him, as she had initially intended.

''So what's the answer, Amy?'' he prodded. ''Do you want to come home with me?''

''As your wife,'' she murmured.

''As my wife.''

Amy shook her head, still not knowing what to say. ''Could I have the night to think on it, sir?''

His answer surprised her again, as he grinned with a hint of devilishness. ''No. I want your answer tonight.''

"Tonight?" she gasped. "But by morning you might change your mind."

He shook his head again. "Your ma didn't put any whiskey in my coffee tonight, not that I know of." His eyes flicked over her with frank ardor, and his voice was slightly husky as he said, "I ain't changing my mind, Miss Amy."

Struggling to control her wildly surging senses, Amy stammered, "B-but have you thought that I might be more likely to say yes in the morning, after I've had a chance to think on it?"

"Nope. I think you'd be more likely to say no."

Despite herself, Amy laughed. Doubtless he was right, and again, she found his charm had her weakening. "You're certainly a man who likes to put things on the line, take chances, aren't you?"

"I don't mind a good gamble now and then," he acknowledged. "But there's more to it than that. If you're not coming with me, then I'll be gone by sunup."

"I see," Amy murmured. As much as he had teased her, he was deadly serious. He wanted her for his wife, but it was all or nothing with him—her immediate commitment, or nothing, and he'd be on his way. No nonsense, no wasting of his time, this man. Amy swallowed hard and thought furiously. Matt Kendall was very attractive, and he could provide for her well. He might even be willing to take on Hannah. In any event, the two of them would no doubt get along well enough, and as he had pointed out, the marriage would serve a practical purpose for both, as well. Oh, the mere thought of living apart from her cruel mother filled Amy with a joy approaching euphoria.

Yet what about Lacy? Even as the softer side of Amy's nature posed this question, her pride, her bitterness, rose up in defiance. What had Lacy Garrett ever done for her except to let her down? What could she expect from him in the future except more disappointment? Wasn't she deserving of a man whose word was his bond? A man like Matt Kendall? And didn't the weak-willed Lacy deserve no less than for her to accept another's suit?

"Well, girl?" Matt now prodded. The look of perplexed

concentration on her pretty face, the unexpected glint of bitterness in her bright brown eyes, had him worried.

Amy looked at Matt and blinked hard. It was now or never; she knew it. Take that leap of faith, trust this man, or lose the chance forever. With a calm in her voice that surprised her, she said to Matt Kendall, "Yes, Mr. Kendall, I accept your proposal."

"Well," he said after a moment, grinning broadly, his eyes shining with happiness. "Well, ain't that just fine."

"You'll speak to my mother in the morning, then?" Amy went on shyly. "I mean—as a matter of tradition."

"Of course," he replied. "I'll want us to marry right off—tomorrow, if possible."

Amy's heart hammered. "Tomorrow?"

"You're not backing out, are you, girl?" he chided.

"N-no."

"Then why would you want to spend another day here?"

He had her to rights there. "No reason, I guess," she murmured.

Having said the words, Amy stood. All at once she felt emotionally exhausted. She needed time alone, time to consider what she had just done with her life. Stiffly, she asked the man who was soon to become her husband, "Well, then, Mr. Kendall, do you have everything you'll need for the night?"

He was standing now, too. "Yes, ma'am."

"I'm sorry you'll have to sleep on the back porch. You see, we've only two bedrooms, and—"

"Ma'am, I'll be fine. The night is mild, and it'll be a pleasure just looking up at the stars."

"I see." Hearing his words, Amy inanely wondered how many nights she would spend staring at the stars with this stranger. She looked at him awkwardly, and he back at her. It was odd. Now that they had decided to marry, they seemed shy as two colts with each other.

"Well, then," she said, twisting her fingers together. At last she gathered the courage to extend a trembling hand to him. "I guess it's good night, then."

Yet again he surprised her. He took her hand, all right,

but said softly under his breath, "I believe it's customary to seal such an occasion with a kiss, Miss Amy."

Although she did not at first fight him when he pulled her into his arms—it was proper for him to kiss her, under the circumstances—Amy was scandalized by the brazen assault of Matt's hot, sensuous lips. Never had a man kissed her this way; his mouth was so hard and demanding on hers, his tongue so insistently burrowing against her lips, seeking to wantonly part them! And he held her so very tightly that she could not catch her breath. Most frightening of all were the feelings aroused by his devouring mouth and muscled body— the treacherous softening in the pit of her stomach . . . Amy struggled against her emotions and finally managed to push Matt away, catching her breath with a gasp.

That seemed to anger him, and somehow to arouse him even more. "No," he scolded, his eyes blazing above her, his voice full of soft menace as he pulled her close again, ruthlessly close. This time, Matt Kendall kissed her with frightening intensity, bruising her tender young lips with his own until her mouth opened, until she let his eager tongue penetrate inside, until she moaned and sagged against him, clinging to him to keep from falling. His tongue brazenly explored the warm inner surface of her mouth in a slow, sensuous circle, and she moaned deep in her throat, her entire being traitorously melting into his hard arousal, his need. Frightened before, Amy now felt dizzy, euphoric, reeling with new, electrifying sensations, burning with the heat he stirred in her. . . . Then, at last, mercifully, his searing mouth moved away, grazing her ear. "Oh, yes, that's much better," he whispered huskily as both of them fought to breathe. He drew back slightly, and his eyes were bright with passion as he gently caressed her face with a rough fingertip. "You go to bed now, Miss Amy, before I do something really scandalous. We'll make our plans in the morning."

He released her, and Amy walked out of the room wearing a dazed expression, the taste of him still on her lips. She didn't dare look back at him; she knew she would collapse in mortification if she did. As she went down the dark hallway, she tried to understand the animal encounter that had just occurred between them. It was obvious now, so obvious, why Matt Kendall wanted her as his wife, the fierce male attraction he felt for her! She had felt the overpowering wanton pull as well. The mere thought of sharing such intimacies with a man both terrified and fascinated her. . . .

At the door to her and Hannah's room, Amy paused to steady herself. Oh, heavens, what had she done? What had she gotten herself into?

Who had she given herself to?

In the parlor, Matt watched Amy leaving, her expression dazed, and he felt a hard stab of conscience. Oh, damn, why had he ruined it all by kissing her so ruthlessly? God, one taste of her had driven him wild, and when she'd pushed him away, he'd reacted like a madman, losing all control. Now she might well wake up fighting mad in the morning and beat him off with a broom!

The very thought set him pacing. If she balked tomorrow, he'd just have to be firm with her, point out that a promise was a promise, after all. He was sure that mother of hers would make her go with him anyway, and would doubtless expect a monthly stipend from him, to boot. But what the hell! He didn't care.

Gravely disappointed that he hadn't found Abel here, Matt felt he could do right by the man in taking care of Amy. And he felt comfortable with the girl already; he could see that she had a lot of her father's goodness in her.

From a purely practical standpoint, the girl was simply perfect for his needs. Considering what she was up against here, the demands of farm life would surely come as no shock to her; indeed, she had all the spunk and grit a good farmwife needed.

And never had Matt Kendall felt so deeply stirred by a woman! In just a few, brief hours, the girl had turned his senses topsy-turvy. Amy was so beautiful—tall and willowy, yet voluptuous in all the places that counted. And such mettle! The defiance on her adorable face when her ma had talked about what a subservient little wife she would make some man! The things that pouting look did to him! And when she'd flat told him later that she wasn't nearly that nice! . . .

Nice. That was it, he realized. He didn't want nice. Sitting down on the settee, Matt reached into his breast pocket and pulled out the picture of the Virginia girl his sister had recently sent him. Pretty enough, the girl was— curling black hair, pleasant features—but something about her visage had always troubled him. It was the eyes; he knew that now. Flat, lusterless, meek—so different from Amy's. No depth, that girl in the picture. No spirit. Unlike the lovely, enticing Miss Harris.

Matt returned the picture to his pocket. His mind was set. He wouldn't go to Virginia at all now. Couldn't chance it. After all, he owed his sister's friend nothing; he hadn't even met her yet. And anyhow, what manner of woman would be willing to marry with a man sight unseen?

Not a creature of passion, he thought. Not a woman like Amy. That was why he had kissed Amy. Yes, he had been ruthless, but he had to know if it was in her to respond—and oh Lord, it was! Her music had smoldered with feeling, and her lips had left no doubt. With his mouth devouring hers, he had sensed the melting in her, had discovered the woman inside her waiting to open up for the first time, to blossom at his touch. . . . Just as he had told the girl, his male urges were strong, so strong they sometimes scared him. She would have to like it, or she'd end up hating him.

It would take time. He would have to woo her, make her willing, and more gently, too.

But this was the way he wanted it. He would do the bidding . . .

Four

✦✦

After tossing and turning through much of the night, Amy awakened early the next morning in the bed she shared with Hannah. She watched the first pink rays of dawn steal through the curtained window as a narrow, golden shaft of light came to rest upon Hannah's cherubic sleeping face. The child frowned in her sleep and turned away from the intrusive sunshine, but she did not awaken.

Amy sighed, sitting up and wrapping her arms about her linen-clad knees. The night had not changed anything, had not altered the fact that she had promised herself to the man who had come to their house an utter stranger yesterday in search of her father. Now, no doubt, Matt Kendall would want her to leave with him, perhaps today. Any hope that he might change his mind had been obliterated by their kiss, and she trembled just thinking of it. . . .

Yet Amy knew she would go through with the marriage. Despite the turbulent emotions aroused within her, she somehow trusted this man more than she had ever trusted Lacy Garrett. Amy wondered what it would be like living with Kendall alone on his farm. It would probably be isolated, she mused; yet there would also be the richness of country life, the growing season around them. St. Louis had its modern conveniences and attractions, it was true—Lacy had occasionally treated Amy to a melodrama or minstrel show, had taken both sisters to view P. T. Barnum's fabulous traveling circus. Yet as interesting as the city could be, Amy relished the thought of not having to worry where her next meal would come from! And to have her very own home—the thought was so wonderful, it was dizzying!

Hannah again shifted in her sleep, rattling the springs in the old iron bed, and Amy studied her sister beside her with a heart suddenly grown heavy. How could she leave Hannah here alone, at their mother's mercy? Amy knew she possessed a certain strength and stubbornness that her younger sister lacked. Oh, Hannah could show a surprising flash of spirit on occasion, but for the most part, the little girl was too guileless and gentle to survive life with Esther without the protection of her older sister.

Amy distractedly drew a hand through the girl's blond curls. Perhaps it was her own fault, she thought; perhaps she should have done more to toughen up her little sister. Yet it hadn't been in Amy to deliberately try to engender a hard side in this dear little girl. And she had always assumed she would be there to protect Hannah.

Oh, if only the child could come with her and Matt to live at his farm! Amy experienced a rush of new hope. Could Matt be convinced to take Hannah on? Amy thought back to yesterday, recalling how Matt had seemed quite taken with the child. And he had a farm to tend, hadn't he? Amy had always admitted that Hannah was a much more industrious and willing worker than she. Wouldn't Matt, with his concern for practical matters, be delighted to have an extra pair of helping hands?

Yet what if he said no? she thought with a sudden wave of depression. What if he wanted his new wife all to himself, so he could continue to do with her that thing he'd begun last night, this time with no one there to interrupt, to stop him? The very thought set her trembling again. Matt Kendall had promised he would be patient in asserting his husbandly rights, yet his ruthless lips had seemed to demonstrate otherwise last night. What if he did want her alone with him, at his mercy, so he could take what, legally, would be his due?

Amy shuddered. If Kendall did say no regarding Hannah, could she tell him the truth, convince him of the true peril the child would be subjected to if left alone with her mother? Oh, Lord! How could she tell Matt of the shameful things her mother had done? Worse yet, how could she ever relate to him the one terrifying memory that made her fearful not just for Hannah's safety, but also made her tremble at the mere thought of sharing the marriage bed with a man?

Though it doubtless wasn't his fault, Matt's electrifying presence brought that memory to Amy's mind with a vengeance. Somehow, Lacy Garrett had never affected her that way. She had always known that she could manage Lacy, that she could take charge of their physical relationship. She was stronger than Lacy, and she had always liked it that way—when his advances moved beyond the most chaste kisses, she could send him away, shamefaced, with a mere look. Not so with Matt Kendall. He frightened her. He fascinated her.

He made her remember.

Amy got out of bed and wrapped a faded afghan about her shoulders for warmth as she went over to the window and stared out at the backyard, at the neat rows of fall vegetables she and Hannah had recently planted.

It happened eleven years ago. She had been a child at the time, yet sometimes it seemed like yesterday. Her father came home on leave from the war for the first time that fateful day in May 1862. Seven-year-old Amy was overjoyed as her tall, handsome father hefted her over his head, hugging and kissing her. Esther Harris, however, was much more restrained with her husband; Amy remembered watching her mother's body stiffen when her father kissed his wife. That night at dinner, Amy watched her father stare oddly at Esther throughout the meal. Esther's expresssion was cold, proud, even as young Amy babbled on bravely, trying to

close the gap between her parents that she could not begin
to understand.

It was much later, when the house was quiet, that Amy
was awakened by a sudden, crashing sound. She tiptoed to
the dining room, peering through the cracked door to the
kitchen to see her parents arguing inside. On the table sat an
open jug of corn liquor; in the corner lay the shards of a
fiercely shattered bowl. Amy had to throw a hand over her
mouth to keep from gasping aloud as she viewed the
bleeding claw marks on her father's flushed face.

He was furious. Never had she seen him so enraged, his
fists clenched as he shouted at his wife. "So this is the
welcome I get, after being gone all these months, and
sending home all my pay? You're a cruel, heartless woman
to turn out a man who's had no loving for a year!"

"No loving!" Esther had scoffed. "Don't you feed me
that twattle, Abel Harris. I know you've been off drinking,
and fornicating, too! One day, the Good Lord will bring you
to your knees for it!"

At this, Abel lost control, grabbing Esther's arm. "So
you've taken religion while I've been gone, have you,
woman? You cold-hearted witch! It's you who's in need of a
humbling. By God, I'll do it—now!"

As Amy watched, horrified, her father made good his
threat, hoisting his kicking, screaming wife into his arms
and carrying her through the hallway to their bedroom. Amy
followed them, unseen, tears streaming down her young
face as she stood at the closed door to her parents' room
listening to her mother's infuriated cries, clutching the brass
candlestick she'd picked up in the dining room and wondering what she should do. What on earth was her father doing
to her mother? she asked herself wildly. Just when she
decided she could stand no more, that she must burst into
the room and somehow stop them, her mother's muffled
cries of outrage abruptly changed to whimpers of pleasure.
Then there was silence. Amy went back to her room, crying
herself to sleep, feeling bewildered, ashamed for what she'd
witnessed.

But later, toward morning, a scream split the air in the

house—a man's scream this time. Amy jumped awake, creeping back to the kitchen. No one was there; but in the sink was a butcher knife, streaked with blood. Amy didn't know why, but she went to the sink, working the pump vigorously, washing the blood away....

In the morning, Amy's father was gone, and after that, Esther change dramatically. She showed no interest in her daughter; she would not have her husband's name said in the house. She took to spending long hours in her room, emerging only to go to the kitchen for food, her gait strangely staggering.

Amy became gripped by the horrible fear that her mother had murdered her father and buried him out in the garden. When she was alone, she began digging around out back for proof, her hot tears spilling upon the sod.

Then came the day when she stood in the hallway and spotted her mother in the parlor, tearing up a letter and tossing it into the grate. As the light caught her mother's silhouette, Amy noticed three things—the rabid hatred on Esther's face, the several crumpled bills in her hands, and the fact that her mother's stomach was strangely enlarged.

As Esther moved out of the room into the hallway, not even seeing her daughter, Amy rushed into the parlor and knelt by the hearth, burning her fingers on the hot coals as she tried to retrieve the letter. It was hopeless; most of the pieces were charred and could not be read. But she did recover enough fragments to see that the letter had come from her father.

How many other letters had he sent, that her mother had destroyed this way? Amy wondered. In the months that followed, she again occasionally spotted fragments of a letter in the fireplace, usually about the same time money would mysteriously appear in the Harris home once more. At least she knew her father was alive....

That winter, young Hannah was born, but Esther cruelly ignored the baby. Amy tried to raise the child herself, doing the best job that could be expected of an eight-year-old, and despite the fact that her mother tried her best to sabotage her. On several occasions, Amy heard the baby scream—a piercing, bloodcurdling wail. She would rush into the bedroom, frantic, to find the child alone and terrified. There would be no obvious source of the child's distress but for a rising welt on a tiny arm or leg, almost as if she had been savagely pinched. . . .

Things reached a head one fall day when Amy went down to the cellar to fetch vegetables. She hurried back with the produce, having left Hannah sleeping in the kitchen. As she entered the room, she heard the nine-month-old screaming in her cradle. A brief glance about the kitchen revealed Amy's mother standing in the middle of the room, staring from the baby to the boiling pot of water on the stove.

Instantly, Amy made two horrible realizations. The mere sight of her mother terrified Hannah. And Esther Harris wanted the child dead!

Amy dropped the vegetables and picked up the nearest object, an iron doorstop. Even though the weight hurt her arm unbearably, she shook it at her mother in a threatening gesture. As Esther at last noted the presence of her older daughter, Amy drew herself to the fullness of her height. "If you ever try to harm Hannah again, old woman, I swear I'll kill you!" Amy vowed. "Stay away from her—she's mine!"

Surprisingly, Esther said nothing, turned almost contritely and left the kitchen.

After that, Esther left the child alone. But even at four, at five, Hannah would sometimes awaken screaming in the night, and Amy would cuddle her, comfort her. The girls grew in closeness and in trust, and loved each other as the only family either had. . . .

What of Hannah's future now? Amy trembled at the thought. Of course, Hannah was much bigger now, larger than Amy herself had been when she called her mother down that fateful day in the kitchen. But it still worried Amy that the child might not be strong enough to defend herself against Esther. Could she confide these matters to Matt, if necessary?

Amy dressed in the only wool dress she owned—a high-necked, unstylish gray affair with meticulous handstitching covering up the moth holes that had come with age. She headed for the kitchen, but the sound of voices drew her onward to the front of the house.

Amy stood in the shadows of the archway to the dining room, observing her mother and Matt Kendall seated beyond. Neither spotted her, so Amy couldn't resist taking a moment to study the man who was now her betrothed. Matt looked quite handsome this morning in a clean white pleated shirt and dark trousers. The light from the window made fiery highlights dance in his thick, curly blond hair. His silhouette was arrestingly strong, almost chiseled in the sunlight. Amy couldn't control a surge of pride that this compelling man was to be her husband.

Yet her feelings of joy turned to curiosity as she studied what he was doing. Matt was dipping a pen in an inkwell and writing something that Amy could not, from this distance, make out.

Meanwhile, she glanced at her mother, spotting that familiar, greedy gleam in Esther's eyes. "It will be a fine match, Mr. Kendall—my Amy Louise will bear you many sons," Esther was telling Kendall. Extending her hand to Matt across the table, her mother added, "You've my consent and my blessings, of course."

"Fine. I think we understand each other," Matt returned efficiently, handing Amy's mother what she now realized could only be a bank draft!

As Esther eagerly snatched up the money, Amy could not restrain a horrified cry, whirling and dashing for the front door.

She stopped out on the porch, in tears, not knowing what to do next, where to go. Then she felt Matt's strong, warm hands on her shoulders. "Amy, I'm sorry you had to see that," came his contrite voice from behind her. "Look, your ma needs the money, and I don't mind, really I don't."

Despite the fact that his touch, along with his using her Christian name, affected Amy more than she cared to admit, she nonetheless turned to face him, eyes blazing. "*I* mind! I'm not a brood mare being sold at auction!"

Matt fought hard not to smile at Amy's words. "Oh, lady, indeed you're not," he assured her. "If you think that was why I was . . ." He took her hands, squeezed them earnestly. "Look, Amy, don't you want your little sister provided for?"

"Yes, but—" Amy bit her lip in total misery, then tried a deep breath, which only filled her lungs with the enticing scent of Matt's shaving soap, making matters so much worse. She stared up at her fiancé, at the deep-set, concerned brown eyes magnetically pierced by the sun, even as his comforting hands on hers provided their own potent brand of electricity. Seeing his sincerity, absorbing his touch, she simply couldn't be angry at him anymore. Abruptly, she asked, "Matt, could Hannah come live with us?"

He smiled reflectively, as if he, too, liked the sound of his Christian name coming from her lips. After a moment, he nodded. "Sure. Why not? I have no objection."

"Oh, Matt!"

And Matt Kendall was no less than stunned as Amy threw her arms about his neck and hugged him tightly. "Whoa, lady," he teased her after a moment, chuckling. "You're going to scandalize the entire neighborhood here, before we even get the knot tied."

Amy backed off shyly, shocked at her own spontaneous outburst, fearing Matt thought her disgracefully forward. "I'm sorry," she murmured, her eyes lowered.

"Don't be sorry," he scolded. "I'm not, especially not since I was scared that I'd frightened you off last night."

She looked up at him quickly and blushed at the memory.

"You haven't changed your mind, have you?" he added, still sounding worried.

She shook her head.

"Great," he said, grinning. Drawing closer, he placed his broad hand on her shoulder again. "Girl, I promise, I'll try to be gentler with you from now on."

He stared down at her with soulful sincerity. Amy's face was smarting now at the indelicate thoughts and feelings both his words and his heated look elicited in her. Having him this close to her again filled her with frightening urges. She asked, "Matt, may I go ask Ma about Hannah now?"

"Of course," he said with a grin.

She dashed for the house.

Esther burst Amy's beautiful bubble. "Not on your life, missy! The child stays here with me, and that's that. Otherwise, who's to take care of me?"

Amy argued, she pleaded, to no avail. Esther was adamant. She would keep Hannah, her young slave, with her.

"All right!" Amy cried at last. "But I'd better hear of no evidence that you're harming my sister. If I do, I swear I'll tell Matt everything. Then you'll have both of us to reckon with!"

Afterward, Amy went out back to the woodshed and cried about it, allowing herself ten minutes to be totally broken up inside, defeated.

She considered telling Matt she had changed her mind regarding the marriage, but knew she couldn't. She'd given him her promise already.

So Amy pulled herself together. She had to go with him, she knew that now. Besides, if she didn't leave, if she didn't take the first step, there would be no hope for Hannah, either.

Five

✝✝

O nce Hannah awakened, Amy explained her decision to marry Matt. Hannah took the news well; she already liked Matt tremendously. But the child did shed a tear or two over Amy's leaving. Amy didn't have the heart to tell her sister that their mother refused to let Hannah leave with them, but she did say sincerely, "Matt and I can't wait until you come visit us," which left the little girl glowing.

When Amy later related to Matt her mother's insistence on keeping Hannah with her, he shook his head grimly. "I figured your ma might say as much. I think she's holding Hannah over us, Amy, to see how much she can get from me. Not that I mind," he added quickly. "I don't at all—if the money will be used to help the child."

"We both know it won't," Amy told Matt bitterly. "Ma doesn't care about Hannah. She uses my little sister as slave labor."

Matt nodded, looking perturbed. "We'll just have to do our best to get Hannah out for a visit, then." Hearing his words, Amy blinked back tears, feeling warmed by his solicitude.

By midmorning, Esther and Matt had completed the arrangements for the wedding. Early the next day, the pastor from the Harrises' church, Central Methodist, would come to the Harris home and perform the service. At one o'clock, Amy and Matt would take the train back to Rolla.

Amy found it odd that Matt had decided not to take his bride on with him to Virginia for the planned visit with his sister, and late that morning as they sat in the parlor questioned him regarding this. "I don't see why you should postpone visiting your sister on my account," she said. "You haven't seen her in—what did you say?—seven years?"

Matt looked uncomfortable at Amy's questioning, but would only say, "That's no way to treat a new bride— taking her off to visit family." Even though Amy argued that she wouldn't mind if they went on to Virginia, Matt was adamant on the point. Again, Amy thought that his attitude was quite strange. Why should he insist on being alone with her, when he'd promised her he would be patient in asserting his husbandly rights?

Why, indeed? she asked herself in a flash of fear. Hadn't Matt's demanding kisses last night revealed his true intentions?

But Amy's trepidation quickly gave way to logic. She knew she would simply have to trust Matt's word. He was to be her husband, after all, and any other attitude would be demeaning for a wife to have. He was surely an honorable man to show such concern for Hannah. Matt was there, and he was living up to his promise to marry her, which was more than she could say for the only other man she'd ever been romantically involved with!

After all the plans were made, Matt announced that he wanted to take Amy shopping for new clothes. "You're a city girl, my dear," he told her tactfully, "and it's not right that I should expect you to have the proper clothing for a farmwife."

While touched by the kindness of Matt's offer, Amy lowered her eyes in mortification at his words, knowing that he had noticed her shabby assortment of clothing. City clothes, indeed! The most modest farmwife's wardrobe would greatly outshine her meager collection of rags! At first, Amy refused Matt's invitation to go shopping, but when he told her firmly that she must have, at the very least, some serviceable bonnets and strong, plain dresses to protect her from the elements, she found herself weakening. Then, when Matt insisted that they should take Hannah along on the jaunt as well, Amy had to give in. It was bad enough that she had to leave the child the next day. She couldn't deny her sister a well-deserved and rare excursion.

So Amy swallowed her pride as best she could and accepted Matt's offer. The fall weather could not have been more perfect—crisp and cool—as the three went off toward downtown St. Louis in Matt's rented carriage.

Whereas a century before, St. Louis had been only a small fur-trading center, the city was now a bustling industrial hub with well over three hundred thousand people. Amy smiled with glee at the medley of sights, sounds and smells surrounding them as they passed iron foundries, flour mills, furniture- and wagon-making factories, meat-packing plants, breweries. The list of enterprises in the burgeoning metropolis seemed endless, and every bit as fascinating as the quaint clothing and dialect of the people on the streets, many of whom were emigrant laborers from Germany, Ireland and other European countries.

Before they started their shopping, Matt stopped off at a Western Union office to wire his sister Charlotte that he wouldn't be going on to Virginia. Then he insisted on treating the girls to a fine dinner at the Planters House Hotel, a popular gathering spot for local politicians and steamboat owners. After the meal, as the three left the stately brick hotel with its iron lace balconies, Matt caught Hannah staring wistfully at a horse-drawn trolley car that had paused beyond them at a street corner. "Let's go for a ride," he told the girls, grinning.

"But your carriage!" Amy protested.

Matt glanced back at the horse and buggy, parked in the street near the entrance to the hotel. "It'll be fine. Come on, they're about to leave!"

Laughing, the three ran for the trolley, the girls hanging on to their ribboned straw hats as they climbed aboard. Matt quickly paid the conductor three nickels for fare; then the three took an enchanting ride through the St. Louis streets on the rattling conveyance, going past the Mercantile Library, the stately Customs House, and the historic courthouse where the famous Dred Scott decision had been handed down. Young Hannah was enraptured, bouncing up and down in her seat as they rocked along, her eyes seeming to dart in every direction at once, her hands constantly pointing at attractions they passed. Watching the child, Matt and Amy laughed, themselves impressed as they stared out the window at block after block of two-, three- and four-story brick buildings in the central business district; the reddish-brown structures were quite grand, many with columns, elaborate cornices and seemingly endless rows of tall, narrow windows.

Once the trolley arrived back at the hotel, the three disembarked and climbed into Matt's carriage, still euphoric from the streetcar ride. They went off shopping along Veranda Row on Fourth Street. In a clothier's shop, they carefully scoured the ready-made stock. Matt made several purchases for Amy, starting with a fashionable traveling suit of dark blue serge with braided trim and a small, high bustle. He insisted that she complete the outfit with kid walking shoes and a newfangled, deep-brimmed feathered hat with ribbon ties at the back. Matt's eyes glowed as he studied Amy in the stylish garments, and young Hannah clapped her hands in glee. By now, Amy was so caught up in the excitement that she completely forgot her pride, as Matt also purchased for her several simple, high-necked dresses for everyday wear, made of calico, gingham and muslin, along with an assortment of colorful sunbonnets. Before they left the shop, Matt even insisted on buying three new dresses and a pair of walking shoes for Hannah.

A while later, Amy took Matt aside and whispered to him miserably, "Matt, I'm afraid Ma might . . . might sell Hannah's dresses once we're gone."

"I see," he replied, scowling. "Well, in that case, we'll only give the child one for now, and let her wear it for the wedding, so's it will be broke in. The others we'll keep back for her to wear when she comes out to visit us."

Amy was deeply touched by Matt's words, his kindness

and wisdom. She found her respect for him building as the three departed the clothier's together. He really cared about Hannah, she realized. He wanted the child to come stay with them and would do his best to protect the little girl against Esther's exploitation.

Before they started home, Matt bought the girls an ice-cream soda at an apothecary shop. Then he drove the carriage down by the levee, past the stately high-spired cathedral and on toward the ornate, almost-completed Eads Bridge spanning the Mississippi River. Matt stopped the carriage on the bank, and Amy and Hannah marveled at the river at sunset, the flood of gold across the waterway. The tired stevedores were leaving for the day, having loaded their daily allotment of barrels and bales onto the stately paddle wheelers anchored to the wharves. Hannah stared at the riverboat *Robert E. Lee* towering in white-railed majesty before them and said, quietly, "One day I'm going to get on one of those riverboats and leave and never come back!" Amy and Matt's eyes met over her.

As they journeyed home, with quilted, ribbon-tied boxes piled in the boot of the buggy, Amy felt overwhelmed with gratitude toward Matt. Hannah dozed off now, lulled by the clip-clop of the horses' hooves, her head against her older sister's shoulder. Amy stared at her fiancé across from her in the carriage, studying his fine features beneath the brim of his hat, and she felt a dizzying wave of tenderness toward him. "Thanks, Matt—for everything," she whispered to him over Hannah's head, and when he smiled back at her with special, lingering warmth, she thought she would melt on the spot. . . .

When they approached Twenty-fifth Street, with its familiar row of crackerbox houses, Amy's euphoria faded as she remembered that, despite her new wardrobe, she was lacking in one critical item for the coming day—a wedding dress. She knew of no way to remedy the situation, either—she possessed no money of her own, and it was unthinkable that a bride should ask her prospective husband to buy her a wedding gown. She knew she would feel humiliated the next morning, and might embarrass Matt as well, by wearing an entirely inappropriate garment, flagrantly breaking the tradition of virginal white.

But as she, Matt and Hannah climbed the steps to the Harris home, each bearing a tall stack of boxes, Vida Peterson, the widow lady next door, waved to them from the porch where she rocked each evening. "Amy, dear, I'd like to have a word with you after supper, if you're free."

"Of course, Mrs. Peterson," Amy called back.

An hour later, Amy went over to visit the kind lady who had taught her piano when she was five, and who had offered the two Harris girls as much comfort as possible over the years. It was twilight as Amy sat down on a porch rocker next to her friend; the air had turned chilly, and both women wore wool shawls about their shoulders.

Widowed soon after she married sixteen years before when her young husband was tragically killed in a carriage accident, Vida Peterson still presented an attractive picture. Her rich black hair, scooped up in a bun, showed few signs of gray, despite the woman's thirty-eight years; her face was a lovely pink and white, with only sketchy shadows of the wrinkles of age. Despite the tragedy in Vida's life, Amy had never once heard her friend complain or look anything but serene; Vida Peterson was a deeply religious woman, accepting the Lord's will without defiance. The widow played the piano at church each Sunday, and managed to eke out a living by teaching music lessons to St. Louis youngsters. Late each afternoon, with her lessons ended for the day, Vida would come out on the porch and rock, welcoming one and all from the neighborhood to join her.

"Well, Amy, so I hear from Hannah that you're about to marry and move away from here," the widow said in greeting.

"Yes, ma'am," Amy replied shyly to her friend. "This has all been rather sudden. I'll be marrying Mr. Kendall in the morning, and we'll be taking the afternoon train to Rolla, where he lives."

"Congratulations, dear," Vida said in a warm, nonjudgmental tone that put Amy at ease. "I'm sure Matt Kendall has grown into a fine man. You know, I remember him from when he and his family used to live here.''

"Do you?'' Amy questioned eagerly. "Then you must recall that he lost both his parents.''

"Oh, yes, that really was tragic,'' Vida concurred, shaking her head. "I felt so sorry for young Matt back then, and for his younger sister, too.''

"Do you recall what happened then? I mean, how Mr. Kendall's parents died?'' Amy prodded.

The widow frowned thoughtfully. "Well, as I recollect, young Matt lost his father and uncle during the Camp Jackson Affair.''

"Camp Jackson Affair?''

"That was back at the start of the war, honey,'' the widow explained. "You see, Missouri's governor favored secession, and organized a Pro-Confederate militia right here in St. Louis at Camp Jackson. Matt's father and uncle were both members of the garrison, even though most citizens here sided with the North. There was quite a public outcry regarding the rebel camp, as you might imagine. The pillars of our community decided the Camp Jackson militia had to go, and organized an opposing force.'' Vida paused, scowling, an index finger alongside her mouth. "If my memory serves me correct, young Matt was there during the clash that followed. He went to where the fighting was, unarmed, hoping to persuade his father and uncle to give up the conflict and come home. Then that poor boy arrived just in time to watch both men he loved get killed in the crossfire.''

"How awful!'' Amy gasped.

"Yes, it was terrible, dear, but you must remember that there was wronging and killing on both sides back then. Anyhow, Matt Kendall became a very embittered young man,'' Vida continued, shaking her head. "Two buryings all at once, then his ma died of a broken heart not long after, too.''

"Merciful heavens!'' Amy gasped.

"I know, dear. It was a hurtful time. If it hadn't been for

your father lending young Matt a hand, who knows what would have become of him?''

"Yes, Matt told me my father was quite helpful to him when he lost his parents," Amy put in. "In fact, that's why he came here yesterday, hoping to find his old friend."

"I see," the widow murmured thoughtfully. "And he found you instead?''

Amy felt herself blushing. "Something like that," she admitted.

Vida reached across the porch chairs to pat Amy's hand. "Want to tell me about it, honey?"

Amy found she truly did; she really needed an older person to confide in at this point. As Vida listened sympathetically, Amy related to her how she became Matt Kendall's betrothed, describing to the widow the flurry of activities and emotions she had become enmeshed in during the last twenty-four hours. When Amy finished her account, Vida shook her head and said wisely, "Sounds like Matt Kendall knows his mind where you're concerned, my dear, and that he has developed into quite an honorable man, just like I thought he would. But one thing troubles me. I hate to interfere—but don't you think you should take more time to consider this decision?''

Amy sighed raggedly, her eyes stinging as turbulent, conflicting emotions welled up inside her. Vida was right— things were going frightfully fast for her! But did she really have any choice in the matter? Oh, if only she could have a mother who would be this concerned about her!

But the fact was, she didn't have such a mother. She and Hannah were, for all practical purposes, alone. To Vida, Amy said, "I realize this is all happening quite hastily, but Mr. Kendall needs a wife to help him with his farm out at Rolla. I think he'll stand by his word and provide for me well.''

Vida nodded with a sigh, realizing that the girl had a point. "I'm sure he will, child, and I must admit that Matt Kendall seems a much more appealing prospect than that Mr. Garrett of yours.''

Amy had to smile at this comment. Vida was very

protective of Amy, and had never approved of Lacy. And even though Amy had not let Vida's feelings stop her from planning to marry Lacy at one time, she did respect her friend's opinions.

"But, Amy," Vida now went on, "have you thought about what it might be like being a farmwife?"

Amy shrugged. "It couldn't be much worse than living here."

"That's true in a sense," Vida conceded. "But I was raised on a farm, girl, and I think it's only fair to warn you that the work is never-ending—sunup to sundown, and into the night, as well. You have to have a strong backbone, and you have to like animals, too."

"Animals?"

"Yes. Horses, pigs, chickens, mules."

Again, Amy shrugged. "I'm sure I'll adjust." The Harrises kept a few chickens in a coop in the backyard, and it all seemed quite uncomplicated.

Next to her, Vida secretly smiled at Amy's glib attitude. The girl would doubtless be in for a few surprises once she arrived at the farm with her new husband. But Amy would be cared for and safe, which was much more than the child could count on here. So Vida decided wisely to keep her peace.

The two friends slipped into silence for a moment, then Amy ventured, "Something's been troubling me, Mrs. Peterson. I have a favor to ask of you."

"What can I do, dear?" the older woman asked, looking concerned.

"I was wondering if you'd—if you'd kind of keep an eye out for Hannah once I'm gone, and write me if anything should—I mean, with my mother . . ." Amy stopped, at a loss for what to say next.

Fortunately, Vida understood completely, and reached out to place a reassuring hand over Amy's. "My dear, I was planning on doing just that already. You know you girls are like family to me. But you'll have to let me know how to get in touch with you."

"Oh, of course!" Amy breathed gratefully. "Let's see—I

guess you could write me general delivery. That would be to . . . to Mrs. Matt Kendall in Rolla, Missouri." Saying the words, Amy blushed. Hearing her married name was sobering, to say the least!

Removing her hand from Amy's, Vida frowned. "Very well, dear. I'll be sure to write—and not just if things are going badly for your sister." More cheerfully, the widow added, "So what time is the wedding to be tomorrow?"

"Eleven o'clock," Amy replied bravely. She added, "Mrs. Peterson, would you come?"

"Why, I was just sitting here with bated breath, praying that you'd ask!" the widow exclaimed. "In fact, I'd love to provide some music, if you think that would be fitting."

"Oh, that would be lovely!" Amy replied. Then she lowered her eyes, suddenly remembering again that she had no wedding dress. It would be doubly humiliating for her to have Mrs. Peterson see her that way.

"By the way, dear," her friend went on casually, "could you come inside with me for a moment? There's something I would like to show you."

"Of course," Amy replied, intrigued.

She followed Vida through the front door, directly into the darkened parlor of the house, where Vida's ornately carved Pleyel piano stood. The widow lit a kerosene lamp, then led Amy to a back bedroom, where the older woman went straight to a mahogany armoire, drew open the doors and pulled out a dress protected by a shroud of unbleached muslin. Pulling off the protective cover, Vida held up a long satin wedding dress for Amy's perusal. "My dear, I would consider it a great honor if you would wear this gown tomorrow."

Amy felt tears stinging her eyes. "Your wedding dress? Oh, Mrs. Peterson, I couldn't!"

The woman drew closer, still holding the dress. "And why not, pray tell?" Vida demanded stoutly. "I'll have you know, Amy Louise, that I always wanted to save this gown for my daughter. But the Good Lord had another plan for me. He wants you to wear this dress tomorrow, my dear, and let an old woman pretend, just for one day, that you're the daughter she never had.''

"Oh, Mrs. Peterson!" Amy tearfully embraced her friend. Under these circumstances, how could she refuse to wear the dress? "You're not old at all," she assured the widow, fighting back more tears. "I don't know anyone younger at heart!"

As the two women awkwardly stepped apart, Amy gazed at the wedding gown with glowing eyes. The satin had yellowed slightly with age and the gown was not stylish, but to her, no finer garment had ever been made!

Vida helped Amy try on the dress. It was a near-perfect fit, except for being a trifle short and a bit too full through the waist. The widow insisted that she would take a tuck in the waist, let out the hem and steam it that night, despite Amy's protestations that she herself should do the work. "A bride should have her mind on other things," Vida pronounced firmly.

A bride, Amy thought to herself sinkingly. Oh, yes, it seemed that she was soon to be a bride in every way!

Six

✦

Morning came all too quickly, even though Amy was up half the night packing and fretting about Hannah. Early on her wedding day, as Amy dressed for the service, she gave the little girl a sound lecture. "If Ma gets to acting crazy, now, you go see Mrs. Peterson, just like I told you."

"I will," Hannah said bravely. "Oh, Amy, I'll miss you so!"

Amy hugged her sister and struggled not to cry. The child looked darling this morning in one of the outfits Matt had bought her the day before—a white pleated blouse with lace collar, and a mauve-colored poplin pinafore with blue velvet ribbon accenting the skirt and sleeves and mounded into a bustle bow at the back. A matching bow held Hannah's lush blond curls in place. She made a delightful picture Amy would never forget.

Once Amy was dressed, she sent Hannah on out to the parlor, then took a moment to examine her own appearance in the beveled mirror over her dressing table. The white satin gown fit her perfectly now, thanks to the ministrations of Vida. The style was from another age—with the bodice section forming a V to the waist, slashed vertically by a long row of tiny mother-of-pearl buttons. The sleeves were full, cuffed at the wrist, and the skirt was long and straight, with two lines of buttons traveling downward from the waist to form a reversed V. Amy wore a simple veil of lace, pinned to her hair. She had to concede, as she stared into the mirror, that her cheeks held a rosy flush of excitement, her eyes a glow of adventure. Change could be frightening, all right; but Amy found herself accepting the fact that she had to make a major move in her life. She felt closer to Matt this morning, after their shopping excursion of the day before, after learning things about his background last evening. She could now understand the wounds of his past, why he was quiet, rather reticent on certain subjects, and she hoped the coming days would be a healing time for them both.

Amy regretted that her father couldn't be here to see this day, that she couldn't walk into the parlor on his arm. She hadn't seen him in eleven long years, yet he remained a well-defined figure in her mind—a kind, soft-spoken man who used to take her to the park and help her with her lessons. She loved her father still, yet there was a spark of bitterness there, she acknowledged, for the years after he left, when Amy was a love-famished child who had cried herself to sleep each night, praying that he would come rescue her from all the harsh trials that had been forced on her.

Her father hadn't come then; nor would he miraculously appear today, she knew. While his absence saddened her almost as much as leaving Hannah did, Amy realized she must look to the future if there were to be hope for either of them. . . .

A discreet knock at the bedroom door pulled Amy from her reverie, and she went over to crack the door, finding Vida outside, elegant and serene-looking in a full-skirted rose-colored silk frock. "My dear, you're a vision!" the widow exclaimed, entering the small bedroom and handing Amy a fragrant bouquet of flowers. "From Matt," Vida explained simply. "He rushed out and bought these from a street vendor this morning. And you should see the ring he purchased for you, too!"

Amy fought back a tear as she heard Vida's words and stared downward at the spray of exquisite pink roses. "How lovely," she murmured, unbearable happiness welling up inside her. Until two days earlier, she could recall no one in her life thinking of her with such sensitivity and thoughtfulness as Matt Kendall did.

"Are you ready, dear?" Vida went on with excitement. "The minister's here, and everything is set in the parlor."

"I'll be right there . . . and thanks so much for everything," Amy told her, giving the widow a quick hug. As Vida hurried off for the parlor, Amy took a final moment to say good-bye to the tiny room she had shared with Hannah for so many years. The next time she slept in the same bed with someone else, she thought to herself with a mixture of anticipation and dread, it would be with her husband. . . .

Moments later, as Amy stepped into the parlor for the service, Matt watched her, his dark brown eyes glowing. Amy looked enchanting to him, radiant, the sun shining in her curling layers of blond hair, even through the gauzy veil. When he studied her dress, not a single thought of its style crossed his mind—instead, he thought only that she was the most beautiful bride he'd ever seen. Pride rose up in him as he noted the spray of roses he'd bought her, clutched in her lovely tapered fingers.

Even though the minister and his wife, Vida, Hannah and Esther were assembled in the parlor with Matt, Amy had eyes only for her fiancé. He wore a different suit today, she noted, obviously his finest—smartly cut of black wool, with a matching vest, an elegant white linen shirt, and white lace jabot. His eyes smiled when he saw her, locking with hers in a meaningful, tender way as she walked over to join him before the pastor. In the background, Vida played a refrain of "Blessed Be the Tie that Binds," and then the gray-haired minister, Reverend Chandler, cleared his throat and began to read from his order of service. "Dearly beloved, we are gathered here in the presence of

God to witness the joining of this man and this woman in holy matrimony..."

It all went so quickly. Amy repeated the vows mechanically, conscious that Matt was watching her in fascination, that her mother, dressed decently for once in plain black silk, was looking on greedily from the settee behind them, that dear little Hannah was struggling not to cry.

Soon enough, a heavy gold band was slipped on Amy's finger, and then came the words, "I now pronounce you man and wife," along with the traditional, "You may kiss the bride."

That was when everything at last seemed to slow down, when Matt turned to her and gently drew back her veil, taking her into his arms and gracing her lips with a whisper of a kiss that somehow left her hungrier for him than his first passionate embrace had. She looked up and saw the ardor, the need in his dark eyes and felt weak....

Then the spell was broken, as everyone gathered around to congratulate the newlyweds. Amy's mother offered her guests punch and white cake, which she'd actually baked herself. Amy embraced Hannah and promised her, "I'll find some way to get you out to be with us at Rolla. Please try to be patient." The little girl nodded bravely to her sister through her tears.

As Amy released Hannah, she felt a comforting hand on her arm, and turned to see the minister's wife, Mrs. Chandler, standing next to her. The sweet-faced little woman wore gray silk, and she was smiling serenely as she watched the two sisters. "My dear, I wish you every happiness," the minister's wife said sincerely, giving Amy a quick hug. "I spoke with your new husband before the service, and he seems such a fine young man. And I know you'll love living in Rolla, too. Quite a picturesque little town."

"Have you been there?" Amy asked eagerly.

"No, but Reverend Chandler and I often pass through there on the train when we go to visit our married daughter in Springfield." Watching Hannah walk off to the serving table where Matt was talking with Reverend Chandler, the older woman lowered her voice and added, "My dear, I couldn't help but hear you telling young Hannah that you want her to come out for a visit. Perhaps the Reverend and I might drop the child off at Rolla the next time we head west to visit Margaret."

"Oh, Mrs. Chandler, could you?" Amy cried, feeling a surge of new hope. Mrs. Chandler was evidently aware that the two Harris girls were inseparably close, and Amy felt quite touched by her sensitivity and thoughtfulness.

"I'll certainly try," the minister's wife now replied. "In fact, I'll be sure to mention the idea to Esther the next time Richard and I are planning the journey."

As Mrs. Chandler offered her kind promise, Matt joined his bride, grinning happily at both women. The minister's wife extended her hand to the bridegroom with a warm smile. "Congratulations, Mr. Kendall. I was just telling your bride that Reverend Chandler and I do pass through your town on occasion. . . ."

While Matt and Mrs. Chandler chatted more about Rolla, Vida came up. She took Amy aside, congratulating the girl and pressing a ten-dollar gold piece into her hand. Amy protested, but the widow told her sagely, "Every bride should have money of her own. What are you going to do if Hannah needs you, or, heaven forbid, if things don't work out with Mr. Kendall? You must take this, or you'll have no train fare to get back."

Amy stood struggling between her pride and the logic of Vida's warning. Yet before she could make up her mind, she felt a hand on her shoulder. "Time to get ready to leave, Mrs. Kendall," her new husband informed her with a smile. "We mustn't miss our train."

Amy swallowed hard, catching herself just in time to keep from pulling away from Matt's touch, as the magnitude of what she had just done overwhelmed her. She was Matt Kendall's wife now, and he had every right to touch her. While she trusted him in many ways, she also realized that she had put herself in the hands of a man who was a virtual stranger to her. Vida was right. The ten-dollar gold piece, the sum total of her savings, was the only recourse she had if things didn't work out with Matt Kendall. The gold still clutched in her hand, Amy hugged the widow. "I'll pay you back."

"Pay me back by being happy, Amy Kendall," Vida whispered.

The Good Lord knew, she would try her best!

Seven

✚

A my Kendall stared out the window, fascinated, as
the A. & P. Flyer chugged through forests of pine
and hardwoods in the rolling hills west of St. Louis.
The landscape was ablaze with the fiery colors of autumn—
the yellow of hickories, the scarlet of sweet gum, the russet
of sycamores, mixed in riotous splendor with verdant short-
leafed pines. The afternoon breeze blowing in the window
was cool and crisp, smelling deliciously of pine, a pleasant
contrast to the dustiness of the passenger car and the
hardness of the seats. Gazing raptly out the window, Amy
made quite a picture of the proper young bride wearing her
new, stylish serge traveling suit, with its coordinating deep-
brimmed hat. The gold curls blowing all about added a
femininely enticing allure to her visage.

While not crammed, the passenger car was well filled
with families and a number of men traveling alone. Matt,
sitting next to Amy, was involved in a conversation with a
federal marshal who sat across the aisle from the couple.
The gray-haired lawman, in striped trousers and dark jacket
with black string cravat, was heading toward western Missouri where he had been called in by local authorities to
help track the James and Younger brothers, who had recently
been active robbing banks and trains in the border region.

Amy had, of course, read about such outlaws in the *Missouri Republican*; while the banks in western Missouri had hired the formidable Pinkerton Detective Agency of Chicago to track down the desperadoes, unfortunately many of the citizens of Missouri seemed to view the brothers as folk heroes, and progress in the case had been practically nonexistent. Amy did wonder that her new husband found the subject so fascinating.

But, staring at the wide gold band on her hand, she soon found her thoughts drifting back to her own situation. She again thought of her wedding mere hours earlier, and remembered with poignance kissing her little sister goodbye. Amy had worried about Hannah off and on from the moment she left with Matt, but Mrs. Chandler's promise that she and the Reverend would try to bring the child out with them on the train in the not too distant future eased Amy's mind at least a little.

The journey itself had offered distractions. Amy was finding her trip with Matt to be an adventure in many ways. She had never before traveled by train. The only trip she could remember ever taking with her family was a wagon journey they had made when she was five years old. Amy vaguely recalled traveling across country with her father and mother to a family reunion in Steelville, Missouri, the event organized by a first cousin of Amy's father. She remembered Cousin Josie, the sweet-faced, plump matron who had opened her home to the Harrises and to other members of the family from such far-flung places as Kansas City and the Boothill Country. If Amy's memory was accurate, Steelville was not far from Rolla. She reflected on this now, finding that the idea of having family, even a distant relation, not too far from Rolla was a distinct comfort. She also thought of Vida's gold piece, even now safely tucked away in her crocheted reticule. The widow had been right, bless her heart; it was good for Amy to know that she would have some options, the wherewithal to at least get away, should things not work out with Matt.

Amy eyed the handsome stranger next to her. Like Amy, Matt had changed clothes following the wedding; he now wore a plain brown suit and a pair of worn everyday boots. Yet, still, her new husband looked quite imposing and masculine to her, especially as she thought of the night to come. By nightfall, they would be at his farm alone. Would he adhere to his promise and not expect her to come, at once, to his bed? Again, she thought of his seemingly contradictory cancellation of his planned trip to Virginia to visit his sister. Why was it so critical to him that he have his new wife alone? The man appealed to her mightily—but, oh, he frightened her, too!

The sound of the U.S. Marshal's voice interrupted Amy's thoughts as the man told Matt, "The Missouri legislature is sure to appropriate the money needed for more agents to track down them varmints, and between the governor's men and the Pinkertons, I think the James and Younger boys will find their days are numbered."

Observing the two men, Amy noted a rueful smile on her husband's face as he asked the older man, "Have the Pinkertons found anyone yet who knows what the outlaws look like?"

The marshal shook his head. "No, that's been a real pickle. But as the gang grows more daring, they're sure to seal their own fate."

"You know, there should be quite a few around who can finger the brothers, seeing's they rode with Quantrill and Anderson back during the war," Matt interjected thoughtfully.

The marshal took a pouch of chewing tobacco from the pocket of his jacket and replied, "Well, whoever knows is keeping his peace, that's for sure."

"So it seems," Matt Kendall agreed.

The men shifted conversational topics then, discussing the scandal-ridden Grant administration and the panic that had recently hit the stock market, affecting many farmers adversely, particularly those who had bought extensively on credit. "Cash on the counter, that's always been my motto," Matt now stoutly informed the lawman.

Amy turned away and stared out the window again.

* * *

Two hours later, the conductor shouted out, "Rolla!", and Amy grew tensely alert in her seat. As the A. & P. Flyer snaked over a rise, its whistle blowing, its smokestack billowing soot and cinders, the town appeared, a prosperous community nestled between rolling hills.

Amy's first glimpse of industry in the town was a stockyard she now spotted off to the west of them, with cattle crammed in pens, cowhands milling about on the November landscape. "The yard just opened up last March," Matt informed her. "It's for fattening up stock from the railroad before they're hauled on to the yards in St. Louis."

Amy wrinkled her nose at the heavy odor of manure, but as they moved on past a large, tree-shaded pond with an excursion boat sitting at its edge, she smiled to herself at the picturesque scene. Now the train slowed, approaching the depot, which was a handsome frame structure surrounded by warehouses, a flour mill and a barrel factory. Amy felt a building excitement. She and Matt had to chuckle at the marshal, who was now stretched out across from them, snoring, dead to the world, the chugging of the train accentuated by his rhythmic snorts and the whining of a baby at the rear of the car.

"Rolla's a right fine community," Matt told Amy. "Good size, too. The stores are well stocked, and of course, there's the train for taking my crops to market."

Amy nodded, disturbed somewhat that Matt's comments had to do only with the practicalities of life and not with the social functions of the community. But then, that was a man for you, wasn't it?

Now, the train was squealing to a halt, the acrid odor of smoke wafting through the dusty car. As all motion ceased, the marshal across from them at last stirred, shrugging awake. Matt helped Amy out of her seat, nodding to the lawman as they left. "Good luck to you, sir."

The man called back a polite farewell, and Amy and Matt, along with five other passengers, disembarked. In the yard of the depot, the wiry conductor unloaded half a dozen portmanteaus from the baggage compartment. Matt insisted on carrying both of their bags, shaking his head when Amy offered to help. As the two crossed the yard and headed for the station house with its sawtooth cornice, Amy knew another moment of unease. At their backs, she could hear the train chugging out of the yard to continue on its journey, and the shrill sound of its whistle seemed a final cutting of her ties with the outside world.

They walked through the paneled depot and out the front door, onto the cool streets of Rolla. Amy was surprised at the industry she saw around them—the wagons and buggies clattering down the dirt thoroughfare, the farmers with their loads of wheat and corn waiting for service at the mill, the workers stacking spanking-new wood barrels in the yard of the cooper shop nearby.

As the two started down Ninth Street, a farmer wearing a huge straw hat passed them on the boardwalk, heading toward the depot. The unshaven man, in baggy pants, home-made shirt and suspenders, nodded politely to Amy, but made no sign of recognition toward Matt. Matt didn't greet the farmer either, and Amy found this strange. She remembered her new husband's reticence around the other passengers who had just disembarked with them—some of whom were surely citizens of this town. She recalled that Matt told her he had only owned his farm here for ten months; yet still, he should be better integrated into the community by now, she thought. Maybe it was the shyness of his nature that kept him from getting to know people; perhaps that was one reason he wanted a wife. One thing was for sure, though, she decided. If this community was to be her home, then she was not living here as a stranger! She recalled how much she had enjoyed the church socials back in St. Louis, the occasional croquet parties given by friends. Such activities frequently had saved her sanity, and she figured that no matter where she lived, community life would be somewhat important to her.

They turned a corner, passing a stylish-looking man in long sack coat with ascot tie and checked trousers. "Afternoon, ma'am," the gentleman said, doffing his derby hat to Amy. While the man also nodded to Matt, there was again no spark of recognition between the two men, and Amy felt even more unsettled.

As they walked past a charming-looking country store, Amy paused, inhaling the delicious aroma of jerky, pickles, and leather. Inside, several men with mustaches and long sideburns, wearing suspendered trousers and homemade broadcloth shirts, were talking near the wood stove. Beyond, two women were discussing yard goods with a clerk. As Matt, too, paused, giving his wife a quizzical look, Amy asked him shyly, "Oh, Matt! Could we go in for a moment? It's such a delightful little store."

In reply, her husband shook his head. "There's nothing we're needing at the moment," he told her. "The larder's well stocked at the farmhouse. Besides, if we don't start for the farm now, we'll be past sundown getting home."

Amy sighed and nodded, unable to refute his logic. With one final longing glance toward the inviting store, she fell into step beside her husband once more. She realized that one reason she had wanted to stop was to postpone as long as possible the moment when she would be alone with Matt Kendall.

Crossing a dirt street, they approached a weather-beaten stable with a horseshoe-shaped sign above the door bearing the words, "Emmett Teague, Livery and Harnessmaker." "My horse is boarded here," Matt explained to Amy.

As they approached the ramshackle building, it became obvious to Amy that this establishment also housed the community blacksmithing operation. In the center of a cluttered yard stood the blacksmith's furnace, along with bellows, a hammer and anvil, and the grinding wheel, which looked so much like the newfangled highwheeler bicycles Amy had sometimes seen people riding in St. Louis.

Inside, the dark structure smelled unpleasantly of animals, dirt and decaying hay. Standing just inside the opened doors with Matt, Amy studied the interior, cluttered with various conveyances, the walls studded with tools and harnesses. No one was in sight, but from a distant stall Amy could hear the sounds of a hammer hitting iron and the nervous whinnying of an animal. Obviously, someone was shoeing a horse.

"Emmett? Emmett, are you there?" Matt called out.

They heard muffled cursing, then a stall at the rear of the building creaked open, and a barrel-chested man, dressed in a ragtag shirt and dark trousers, lumbered out. "Why, hello, Matt." The man greeted them with a gap-toothed smile. "That was the quickenist skip to Virginny I done ever heard of," he added, eyeing Amy with unabashed curiosity.

"I didn't make it to Virginia, Emmett," Matt told the blacksmith self-consciously, shifting from foot to foot. "I stopped off in St. Louis to see an old friend and met his daughter and well . . . meet Mrs. Kendall."

"Well, I'll be a turkey's gizzard," the man named Emmett said with a dry laugh, drawing closer to the couple. Eyeing Amy frankly, he added, "Hello, young lady. If you ain't the prettiest thing I ever laid eyes on. No wonder old Matt didn't make it no further than St. Louie!" Jabbing Matt in the ribs with a heavy elbow, the man added slyly, "You old snake, Kendall! Wait till I tell the boys about this down at Salter's Store!"

While Amy found herself smiling at Emmett's quaint humor, Matt seemed to see no reason for levity in the situation. Clearing his throat, he told the harnessmaker tersely, "Now, if you'd just hitch Ginger up to my buggy, and let me settle up with you for the board—"

"Sure, Kendall," the man said with a grin, undaunted. Scratching his head with a smutty hand, he added, "Well, I cain't hardly charge you for board, seeing's your mare ain't been here a week—"

"I'll pay you for a week, then," Matt said stiffly, and Emmett merely shrugged as the younger man dug into his pockets.

The two men settled their account. Emmett Teague was heading off toward a stall at the back of the building to fetch Matt's horse, when a tall man, dressed entirely in white, entered the structure and headed toward Matt and Amy. To Amy, the newcomer looked almost like a showman in his impeccable suit and matching white Panama hat. "Why, Matt Kendall," the man called out as he strode assuredly toward the couple. "Imagine running into you here."

Though it was a relief to Amy to know that her husband knew at least two people in this town, her pleasure quickly turned to distress as she studied Matt's expression. Her husband's strong jaw was set in hard lines, his dark eyes narrowed in suspicion. "Afternoon, Reverend Fulton," he finally, grudgingly acknowledged. To Amy's surprise, Matt moved closer to her, even took her hand protectively.

Now standing in front of them, the brown-haired, wide-faced man stared keenly at Amy. "And who might this young lady be?"

"Meet Mrs. Kendall," Matt said stiffly.

While the reverend's eyebrows shot up in surprise at this revelation, he nonetheless doffed his elegant hat with exaggerated form and shook the soft hand that Amy graciously extended. "Pleased to meet you, ma'am," he drawled. To Matt, he added, "Isn't this marriage right sudden, Kendall? I was never told—"

But Emmett Teague's voice cut into the reverend's remarks. Evidently having trouble leading Matt's nervously whinnying horse out of the stall, Teague called out irritably, "Kendall, would you come give me a hand with this filly?" Spotting Fulton, Teague added, "Afternoon, Reverend. I'll have Jezebel shoed directly."

"Mighty fine, Emmett," the reverend called back to Teague.

As Matt hesitated to leave his wife's side, the harnessmaker called out with strained patience, "Kendall, do you mind?"

Matt scowled in uncertainty, then strode off for the back of the building. Meanwhile, Reverend Fulton turned his curiosity toward Amy. "Well, if this ain't a nice surprise. Emmett told me Kendall was going off to Virginny fer a visit, then he shows back up in nothin' flat, with a new wife, to boot."

The man's inquisitiveness had Amy blushing. Watching Teague and her husband struggle with the horse through the corner of her eye, Amy explained to the reverend that Mr. Kendall had met her when he stopped off in St. Louis hoping to see her father, and that she and Matt had decided to marry rather quickly.

"Makes sense, I suppose," the man commented when she finished. "If anyone were needin' a wife, I suppose it's Kendall there, with that farm to run all by hisself."

"Why, yes, I'm really looking forward to seeing Mr. Kendall's farm," Amy replied eagerly.

At her words, the reverend surprisingly snorted. "Hmmph. If you're wanting my thoughts, young lady, I'm bettin' you'll be right sick of that there farm before a fortnight passes. You have my sympathies, too."

"What do you mean?" Amy asked, watching Matt and Emmett hitch the chestnut-colored mare to a small, black buggy.

"Well, he's a right peculiar breed, that husband of yourn," Fulton informed Amy. "Be here right onto a year, but stays to hisself most of the time. Only comes to town twice a month or so for supplies. When he first got here, I rode out to the place personal to invite him to church." Hooking his thumb in his lapel with pride and smiling from ear to ear, Fulton explained, "Got me a right nice little congregation here at Rolla Presbyterian—decent, God-fearing folk. But that husband of yourn," the reverend went on with a perturbed look, "he told me flat out that he don't hold with religion, nossir. Didn't even offer me a gourd to wet my whistle nor a drink for Jezebel, neither."

"Jezebel?"

"My horse."

"Oh, yes. I believe Mr. Teague mentioned the name," Amy muttered.

"Right unneighborly, if you ask me," the reverend grumbled on.

Amy listened to the reverend's words with dismay. Her fears that Matt was something of a loner in the community were being confirmed. Indeed, her husband was now glaring at the minister sideways as he harnessed his mare to the buggy. His expression suggested that he suspected what the reverend was saying to his bride.

Amy's pride and her feelings of loyalty as a wife forbade that she say anything against her husband, so she explained to the reverend simply, "I'm sure that when you came calling, Reverend Fulton, my husband was feeling the strain of running the farm himself, and embarrassed that he had no suitable repast to offer you. However, if you wish to call again, I assure you that it will be my pleasure to receive you.''

The man beamed at her words, his face again split by a wide, buck-toothed grin. ''Well—well, ain't that neighborly of you.'' More soberly, he added, ''It seems you've come in the nick of time, too, young lady. You look like a God-fearing type to me. If I were you, I'd be thinking of the soul of that husband of yourn and get him into church right quick.''

With the buggy readied and Matt approaching her with a determined gleam in his eye, Amy nodded and whispered under her breath, ''I'll do my best, Reverend Fulton.''

Soon thereafter, Matt and Amy left the town of Rolla in his buggy. He made no comment regarding her conversation with Fulton, instead politely pointing out to her the various sights on the way, including the Rolla Fair Grounds and a large, stately building sitting isolated on a rise to the north of them, which Matt explained housed the newly established Missouri School of Mines.

The two fell into silence as they left the town behind them. They proceeded west on Springfield Road, entering a terrain of closely grouped blue hills adorned with autumn's bright fire. Amy looked around eagerly at the glorious countryside. Matt had told her before that this part of Missouri was in the foothills of the Ozarks. The area was a mixture of glades, with their sparse vegetation and rocky outcroppings, along with lush hillocks, grassy meadows and rich creekbeds. The road followed a sparkling stream now, snaking with it between the hills, and Amy smiled as she looked downward and watched a rainbow darter streaking over the rocks. She enjoyed the quiet music and invigorating purity of nature after the roar and smoke of the train; taking deep breaths of crisp air, she listened to the rush of the brook, the murmur of the wind, the song of robins and the calling of meadowlarks. The afternoon had grown colder, but the day was still bright and lovely. Amy imagined what the landscape would look like during the coming spring, when the trees she recognized as redbud and dogwood would come into full bloom, when wildflowers—buttercups, daffodils, jonquils—would poke their lovely parasols above the turf.

But the thought of spring brought its own particular chill. Come spring, what would things be like between her and Matt? Would she be his wife in every way then?

She turned to her husband, and while she couldn't read his expression beneath the brim of his felt hat, she decided it was time to break the silence between them. "So you bought your farm here around the beginning of this year?" she ventured.

He nodded, clucking to the horse as they navigated a steep turn around a small hill. "January tenth, to be exact. It's a nice little place," he continued with pride. "The glades are mostly worthless, 'cept for grazing the stock, but there's a good bit of creekbed, rich bottomland, and I've had me one good season of corn already."

"I see," Amy murmured. "If you don't mind my asking, what made you decide you wanted to be a farmer in the first place?"

He turned to her and smiled quickly. "I don't mind," he said. "After the war, I spent several years down in Texas, working as a ranchhand. I learned a lot down there—how to care for livestock, how to grow crops for feed. And one day—I don't know, I just got me a hankering to come back east, put down roots, find a spread of my own. I got as far as Rolla and heard of this farm. Then, when I laid my eyes on the place . . ." He shook his head with a sort of wonder, then smiled at her in a tender, fervid way. "I guess you know that when I see something I want, I make it mine."

At his words, Amy felt her cheeks flaming, and she turned away in acute embarrassment. Matt's comment was totally unexpected. It set her senses reeling. Again, she wondered about putting her trust in this man. The rest of the way to the farm, his words reverberated through her brain, like a prophecy: *When I see something I want, I make it mine. . . .*

Even though it was near sunset when they finally approached Matt's land, Amy's first glimpse of the farmstead delighted her. As they went down into a valley and crossed a brook Matt informed her was called "Little Beaver Creek," his spread appeared beyond them, the house sheltered beneath a craggy limestone bluff, a sparkling spring meandering off to one side.

The two-storied farmhouse dominated the landscape; it was neatly whitewashed, with a tin roof, black shutters and a huge front porch complete with swing. Scattered about the grassy landscape were the other outbuildings—the barn, smokehouse, springhouse, various pens and cribs.

As Matt navigated the horse across the stream and drew them closer to his property, Amy spotted chickens and pigs in the farmyard and cows and horses grazing on a glade off to the west. Mixed in with it all was the whimsical, almost eerie rustle of the wind. It rattled the chains of the swing and the doors of outbuildings, even as the glorious light play of the setting sun showered the atmosphere with an almost phosphorescent glow. To Amy, the scene was pure enchantment. "Oh, your farm is so lovely!" she told Matt.

He smiled with pride and snapped the reins. "Our farm," he corrected. When she glanced at him quickly and warmly, he nodded and remarked, "Looks like Lyle kept things well tended while I was gone."

Amy eyed him curiously. "Lyle? Would he be your hired hand?"

Matt shook his head. "I don't hold with hiring on help, not when a man and his missus can see to a spread of this size themselves."

"I see," Amy replied, rather taken aback. "But Lyle—"

"Lyle Stockton's my neighbor," Matt explained. "He promised to come by daily to feed and water the stock while I was gone."

"Oh," Amy murmured, rather disappointed. It was nice to know Matt knew one of his neighbors, but considering the warnings she had received about how much work was involved in running a farm, she would have welcomed a hired hand, too. "Does Mr. Stockton have a family?"

"Yes. A wife and two boys. They live two miles west of here."

Amy smiled with relief. Another farmwife she could talk to—even visit! "Do you see them often?" she asked her husband eagerly.

"Nope," he said.

Just as Amy's heart thudded in disappointment at his reply, Matt stopped the buggy before the house. He quickly alighted from the conveyance and came around to her side to help her down. He caught her beneath the arms with his strong hands and effortlessly eased her to the ground. "Welcome home, Mrs. Kendall," he said, smiling.

There was a huskiness in his voice as he drew her down beside him, and he kept her there, pressed between the buggy and his hard masculine body, a bit longer than necessary. She looked up tentatively and at last got a good look at his face, his eyes. She saw the setting sun reflected in those dark orbs, which showed tenderness, too. Amy felt a hard stab of guilt for ever doubting Matt's motives or his sincerity, for she could not look at his face now without seeing the pride he took in having her with him and his protectiveness toward her, too. For a moment, she was almost sure he was going to kiss her, and, wantonly, she welcomed the thought.

But then the spell broke as Matt cleared his throat, wrapped an arm about Amy's waist and led her toward the house. They climbed the steps together, and Amy, looking around, noticed a fine scattering of leaves on the porch. All at once, it struck her that this was her house now, her very own home! She would take pride in this house, sweep the porch with joy in her heart, be filled with love for every plank. Never had she known something so fine that was truly hers before, and the thought was so exhilarating that it almost made her dizzy.

Matt had taken out his key and opened the front door now, and Amy stepped forward, eager to see more of this delightful home. But that's when Matt caught her firmly by the arm and asked with laughter in his eyes, "Don't you know that it's customary for a bridegroom to carry his bride over the threshold?"

He lifted her up against his hard chest as if she were a feather. She could smell the bay rum in his hair, the slight odor of smoke from the train car on his clothing, and it seemed so very masculine, so right. He carried her so effortlessly that she felt she was floating on a cloud, and her euphoria, her feeling of being—for once in her life—entirely at home, overwhelmed her, and a laugh of pure joy bubbled up from her throat.

His eyes lit in return as he carried her into the darkened front hallway of the farmhouse, kicking the door shut behind them. That's when she got her kiss. Matt stood there, holding her in the shadows, and kissed her as if he would climb inside her. His mouth was demanding, almost bruising, and she found her lips softly opening to him, welcoming his ravishment. Her heart was beating so frantically she thought she would faint, but she embraced the giddiness, soaring with it, even as she wrapped her arms about his neck and clung to him.

After a leisurely moment, he set her on her feet, pulled her tighter against him and kissed her once more, his tongue penetrating her mouth again, this time with a blatantly intimate message. When his hands reached boldly upward to caress her breasts through her traveling suit, she at last realized that things were getting out of hand. With a low cry, she pushed him away.

He cursed under his breath but didn't pursue her. His expression was difficult to read in the gathering shadows of the hallway, yet the sound of their labored breathing seemed to scream out in the void.

After a moment, Amy heard the hiss of a match. Then Matt was standing across from her, holding a lighted kerosene lantern, his eyes impaling her with challenge, his strong chest rising and falling as he struggled to control himself.

It was a terrifying moment for Amy, a moment filled with

stark fear and debilitating desire. She was totally alone with this man, powerless, and she had no idea what her husband would do next. In a moment of reckless joy, she had forgotten herself, brazenly welcoming him with her mouth, her arms, only to then push him away like a cheap tease. No man, much less a husband, could be faulted for giving a woman just what she deserved under the circumstances.

Would that be so terrible? a perverse inner voice demanded. Matt Kendall's physical needs frightened her, yet that look in his eyes now . . . so dark, hot, soul-searing. It drew her like a beacon. He seemed to need her so much. . . .

Nonetheless, Amy remained immobilized, her fear of the carnal unknown ultimately winning out as memories of the violence in her parents' marriage again assaulted her. For a charged moment, Matt said nothing, just stared at her until she feared his gaze would leave scorch marks on her person. Then he muttered in a strained tone, "I'll show you the house."

Mechanically, they both hung their hats on the pegged rack near the door. Then, like two strangers, not touching, hardly daring to look at each other, they navigated through the spacious, homey interior, with Matt, lantern in hand, leading the way.

The downstairs boasted two large rooms on either side of a central hallway. The kitchen was spacious and full of windows. The parlor had quite serviceable Victorian furniture, cozy braided rugs, and a beautiful native stone hearth with a large central supporting block Matt told her was called the keystone.

Upstairs were four smaller rooms. The first had an oak bed and matching dresser. "This is my room," he told her.

When she stared back at him, at a loss, he took her arm and led her to the room next door. "I suppose you'll be wanting to stay in here for now."

Amy stared gratefully at the small room, with its iron double bed, plain wooden dresser and wardrobe. Whereas the room would appear stark and cramped to many an eye, it looked like heaven to Amy, and she was relieved and grateful that Matt evidently planned to keep his promise, and wouldn't expect her to come immediately to his bed.

The other two upstairs rooms, while quite tiny, surprised Amy. One was a sewing room—complete with dressmaker's form and an elaborate Singer Family Sewing Machine. "Oh, Matt!" Amy breathed.

"Do you enjoy sewing?" he asked.

She smiled shyly, her eyes aglow. "Very much."

"Good," he replied with obvious pride. "We'll get you some dress lengths in town later on. You'll be needing more dresses for everyday wear, and maybe you'll want to redo some of the curtains, too."

Matt's solicitude left Amy flushed with appreciation as they went to the remaining room upstairs. She gasped in pleasure. A nursery! She was enchanted by the small, obviously handmade spindle cradle. Going over to the dresser, she opened a drawer and held up a small linen baby dress with beautiful blue cross-stitching on all the seams. "Matt?" she questioned her husband, her brow puckered. "Gracious, this dresser is full of baby clothes!"

He nodded, moving closer to her. "The couple I bought the farm from had just lost their child before they left here."

"Oh, Matt!" Amy cried in dismay. "You mean, she made all these clothes for—"

"Yes," he replied sadly.

"But she should have taken these things with her. Why, the hours it takes for this kind of handwork—"

"I know. That's what I told her. But she and her husband wanted to start over out west. Couldn't take along any memories, she told me. She wanted to leave the sewing machine and the clothes for someone who could use them fresh." Moving closer to Amy, Matt added, "She told me she thought I'd need them." He touched her arm and said tenderly, "I think she was right."

Amy stared up at him, mesmerized by his look and his words, weakening once more. Oh, Lord, this situation was dangerous! The tension was always there between them, waiting to well to the surface, to explode between them once more. And what such an explosion might mean frightened her terribly. She must never fool herself about that; she must never let her guard slip.

With these stern inner warnings, Amy managed to tear herself from the sensual message in Matt's eyes. She shut the dresser drawer. Avoiding his perplexed scowl, she left the room ahead of him.

"I'll be bringing in our bags," he said as they headed down the stairs.

"Fine," she returned stiffly.

At the bottom of the steps, they both paused and merely stared at each other for another awkward moment. Finally, Matt said, "You'll be wanting to fix supper, then."

And he walked out the front door with the lantern, leaving her alone in the shadows.

That angered Amy. She glowered at the door he'd just practically shut in her face, then turned on her heel, heading for the kitchen, rubbing her arms to stave off the deepening chill in the house. As she located a box of matches and a kerosene lantern on the table in the center of the large room, it didn't occur to her that perhaps Matt felt as uncomfortable as she did, that perhaps he had told her to cook supper simply because he didn't know what else to say. Instead, she thought of how cold, impersonal, even arrogant his parting order was. Here she had just arrived, and he expected her to go to a kitchen she had never before seen and miraculously produce a meal!

As the light illuminated the room, she stared at the cold cast-iron stove. She may as well go on outside, she mused, find kindling for the fire box, hunt up eggs in the henhouse and meat in the springhouse. Her new husband wanted a fiery kiss and a hot meal, in that order, so it seemed. At least she should be grateful that he wasn't demanding she immediately come to his bed.

Moments later, stumbling around outside looking for kindling, almost dropping her smoky lamp, Amy wasn't grateful.

Matt mentally kicked himself as he went out the front door to fetch in their luggage. He felt he had acted like a fool around his new wife. But the girl was peculiar. First she had kissed him as though she wouldn't let go of him for a month of Sundays, then she had backed off like a spooked deer. He had been strongly tempted to take her upstairs then and make this marriage a marriage in every way from the beginning. But something in her eyes had at last reached him, penetrating his frustration, telling him that she wasn't merely playing a game with him. The girl was frightened, really scared, he knew now. What was the cause of that horrible fear in her eyes? Was it him?

He knew the potential for violence was in him, had been there ever since the day he had watched his father and uncle being killed back at the start of the Civil War. He was never to forget that day; his mother had sent him to fetch the two men home from a confrontation going on in the streets, and instead, he arrived in time to watch both men die, killed in the crossfire of a skirmish between Confederate sympathizers and the St. Louis Home Guard. He would never erase from his mind the look on his mother's face when he told her of the killings—it was like watching her soul fold up and die right there in front of him. Weeks later, he watched his mother die, and the rage had been inside him ever since. The rage even the violence of the war couldn't cure . . .

But Matt controlled it around Amy, didn't he? He knew his bride was a lady and virginal, and he sure didn't want to scare her away. This afternoon, when Fulton was sidling up to her, his first instinct had been to wrap a few horseshoes around the neck of that sanctimonious bastard!

The truth of it was, he wanted Amy so badly, he wasn't sure he could control it at all. After he saw her today in that white dress, and they repeated the vows that made them legally one . . . The girl would have to be persuaded to come around, to satisfy the unendurable desire he felt for her, before his body took charge and did all the persuading, whether she liked it right off or not.

Still holding the lantern, Matt gripped the handles of both bags in his other hand and headed back for the house, his spirits sagging in the darkness. That was poor, telling the girl straight off to go fix supper, knowing how tired she must be, and without giving her a hint of where things were. He thought of going in to the kitchen now to lend her a hand, then saw the light from another lantern bloom and spill out through the kitchen window. He smiled to himself. The girl had grit. She'd make out just fine. Besides, it wouldn't be manly for him to do kitchen work for his new wife, now would it? It might start the marriage off on the wrong foot.

Then why was it he could hardly keep himself from dropping the bags flat out, rushing inside to help her stoke up the stove, fry up some ham and eggs?

He clutched the bag handles in a hardened fist and started up the steps to the house. "Women," he gritted under his breath. He had no idea what to do with his new wife.

But on the porch, he paused to smile to himself ruefully. Well, he did have some ideas. Yes, indeed.

Eight

✛

Early the next morning, Amy awakened with a start to a loud banging sound from downstairs. Before she even fully realized where she was, instinct made her move. She bolted out of the room in her nightgown, grabbed a man's umbrella from a hallway stand and hurried down the stairs, searching for the source of the unsettling noise. Back in St. Louis, it wasn't unusual for vagrants or drifters to come knocking at their door, to even steal vegetables from the garden on occasion; thus the first thought that penetrated Amy's sleep-drugged brain was to try to prevent a possible break-in. In her haste, she didn't pause to consider what she looked like—scandalously attired in a handkerchief linen gown, the thick blond curls she had been too tired to plait the night before tumbling in riotous dishevelment about her face and shoulders.

Arriving downstairs, however, Amy immediately regretted her rash flight. Matt was at the front door wearing denim trousers, boots and checked shirt. Scowling murderously, his clenched fist on the doorknob, he was obviously having a devil of a time trying to get the heavy oaken panel to shut properly. Glancing down at herself and realizing at last how improper her wispily thin attire was, Amy smothered a gasp and tried to retreat unnoticed.

Too late. "What the hell!"

Matt Kendall had turned and was staring, flabbergasted, at his wife, his smoldering brown eyes rooting her to the spot. Amy felt her heart begin to pound frantically as her husband's dark eyes examined her from head to foot, pausing to burn the curves of her womanly torso, making the nipples of her breasts go taut at the heat of his perusal, then raking over her mussed hair and flushed features with an animal hunger that was heartstopping. Yet just as quickly, the yearning in his eyes became sparkling anger. "What the Sam Hill do you think you're doing down here, woman, half-clothed?"

Amy felt her pride prickling at his accusatory tone. Leaning the black umbrella against the newel post of the staircase, she protectively crossed her arms over her breasts and restrained a shudder at the coldness of the breeze blowing in through the ajar door, penetrating her bones. "I was just investigating the sound of the noise," she replied, her chin tilted as she faced him down. "I thought maybe someone was breaking into the house."

He turned back to his task and grunted self-consciously. "You thought someone was breaking in, out here in the middle of nowhere? And you were going to coldcock them with that umbrella, you in your nightgown?" He tried unsuccessfully to shut the door; it stuck again, and he cursed under his breath.

"What's the problem, anyway?" she asked, nodding toward the oaken panel, trying hard to keep irritation out of her tone.

His answer was muffled and hoarse. "The door's gone cantankerous on me. Won't shut. Must be the damp. Guess I'll have to take it down and plane it proper."

Now Amy restrained a smile as she eyed him struggling so earnestly with the door, finding the fierce frown on his face rather endearing. Moving closer, she offered, "Maybe you're just trying to force it too hard. Here, let me—"

She touched his sleeve, and that was when he whirled, his face tight with suppressed emotion. "Woman, will you kindly get upstairs and put on some clothes? You act like you've got no sense of decency!''

A cry of outrage burst from Amy's lips at Matt's unjust charge. She would have set him straight in no uncertain terms, but she didn't get the chance. He turned and stalked out the front door, slamming it behind him. It banged shut perfectly this time, tight as a tomb.

While Amy stood seething in the hallway, Matt stormed out to the barn. He'd made a great start with the girl this morning, he told himself ruefully, surpassing even his dismal performance last night. Keep this up and Amy would be packed and gone by sundown.

He knew he'd been unnecessarily short with his bride. But when he saw her at the foot of the stairs, feasting his eyes on her luscious curves taunting him through the thin cloth of her gown, it had taken all the restraint in his body not to drag her off by that wildly curling, seductive hair of hers and drink his fill of her womanly charms! God help the girl if she tried that again! Had she no idea of the effect she had on his senses?

Still, it had been poor of him, telling the girl she acted as if she had no sense of decency. Truth was, he was all too accustomed to women with no sense of decency. During his days as a ranch hand down in Texas, there had been many a barroom brawl over females of questionable moral character. One woman in particular, a barmaid back in San Antonio, had made a habit of taunting him needlessly by flirting with every vaquero in the cantina. The girl had liked her men mean and rough and liquored up, and when he had invariably obliged her by carrying her off and giving her just what she wanted in a squalid upstairs room, she had purred just like a kitten.

But Amy wasn't like that—oh, no, she wasn't anything like the others he'd known! His wife was young and pure, just as he had wanted. Actually, it had probably been her very innocence that had sent her rushing down the stairs earlier, with no thought to her attire. The evil thought had been in *his* mind, not hers. What a jackass he'd been!

''Mornin', Sampson,'' Matt muttered to a huge draft horse. He had entered the barn now and was nearing the stall of the docile gray animal. "You got any thoughts on how to deal with women, old boy?" he asked the horse wryly. When the horse shook his head and neighed, Matt had to chuckle to himself at the humanlike response. He grabbed the silage fork and hefted fresh hay into Sampson's stall, checking the animal's supply of water and feed. "Now, don't get restless, partner," he soothed in parting, stroking Sampson's coarse flank. "We'll get busy with the fall plowing in a few days' time."

Shutting the stall door, Matt went over and picked up a heavy harrow that was leaning against the planked wall. As he had said aloud to the horse, he would soon start the fall plowing, turning under the stubble of the recently harvested corn crop. The harrow would then be dragged over the plowed furrows to break up remaining clods. The crude implement was basically just a log into which nails had been driven, many of which had loosened during the last plowing. Matt had been meaning for some time to throw the tool into Little Beaver Creek so the wood could swell around the prongs, and he headed out the door to do that now.

Carrying the heavy log down the hillside was difficult, and Matt felt some of the horrible tension in him easing as a result. By the time he had thrown the harrow out into the shallows of the sparkling stream, he felt almost relaxed.

There was something so calming about hard work, he reflected, wiping his sweaty brow, something so soothing about being part of this fine land. Throwing himself into the routine of the farm might ease his frustration somewhat regarding Amy. There was also much his bride needed to learn about her new duties—not the least of which was that she sure as hell better be up, dressed and about her business at sunup! Lord, if he could just keep his mind off that tempting body of hers long enough to help her get acclimated!

Now that his tension regarding their earlier meeting had subsided, he realized that her fright at the noise he had made was rather odd. What had gone on at her home to make her so edgy and fearful? He hoped in time she would come to realize that she was safe here.

And wanted!

* * *

All morning, Amy fumed about Matt's unfair outburst at
sunup. She didn't see him. By the time she had dressed in
one of her high-necked calico day dresses and gone down to
the kitchen, she found only the evidence that he had already
prepared and eaten his own breakfast, and left his dishes
stacked on the dry sink. An odd man, she thought. She ate a
hasty repast of biscuits and gravy, tidied up the kitchen, then
went upstairs, aired the rooms and made the beds. The iron
bed in her room was similar to the one she had shared at
home with Hannah, and worries about her sister's welfare
kept flitting to mind as Amy smoothed down the covers.
Finally, growing restless, she grabbed her wool shawl and
headed outside in search of Matt.

The November morning was cool, and the balmy breeze
felt pleasant on Amy's skin. Two chickens scurried across
the path as she walked, cackling at her importantly. Smiling, Amy paused and turned around, studying the two-
storied farmhouse that was now her home, feeling a renewed
rush of pride. In the spring, she must plant marigolds across
the front, beneath the long gallery. Marigolds kept pill bugs
out of the house, Vida had always told her.

Approaching the outbuildings, Amy glanced about at the
pens and cribs, but Matt was nowhere in sight. She finally
located him inside the barn, standing next to a fenced
enclosure, feeding corn to several snorting black and brown
pigs. "Good morning," she called.

When he heard her voice, he turned, holding a burlap
sack full of feed and watching her approach. His expression
was guarded, unreadable, but at least he didn't look angry
as he had before, she thought to herself. She moved closer,
inhaling the mixed aromas of hay, manure and hogs.

"Good morning," he returned at last, his words accentuated by the snorting of the feeding pigs in the pen beyond.
"I see you slept in a bit this morning," he added, as if
their altercation in the downstairs hallway had never taken
place.

"I did?" she countered, taken aback. It had barely been
dawn when she had been awakened so rudely by Matt's

banging, and she hardly considered being roused at that hour "sleeping in."

"But I reckon you'll be wanting to get up earlier from now on," he continued.

Amy felt her back automatically stiffen. "I will?"

"I had to fix my own breakfast," he further edified her, scowling.

"You mean you've never done that before?" she asked conversationally.

His brow tightened, as if he weren't quite sure how to interpret her comment. "I had to feed your chickens, too, but I'm sure you'll be wanting to see to that yourself from now on."

"My chickens," she murmured. "Gracious, I've never had my very own chickens before."

He turned and leaned over, reaching through the rails of the pen to pour more corn into the hollowed-out log that served as a feeding trough for the pigs. "In the meantime, I reckon you'll be wanting something to do," he went on with bravado.

"Most assuredly," she muttered back, her eyes narrowing.

Pivoting to look up at her even more suspiciously, Matt stated, "The root garden needs tending something bad, and you'll be wanting to haul up water from the creek to soak it good. After that, there's a big kettle out back behind the barn that you'll want to scrub. We'll be scalding hogs tomorrow, and of course you'll be wanting to help—"

"Scalding hogs?" Amy was appalled, her stomach rearranging itself.

Setting down the bag of grain, Matt straightened, dusting off his hands. "It's November, woman," he explained, as if he were talking to a simpleminded child. "We can't put off the hog butchering no longer—that is, if we want cured meat come springtime. We should have started today, but I figured you'd need some time to sort of get acclimated—"

"Yes, while I pull weeds, haul water, and scrub kettles," Amy provided generously.

He scratched his head, obviously perplexed. "Were you expecting something else?"

"Oh, no, no," she replied blithely. "But I do so like the way you have, Mr. Kendall, of telling me what I'll be wanting to do. Like I'll be wanting to make your breakfast. I'll be wanting to feed your chickens and scald your hogs."

"Woman, are you mocking me?" he asked at last, looking stunned.

"Yes," she replied, and walked out of the barn.

With teeth clenched, Amy strode out into the yard, muttering unladylike comments under her breath. Just on the other side of the large frame building, she spotted the root garden, bone dry and overrun with weeds, begging for someone to take a good five hours, clean it out and recultivate the soil. "Mercy!" she gasped.

What had happened to the charming man she had met in St. Louis only days before? she asked herself irritably. Now that they were alone here on his farm, he had been a combination of curt, rude and imperious with her.

She supposed that now that they were married, Matt had decided the time for gallant wooing was past. She was his wife now, his chattel, his to do with as he pleased . . . and it galled her that in her naiveté, she had evidently been so deceived.

Tapping her foot, she glared down at the errant vegetation tangled across the cracked ground. Whatever had made her want to go hunt up Matt Kendall this morning anyway?

At midafternoon, Lyle Stockton, their neighbor, came by, riding a reddish-brown horse. "Howdy, neighbor," the robust, middle-aged man called to Matt. Matt put down the ax he was using to chop wood and came over to greet his visitor. "Wasn't 'specting you back for several more weeks," the overall-clad farmer added, dismounting and shaking hands with Kendall. "Just come by to tend your stock."

"Well, I sort of had me a change of plans." Matt watched Amy approach from the garden, where she'd been struggling with the weeds after recovering from her fit of temper toward him. Lyle Stockton doffed his straw hat and watched with shocked pleasure as the pretty young woman in calico dress and bright sunbonnet drew near. Matt told his neighbor simply, "Meet Mrs. Kendall."

Stockton threw Matt a purely amazed glance. "Well, if that ain't the beatenest . . . I'll be dogged, Kendall!" Grinning from ear to ear, the farmer said eagerly to Amy, "Lyle Stockton, ma'am." The big man then transferred his hat and the horse's reins into one hand and with a smile took the delicate hand Amy had offered. "May I say, ma'am, that Kendall here is a very lucky man?"

"Thank you, sir," Amy graciously replied, shaking the rough, beefy hand of the ruddy-complected farmer. Turning to Matt, she inquired, "Aren't we going to ask Mr. Stockton in?"

Matt looked positively blank at this suggestion, while Stockton interjected hastily, "Oh, no, ma'am. I can't stay. Got me a day's work still waiting for me back to my spread. Just wanted to check on your stock here, but since you folks is back, I won't trouble you no more."

"It's no trouble," Amy insisted. "Wouldn't you like a glass of tea before you start back?"

"Oh, no, ma'am; thank you, ma'am," the big farmer said awkwardly, shifting from foot to foot. "But I'm sure my wife'll take you up on the offer." He grinned. "Nell'll be hard to tie down once she hears there's another woman in these parts."

Amy's dark eyes lit up. "Oh, yes, please urge your wife to come see me soon, and bring your children, too, if she'd like to. You do have children, don't you?"

"Yes'um, two sons," Stockton replied proudly.

Amy nodded. "I thought Mr. Kendall mentioned them."

Matt, who had been scowling at this exchange, now remarked, "Stockton, we'll be butchering hogs tomorrow, and once the curing's done, I'd be right proud to have you pick out the best ham for your troubles."

The big man waved Matt off with his straw hat. "No way, son. What are neighbors for, anyhow? 'Sides, I've been promising Nell I'd take her for a lark to St. Louie, ever since the railroad come through. Sooner or later, she's bound to call my hand on it, and I might just be needing you to return the favor, if you know what I mean.''

"Well," Matt said, his pride satisfied by the idea of reciprocating, "that'll just be my pleasure. Say when, neighbor."

"Mighty fine," Stockton agreed, and the two men shook hands on it. "Say, would you be needing some help with the butchering tomorrow?" the farmer added.

Matt shook his head, saying casually, "Much obliged, but the wife and I can handle it just fine," even as Amy stared at him in wide-eyed horror.

"Well, if you change your mind, just holler. Guess I'll be going, then." Stockton nodded to Amy as he pivoted toward his horse. "A pleasure meeting you, ma'am. And I'll be sure to tell Nell of your invite."

"Please do," Amy replied eagerly, heedless of the fact that she caught Matt glowering at her again through the corner of her eye.

As Stockton remounted and rode off down the crude road curving off to the west, Amy noted that Matt still wore his brooding, resentful expression. Finally, she asked him, "Why didn't you accept Mr. Stockton's help with the butchering tomorrow?"

"I don't own with being beholden to no one," he replied stiffly.

"But couldn't we return the favor, help them out sometime, too?" Amy argued. "I think it would be fun, a good way to become acquainted with Mr. and Mrs. Stockton—"

"If a man can't work his own spread, then he has no business buying land in the first place."

"Meaning we don't need neighbors at all?" Amy challenged, rapidly losing her patience.

"I didn't say that," Matt hedged. "It was right fine of Stockton to feed the animals while I was gone, and I'll do the same for him sometime. And of course, I'd call on my neighbors, if there was a fire or something—"

"Then if I want to meet the neighbors, I'd best set the house on fire?"

Matt looked flabbergasted, his handsome brow deeply

furrowed. "Woman, what's got aholt of you today? Damned if you don't seem to have an ornery streak."

"Maybe I just never realized I was marrying a hermit," Amy snapped, her patience gone.

"And maybe I never realized I was marrying a spoiled city girl, who'd weep at the sight of dirt under her fingernails and want to spend all her time calling on the neighbors."

That comment infuriated Amy. "Spoiled city girl? Just because I want to meet Nell Stockton?"

Matt stood his ground, scowling, crossing his arms over his broad chest. "I think you got better things to do than gossip all day."

"Gossip all day? Is that all you think women do when they get together?"

That question seemed to take him aback a bit, but he recovered and nodded firmly. "Yes."

"Why, of all the—What's wrong with *you*?" she finally demanded, exasperated. "You seemed so different in St. Louis, so—so kind, soft-spoken . . ."

His answer confirmed her fears. "That was courting time. A man can't spend his whole life sparkin', not when there's plenty of hard work for him—and his wife—to do."

That did it for Amy. "Work!" she scoffed, throwing up her hands. "I swear you're beginning to sound like my mother. Oh, yes, Mr. Kendall, you've made it crystal clear that I have *plenty* of work to do."

Amy whirled and, with a mutinous glance at the recalcitrant garden, decided it was high time she went inside the house and had a leisurely nap.

Amy's revolt did not last long, for soon enough she realized she would have to prepare supper. She was hardly in the mood to cook for Matt; he deserved no less than a bare soup bone for accusing her of out-and-out laziness. In fact, part of her wanted to ignore him completely, let him stew in his juices for a while. But she knew that would solve nothing, and she did need to eat herself.

She decided to butcher a chicken for dinner. She considered first asking Matt's permission, but then remembered ruefully that he'd called the chickens hers earlier. Heck, she could slaughter them all if she wanted to! Not that she would—it was all she could do to get through beheading just one bird. At home they had kept a few chickens, and it always swept Amy with a wave of nausea to watch the headless bird flap about for several seconds following decapitation. She realized as she sat near Matt's chicken coop, plucking feathers from a just-slaughtered hen, that butchering hogs must be a hundred times worse. Being brought up in the city, she had never observed the process, but even Matt's reference to "scalding" the animals was enough to make her cringe. Surely that was not the way the pigs were killed! She heartily resented the fact that Matt had blithely refused Lyle Stockton's offer of a helping hand tomorrow.

Amy fricasseed the chicken for supper and served it with spoon bread, some string beans and stewed apples she'd found in mason jars in the root cellar. Matt praised the meal, ate huge quantities and drank several glasses of tea. Amy was secretly pleased that he enjoyed the repast, even though she still resented his earlier high-handed treatment of her. He did try his best to be charming during the meal, and she wondered if this weren't his way of making amends for prior sins.

After they finished, he surprised her by helping her clear the table, though he didn't assist with cleaning the dishes. It was near sunset, and, thanking her for the meal, he retreated to the front porch swing. Through the open kitchen window, Amy could hear the creaking of the chains that held the swing, and smell the pungent aroma of tobacco from the corncob pipe her husband was smoking.

Actually, Matt was not just smoking but brooding as he rocked out on the porch, looking back over his day with Amy. Perhaps he had been too hard on the girl, expecting her to pitch right in with the chores. But running a farm was hard work, and there was much expected of a farmwife. He loved this land; it was something he could truly call his own. The farm represented something clean and wholesome, even idyllic, in his life, much needed after years of

.violence and pain. He fully intended to make this spread a success, and Amy had best get used to doing her part of it.

There was something else she'd best get used to, and that was doing her part as a wife. Matt was dismayed by the glint of fear that flashed in Amy's eyes every time he touched her. He hoped that, in time, she would come to think of the marriage act not as a dreaded duty but as a pleasurable experience to be anticipated. He wouldn't break his word to the girl; he wouldn't force her. But the frustration of being alone with her was driving him crazy, making him act as downright ornery as he'd earlier accused her of being!

How could he get her to come to him? Obviously, she was greatly reluctant. Couldn't he somehow make a beginning, weaken her defenses a little?

Suddenly, he smiled, as a devious thought sprang to mind. It might work, if he could endure the torture of it. It would require patience, but he knew the girl had responded to him before. There was a sensuality there, waiting beneath that prim, guileless surface, hidden beneath those taunting brown eyes. Surely he could wear her down in time. . . .

When the sounds of dishes being washed in the kitchen ceased, he set his pipe down on the porch railing and called out softly, "Amy, come join me. The sunset's right fine."

In the kitchen, Amy heard him. Hanging her apron and smoothing down her hair, she went out onto the porch and shyly sat down next to her husband on the swing. He smiled at her, and an unexpected weakness slammed her stomach. It was almost as if their earlier spats had never occurred. Amy felt near-giddy at Matt's closeness. She couldn't help but notice how his shirt and trousers pulled at the powerful muscles of his torso and legs, how his wind-ruffled blond hair caught the fading light. Hoping to distract her errant eyes, she turned and studied the sunset. It was, indeed, spectacular, an amber-red fireburst on the hilly horizon.

After a moment, Matt cleared his throat and remarked, "Well, you did right fine today."

Amy did not reply, but turned to her husband sharply,

pride clenching her lovely features. Matt realized his attempt to smooth things over had failed, and he hastily changed the subject. "You like it here?"

She sighed, staring off at the pink and gold horizon. After a moment, her features relaxed, and she replied, "The farm is quite lovely. But it's isolated."

Her words left him scowling. "I thought the idea was for us to become a real family, you and me."

"Well, we are. I mean, we will be in time, I'm sure," Amy stammered. "But"—she took a deep breath, then bravely met his questioning eyes—"that may not be enough for me. I want to become part of the community, too."

"There's no need for you to be lonely, woman," he said with sudden fierceness, and kissed her.

Amy stiffened as Matt bestowed upon her lips a brazenly intimate kiss, which tasted potently of tobacco and carnal need. Her heart skidded crazily as she realized it was growing dark and he might not want to stop this time. Despite the devastating temptation of being so close to him, she pushed him away and stood, trembling.

"What's wrong with you?" he demanded. He, too, stood now, looking very frustrated, his eyes blazing, his jaw clenched.

She trembled at his ire. "There's nothing wrong with me that some patience won't cure," she railed back, trying her best to face him down. He was formidable, standing before her so menacing and tall, every male muscle in his body taut and ready for action.

"I don't believe you," he countered savagely, advancing an ominous step toward her. "There's something wrong with you. Every time I touch you, you bolt like a shy deer. Whatever it is that ails you, you should have told me before we married."

Though his words hit brutally near the truth, Amy was not about to tell him what he wanted to know. With bravado, she insisted, "There's nothing wrong with me."

His eyes glittered with triumph that barely masked smoldering desire. "Oh? Then you won't tell me not to kiss you."

"What?" she asked, the word a barely audible gasp.

He advanced steadily, an implacable gleam in his dark eyes. "You're not ready to come to my bed," he said bluntly. "But surely you're not going to tell me a husband can't kiss his wife."

"I—I . . ." Wretchedly, she clenched and unclenched her fists. "Matt, you promised me more time. We've only been married a little over a day."

"Have you thought, woman, that one day alone with you could be a never-ending hell for me of wanting you?"

His words were electrifying, and the raging need in his eyes left no doubt. But she managed to hold her ground and demand, "Of wanting me or wanting children, heirs for this farm?"

"Both," he said without batting an eyelash.

"Matt . . ." She extended her hands to him in entreaty, her heart pounding in her ears, and all she could say was, again, helplessly, "You promised me. . . ."

Yet he drew closer still, smiling in a determined yet tender way. "Easy now. I'm not going to force anything on you. For the present, Mrs. Kendall, I'm only asking for a kiss." Huskily, he added, "I must gentle you to my touch."

She stared at him scornfully. "I'm not a horse!"

Her retort backfired, for he laughed heartily. "Indeed, you're not." Persuasively, he went on, "But don't you agree that a wife, whether she's ready for the marriage bed or not, has no right to refuse her husband a kiss?"

Amy hung her head in misery at this new, dangerous tack on Matt's part. He had her to rights on this one. Even the parson had told Matt to kiss his bride. She might deny him her bed, but she couldn't justly deny him any display of wifely affection. Forlornly, she nodded.

He chuckled softly and asked, "What's that? I didn't hear your answer."

She looked up at him defiantly and said, "Yes."

Smiling, he turned and went back to the swing, sitting down and patting the place beside him. He looked quite satisfied with himself as he whispered, "Come here."

Amy had no choice. She walked unsteadily to the swing,

surprised her legs supported her at all. When she tried to sit down, Matt surprised her by pulling her down into his lap. And she couldn't protest, because he immediately and hungrily fastened his mouth on hers!

What followed was unendurable torture for Amy. Matt kissed her until she was weak with wanting him, until sensations stirred in the pit of her stomach that were so powerful they frightened her. His tongue tasted every recess and texture of her mouth, its heat draining her will. He rocked her gently as his lips worked their sensual magic, and she clung to him, fearing she would slide off his lap into oblivion if she didn't. His strong, warm hands roamed her back, eventually teasing the sides of her breasts through the cloth of her gown. She bucked and tried to pull away from his boldness, but he scolded, "No," kissing her again, swallowing her moan of protest as he firmly replaced the insistent, titillating fingers near her bodice. When she felt his manhood rise and grow brazenly hard against her bottom, she thought she would die from mortification mixed with desire. Yet she had no way of telling him how indecent their position was, not without making matters so much worse!

Having ravished her mouth to bruised tenderness, Matt's lips moved to torture the fevered flesh of her face and throat, the friction of his whiskers, combined with the hot, delicate flick of his tongue, making her break out in shivers all over. He continued nuzzling her with exquisite skill, until she relaxed and grew limp, until the fight in her died. Then he sighed deeply, snuggling her head beneath his chin and just rocking her, holding her in his strong embrace.

Amy felt touched—no one had ever held her this way, and she buried her head against his shoulder to hide her tears. She was relieved, too, the wild thumping of her heart at last subsiding. She had feared he wouldn't stop, that he might become violent, as her father once had with her mother, that he'd want to bed her then and there and would grow enraged if she resisted. Yet even though he'd pressed the boundary of their agreement so far that she had almost succumbed to his desire, he had, ultimately, kept his word.

Amy could breathe more easily, reprieved for the moment, as she realized that her meeting him halfway—letting him kiss her in the passionate, leisurely way he had wanted—had somehow eased the horrible tension within him.

After a moment, Matt tenderly pressed his lips against the golden curls on top of her head and said, "There. It's not so bad being touched by me, is it? You know you're safe here, Amy."

When she didn't reply but tensed slightly, he stroked her arm with his skilled fingers and continued, "I don't know what all happened to you before, but I'm here to take care of you now, to protect you. Remember that, love."

His words made fresh tears sting her eyes, tears of gratitude and new understanding. He continued to rock her in the silence, and Amy savored the closeness. The motion of the swing was so soothing, the scent of the breeze so sweet, and the stranger who rocked her seemed oddly not a stranger at all anymore. . . .

After a while, Matt nudged her awake. It was night, cold, the stars twinkling in the vast black sky above them. Amy blinked groggily; she hadn't realized she had drifted off to sleep. "Time for bed," Matt said, leading her into the house, lighting a lantern before he led her up the stairs.

Once they arrived at her door, Amy's heart pounded with renewed fear and anticipation, but Matt merely handed her the lantern, kissed her quickly on the forehead and continued on to his room.

Sleep was elusive for Amy. She found she ached all over, burning as if she had a fever, and she hurt to be held in the strong arms that seemed like a part of her cruelly wrenched away. . . .

But most of all she knew that this was where she belonged now, here with this fine man she was learning to trust. And she was glad now, so very glad, that Lacy Garrett had never come back to get her!

Nine

+·+

The Boothill Country, Missouri

While Amy Kendall slumbered safely hundreds of miles away, Lacy Garrett lay in a dark, cold jail cell in a small town in the Boothill Country of Missouri. The stark moonlight, cutting through the bars on the cell's small window, cast long slashes across the moth-eaten cot where Lacy lay, his fingers laced together behind his dark head, his long legs and booted feet crossed.

It had been a damn long night, Lacy thought to himself irritably—cold, with no whiskey or women to comfort him. After the card game at the saloon earlier that night, when he and his traveling companions, Charlie and Jim, had won so big at draw poker, several of the locals were riled. Guns had been drawn, accusations had flown, and only the quick action of the town sheriff forestalled a full-fledged saloon brawl. Unfortunately for Lacy, Jim and Charlie—the slippery skunks!—had managed to sneak away during the confusion, leaving Lacy alone to answer to their irate poker companions, as well as to the sheriff. When three of the locals insisted Lacy had cheated, Sheriff Bridges informed Lacy he would lock him up in jail for the night, "for your own protection," even though the others could supply no actual proof that he had bamboozled them.

Now, sitting behind bars in an unheated cell this November

night, Lacy felt far from protected, especially with all his winnings locked in the sheriff's desk drawer in the outer office! Damn Charlie and Jim for leaving him to face this mess alone. What a couple of low-down cowards!

Maybe he should have gone on back to St. Louis, as he had promised Amy in the first place, he thought grimly. The thought of his pretty young fiancée spurred Lacy to his feet and set him to pacing in the narrow enclosure. By now, he was sure Amy was mad enough to chase after him with a fireplace poker. They had set a firm date for their elopement this time—he had promised her good and proper on her mother's Bible that he'd be there. Yet instead, he'd hidden out again, let her down again, just like the other two times. What the hell was wrong with him, anyhow?

It was the marrying, he decided, his bootheel pivoting on the clammy stone floor. He just wasn't ready to settle down. Yet the girl was so lovely, so desirable—the thought of her warmth all the more appealing in the cold starkness of his current surroundings. He wanted the girl, all right, and he knew she would never give him what he craved until the knot was tied. Oh, he'd pleasured himself with many a woman before, but it was her that haunted his dreams—the kissable mouth, large eyes, the luscious breasts he'd only gotten to see a glimpse of previously. One day he would have her; he'd promised himself that long ago. But once he tasted her fully, quenched his hunger thoroughly on her voluptuous young body, he wasn't even sure he'd be able to stay with her. Not even if she bore his name—or his child. Lacy was a peddler by trade, but he was also a gambler's son. He possessed the wandering nature and the quicksilver soul of the seasoned cardsharper.

Anyway, why even think about her? he asked himself ruefully, hugging himself and stamping his boots to stave off the cold. She'd probably never speak to him again, not following this third desertion. Still, he knew something would not rest in him until he went back to her, tried to make her his, satisfy his hankering for her once and for all. Until then he'd never completely get her out of his blood.

Muffled sounds in the outer office now startled Lacy from

his thoughts. He instantly paused in his tracks and cupped his ear with his hand, listening alertly. It sounded as though there was a scuffle out in the sheriff's cubicle!

All at once, the door to the cell area creaked open and a narrow beam of light spilled inside. "Get your ass in there, cracker!" Lacy heard a familiar voice hiss from the other room. "One sound outta ya and yer a dead man!"

Now three men entered the small block of cells. The first, a potbellied man Lacy assumed was the deputy sheriff, walked down the narrow aisle with arms raised and keys jangling, a look of stark terror on his face. Behind him were two armed men wearing hats and dark jackets—Lacy's friends Charlie and Jim! "Well, it's about time," Lacy greeted his companions disgustedly.

"About time?" Jim hooted back, nudging the deputy forward with his pistol. "What you make of that, Charlie? Here we are breaking the law for this bottom-dealing card-sharp, and he tells us it's about time!"

"Since when have you given a tinker's damn about breaking the law, you lowlife clay-eater?" Lacy scoffed back, drawing his jacket tightly about him and stamping his feet again. "Now quit jawing and get me out of here! I'm freezing my ass off."

"You heard the man, cracker!" Jim said with a chuckle, again nudging the deputy forward with his pistol. "Unlock the cell."

The frightened deputy hurried forward, extending his key ring, which rattled from the force of his trembling. After two unsuccessful tries, the white-faced man managed to jam the key into the lock, twisting it until the door clicked open. Lacy instantly flung back the door and left the cell, even as Jim and Charlie pushed the deputy inside. The two armed men stuffed a handkerchief in the deputy's mouth, then secured the gag with a bandanna around his head. Charlie grabbed the deputy's keys and left the cell, while Jim followed. As Charlie turned back to lock the cell door, he announced, "All right boys, let's make tracks."

In the outer office, Lacy made the others pause so he could recover their poker winnings from the sheriff's desk drawer. The drawer proved to be locked, and when Jim got ready to shoot it open, Lacy's reaction was immediate and savage. "You tarbrain!" he hissed, shoving his friend out of the way. "Put that damn pistol away before I cram it down your throat. You want to wake up the whole damn town?"

Jim, looking suitably chastised, retreated, holstering his gun, while Charlie came forward with the keys, trying each one on the drawer lock. At his side, Lacy shook his head and complained to both men, "The way you two fools operate, it's a wonder you ain't got me kilt yet tonight."

Jangling the keys as he struggled to open the lock, Charlie shot Lacy a dark look. "Look, Garrett, if you still got a burr in your britches 'bout me and Jim making a break for it back at the saloon, you'd best recollect that Jim here was wearin' the holdout vest tonight, while I had the marked deck in my back pocket. All you was holdin'—as usual—was all our loot! Just remember if'n we'd a'stayed back there to have our pockets turned out by the sheriff, we'd all three of us be hangin' from the nearest oak right now, pretty as ducks in a row! So I reckon you'd best be damn glad me and Jim made a run for it. There, by Jesus!" Charlie finished, tossing the keys aside as the drawer finally opened.

The men eagerly scooped up the coin and currency inside the drawer, then rushed to the front door, where Lacy grabbed his hat from a nearby rack. After creaking open the heavy panel and checking to make sure no one was about on the dark streets outside, the three men hurried for their horses and Lacy's peddler's wagon, all of which had been left at the end of the street in the shadows of a large tree. Guided only by the moonlight, the threesome rode out of town, one horseman on either side of Lacy's wagon.

"Where you boys headed?" Lacy asked the other two as soon as they were safely out of the burg, traveling down the dark, crude road.

"West," came Charlie's answer. He grinned, his teeth flashing in the moonlight. "Things have got kinda hot out there to the border, but reckon we'll head home first, anyhow. How 'bout you, Garrett? You ready to come with us—take a breather from suckering half the Missouri countryside?''

"I ain't suckered no one that wasn't out to make a quick buck hisself,'' Lacy defended stoutly. "Thanks for the invite, boys, but I reckon I'll be headin' north,'' he added.

"Pinin' away for that pretty lady of yours back to St. Louie?'' Jim taunted.

"I conjure I could use some female companionship now that the weather's turned cold,'' Lacy replied with a grin.

"Don't hightail it too fast now, Garrett, or you'll break the wind of that old nag pulling your wagon,'' Charlie advised sagely, nodding toward the old draft horse that ploddingly pulled along Lacy's rickety collection of wares and peddler's samples.

"I ain't in that big a rush, boys,'' Lacy assured his companions. "Got me some money to make between here and St. Louie, anyhow. Reckon I'll be taking my time.''

"Sure, while you screw up the courage to face that feisty female you stood up!'' Jim needled.

"Oh, I'll be facing her, all right,'' Lacy bragged back to his cronies. "But in my own good time, boys. Amy'll welcome me back, just like she always does, you can bet hard cash on it. Like it or not, that little lady ain't seen the last of Lacy Garrett. Nossir.''

Ten

+ +

The next morning, Amy was up before first light, and by the time Matt came down the stairs she had already prepared a breakfast of eggs, bacon, biscuits with gravy and steaming coffee.

Matt's eyes took on a tenderness as he walked into the warm room and surveyed the repast laid out on the square oaken table. Then he spotted Amy pouring coffee at the dry sink. She wore an ivory-colored muslin frock, its boat-shaped bodice displaying to perfection her high, rounded breasts, and a red-and-white-checked apron becomingly accenting her slim waist. She looked like female perfection to him, her cheeks flushed from the heat radiating from the iron stove, her thick wavy hair caught by a red satin ribbon at the nape of her neck. Glancing with pride from his wife to the table she had set, Matt grinned and said, "Well, ain't that fine."

Amy turned, smiling shyly as she noted Matt's presence. Walking to the table with two steaming cups of coffee, she asked him innocently, "Sleeping in a bit this morning, Mr. Kendall?"

He had the grace to grin sheepishly as he held out her chair for her. The two were reserved as they began eating the delicious meal, speaking only to exchange pleasantries or pass the food. Amy covertly watched Matt as the morning sun streamed through the window behind him, outlining his muscled torso and dancing fiery highlights in his rich blond hair. It struck her again what a handsome man she'd married, and joy welled up within her. Matt's face was so masculine, the lines of his nose and mouth so cleanly etched, his eyes so deeply set and compelling. His hands were beautiful, finely shaped, tanned and full of strength, whether he was holding a cup of coffee or wielding an ax.

Amy thought of the intimacies they'd shared last night on the porch swing—how they'd made a start at communicating, in every way—and felt herself blushing. She lowered her eyes and buttered a biscuit, hoping Matt would not note her trembling fingers. Had he forced himself on her last night, she knew she would hate him now. But he was far too wise for that. He was courting her, wooing her, and it had a devastating effect on her senses. She realized that never had Lacy Garrett tried to seduce her with drugging kisses. Oh, Lacy had kissed her on occasion, rather artlessly, and she realized now that his fumblings as a bridegroom would have been equally lacking in finesse. But this man, on the other hand . . . He was subtle, he was hard to figure out. But most of all, even if he exasperated her at times, he was irresistibly sensual, determined to make her his—and that electrified her most of all!

As they finished eating, Matt shattered the romantic spell Amy was drifting in by clearing his throat and remarking, "You know, girl, you never did scrub up that kettle yesterday."

Amy's coffee cup clattered into its saucer. "I beg your pardon?"

Looking slightly taken aback at the indignation in his wife's bright eyes, Matt nonetheless braved on. "The kettle out back behind the barn. You never did scrub it out. And, like I told you, we'll be needing it today for scalding hogs—"

"Well, maybe I just was waiting for you to offer me a hand, Mr. Kendall," Amy interjected in challenge.

At that, surprisingly, Matt laughed. "Well, you got me to rights this time, girl. Sure, I'll lend a hand."

Amy's eyes widened in shocked pleasure.

After she tidied up the kitchen and changed into an older dress, Amy and Matt left the house together to go scrub out the kettle. As they attacked the mud-caked cauldron with steel wool and bristle brush, Amy was still stunned that Matt was actually helping her.

Yet there was a lot he wanted to help her with. But he didn't really know how to offer.

And she was just beginning to learn how to ask.

Despite Matt's assistance with the kettle, hog butchering was just about the death of Amy. Cleaning the kettle was no problem, nor was setting it on the cast-iron trivet, hauling up water from the creek to fill it, or starting a fire beneath it. Amy was quite relieved to learn that the hundred-and-fifty-pound hog would not be scalded alive but would be killed earlier on. Matt spared her this grisly event by going to the barn alone as she added more wood to the fire. Whatever he did to kill the animal, there was no sound, not until he called out for her to come help him drag the animal to the cauldron. What followed wasn't too traumatic either, a process of dipping the hog in the water and then scraping the coarse hair from its hide. Matt was amazingly strong and needed little help lifting the animal.

But when the scalding and scraping were done, Matt, with Amy's help, hoisted the pig by its hind legs to a beam jutting out from the barn. He then cut off its head and gutted the animal from end to end, and Amy ran for the spring, clutching her sides.

After she relieved her nausea, she ran back to the house and hid upstairs in her room. She couldn't go back, she just couldn't! Curled up in a ball of misery, she tried to erase from her mind the horrible image of the pig's guts spilling out, Matt expecting her to stand beneath the eaves and catch the animal's innards in a pan! A new spasm of nausea gripped her at the very thought, but she managed to steady herself with deep breaths. How could Matt do this to her, a new bride? she asked herself, seething. How could he refuse Lyle Stockton's help, then let his wife be subjected to this trial instead? The intimacies she'd shared with him last evening might have never existed, she was so furious with him now.

The minutes passed, but Matt did not come upstairs to get her. That was lucky for him, she reflected, for if he did try to fetch her, she was sure as Sunday determined to give him a piece of her mind he'd never forget! After satisfying moments spent reflecting on the scathing remarks she'd hurl at him if he dared darken her doorway, she felt a little better. She got up, changed out of the dress the butchered hog had not left unblemished, washed her face and fixed her hair. Smoothing down the crisp folds of her muslin gown, she firmly decided that she really needed to go downstairs to the parlor, hunt up paper and pen and write letters to both Hannah and Vida. She would spare them both the harrowing details of her current ordeal, however!

Amy was leaving her room to do just this, when, surprisingly, she heard the sound of a wagon approaching. She whirled, raced to the bedroom window and parted the chintz curtains. Below her in a buckboard was Mr. Stockton with a lady, obviously his wife, sitting next to him. In the bed of the conveyance were two laughing boys.

Amy fairly flew down the stairs and out the front door. "Welcome!" she called breathlessly to the newcomers, her brown eyes glowing.

Lyle Stockton, wearing yesterday's overalls and straw hat, climbed down from the wagon and helped the lady down. "Mrs. Kendall, this here's my missus, Nell," he said as Amy eagerly approached.

Nell Stockton was a sprightly middle-aged woman wearing a yellow and green calico dress, a matching slat bonnet on her head, a wool shawl about her shoulders. "Howdy, honey, welcome to Rolla," the woman said cheerfully, shaking hands with Amy.

The boys, one a redhead, the other blond, now scampered down from the wagon, wearing suspendered trousers, high-topped buttoned shoes and flannel shirts. "These are our young'uns," Nell told Amy proudly. "Ben here is eight, and Pete's ten."

"Hello, boys," Amy said warmly, leaning over to study the youngsters, enchanted by the boys, both of whom had freckled faces and bright blue eyes.

"Kin we go fishing, ma'am?" the oldest asked. "We got our poles in the back of the wagon."

"You boys gotta ask Mr. Kendall that," Lyle Stockton informed his sons sternly. "It's his spread."

Matt now approached from the barn, blood on his shirt, wiping his soiled hands on a rag. "Well, hello, folks," he told the newcomers cautiously, tucking the rag into his waist. "If this isn't a surprise."

"Howdy, neighbor." Stockton cleared his throat self-consciously and shook the hand Matt offered. "Don't know what possessed the wife here this mornin'. Nell was up afore dawn, fixin' enough chicken and dumplings fer half the county. I reckoned we'd best share the pot with you folks, else it'd spoil. And we wuz thinkin' mebbe we could lend you a hand with the butcherin', too."

"That's right neighborly of you," Matt replied, still looking perplexed and rather wary.

"Of course, we'd be delighted to have you stay," Amy interjected, smiling at the Stocktons. "But it wasn't necessary for you to bring a meal."

"'Tain't nothin', honey," Nell assured her.

An uneasy silence followed. The older couple looked awkwardly expectant, since Matt had yet to invite them to stay, and by tradition, they would not remain on a spread without the landowner's blessings. Amy beseeched Matt with her eyes; while he appeared far from unaffected by her unspoken plea, he continued to struggle silently, his jaw tight.

Suddenly, the older boy, the redhead, approached Matt with eyes full of eager anticipation. "Mister, kin we fish in yer crick?"

Abruptly, Matt broke into a grin, ending the horrible tension. Even he was a goner to the boy's winsome charm. "Sure, son," he told the youngster. As the boys grabbed their poles along with a pail of bait and ran, squealing with laughter, down to Little Beaver Creek, Matt nodded to

Stockton and said, "Much obliged, neighbor. I reckon we could use a hand today. But now I must insist you take your pick of the hams."

"We'll talk on it, son," Stockton replied with a hearty chuckle, slapping Matt on the back. The two men headed toward the barn together, leading off the horse-drawn buckboard.

Amy was thrilled to have female companionship. She invited Nell into the house, helping her guest carry in the large basket she'd brought. "It really wasn't necessary for you to bring a meal," Amy reiterated as they moved down the central hallway to the kitchen door, each gripping a handle of the wicker basket which swung between them.

Nell scolded back, "I wouldn't dream of not bringing something to welcome a new bride to the community."

In the kitchen, Amy stopped in her tracks, gasping with dismay. On the drainboard was the hog's head, complete with bulging eyes! Nearby were two large pots, one filled with grisly-looking pork trimmings, the other overflowing with raw fat! Mortified, Amy helped Nell place the basket on the table, then turned to her guest abjectly. "Oh, Mrs. Stockton, I'm so sorry you have to see—"

The older woman stopped the bride short with a laugh as she untied her bonnet and hung it on a wall peg. Turning to Amy as she smoothed down several wisps of grayish-brown hair that had escaped her bun, she retorted, "That ain't nothin', honey. And call me Nell. What's your Christian name, anyhow?"

"Amy."

Nell dismissed the frightful scene before them with a wave of a bony hand. "Well, Amy, you think this is somethin' I ain't seen a hunnard times before? Law! Fact of the matter is, we'll be needin' to set that fat to renderin' in short order and the sausage pot to simmerin', too, but since the sight of it is turning you right green, why don't we set a while in the parlor first?"

Amy's mouth fell open. "Why, of course," she said after a moment, recovering her composure with a laugh. "That sounds—most excellent."

In the parlor, Amy gratefully sipped coffee with her new

friend. She immediately liked and trusted this wholesome, unpretentious lady. "I'm—just so glad you've come," she remarked, embarrassed to find her voice cracking with emotion.

Nell, across the room, nodded and asked wisely, "Want to tell me about it, honey?"

Amy poured out her heart to the motherly Nell Stockton, heedless of the fact that she had just met the woman. She was desperate for a sympathetic ear and held nothing back, telling Nell of meeting Matt in St. Louis, of how bad her home situation was there, and how the stranger from Rolla had seemed her savior. She spoke of their marriage, and then of the rude awakening when she arrived at his farm. "He can be so charming at times," she confessed to Nell, "and then at other times, I think he wants me only as his servant, and to raise a new generation of farmhands."

Nell nodded compassionately when Amy finished, leaving the wing chair to come sit by the younger woman on the settee. Amy noted the lines of wry humor and deep experience on her neighbor's kind face as Nell replied, "Honey, I know it's right rough, this marriage being so new and the two of you hardly knowing each other. A man being a man, he feels he needs to show his new wife right off who's the boss. You got to give it some time and some patience."

"I'm trying to," Amy said earnestly, fighting tears. "But it seems Mr. Kendall has none. I mean, expecting me to—to butcher hogs, me right off the train from the city—"

"I knowed it honey, I do," Nell said soothingly. "If you're asking me, that was right poor judgment on his part. In fact, that's just what I told Mr. Stockton last evenin', and he was of a sim'lar mind. That's why we come, honey."

Amy smiled, her spirits improving. "I'm just so glad you did!" Shyly, she added, "He seems a fine man, your husband."

Nell waved her off with a laugh. "You think we didn't have our troubles, too, startin' out? Honey, I was reared in a right fine home for these parts, but when Lyle up and married me, I'll have you know he took me off to a dirt farmer's shack that weren't no more'n a lean-to chinked with mud, with rats running in and out, not to mention snakes, even a polecat.''

"A skunk?" Amy queried, and both women laughed.

"How'd you like to be a new bride chasing one of them varmints outten your house with a straw broom?''

Amy continued laughing until tears sprang to her eyes as Nell pointed out, "Honey, look around at what you got here, and you just startin' out. This is the right finest farmhouse in these parts—and a goodly spread come with it, too.''

"I know," Amy agreed, looking with pride at the spacious parlor. "I'm grateful. Believe me, I am. It's just that Mr. Kendall—''

Nell placed a reassuring hand over Amy's and told the younger woman confidentially, "Honey, that boy is green as grass when it comes to husbandin'. Have you thought that this might be just as bewilderin' to him as it is to you? Maybe he just don't quite know what to do with a wife yet.''

"Oh," Amy said, blushing to the roots of her hair, "he knows what to do all right.''

Both women laughed their delight, fast friends now.

The rest of the morning was quite enjoyable for Amy. She and Nell visited in the kitchen as the older lady schooled her in "women's work" at hog-butchering time. Under Nell's tutelage, Amy learned how the hog's head was processed, how the fat was rendered into lard, even how to grind and season sausage, sealing it up in the cleaned intestines. None of these activities seemed nearly as distasteful now, with Nell's guidance and patience to see her through. Whenever Nell caught Amy "greenin'" again, the woman would insist the young bride sit by the window and take deep breaths of crisp fall air until the nausea passed. The older woman was well aware that the girl would have to learn the rudiments of hog slaughtering and processing if she were to survive here in the country, where pork was the mainstay. But Nell also knew a gentle initiation was called for, not the trial by fire Matt seemed to prefer.

Nell's presence was so calming to Amy that after a while she even found herself humming a Stephen Foster melody, "Come Where My Love Lies Dreaming," under her breath as she worked. When Nell complimented her on the soulful tune, Amy admitted to her new friend that she missed her piano back in St. Louis. "Why not get Mathew to buy you a pianer, then?" Nell suggested. "He's well fixed, from what I hear."

"Oh, I couldn't," Amy murmured back, embarrassed. "Anyway, how on earth would my husband get a piano out to this farm?"

"That might be a real pickle," Nell admitted with a laugh. "We'll have to think on that one, won't we, Amy?"

While the women continued to chat and work in the kitchen, Lyle Stockton and Matt were out at the smokehouse. They dipped hams and various pork pieces in a vat of salt, then arranged the slabs of meat on the smokehouse shelves to cure. "Again, Lyle, I really appreciate the hand today," Matt felt compelled to tell the older man as together they lifted a pork shoulder onto a cedar ledge.

"Thought it might be somethin' extry, the butcherin', you with a new city bride," Stockton returned, wiping his sweaty brow with the smutty sleeve of his shirt.

Matt paused, realizing the man was right. In fact, he shuddered at the thought of him and Amy trying to get through all this, without the Stocktons' help. Butchering had seemed so simple back when he worked on a ranch. Two trained hands could dispense with several hogs in a day's time. But with a new, unskilled wife—damned if that wasn't something else again! To Stockton, he said with a grin, "Guess maybe I made a mistake."

"Have you told the girl that?" the older man questioned.

Matt automatically tensed. "It wouldn't be seemly for a man to humble himself to his wife that way."

Lyle Stockton straightened to take a deep breath and again wiped the sweat trickling into his eyes. "You know, son, it takes an awful big man to admit he's wrong," the farmer pointed out gently.

Matt leaned over, grabbing a small ham and rolling it in

the salt. "Guess I'm not that big a man—not yet," he mumbled.

At noon, Nell served up a dinner of chicken and dumplings, along with fresh bread and strawberry preserves. Everyone ate the repast with relish, having thoroughly enjoyed their day together thus far. One of the boys had even caught a black bass, which the Stocktons would be taking home for their evening meal.

By early afternoon, the men had butchered another hog, a two-hundred-pounder this time, and the process of cutting up, curing and rendering began again. All were exhausted by the time the last of the slabs of meat had been placed on smokehouse shelves. Toward sunset, Amy and Matt saw the other family off at their buckboard. The tired, happy boys climbed in the back and were dozing on a blanket before their folks had even said good-bye. Amy warmly took Nell's hand. "I can't thank you enough."

Nell smiled back, her angular face weary but serene. "Honey, you can thank me by coming to see me—soon. Gets right lonely in these parts, 'specially come spring, with Lyle and the boys in the fields most the time." Suddenly, Nell snapped her fingers. "Say, mebbe I'll see you folks at church, too. You'll be drivin' into town come Sunday, now won't you?"

Amy glanced at Matt, who was on the other side of the buckboard, shaking hands with Lyle. Her heart sank as she remembered her talk with Reverend Fulton back in town. She realized it was unlikely her husband would escort her to church, and she muttered to Nell, "I don't know. But I'll try."

Following the direction of Amy's gaze, Nell seemed to sense the problem. "You work on him, honey."

"I will," Amy promised with a smile. Impulsively, she hugged the older woman. Then the wagon lumbered off.

While Amy prepared supper, Matt went off to wash at the spring. He appeared in the kitchen soon enough, wearing a clean shirt and a self-satisfied smile. He and Amy exchanged awkward small talk over the meal, which was actually leftovers from dinner. Neither was very hungry after eating Nell's luscious noonday repast.

After Amy did the dishes, Matt invited her to join him in the parlor, and they sat stiffly, side by side, on the settee. Studying Matt's scowling, preoccupied face, Amy sensed strongly that he wanted to tell her something. She hoped he was planning to apologize. While her anger had abated somewhat, she realized she would doubtless be ready to murder him by now had Nell and Lyle not arrived to rescue her. She still felt that her husband could have chosen a much better way to introduce her to the rituals of country living than expecting her to watch a hog's belly be opened up before her very eyes!

At last he spoke, each word coming like a pulled tooth. "You did right good today, Amy."

She wasn't pleased by his remark, any more than she was thrilled by his similar statement the night before. She set her arms akimbo and stared off at the fire he'd set earlier in the grate.

"Looks like you survived it all, and in fact, you're stronger for it," he braved on.

At this, she turned to glower at him, and was pleased to note that his expression folded at the ire in her eyes. For a moment, neither spoke. There was only the sound of the fire crackling, the wind rattling the house.

Finally, Matt cleared his throat and tried a new tack. "Those boys of Lyle's were something today, weren't they? I know they must really help their pa out at his spread."

Amy was not placated. While she thought Nell's boys were "something," too, she resented Matt's reference to the workaday convenience of having children. His preoccupation with practicalities seemed cold. "I suppose you'd like a dozen or so strapping boys just like them to help out around here," she muttered.

"Not a bad idea," he rejoined with an infuriating chuckle. When she glared at him in return, he offered her a supplicating gesture and coaxed, "Come on, woman, cut me some slack, will you? Everything I say seems to come out wrong tonight."

She laughed shortly. "Actually, Mr. Kendall, that's the first statement you've made tonight that has come out *right*."

He sighed heavily. "Amy, honey . . ." His hand gently reached out to turn her face toward him, and his dark eyes beseeched her. "Please don't be angry at me like this."

His fervid eyes threatened to melt her, but she wasn't satisfied. He hadn't apologized, and that made her more determined than ever to resist his magnetism.

"Amy . . ."

All at once, he pulled her into his arms and kissed her. A startled moan died in her throat as his warm, demanding lips ravished her mouth, then moved hungrily to her face, her neck. She didn't fight him—she couldn't; that was their tacit agreement, as long as he just kissed her. And besides, it was too much hell just fighting herself as the potent arousal of being in Matt's arms again threatened to engulf her with its lethal magic. He smelled of good, earthy things—male sweat, the autumn woods. His face was slightly rough against her delicate throat, and she longed to stroke that wonderful texture of his skin with her fingertips, to run her hands through his still-damp hair.

"Damned if you aren't the most adorable thing I've ever seen," he now said hoarsely, his dark eyes ablaze with passion as he nibbled at her throat and the lovely contour of her jaw. When he latched his mouth on hers again and kissed her more deeply, snaking his tongue in and out of her mouth in brazen imitation of the total intimacy he sought, she thought she would die if he did not still the exquisite yearning within her.

His lips moved to gently torment the lobe of her ear, and he whispered, "Oh, darling. Oh, love. Please relent. I can feel you breathing, feel your heart beating so hard, feel you responding to me. Come with me to my bed now, before I lose my mind with wanting you."

She was tempted, she was deliriously tempted, to give in to the powerful urges that seemed so natural and right. But then a small voice in the back of her mind reminded her that, still, he hadn't apologized. "No—please let me go," she murmured breathlessly.

Surprisingly, Matt released her. But as she pulled away, his dark eyes softly scolded her. "You know, my father once told me that a man and his wife should never let the sun go down on their anger."

She looked at his eyes, eyes desperate with desire for her, and almost threw herself back into his arms. Yet she said simply, "I'm not angry with you anymore, Matt," and got to her feet. It was true, she told herself. She really wasn't angry with him anymore. But that didn't change the principle of the thing.

As she turned to leave the room, he followed her, venturing in a lighter tone, "You did do me proud today, Amy. Guess you'll be ready to take on butchering another hog tomorrow, just the two of us."

At that, Amy, looking horror-stricken, raced out of the room, her hand over her mouth.

Matt stayed behind, pacing and mentally kicking himself. What had made him do a fool thing like mention hog butchering to the girl again, just when she was starting to soften a little? Actually, the butchering was done now, with plenty of meat stacked in the smokehouse. He'd meant the comment as a joke, to lighten the tension between them, and it had backfired mightily right in his face. He continued to pace, his boot angrily kicking a basket of wood near the hearth.

Eleven

⁑

The next morning, Reverend Fulton came to visit. Matt was gone at the time, having ridden off to check on some of his cattle that were grazing on a distant glade. Amy was tidying up the kitchen when she heard the knock at the front door. She removed her apron and smoothed down her hair as best she could, hurrying for the central hallway. Seconds later, as she swung open the heavy oaken panel, the tall preacher smiled in greeting, removing his white hat. "Good morning, Mrs. Kendall. May I have a few words with you?"

"Certainly, Reverend," Amy replied graciously. "Please come in."

The minister stepped inside, and Amy took his hat and hung it on the hallway rack. "Mr. Kendall around?" he casually asked, straightening the lapels of his white coat.

"No. He's out hunting up some of our stock."

Amy showed Fulton into the parlor, then hurried to the kitchen to fetch coffee for them both, regretting that she had no cookies or cake to offer her guest. Reentering the drawing room with a tray bearing two cups of coffee, cream and sugar, she also hoped Matt would not be returning to the house anytime soon. The memory of his curt behavior toward Fulton at Emmett Teague's livery had not left her.

118

"Well, now, mighty fine, mighty fine," Fulton remarked moments later as he sat across from Amy, sipping the strong brew. His eyes flicked over her, and she knew a moment of uneasiness, regretting that she had worn one of her older dresses, a faded blue gingham frock with low rounded neck that fit perhaps too snugly across the bodice. Indeed, she felt her cheeks smarting at the clergyman's perusal, for she could almost swear his eyes lingered for a moment on the just-visible cleft of her bosom! "I can tell you're a fine Christian wife, Amy Kendall," the reverend at last pronounced with a self-satisfied gleam in his eye.

Amy stared at the man for a moment, inwardly resenting his comment, which seemed to have been delivered with a sanctimonious, condescending air. That, along with the suspicious, almost prurient glimmer in his eyes, unsettled her. Smiling stiffly, she inquired, "If I may ask, what brings you out here this morning, Reverend Fulton?"

He grinned. "Why, I've come to invite you folks personal to church, a' course. I know I done so back to Emmett's the other day, but an official visit is always in order, don't you think?"

"Certainly, Reverend Fulton, and I really appreciate your coming—"

"Got me a fine group of Christians there at Rolla Presbyterian," Fulton went on, leaning back against the settee and crossing his legs. "A goodly Circle for the womenfolk, too. Say, maybe you can come the next time the ladies hold quilting bee. You did belong to Circle back home to St. Louie, now didn't you?"

"I—we were Methodists at home, although I occasionally attended the Women's Society."

"Methodists, were you?" The reverend winked at her and remarked, "Don't worry, young lady. I won't hold it against you. We'll convert you to the Presbyterian way soon enough."

Now the reverend laughed, offering Amy a conspiratorial smile, and while she was pleased to see that the man possessed at least some sense of humor, the subject of his mirth was hardly comforting to her. In fact, there seemed a less than honorable double meaning in what he was saying. Feeling her back automatically growing rigid, she told him, "Reverend Fulton, I truly appreciate the invitation. But please do not expect too much involvement in church affairs from Mr. Kendall and me, at least not right away. My husband—"

"That's just what I come here to talk to you about," Fulton interrupted, leaning tensely forward, "and I'm right glad Kendall ain't here at the moment. Look, young lady, just because Kendall's of a heathen bent don't mean he has the right to keep you here like a shut-in, too."

Now the man had gone too far! "Reverend Fulton, I'll not have you say such things about my husband!" Amy retorted vehemently, struggling to keep hostility out of her tone. While she conceded that Fulton had his role as spiritual adviser for the community, and while she was concerned that Matt might indeed forbid her to attend church, she realized that she still owed her first allegiance to the man she had married. The reverend had absolutely no right to interfere in private matters between husband and wife, not unless his guidance was requested! Stiffly, she informed him, "If I decide I want to attend church here, that's something I'm sure my husband and I will work out."

"I'm not so sure," the reverend countered, undaunted. "I'll have you know, girl, that I've buried many a wife whose husband used her up out to the farm, and I've seen just as many look fifty at twenty-five. Your husband may not avow it, but he owes you a day for the Lord." Suddenly, the man snapped his fingers, his dark eyes lighting up with zealous resolve. "You know, young lady, I'll be seeing your neighbor, Lyle Stockton, at the deacons' meeting tomorrow night. I'll have him and Nell fetch you in on Sundays, that's what I'll do."

Before Amy could respond to this audacious dictate, an adamant male voice interjected, "If anyone's taking my wife anywhere, it'll be me."

Amy gasped and turned in her chair to see Matt standing in the archway to the parlor, his features rigid with anger. She hadn't even heard him come in!

Spotting Kendall, Reverend Fulton immediately stood, facing the other man grimly. "I've come here, Kendall, to invite you two personal to church on Sunday."

"Fine," Matt snapped back. "You issued that same invitation in town the other day, and the answer's still no."

"Look here, man," Fulton scolded, shaking a finger at Matt, "you got no right to keep this girl here—"

Matt cut in thunderously, "I have every right to throw you out of my house for sneaking in here while I'm gone, trying to cozy up to my wife!"

"Matt!" Horrified, Amy sprang to her feet. Her husband was looking murder at both her and Fulton, his fists clenched, veins standing out on his forehead. She was stunned that he should become so enraged at the preacher's mere presence in their home.

"Now, get out of my house, Fulton," Matt ground out, taking a menacing step toward the preacher.

Amy felt compelled to intercede. "Matt, please . . ."

"You leave the room, woman," her husband barked, turning on her savagely.

With an incoherent cry, Amy did just that. Running up the stairs, she heard Fulton exclaim, "You haven't heard the last of this, Kendall!" then her husband's retort, "If I were you, *Reverend*, I wouldn't be laying bets. . . ."

Upstairs in her bedroom, Amy, sobbing, threw herself on the bed. She heard the door slam downstairs. How could Matt do this to her, disgracing her in front of company, acting like such a beast? Why was he so suspicious of Fulton, so distrustful of her? It wasn't fair, it just wasn't fair! She had done nothing to merit this lack of faith!

"Amy?"

She heard Matt's voice outside her door, accompanied by a soft knock. When she didn't respond, she heard him open the door and step inside. She turned on the bed to face him with eyes defiant, and even though he looked somewhat contrite now, her visage did not soften one bit as she stared him down.

He sighed and raked a hand through his hair before he informed her softly but firmly, "Amy, look, I'm sorry about what happened just now, but I won't have his kind in our house. I won't.''

She struggled to her feet. ''Do you realize you humiliated me, not to mention that you were unpardonably rude to the reverend?''

Matt's jaw clenched, and his eyes flashed with renewed resentment. ''He deserved it for sneaking in here—''

''Sneaking in here?'' she half shrieked. ''Do you think he and I arranged a private tryst back at the livery the other day, while you were hitching up the buggy?''

Matt had the grace to look taken aback at her incisive challenge, swallowing hard. ''No, of course I don't think that,'' he said, moving a step closer. Passionately, he added, ''But his kind can't be trusted. They're nothing but charlatans—''

''What makes you say that?'' Amy cut in. ''What proof do you have?''

Matt's countenance darkened dangerously. ''I saw the way he looked at you.''

''*What?* Matt, he's a preacher, for heaven's sake!''

He set his arms akimbo. ''He's a man, and as full of lust as any other, I'll wager.''

Amy could only gape at her husband in dumbfounded horror. Finally, she asked incredulously, ''Matt, do you actually think I could be persuaded to—to . . .''

He stared at her with the grim, implacable eyes of a stranger. ''You agreed to marry me quick enough, didn't you?''

By now, Amy was beyond speech, totally stunned, as Matt announced tersely, ''I've still a heifer and her calf to search for south of the creek, but I'll be back directly for dinner.''

Amy glared at him in livid silence as he left the room. How dare he treat her this way, intimating that she would bestow her affections so capriciously on another! She paced, her fists clenched so tightly they hurt. Did accepting Matt Kendall's suit make her a loose woman? It was so unfair!

As for his dinner, let him stew in his own damn juices for a while!

* * *

Amy started down the rocky, crude road on the large plow horse. Matt had told her he would be searching for the heifer south of the creek, and she was traveling to the west, putting as much distance between her and her husband as possible. She had decided to take Nell Stockton up on her invitation and go to the neighboring farm for a visit. Defiantly, she had not even left her husband a note; she fully intended to return later that day, but, in the meantime, she cared not one whit if Matt became worried about her. Let him think of someone besides himself for a change!

Amy knew but the rudiments regarding tack and riding, and thus it had been some chore saddling and bridling the draft horse back at the barn. The plow animal was obviously rarely if ever ridden, and the spare saddle Amy had finally located in the barn loft fit the huge gray poorly. Yet the old horse had been quite patient with Amy. Now, the animal's gait could only be called a trudge, but at least he was taking her to the neighboring farm faster then her own feet could!

As horse and woman lumbered along, Amy tried to calm herself by looking closely at the countryside she was traversing. The landscape possessed an intriguing diversity— rolling hills dotted with pines and hardwoods, rocky glades, rich creekbeds, and meadows full of dewy grass. Amy enjoyed seeing an occasional cottontail rabbit hop by as she rode along, and a red-tailed hawk circled gracefully above her. The weather was crisply cool, and she gathered her shawl more closely about her shoulders, realizing that winter would be upon them soon.

Things would slow down at the farm during the coming cold months, she reflected. Amy was not that familiar with farm routines, but she realized that the main function of a farm was the production of food. Since little could be accomplished in that vein during the cold winter months, it followed that both she and Matt would have much more time on their hands then.

Time for what? Her hands tightened on the reins at the very thought. Doubtless, Matt would expect her to warm his bed during those cold winter nights. She wanted so much to be a good wife, to fulfill her part of their bargain. But, damn it, the man made it so hard! And in many ways, he was a stranger to her. His past was a mystery—what was it about him that made him so very suspicious, so distrustful of others? Why was he trying to isolate both of them against the world?

The long ride brought no answers, and Amy's mood was further dampened by the thought that, with Matt angry at her now, it looked unlikely that Hannah would get to come out for a visit anytime soon. Amy could only hope that Reverend and Mrs. Chandler would somehow make arrangements with Esther Harris to bring the child out.

Despite these concerns, Amy found her spirits improving considerably as she crested a rise and spotted a sprawling homestead in the hollow below. She knew immediately that the spread must be the Stocktons' farm—Nell had told her yesterday that their place was the first farm down the road to the west!

The Stockton farmhouse was not nearly as fine as Matt's place, the single-story, square-log dogtrot having a weather-beaten appearance. Yet the house looked quite homey with its neat, swept yard, blooming marigolds spanning the porch and smoke curling from the limestone chimney. In the dogrun, two long-eared hounds dozed in the morning breeze. Beyond the house, the outbuildings dotting the yard looked precariously ramshackle, but numerous fat pigs and cackling chickens testified that the farm was prosperous.

Amy knew she'd come to the right place when she spotted Nell's two boys come tearing around the side of the house, the youngest screaming with fear, the older one chasing his brother with a dangling snake! While she tried to figure how she could get down from the huge horse to go to the younger boy's aid, Nell herself came rushing to the rescue, sprinting around the side of the house in a wool dress, white apron and lacy housecap, pursuing the boys with a wooden spoon in hand. Amy chuckled to herself as she watched the angular matron grab the older boy by his suspenders and give his bottom several sound swats with the spoon, delivered with enough force to send the small snake flying out of the youngster's hand. "Don't you *ever* spook your brother like that again!" Nell scolded the child, even as the redheaded boy squealed, "Ma, it was only a garter snake!"

"Don't you sass me neither, young'un! Now, git in the house!" Nell retorted stoutly. Shamefaced and rubbing his bottom, the older boy trudged off to reflect on his sins, and it wasn't until the farmwife turned to comfort her smaller son that she noticed Amy sitting on the horse in front of the house. "Well, howdy, honey!" she called out with happy surprise, quickly approaching her guest, leading her younger son by the hand. "My, but if you don't give a body a start, Amy Kendall!"

"I hope I haven't come at a bad time," Amy called back awkwardly as Nell and the child grew closer.

"Honey, we're plum delighted to have you," Nell retorted cheerfully.

The matron drew closer, offering Amy an assisting hand as the younger woman gingerly slid to the ground. She was grateful for Nell's help, since back at the barn, she had had to stand on a barrel to saddle and mount the old gray horse.

Nell persuaded her younger son to take Amy's horse off to the water trough near the barn, and invited her neighbor inside for coffee. Sitting in the cozy kitchen, Amy felt at home. She glanced about at the huge iron stove, the wooden pie safe with punched metal doors, the windows curtained in cheery green and white gingham. A massive limestone fireplace lined one entire wall of the large room, the fire crackling as delicious-smelling bread baked nearby in a tin kitchen. Even the chairs at the oaken table creaked with a comforting sameness. Sipping the strong, delicious coffee and warming her cool fingers on the ironstone cup, Amy asked her hostess, "Do your boys fight often?"

Nell turned, smiling, from the wood stove, where she was stirring a succulent ham stew. "Oh, honey, you know how boys are. But the older one, he don't realize Ben is still a baby in some ways." Through tending the pot, Nell moved over to sit beside Amy at the table, brushing a wisp of gray-brown hair from her eyes. "You look right peaked. Is somethin' wrong?"

Amy nodded, and found, to her horror, that Nell's question had brought tears perilously close to the surface. To her friend, she spilled out the story of what had occurred when Reverend Fulton visited her home earlier that morning. Nell shook her head when Amy finished. "If that don't beat all. I'll grant Preacher Fulton's been known to meddle, but still . . ."

"Matt's behavior was totally unjustified," Amy told her hostess.

Nell nodded with motherly concern. "What do you reckon made him like that? Why, Lyle was saying just last night that Matt seemed right standoffish, even around us. It's like he wants you all to hisself."

Nell's perceptive words unwittingly touched a nerve in Amy, and she stood and moved to one of the cheery windows, her fingers gripping the starched gingham curtain as she stared out at the fall garden behind the house. "Nell, there's something I haven't told you," she admitted, blushing miserably. "My marriage to Mr. Kendall was quite sudden, and we haven't, I mean we agreed to wait . . ."

"You don't have to explain nothin' to me, honey," came Nell's comforting voice from behind her. "I figured as much already. That's the way it is in these parts, honey. Folks marry 'cause they got to to survive, and love comes later. I knowed it did with me and Mr. Stockton."

Amy turned, her face flooded with relief. "Then you know what I'm going through?"

"Oh, yes, honey, I do, indeedy." Nell patted the seat next to her. "Now, come finish your coffee." After Amy had seated herself and taken a few more soothing sips, the wise older woman went on, "Honey, I'm not one to meddle, but I do have a suggestion, if you're wantin' to hear it."

"Oh, yes. Please," Amy urged.

"I know it's hard on you, 'specially the way he's hurt your pride, even suggestin' you were hankerin' after the preacher. But have you thought that maybe if you give him what he wants, he might lighten up on the reins a bit?"

Amy blushed. "I . . . hadn't thought—"

"Honey, I've seen many a stamping wild stallion grow docile once he's mated proper."

Amy couldn't help but laugh, her cheeks now blooming with high color. "Nell! You make men sound as if they're wild animals or something!"

Nell playfully nudged Amy with her elbow, winking confidentially. "Well, ain't they?" As both women giggled, Nell added, "You think on it, honey. But for now, I'd sure consider it an honor if you'd stay and take dinner with us, Amy."

Mulling over Nell's kind invitation, Amy couldn't repress a self-satisfied smile as she thought of Matt coming back to the farmhouse for his expected dinner, finding nothing prepared for him—and her gone! Wouldn't that knock him on his heels a bit? "Thank you, Nell, I'd be delighted to stay," she told her hostess with bravado.

Amy assisted Nell in preparing the noonday meal—setting the table, slicing the mouth-watering, just-baked bread. She was unable to resist eating a large hunk smeared with the sweet butter Nell had set out in a crock. When Lyle came in to join them, he at first looked shocked to see Amy; but he quickly recovered, greeting their guest with his friendly, accustomed "Howdy." The three adults were seated with the boys in the kitchen, in the midst of the hearty meal, when the dogs began barking out on the adjacent breezeway. Amy and Nell exchanged quizzical glances as Lyle left the kitchen to investigate. Amy's stomach fluttered as she heard tense, muffled voices outside in the dogrun. Seconds later, her husband burst into the room, storming toward her.

Amy's stomach churned violently. Never had she seen Matt this furious! His face was rigid with ire, his chest heaving, his dark eyes scorching her with the heat of twin branding irons. The tension in his tall masculine body was totally lethal in its menace as he arrived at her side and glared down at her. "Mrs. Kendall," he gritted through clenched teeth, "what the hell do you think you're doing here? Running off without a word? My dinner nowhere in sight?''

His tone of voice was so fierce, Amy automatically shot to her feet, her heart beating frantically. "I was just—just visiting with the neighbors," she told him defensively, mentally reeling at his formidable visage. While she realized she had riled him mightily, she couldn't believe he would forget himself to this degree, cursing in front of Nell and the children! There'd be the devil to pay for her demonstration of independence, she knew that now. She looked at him, swallowing hard, not knowing what else to say as he continued to stare murder at her.

Nell immediately took up the slack. "Matt, please join us for dinner. There's plenty of food. Pete, fetch Mr. Kendall a chair—''

"No, thanks, Nell," Matt retorted in such an obdurate tone that even the normally unflappable Nell was instantly rendered silent and could only glance at Amy lamely. Meanwhile, Matt added to his wife in a dangerously low voice, "Mrs. Kendall and I are going home. Now.''

At this, Lyle Stockton moved forward from the doorway, interjecting a tempering, "See here, Mathew . . .'' even as Amy herself opened her mouth to protest. But Matt stymied them both by grabbing Amy's hand and dragging her out of the room, without giving the flabbergasted Stocktons a backward glance.

She exploded at him out in the yard, wrenching her hand from his as he tried to pull her toward the horses tethered near the barn. "How dare you come here like this, Matt Kendall, acting like a madman—''

"How dare I?'' he hissed, turning to face her with eyes blazing. "So you think you got every right to just walk out of the house, not give anyone a hint of where you're going—''

"Well, perhaps, as you so kindly suggested earlier, Mr. Kendall, I can't be trusted, I'm loose with my loyalties,'' she snapped back, hands defiantly on her hips.

"Woman, you're loose with your tongue,'' he growled back, grabbing her hand and yanking her off again.

Matt dragged her to the horses and practically threw her onto the old gray, keeping the reins in his hand as he mounted his own horse. "Giddy-ap, Sampson," he called back to the gray as he spurred his own horse and started them off at a brisk trot. The plow horse reluctantly fell into step behind Matt's sprightly mare, and Amy's bottom was soundly pounded during the long ride. She gripped the saddle horn with both hands to keep from falling off, and glared at Matt's broad back before her.

When they arrived at home, Matt summarily pulled her from the horse and led her inside. In the front hallway, he took her firmly by the shoulders and lectured, "I've had just about enough of your willfulness, woman. First you shirk your chores, then you flirt with the preacher, then you traipse off visiting, not telling a soul in hell where you're going." Amy opened her mouth to protest but was silenced by Matt's scolding finger. "No more gallivanting for you, girl," he pronounced, "until you start performing your wifely duties. *All* your wifely duties," he added meaningfully.

Amy was appalled, shrugging away from his touch, her eyes huge with incredulity. "You mean you're keeping me here your prisoner until I go to bed with you?"

"Yes," he said baldly.

Her mouth dropping open, Amy couldn't help but remember Nell's comment, that perhaps Matt would soften a bit if she gave him what he wanted. Yet Nell had no idea what it was like living with this exasperating man! "You may as well wish for hen's teeth, Mr. Kendall," she snapped back, turning on her heel and going up the stairs.

Climbing upward angrily, Amy wished she'd been able to come up with a much more scathing rejoinder. But she was a Christian woman, after all.

Twelve

✛

The next couple of weeks passed for Amy and Matt in strained courtesy. Matt did not back down from his dictate that his wife couldn't leave the farm until she came around to his way of thinking, but Amy didn't give in, either. She refrained from out-and-out hostility toward her husband, and he was evenly civil toward her. But the two were, at best, polite strangers, all the closeness and attraction they'd once felt suppressed beneath cool facades of pride.

Matt spent the time preparing the farm for the winter months—cleaning out the barn and animal cribs, laying in fresh hay, grinding cornstalks and husks for fodder, chopping an ample supply of firewood. He had planted a field in corn the previous spring, and thus fall plowing also had to be done in order to turn under the dried stubble remaining in the fields after harvesting. Matt's modest first gathering of corn would be used mainly as animal feed, he mentioned to Amy. But next season, his plans for the crop were much more ambitious; he would seed all his fields this time, raising enough corn to sell some of it for profit. Amy respected his enterprising nature, especially since he was a new farmer. When the brood sow had her litter, he took the piglets they would not raise for pork and sold them off in town. She felt hurt that he didn't ask her along on his trips into Rolla; each time he left, it was all she could do to swallow her pride and hand him a list of badly needed supplies, or letters for posting to Hannah or Vida.

Matt always checked the mail in town, yet as the weeks passed, there was no reply from St. Louis. This worried Amy, for she was most anxious to hear news of Hannah's welfare. She thought of her sister frequently, and would often wipe a tear as she realized that, considering the distance between her and Matt, her chances of getting Hannah to the farm for a visit were looking increasingly slim.

Amy tried to keep herself busy with the house. While her new interest in her surroundings was spurred in part because she didn't want to rile Matt again, on a deeper level she realized that this was her home now, come better or worse, and she'd best start making the most of her situation. The incident at the Stocktons' had dashed any hopes of escape or independence. Even if she could somehow travel to her second cousin in Steelville, what could she tell the woman? That her husband was demanding she live up to her part in the marriage, do her chores and come to his bed like a dutiful wife? There was certainly nothing unusual or reprehensible about that attitude on a man's part!

Yet it was Matt's reason for wanting her that galled her the most. Her pride refused to let her become a mere object of his lust, another member of his brood stock! She'd stay here his prisoner forever before she stooped to that! If only he would tell her he wanted her just for herself. Yet that seemed a foolish dream, every bit as whimsical as her hopes of leaving!

So she worked about the house and tried not to think of how unhappy she was. She realized that the house, while basically neat, had not had a thorough cleaning in many months, and that now was the time, before winter set in. Amy rolled up rugs and beat them outside on the line, took down curtains, scrubbed them in an iron pot, then later starched them, laboriously ironing them in the kitchen, using one heavy iron while the other heated on the wood stove. She washed windows, swept floors and whisked cobwebs from corners, giving the hearth in the parlor a good cleaning as well to prepare it for heavy winter use. She aired pillows and feather mattresses, plumping them and returning them to the beds, and she turned out the wardrobes in both bedrooms, to air her clothing as well as Matt's outside.

It was on one of these fall cleaning days, when Amy was taking Matt's brown frock coat from his wardrobe, that she felt something stiff through the fabric of the breast pocket. Thinking that he may have forgotten some important papers in his suit, she took the item out, and was appalled to find herself staring at a photograph of a dark-haired young woman, dressed in a high-necked, prim frock, her thick hair piled in a bun on top of her head. A hard stab of jealousy assailed Amy as she studied the picture. Who was this young lady? Could she be Matt's sister? Amy shook her head grimly. There was no familial resemblance whatever between Matt and this dark-haired beauty, and besides, why would a man secrete his sister's likeness in his breast pocket?

That particular thought spurred a welling sense of outrage in Amy, as she realized Matt had courted her while all the time carrying another's image next to his heart. How dare he!

"Amy, what are you doing in here?"

Amy whirled to find her husband standing in the open doorway to his room, staring at her curiously. He eyed the pile of clothing laid out on his bed; then his eyes shifted back to her. Spotting the photograph in her hand, he paled, swallowing hard. "What are you doing with that photograph?"

"I—I was turning out your wardrobe," she began defensively, "and this was in the breast pocket of your coat—the same coat you wore when you met me in St. Louis." She held the picture up to him with a shaking hand. "Who is she, Matt?"

He took a step closer. "Amy, I've never met her," he said lamely.

"Then what are you doing with her picture in your coat?"

Edging nearer, Matt studied his wife curiously. She was trembling with anger, and unwittingly he felt the beginnings of a smile pull at the corners of his mouth. "Why Amy, I do believe you're jealous."

That comment enraged Amy, mainly because it was true, and she shook the photograph at him. "There's a difference between being jealous and feeling betrayed, Mr. Kendall. I thought we had a commitment, you and I, but now it seems that *this* is how seriously you have taken what's between us!"

"Amy . . ." He extended his hands in supplication. "Look, she means nothing to me. My sister sent me her picture. She's just a girl Charlotte wanted me to meet when I went to Virginia—"

Matt's attempt to smooth Amy's ruffled pride backfired disastrously. "So *that's* why you were going to Virginia!" she cried, her eyes bright with anger and realization. "You had a marriage all arranged there! Then, when you stopped off in St. Louis and met me, you decided I looked strong and healthy enough for a farmwife, so you'd save yourself some time and trouble and hitch up with me instead!"

"Amy!" His expression showed he was crestfallen. "That's not how it happened at all."

"Then why have you kept her photograph?" she demanded, trembling with the force of her fury. "Of all the cold, calculating . . . Are you still wondering which one of us would have made the more efficient wife?"

By now, Matt was visibly struggling to control his patience, his jaw tight, his fists clenched at his sides. "The God's truth is, woman, I plum forgot the damn picture was in my pocket."

"I don't believe you!" she cried. To her horror, she felt tears burning, and she lowered her head in shame.

"Amy." Matt came to her side, gently taking the picture from her hands and then tearing it to small pieces before her very eyes. The fragments fluttered to the floor, and Amy watched them through the blur of her tears. "Forget the picture, please," Matt's soft voice entreated her. "If you'd only let me, darling, I'd love you till there was no doubt in your heart which one of you I wanted."

She looked up at him then, mesmerized by his words. The sheer sensual magnetism in his dark eyes was so intense as he waited for her response that she was sorely tempted to forget everything. Yet she was still so hurt and confused, her pride perversely reminding her that if she went to him now, he would win—he would think he could bend her to his will simply by keeping her his prisoner here. No, no! an inner voice rebelled. As much as she was drawn to him, as much as she hurt to be sheltered in his strong embrace, she would give herself to him only when she could do so of her own free will, not bow to the pressure of his unjust dictates. Wounded pride made her demand of her husband, "And if I come to you, Mr. Kendall, will I be privileged to sit by your side the next time you go into town, or will I be left behind again, like one of your cattle?"

That infuriated him, and he threw up his hands, turning on his heel to leave her. "Maybe I should have married her," he growled under his breath, pivoting to glare at her from the doorway. "My sister said she was eager to be a farmwife, eager to rear a family, not muleheaded and full of pride, like—"

"Get out of here—I hate you!" Amy cried, not allowing him to finish.

With eyes blazing, he left her, and she could hear him swearing vehemently as he stomped down the stairs. Amy rushed to her own room, collapsing on the bed in tears. The hell of it was, she didn't hate him, she thought, beating her fists upon the coverlet. Oh, no, she didn't hate him at all. In fact, her feelings for him were so far from hatred that it sometimes scared her to death. Nevertheless, she refused to be humiliated at his hands.

After a while, she heard his soft voice at her door. "Amy . . ." His words came almost helplessly. "Look, love, I'm sorry. Would you let me in, please?"

Again, she was tempted to abandon her pride, seek the comfort she so desperately needed in his arms. Yet nothing had changed. She was still his prisoner. "Go away!" she called out, and heard his defeated footsteps trudge off. . . .

Following the scene with Amy, Matt went out to the barn, grabbed the silage fork, and began tossing hay into the cast-iron baler. He tried to mull over his unhappy relationship with his bride.

He'd done it now. He'd really done it. His wife was mad enough at him to stuff hot coals in his drawers. But what was he to do with the girl? What did she expect of him? How long did she think he could last, being around her all the time—her eyes, her hair, her smile, that tantalizing body of hers—before he completely lost control and gave vent to the passions tearing him apart?

Oh, he'd come close in past weeks. He realized he had overreacted when the reverend came to visit, but he didn't trust the man, was convinced that the preacher was as full of carnal urges as any other male animal. Despite that, he knew he'd had no call to intimate to Amy that she might be loose with her affections. That was poor. It was Fulton he distrusted, not Amy. Yet when he was pushed, frustrated that way . . . frightening rage rose up in him, making him do stupid, unforgivable things. Matt had thought he could control those violent urges that had ruled his life for so many years during the war and afterward, and now, when that wildness inside him again surged to the surface, it scared him to death.

That same madness had spurred him to drag Amy home from the Stocktons' two weeks past, issuing his harsh ultimatum that she couldn't leave the farm until she performed *all* her wifely duties. How he had regretted those reckless words! Yet his pride wouldn't allow him to take them back. In his own defense, he knew he was scared of losing her. Why was she seeking the comfort of others when he, her husband, should be enough for her?

He realized sinkingly that she sought the solace of others because he had lost her trust. He had pushed too hard to consummate the marriage, had expected too much of her as a new farmwife, too. Now, the problem of her finding the picture of the Virginia woman made things so much worse. Damn, he wished he'd torn the photograph up in the first place! But what he told Amy was true. He'd forgotten all about the damned picture his sister Charlotte had sent him. Amy didn't believe him, of course, and he couldn't blame her.

He sighed, wiping his sweaty, furrowed brow. Securing the now-compressed bale with wire, he then lifted it into the loft by means of a clawlike structure attached to a rope and pulley. Grimacing as he yanked at the rope and swung the bundle upward, Matt acknowledged to himself at last that he couldn't win Amy over by confining her, crushing her spirit, just as he had compressed the hay. He would have to give her more freedom, he would have to win her trust all over again.

But how? Where to make a start? Grabbing the hayfork, he started making another bale, desperately hoping the answers would come. As he worked, he smiled ruefully at Sampson, who had now poked his long gray muzzle over his nearby stall.

The old horse neighed and shook his head at Matt.

During the rest of November, the impasse between Amy and Matt continued, their relationship as cool as the first winter winds that now blew across the glades. Nell Stockton came by for a brief visit to check on the young bride's welfare, and Amy filled her friend in on the new twists in the story. Nell again urged Amy to be patient, and begged her not to set too much store in the photograph she'd found; but, other than that, the motherly woman could offer no workable solution for the troubled couple. "Guess the two of you will have to ride it out till both of you learn to give a little," was all the matron would say. Amy was not too pleased with the comment, for from her perspective, all the "giving" was expected from her quarter!

Amy fixed herself and Matt a traditional Thanksgiving dinner, complete with the wild turkey her husband had hunted; while Matt politely praised Amy's cooking, the meal passed mostly in strained silence. Amy knew she should be thankful to have her own home, yet the days in the isolated country were long and lonely; she missed the company of others as well as her music and attending church. She did at last receive a letter from Vida, which for some odd reason took several weeks to arrive at Rolla. Yet the correspondence was no comfort to her. It wasn't what was said, but what was left unsaid by Vida's words: "I see young Hannah frequently. Bless her heart. We're making out as best can be expected under the circumstances." Amy shuddered to think of what Hannah's true "circumstances" were now that she was gone. She didn't dare broach the subject of her sister's welfare with Matt, fearing that he would soundly scold her for asking him to intercede in Hannah's behalf before she herself fulfilled her own duties as his wife. Of course, if conclusive proof emerged that Hannah was being abused at her mother's hands, Amy was completely willing to go to Matt, accept whatever terms he laid down in order to get his help; yet she hadn't quite reached that point yet.

Amy did decide that, considering the tension in her marriage, it was high time she made some overture toward her cousin Josie in Steelville. She sent off a letter to her cousin care of general delivery, telling the matron of her marriage to Matt, of how she lived in Rolla now, and offering her relative greetings of the season. To Amy's surprised pleasure, two weeks later she received an enthusiastic reply from the kind woman. Cousin Josie expressed her delight that Amy now lived thirty miles to the north of her, and invited the girl and her husband to come for a visit any time. Although Amy well knew Matt would not be willing to take her off visiting relatives, it was a great comfort to the young bride to know that she had a place to go should her problems with Matt worsen.

She tried to keep her mind off her unhappiness by staying busy with chores. Patiently following Matt's instruction, Amy learned to milk the two cows out in the barn, and how to churn butter, as well. The root cellar was in bad shape, obviously overrun with mice, so she cleaned it out, discarded spoiled and gnawed foods and set new traps for the rodents.

She also busied herself putting up vegetables from the now-harvested fall garden.

Matt made no more physical advances toward her, though she could often see the reproach in his eyes. It was a look that said, "You promised me . . ." She realized that she had indeed not honored her word, and in a perverse way, she almost wished he would push things a little, like by kissing her as he had the first few nights following their marriage. Even the memory of how his strong arms had imprisoned her, how his hard, hot mouth had demanded so much, could make her breathless, giddy. Now all she had left to fill the cold nights were those memories and the comfortless knowledge of her resolve. Maybe Matt was so disgusted with her now, he didn't want her at all, she thought dismally. Perhaps he did wish that he had married the Virginia woman instead. If only she could go to him! They were stalemated. Amy's pride might allow her to go to him of her own free will, but she couldn't crush her own spirit by bowing to an outrageous, unjust ultimatum. He would think she was sleeping with him just so she could get out of the house again—and that, to her, was no better than whoring.

When Matt went off to town alone for the third time since he'd forbidden Amy to leave the farm, her rage was such that she wanted to go into the kitchen and break every dish. Yet she controlled herself with an effort. Amy sat down with needle and thread to mend a stack of frayed sheets, and gritted her teeth, swallowing unladylike curses, when her angry motions resulted in her sticking herself with the needle an uncommon number of times.

Amy lost track of the time, and much later was astonished to hear laughter out in the yard. The mirth sounded almost childlike, and Amy sprang to her feet with a sudden, unfettered sense of excitement, figuring Nell and her boys had come for another visit.

Racing out the front door, she was stunned as a laughing young girl flew up the stairs and into her arms.

"Hannah!" Amy cried.

Thirteen

✛

A cool afternoon breeze whipped about the yard, and sunshine shone brightly on the tender scene near the farmhouse steps. Amy continued to hold her sister, and tears of joy and astonishment welled up in her eyes as she glanced toward Matt, who stood smiling off to the side. She was so touched and warmed by his bringing Hannah to the farm that she felt tempted to give in, to fly into his arms and knock him to the ground with wild, grateful kisses. Amy controlled her reckless impulse, of course; instead, her lips formed the silent, exulted message, "Thank you," as she smiled at him. He nodded back his understanding.

Turning her attention back to Hannah, Amy clutched her sister tightly. "Hannah—oh, praise the heavens—I just can't believe you're here!"

Hannah looked up at Amy. A wide smile brightened her slightly freckled face and her brown eyes sparkled beneath the brim of her hat. "Matt sent Ma the money for my train ticket and told her to let me come out next time with the Chandlers," the child explained gleefully. "So the reverend and his wife brought me, and I can stay for two whole weeks—till they come back through from Springfield. Isn't that wonderful, sister?"

"Oh, yes, wonderful." Releasing her sister, Amy glanced

back at Matt, who was still grinning at the two girls. She realized with an intense wave of shame that her husband had doubtless sent her mother a more than generous bank draft in order to convince Esther to let Hannah come out for a visit. How Amy had misjudged him!

"How were Reverend and Mrs. Chandler?" she asked Matt, smiling shyly.

"Fine—I spoke with them for just a moment before the train pulled out," was her husband's reply. He grinned. "They sure had a high old time with baby sister here," he added, glancing at Hannah fondly.

"The train was such fun!" the little girl chimed in.

"And Mrs. Chandler told me to tell you she'll look forward to seeing you, too, when they come back through," Matt added to Amy.

By now, Amy was fighting tears again, and Matt, evidently sensing that his wife needed some time alone with her sister, cleared his throat and said, "I'll fetch in Hannah's bag, then."

As he grabbed Hannah's portmanteau from the boot of the buggy and headed for the house, the two sisters again embraced ecstatically. "Oh, Hannah, I can't tell you how glad I am that you've come!" Amy breathed. She backed off slightly. "Here, let me look at you." She studied her from crown to toe. "Ahah! You've grown at least another inch."

"Have not!" Hannah insisted, waving her sister off. "It's just these high-heeled walking shoes Matt bought me on Veranda Row. Remember?"

Amy nodded. Then, in a more serious tone, she ventured, "How are things at home?"

Hannah bit her lip. "Let's go inside, sister," the child evaded. "You're shivering."

Amy laughed, glancing ruefully at the thin cotton frock she wore. The afternoon had grown quite frigid and she *was* feeling the cold, now that she thought of it. "You know, I was so excited to see you, I plain forgot about the weather," Amy confessed, glancing with approval at the heavy, if dark and patched, traveling cloak Hannah wore. "Come on, let's get you inside and settle you in."

In the front hallway, Amy hung Hannah's cloak and hat on the pegged rack and again ordered, more firmly, "All right, now. Tell me how things really are at home."

"Oh, Amy, please don't spoil my visit," Hannah cajoled. "You know how it is. Ma is Ma."

"Yes, I know," Amy echoed dully. "It's good she let you come out with the Chandlers, though."

"Yes. They're funny, you know. The reverend and his wife argued all the way out here 'bout whether their grandson is eight or nine months old. The reverend's voice kept getting louder and his nose turned bright red." Hannah scratched her blond head. "I didn't think preachers were allowed to argue with their wives."

Amy giggled. "Oh, I'm sure every man argues with his wife at one time or another," she put in ruefully.

Hannah smiled and grabbed her older sister's hand. "Come on, now. Show me your house! It's so beautiful and tall! Will I have my own room? How many horses do you have?"

"One thing at a time!" Amy laughed.

Amy found her younger sister's exuberance infectious as the two went from room to room. Hannah bounded along, her golden curls bobbing up and down. The little girl adored the two bright, spacious downstairs rooms, so different from the cramped, drab quarters she lived in in St. Louis. Upstairs, Hannah looked awestruck at the nursery. "Amy, are you . . . ?" she asked excitedly.

"No, no," Amy hastily replied, embarrassed. "The previous owners left these things."

Hannah took this in stride as they toured the other rooms. She was astonished by the fine oak furniture in Matt's bedroom, and then, as they went into the guest room, with its iron double bed and plain but pleasant bureau and wardrobe, she spotted her bag and exclaimed, "Amy, will this be my room while I'm here?"

Amy cleared her throat nervously. "Um—yes, dear, but—I hope you won't mind sharing it with me."

"Don't you sleep with Matt?" Hannah asked her sister confusedly.

"Hannah!" Amy gasped, very taken aback.

"Well, Gracie Stallings says her folks sleep in the same bed, in the room next to hers." Hannah smirked in little-girl style and whispered, "And, sometimes, Gracie says, they make the most ungodly racket—"

"Hannah!" Mortified, Amy spoke with loving firmness. "Dear, it's not proper to speak of such things."

"Why not?" the little girl questioned.

"Because . . ." Amy floundered miserably. How could she explain these matters to her sister? She realized that while she had done her best to raise Hannah, there were many gaps in the child's training, gaps that only a parent could fill. Since Esther had ignored the child entirely, Amy realized the little girl's remarks were motivated more by innocence than by any desire to be fresh or mischievous. Nonetheless, Amy knew that this was one gap she'd best fill in a hurry! What if Hannah asked Matt precisely the same question at dinner tonight? The very thought made her shudder.

Amy grabbed Hannah's bag and lifted it onto the bed. Opening the latch, she said thoughtfully, "Sweetheart, while you were growing up, there was a lot expected of me, and I suppose there are some things I should have told you about long ago that I never quite got around to."

"Oh, that?" The little girl waved her off. "Don't worry. I've seen cats doing it out in the yard."

This was too much! Amy collapsed on the bed, next to the open suitcase, laughing until tears filled her eyes.

Hannah joined her, clutching Amy's hand. "Did I say something wrong, sister?"

Amy hugged the little girl, still struggling to control her mirth. "No, no, of course not. You're absolutely perfect, delightful, as always. Oh, Hannah, I've missed you so!" Straightening and wiping a tear, Amy went on with a smile, "But as for the other . . . well, it's not quite like what cats do, dear—"

"What, then?" the child prompted eagerly.

Amy playfully tugged on one of Hannah's golden curls. "Let's get you unpacked and have some tea. Then you and I will have a long talk."

"Great!" But the child's face puckered in a frown as she watched her sister go to the wardrobe and move her own dresses aside to make room for Hannah's. "But if you and Matt don't sleep in the same bed, then how are you going to have a baby?"

Amy whirled, again scandalized. "Hannah, please, not everything at once! I can't endure it. I'll try my best to explain later."

"Oh, all right," the child said rather petulantly. "But if you're sleeping in here all by yourself, it just seems to me that you don't know very much about it."

"Hannah!" Throwing up her hands and shaking her head, Amy went to the bureau, opened a drawer and rearranged the contents to create space for Hannah's underclothes. Her back to the child, she finally dared address the question that had been at the back of her mind ever since her young sister arrived. "Hannah, I've been wondering—did Lacy ever . . . ? I mean, did he—"

"No, sister, we haven't seen him," the child replied frankly. As Amy sighed heavily, turning to face her sister, the little girl seemed to guess her thoughts, adding, "You did right to marry Matt."

Amy nodded. "I know. Even if Lacy had come back, I still know I made the right decision." Taking a steadying breath, she went on sternly, "Now, young lady, I must have your word that you won't mention Lacy's name around Matt while you're here."

"Why, sister?" the guileless ten-year-old asked. "You're married to Matt now, and you just said you made the right choice—"

"No more arguing. Just give me your promise."

"Yes, sister."

With Hannah there, Amy's entire attitude toward Matt changed. She had been deeply moved by his bringing her sister to the farm, and the lengths he had gone to to accomplish it. She felt guilty for having judged him so unfairly before, and for the first time, she laid aside her own anger and tried to see things from his perspective.

Sure, Amy had feared she was being used in the marriage, but what about him? Didn't he have every reason to experience the same doubts, having married a miserably poor young woman, rescuing her from a mother who was cruel to her? Why wouldn't he assume that her desperation to escape her unhappiness was the main reason she had accepted his suit? And wasn't it?

No, no, she would deny to herself. Of course she had wanted to get away from her mother, but she had also felt such an attraction for Matt. She *had*!

Yet how had she showed it? By refusing him his husbandly rights? By balking at her chores? Why shouldn't he feel betrayed and angered by her attitude, when he'd given her a beautiful new home and she'd turned up her nose at her duties? No wonder he forbade her leaving the house! He was right when he had said she wasn't keeping up her end of the bargain. And maybe, just maybe, he was afraid he might lose her!

Of course, in her own defense, Amy acknowledged that Matt had in some ways made things quite difficult for her. Yet they were both so new at this, just as Nell had pointed out. Amy longed to go to Matt and make her peace with him, to thank him unreservedly for all he had done; yet, even though Hannah's arrival had brought her to this juncture, the little girl's presence had subtly altered the intimate atmosphere. Hannah noticed everything and was insatiably curious about it all, from the workings of the farm to the intricacies of her sister's marriage. As a result, Amy and Matt instinctively grew more guarded around each other. They didn't realize that Hannah was not fooled by this. The child caught every secret, longing glance each cast upon the other.

While technically, Hannah had come to the farm to visit her sister, she almost immediately became more of a companion to Matt. On her first full day at the farm, the child bounded down the stairs before dawn, fully dressed, and danced into the kitchen where Amy and Matt were eating the morning meal. "Sister, that ham smells wonderful! Matt, may I help you with your chores after breakfast? Will you show me the baby chicks you told me about yesterday?"

Matt grinned at the child's enthusiasm, nodding as he drank his coffee. "Sure, I'd welcome a hand, honey." And thus it was in the days that followed that Matt taught the child all about the farm—how hogs were fed, how cows were milked, how chickens would sometimes lay their eggs under the house. And Hannah eagerly assisted the young farmer with all his yard tasks, making Amy feel ashamed of her own attitude.

Together, Matt and Hannah rode the old plow horse bareback out to the fields, so Matt could show Hannah all of his lands. As they left together, Amy stood watching on the front porch, and felt an unexpected stab of jealousy. She realized she was resentful partly because she wanted Hannah to herself. Yet how could she tempt her sister with her own largely mundane routine, when the workings of a farm had to be as fascinating as a carnival to a city child?

Part of her jealousy, Amy realized, was on another plane, a man-to-woman plane. Of course, she knew there was no romantic interest between Hannah and Matt; he thought of the child as a daughter, and she thought of him as the father she'd never had. But oh, how Amy wished she could be sitting behind him on that horse, holding on to his trim waist! How she longed to share with him so much easy, healing laughter!

As much as Hannah's smooth rapport with Matt was a surprise to Amy, more shocks awaited her during the oncoming days. One morning a few days after the child arrived, Matt rode off, and returned at noon with a palomino pony! Hearing the high-strung whinny of a young horse, Amy and Hannah raced out to the small corral adjoining the barn, where the good-sized colt was stamping about inside. The girls were enchanted by the animal's beautiful gold coat and cream-colored mane, as well as his stocky build and proud stance. Matt merely grinned at them in greeting, explaining, "Hannah likes to ride, and Charlie Moss was willing to let this pony go for a right good price." Hearing this announcement, Hannah jumped up and down in her glee, while Matt added to Amy, with a wink, "Once the colt's grown, he's yours, my dear. I can't have you ruining a good plow horse trotting off to the neighbors all the time."

Amy turned away at Matt's words to hide her feelings, her stinging eyes. Matt was such a baffling man! Was this his way of saying that he was no longer angry at her for going off to visit the Stocktons, that he was through trying to keep her his prisoner at the farm?

Yet her thoughts took a back seat to watching her husband teach Hannah to ride the frisky animal. At first, Matt avoided full tack, leading the bridled horse around the corral with an exuberant Hannah perched on his blanketed back. Under Matt's guidance, the untrained pony adjusted to a walk and then to a trot, while Hannah laughed with delight and hung on to his thick mane, her own curls flying in the breeze. But when the wind hooked the little girl's skirts, flapping them upward and exposing her pantalets, Amy gasped her mortification.

After the riding lesson, Amy took Matt aside in the front hallway of the house. "Matt, I think it's wonderful about the pony. But—um—Hannah's skirts—"

"I know," he cut in quickly, saving her further embarrassment. "Your sister needs a riding outfit. Do you think you could sew her one?"

"I'd love to—but I don't have any material," Amy replied awkwardly.

"Damn. I should have gotten you some yard goods in town."

"Wait! I have an idea . . ." As Matt watched her in confusion, Amy rushed upstairs. She remembered that one of her housedresses had torn so badly on a loose nail in the henhouse that she had decided to use it for rags. Yet she now realized that there was plenty of cloth left in the skirt to make a smaller divided skirt for Hannah. Amy stayed up late that night making the skirt in the sewing room, and

Hannah, consumed with excitement, assisted her. The next morning, the delighted child raced down the steps and headed for the corral, proudly wearing her new skirt and a short jacket of her own.

Matt and Amy both laughed as they observed Hannah's first attempts to guide the pony around the corral unassisted. Matt had not yet put any more than a blanket on the colt's back, so the child could better acquaint herself with the silent language of the animal's movements. Amy watched proudly, clapping as Hannah successfully maneuvered the pony into a trot. Chuckling at her side, Matt turned to his wife and playfully cinched her chin between his thumb and forefinger. "Don't forget, my dear. Once the colt's grown, you're next."

Early on the first Sunday morning during Hannah's visit, as Amy and Matt sat in the kitchen sipping coffee, the child burst into the room wearing her best dress, the pinafored outfit Matt had bought her back in St. Louis. Spotting Amy in her household muslin and apron, and Matt in his every-day shirt and denim trousers, the little girl stopped in her tracks, looking crestfallen. "Aren't we going to church, sister?"

Amy bit her lip, not knowing what to say. How could she tell her sister that her husband didn't hold with religion? In acute misery, Amy glanced from Hannah to Matt. Her husband was scowling, obviously lost in thought, and she could see the visible struggle etched on his fine features. As he took in the child's bewildered, expectant expression, his countenance wavered even more, as if his visage might simply cave in.

"We won't be attending services, sister?" Hannah repeated to Amy, with the horrified look of one who would ask, *We won't be saving our souls from the devil?*

Fortunately, Matt at last saved the moment, stunning Amy by snapping his fingers and remarking to the child, "By thunder, you're right, Hannah. Dogged if it ain't Sunday." He turned to Amy with a mock scowl. "Mrs. Kendall, how could you forget? We must hurry upstairs and change to our go-to-meeting clothes.''

While Amy started in wide-eyed astonishment, Matt stood, ready to gallantly assist her out of her chair. Amy numbly left the room and went upstairs to change, with Matt following close behind her. Would wonders never cease? She was stunned by her husband's abrupt change in attitude. Matt was actually planning to attend church—Reverend Fulton's church, no less?

This she had to see!

She did. True to his word, Matt hitched up the buggy and took the two girls to town for church. The small conveyance was crowded as the three of them jammed onto the narrow seat, Hannah protectively placed in the middle. But the girls thoroughly enjoyed the outing, taking deep breaths of crisp, invigorating air. The day was chilly, yet mild enough, considering that winter had now officially arrived in Rolla. The season's first frost had yet to come, however, and the still-shedding trees offered splashes of brilliant color—russet, yellow, crimson, mixed in with verdant evergreens.

As they moved up out of the bottomland, cresting a large rise, Rolla appeared before them, grouped between vibrant, late-autumn hills. Amy caught sight of a distant church steeple and knew a moment of intense uneasiness. She glanced at Matt, sitting across from her. He looked quite handsome in his brown suit, his strong hands working the reins, but she found his features unreadable beneath the wide brim of his buff-colored hat. Would she ever figure this man out? Brief weeks before, he had practically thrown Reverend Fulton out of their home for coming for a visit, yet today Matt was taking his wife and her sister to the man's church! Amy knew that her husband had shifted his position for Hannah's sake, and while she delighted that her sister had brought about this reversal, she also couldn't control a pang of jealousy, a feeling of inadequacy, that she, Amy, was obviously incapable of moving Matt to this degree. And she was quite anxious about the coming hours, fearing the change in her husband might be no more than mirror deep. Would Matt's bitter attitude resurface as soon as he came into contact with Reverend Fulton again?

The Presbyterian Church was a small frame structure on Pine Street, north of the main business section of town. A crowd of Rolla folk in Sunday finery were gathered about the steps when the threesome from the Kendall farm alighted from their buggy. As the newcomers approached the board steps of the little white church, Nell Stockton burst forward wearing a dark cloak and an elegant black bonnet lined with a watered silk ruching. She warmly embraced Amy. "Amy Kendall, I do declare! My prayers have been answered!" Nell's fine green eyes then fixed upon Hannah. "Who's this little angel?"

"My sister," Amy explained. "Hannah's here visiting from St. Louis."

"I knowed it! She's your spittin' image! Well, howdy, little missy! Welcome to Rolla!"

Nell Stockton graciously introduced her neighbors around. The townfolk, mostly of farming stock like Matt, were reserved but polite as they welcomed the visitors. While Matt was rather standoffish with the parishioners, Amy greeted the churchfolk warmly and studied them with interest. The women wore fancy "poke" bonnets and dainty gloves, their finest crocheted shawls draped over frocks of silk or calico or dimity. The men wore "Sunday best" suits and a collection of hats, from beavers to Panamas to straw. An assortment of children of different shapes and sizes frolicked about, bobbing in and out of the sea of adults and making eyes at Hannah. Before too much visiting could be accomplished, however, the church bell pealed out and the gathering of parishioners obediently trooped inside.

The small sanctuary was cool but crowded, and the townfolk were crammed onto its hard wooden benches. The hymn singing, done to the accompaniment of a woefully out-of-tune piano, seemed to take an eternity for Amy. She also felt unnerved by the stare of Reverend Fulton; the instant the preacher mounted his pulpit, his shrewd eyes fixed meaningfully upon her and Matt. Amy's uneasiness turned to miserable apprehension as Fulton chose to read the parable of the prodigal son returning home. The minister then expounded at length upon that same theme during his sermon, his fist pounding the pulpit as he alternated screaming then whispering his melodramatic message of salvation from past sins. Matt suffered through the pious discourse in grim silence, and Amy prayed that he wouldn't simply walk out of the service, dragging the rest of them along with him.

Amy sighed with relief when it came time for the closing hymn and benediction. She had a tense moment after the service, when Reverend Fulton stood in the foyer shaking the hand of each departing parishioner. As the threesome from the Kendall farm approached the minister, Fulton's eyes fixed with zealous resolve on Matt. "I'll have you know, Kendall, that it's about time—"

But Matt cut the man dead by pumping his hand briefly and mumbling gruffly, "Mornin' Fulton," not even breaking his stride as he grabbed the hands of Amy and Hannah, tugging the two girls with him out the door. Amy could do no more than throw the outraged reverend an apologetic glance over her shoulder as she half stumbled out of the foyer. She felt annoyed by Matt's actions, but one look at his stony features convinced her to keep her peace.

Outside, the churchfolk enjoyed another informal gathering. Matt did not insist they leave at once, allowing Amy some time to visit with the women, while Hannah freely intermingled with the other children. Matt stood off to the side during the social hour, still resisting any overtures from the men; Amy sighed with relief when Lyle Stockton went over and matter-of-factly engaged her husband in a conversation. At least Matt seemed halfway comfortable around the easygoing farmer.

An older lady named Winifred Wilson invited Amy to come to the church on Tuesday for a quilting bee. The sharp-featured woman in gray silk dress and matching bonnet nodded toward Hannah and told Amy, "Bring along baby sister, too. She kin help the grannies sit with the wee ones while we do our stitchin' and ruminatin'."

"I'd be right pleased to give you a ride in come

Tuesday, honey," Nell Stockton chimed in, adding her firm endorsement to the invitation.

Amy bit her lip, glancing toward her husband. Even though Matt was now laughing with Lyle Stockton, he still looked uncomfortable, shifting from foot to foot. Amy sighed. Matt's bringing them to church had been enough of a concession, for now. She couldn't threaten her fragile rapport with him by throwing in a quilting bee, too! To the expectant ladies, she said, "Thank you so much for the invitation, ladies, but I think I'd best wait until after my sister returns to St. Louis."

"We meet every Tuesday morning, honey, and we'll be expectin' you one of these times soon, then," Winifred Wilson told her in parting.

Catching Matt's stare through the corner of her eye, Amy bid the ladies a cheerful farewell and motioned to Hannah that it was time for them to leave. During the ride home the little girl entertained them with anecdotes about the children she'd met after church. "You know that skinny redheaded boy named Chester Wiggins, the one with no front teeth? He told me one time he put a horny toad in the pocket of Reverend Fulton's robe. The Reverend was reading the Beatitudes and reached for his handkerchief, then he got so spooked he went straight to the Benediction!" As Amy and Matt shook with laughter, the child went on, "And that curly-haired little girl, Frances Parker? She saw a sure 'nough haint out in the woods—twice! Second time it almost took her away with it. What's a haint, sister?"

Matt and Amy again chuckled as Matt explained to the child that haints were ghosts the natives of the Ozarks often swore they saw, and that the spirits could more likely be attributed to the thick mists that sometimes gathered in the hollows of the hills. Hannah took all of this in stride, barely pausing to catch her breath as she excitedly tore on with her discourse. But then, a little better then halfway home, Hannah suddenly grew silent. Amy quietly asked her sister what was wrong, and the little girl grimaced, telling Amy in a low voice, "Back at church, I forgot..."

Amy was embarrassed, but she knew she had to ask Matt

to stop. Her face reddening, she leaned across Hannah and whispered the message in his ear, her lungs filling with the appealing scent of his shaving soap as she caught her breath. Matt chuckled in turn, and seconds later pulled the horse up near a woody thicket.

Hannah dashed for the woods, and Amy sat in awkward silence with her husband. He was studying her with an amused, tender expression that unnerved her mightily and made her feel vulnerable. All at once, her gratitude toward this man welled up inside her, deep and powerful. Matt was so dear to bring her sister to the farm. He had filled a void in the life of a love-starved child who hungered for a father. Amy could well remember being Hannah's age—her anguish, her need, her feeling of being abandoned; how she would have given her right arm to see Abel Harris again. And thus she fully realized how very much Matt meant to Hannah in his surrogate role.

Now, Amy wanted to thank him for everything he had done—for bringing Hannah out, for the pony, for fighting his own distrustful nature and venturing out into the world with them, even for keeping his temper in check during the church service today. She realized, too, that her sentiments toward him now went far beyond gratitude. She wasn't angry at him anymore and didn't want to fight him anymore. She wanted the two of them to be together, in every way. She knew she couldn't express all of her feelings to Matt at once—the emotions were so new, and Amy felt too exposed when he looked at her this way. But at least thanking him would be a beginning, however inadequate.

"Matt?" she ventured.

"Yes?"

The two words seemed to hang between them in the silence, along with the cool swirling of the wind and the chirping of birds. "I—I want to tell you . . ." Amy forced herself to look up at him, and she was almost undone by the ardent smile that still lit his dark eyes. "I want to thank you for today. I want to thank you for Hannah. For—everything."

Impulsively, she leaned over and kissed him on the cheek, felt for a moment the warm rough texture of his skin against her mouth. She drew back, frightened yet fascinated by the instinct rising within her, her desire to close the distance between them and cling to him for dear life.

He smiled at her, yet there was another emotion in his eyes now, a fierce, fathomless yearning.

He knows! she thought to herself with wild joy. He knows.

Fourteen

✦

T hat night, one of Matt's horses took the colic, and Matt was still with the animal in the barn when the clock in the house struck midnight. Since the house was quiet and Hannah was asleep, Amy decided to take her husband a cup of coffee. Wrapping herself warmly with a wool shawl, she filled a tin cup with the hot, aromatic brew, then left the kitchen through the back door. She struggled walking across the cold, dark yard to the barn, the coffee cup balanced in one hand, a smoky lantern in the other.

Amy managed to creak open the weathered door to the barn and step inside, immediately spotting the yellow light from Matt's lantern in the open doorway to a nearby stall. Still shivering from the trip across the yard, Amy hurried over to join him.

"You should be in bed," was the first thing Matt said to her when he saw her enter the stall. He glanced up at her as he kneeled next to the suffering mare, the horse laid out beneath a blanket on the straw-covered floor.

"I wanted to bring you this coffee—I'm sure you're cold out here," Amy explained to her husband, hanging her lantern on a nearby nail and extending the cup to him with a smile. "How is Ginger?" she added worriedly, glancing at the sick chestnut mare, who now neighed pathetically from the floor, her dark eyes glazed and doleful.

"Ginger's about the same, I'm afraid," Matt returned with a sigh, standing. Murmuring "Thanks," he took the cup Amy offered. In the cold silence, with only the sound of the wind rattling the old structure, Amy watched her husband take a sip of the steaming brew. She noted how tired he looked—his face was lined with worry, his hair and clothing were endearingly rumpled and the shadow of his whiskers was prominent. She knew he must be near-distraught with anxiety, and she added his concern for animals to her mental list of the admirable qualities she had discovered in him. It struck her again that perhaps she had not tried hard enough to understand him before.

"What do you suppose caused the colic?" she now asked him, gesturing toward the prostrate, bloated horse.

"Dunno," Matt said honestly. "Could be she got aholt of some crazy weed on the way home from church. Or maybe something else disagreed with her. Horses can be right peculiar, you know. They can take the colic just from eating too much corn."

Having finished his coffee, Matt placed the cup on a vertical stud bracing the planked wall and again knelt by the horse. He stroked the animal's head as she looked back up at him with pain-filled but trusting eyes, neighing softly. "Are you going to stay out here with her all night?" Amy asked.

"Till I get her on her feet," came the adamant reply.

Amy knelt beside him. "Want some company?"

Matt turned to look at her with tender amusement, and her heart hammered in her chest in response. He just looked so appealing next to her, with the lantern light dancing in his golden hair and mirrored in his dark, sexy eyes! For a dizzying moment, she thought he would take her up on her offer. But then he shook his head. "You go on to bed now. Hannah will be up by first light, wanting her breakfast." With a surprising wink, he added, " 'Sides, woman, if you stick around, you might just start kissing me again. Then who would tend this animal?"

Amy shot to her feet, blushing. The twinkle in his eyes
had told her he had not forgotten the kiss she had so
impulsively planted on his cheek earlier that day! ''Guess—
guess I'll go on back to the house, then,'' she mumbled,
grabbing the empty tin cup and her lantern and turning to
leave. Yet she couldn't resist pivoting for one last, anguished look at him as he knelt beside Ginger, stroking the
mare and talking to her soothingly. Oh, to be at the
receiving end of those tender, practiced hands! Never before
had Amy thought she would long to be a sick horse, to
spend the night in a cold, miserable barn stall, wrapped in a
smelly, moth-eaten old blanket!

Matt smiled to himself as Amy left. ''That was right nice
of her, bringing me the coffee, wasn't it, old girl?'' he asked
Ginger, stroking the sick mare's muzzle.

The horse whinnied in response, and Matt had to restrain
a chuckle. He had a way with animals—they responded to
him, communicated with him, almost like they were blood-
tied to him. And now it looked as though his wife was
warming up to him, too! He'd done right, bringing Hannah
to the farm. Not that he wouldn't have brought the girl out
anyway; he was almost as crazy about that little sweetheart
as he was about her sister, and only regretted that the child
couldn't be a permanent addition to their family.

But it had been a good gesture, a good beginning,
bringing the child out. Matt was pleased to be regaining
Amy's trust. He knew he must go slowly with her now, not
risk frightening her off again, *certainly* not chance giving
her the notion that he'd brought Hannah out only as a bribe
to secure his wife's affections! Oh, no. While he had to
admit that lust had consumed his every waking thought for
weeks after he first met lovely Amy, he had recovered his
senses recently, realizing he wanted her to come to him out
of her own free will, not out of fear, nor out of any sense of
duty. Not out of gratitude, either, he added to himself
firmly, remembering her words earlier today.

They were making a start, though, and that was what
really mattered. They could build something good together,

the two of them, if only he could hold on to his patience a bit longer, curb those animal instincts that, unleashed, would surely drive the girl away forever.

Matt coaxed the horse to drink more of the mixture of mineral oil and corn syrup he'd placed in a bell-shaped nursing flask he used. "There, girl," he crooned, as the mare dutifully drank the medicine. "That Amy—Lord a'mighty, isn't she something? She'll come around soon enough—just like you. You both just need some time, some tender, loving care. . . ."

Back in her room, in bed next to the sleeping Hannah, Amy found slumber eluding her as the hours passed. Her mind swirled with images of Matt tending his sick animal—his wonderful touch, his beautiful smile. How she wished that love and tenderness could be directed toward her. Her frustrated wants made her burn even in the cold, and she flipped about restlessly, tangling the covers about her soft, aching limbs. Finally, she got up, wrapped a wool afghan around her shoulders and went to the window to look out at the moon through the clear, cold glass. The large, distant orb was full and bright, a thousand stars shimmering about it in the black heavens.

Amy felt consumed by the heat of every one of those bright stars. She wanted Matt. The realization possessed her like a fever, made her pulses pound, wouldn't let her go. She ached for him in a very womanly way, her yearnings new, potent, undeniable . . . so irresistible that she was ready to forgo her fears and doubts and let him love her in every way. She simply had to be his. She was no longer whole without him.

Yet somehow in recent weeks Matt had become as inaccessible to Amy as the beautiful bright stars now mocking her from the dark sky. He had turned the tables on her, she realized. Matt had stopped pursuing her, and was leaving it up to her to make the next move. But how could she do so, without appearing hopelessly fresh and unladylike? And how could she really be sure he wanted her, too?

God, she knew she wanted *him*. No, she swiftly amended,

she didn't just want him, she loved him! She loved his strength, his tenderness, his steadfast character, even, she acknowledged with a wondrous laugh, his temper. She loved everything about him—Amy knew it surely now—and it only amazed her that it had taken her so long to realize how deeply this fine man had entrenched himself into her heart.

She started, spotting a yellow light spilling out from the distant portal to the barn. A shadowy figure left the barn and approached the house. Matt was coming back! Yet what about the mare? Was she better, or . . . ? The mare was better! Amy decided vehemently, noting Matt's sprightly step, hearing the soft echo of the tune he whistled under his breath. Oh, yes, the mare was fine, she just knew it. Otherwise, Matt would never have left the barn. He must have gotten the animal on her feet!

Watching her tall husband climb the steps to the porch below her, hearing the familiar groaning of the boards as his boots thudded past, Amy was tempted to fly out of her room, down the stairs, out the door, into the moonlight, into his arms. . . .

Then what? she chided herself. Would she tell him what she felt? What if he didn't return her love? Sure, he often looked at her with that magnetic yearning in his eyes. But then, she was a woman and he was a man. What if his needs didn't go beyond the physical?

Yet wouldn't that be a start? she asked herself. Perhaps, she acknowledged. But not tonight. Not with reckless haste and a muddied, unrested mind. If she flew into his arms now, like a hoyden, he might never quite recover. He had already accused her of being too free with her affections, simply because she had invited Reverend Fulton into the house. No, Matt was a conservative man, she decided, and brazenly throwing herself at him would be a mistake.

But she wanted him. Lord, how she wanted him.

She would win his love, Amy vowed. She'd simply have to convince him that it was his idea. . . .

* * *

"Sister, you're not dressed," Hannah gasped, taking her seat at the kitchen table the next morning.

"I'll dress directly, but I must take Matt his breakfast first. He was up late last night getting the mare on her feet."

Amy was at the stove, wearing a handkerchief linen gown and wrapper, tossing flapjacks in a cast-iron frying pan. Her hair fell in wild, lovely curls about her head and shoulders, and her thin, frilly nightclothes did little to hide the full feminine curves of her body. Matt was still in bed, and she fully intended to get upstairs with his breakfast before he awakened!

At the table, Hannah, already dressed in her riding clothes, continued to scrutinize Amy. "Is Matt's horse all right now, sister?"

"She was up drinking water when I went through the barn this morning."

"You went to the barn dressed like that?" the child asked, sounding scandalized.

Amy chuckled. "I wore my cloak, silly. Actually, I only went to the barn hunting eggs. Someone forgot to lock the hen coop again, and as usual, the hens did most of their laying in the hayloft."

Behind Amy, Hannah giggled. "Get me to hunt for eggs next time, sister. It'll be like Easter."

"The chore is yours," Amy called back cheerfully. She took Hannah a plateful of buttered, syrupy hotcakes, then went back to the stove to finish serving up Matt's surprise breakfast. Amy grinned with self-satisfaction as she imagined his reaction when he saw her wearing her suggestive nightclothes. Ah, yes, she had *several* surprises in store for Matt Kendall this morning!

Seconds later, as she was heading out of the room with a wicker tray laden with a plate of steaming flapjacks, honey, butter and hot coffee, Hannah's voice stopped her. "Sister, will you ask Matt if I can ride my pony out alone today?"

Amy turned to frown at the younger girl. "You're sounding a bit big for your riding britches, my dear."

Hannah stood, her chin outthrust, her ribbon-graced yellow hair falling in loose waves about her determined young face and squared shoulders. "I'm ready, I just know I am. Matt's ridden out with me for three days now, and it's time for me to try it on my own. Besides, he won't be able to work his horse today, not with her just getting over the colic."

Amy sighed, unable to deny Hannah's logic. "All right, I'll talk to him. But if he says no, no pouting. Do you understand, young lady?"

"Sure, Amy!" Hannah replied gleefully, and Amy again had to sigh, realizing that the unflappable Hannah was automatically assuming that she, Amy, would be successful in interceding with Matt.

Going up the stairs with the tray, Amy shrugged, smiling. Hannah's request would give her an excuse to stay a bit longer in Matt's room, now wouldn't it?

At the closed door to his room, she knew a final moment of unease. What would he think of her after she . . . ? Well, someone had to make a start to bring the two of them together, she told herself sternly. She knew she loved Matt now, and it was time to get on with the rest of their marriage, end this horrible distance between them. Balancing the tray in one hand, she carefully creaked open the door.

Inside her husband's room, the light was dim, the curtains drawn. Amy slowly approached the bed and laid the breakfast tray down on the nightstand, studying Matt's sleeping countenance. With his eyes closed, she could see how long and thick his brown eyelashes were. Despite the manly shadow of his whiskers, his expression looked vulnerable, almost boyish. Her eyes strayed downward, and she studied a matting of thick blond hair on his chest. The covers had obviously slipped down about his waist during the night, and she wondered with giddy fascination if he wore anything at all beneath the bed linens. He must be quite hot-blooded by nature, too! she thought to herself shamelessly. Even in the cold of the room, there was no gooseflesh on his bare torso. Oh, to be next to that warm, naked chest, and held in those tanned, muscular arms. . . . She stood there for a moment, just watching him, absorbing him, listening to his deep, even breathing, gathering her courage. Then she walked over to the window, drew open the curtains, and raised the sash.

"What the hell?" a sleepy voice grumbled.

As Amy turned to face her husband, Matt awakened, blinking at the sudden brightness. Before he could even think to gather the bedclothes around him, he found himself stunned, totally mesmerized by the vision that stood before him.

Amy stood outlined in sunshine. A crisp breeze billowed about her white, lacy nightclothes, the flooding light delineating every delightful curve of her body. Matt was thunderstruck, his hungry eyes roving her figure. Her beauty constricted his throat, making breathing nearly impossible as he observed her golden, glorious hair undulating in the breeze, falling in tantalizing waves about her youthful face and the perfect column of her neck. She was exquisite. Desire gripped his loins so powerfully that he almost winced aloud with the pain. Finally, he managed to gasp out, "What are you doing here?" The words were distant, full of choked anguish.

She moved closer, smiling flirtatiously, her dark eyes dancing with devilment. "You're sleeping in a bit this morning, aren't you, Mr. Kendall?" Turning casually to the nightstand, she lifted the tray. "I brought you your breakfast."

She leaned over to place the tray in his lap, and one of her breasts, just veiled by the near-diaphanous linen, brushed provocatively against his shoulder. He groaned audibly at the exquisite torment, smelling rosewater, the sachet on her nightclothes, and . . . just her, heavenly her! As she moved backward with innocent grace, he savagely gripped the tray now sitting in his lap to keep his swollen manhood from tipping it over. Damnation! He was responding disgracefully. All his fine resolutions were for naught, and he was lusting after the girl like a wild animal! Matt stared at his wife, unable to speak, a war of emotion on his face.

"Ginger looked fine when I went to the barn for eggs earlier this morning," she remarked conversationally.

"Yes, she's doing right well," came the tortured response

as Matt continued to stare at Amy, not even touching his breakfast.

Amy petulantly noted his lack of interest in the food, her lovely brow furrowed in a scowl. "Don't you like my hotcakes?" she pouted. "I've served them up with fresh honey."

This was too much. Matt's knuckles were white from gripping the tray. Somehow, he managed not to set the infernal dishes flying, grab the girl by the hair and thoroughly devour the one woman in his life he had ever loved.

Loved? Yes, loved. How could he doubt it, looking at her now? She was adorable, delightful, so strong, yet full of humor and vulnerability. Only she could make him so damn afraid of his own feelings. Only she could make him die inside at the mere thought of hurting her, losing her.

Yet did she realize what the Sam Hill she was doing to him now? The way the breeze seductively swept about her, the way her nightclothes clung to those luscious ... Oh, God! What was she was doing now? Sitting on his bed?

She was. Amy planted herself down at the foot of his bed, her lush body flanking him, and wrapped her arms about her linen-clad knees. He swallowed a painful lump in his throat as his eyes devoured her shapely long legs, the firm thighs and hips now seductively outlined through the linen. When she turned to look at him, her expression was dreamy, her face all glowing, rosy and flushed. He felt like the breath had been knocked out of him—by a freight train.

"Hannah told me she wants to ride the pony alone today," she murmured at last, casually. "What do you think?"

"Think?" He couldn't think at all, not as he lost himself in those fathomless brown eyes of hers.

"About Hannah riding the pony alone," she repeated patiently.

"It'll be all right, I reckon, if she stays in sight," he groaned, his hands violently gripping the breakfast tray. Desperately, he added, "Woman, don't you have chores to do? Hadn't you better go get some clothes on?"

"Some clothes on?" she repeated innocently. Undaunted,

she got to her feet, smiling with secret pleasure. She stared at his bare chest meaningfully as he struggled to raise the covers without toppling the breakfast tray or revealing his burgeoning desire. Restraining a giggle, she turned and headed for the door, an alluring sway to her hips that left him biting his lower lip until he drew blood. Opening the door, she tossed back over her shoulder, "You're one to talk, Mr. Kendall."

It was perfect! Amy's plan worked perfectly, and it amazed her that she hadn't thought of it before. Not ten minutes after she left Matt's room, he came bounding down the stairs in his shirt and jeans, looking frustrated, very preoccupied, and rushed off behind the house to go wash at the icy spring. Amy stood at the kitchen window and laughed herself giddy as she watched him strip off his shirt, then splash his bare chest and face with frigid water. Oh, the look on that face earlier when she had brushed her breast against him! She had been wicked, yes—but she had also gotten to him, she just knew it! Actually, he had gotten to her, too. She had just about come undone when she felt his warm shoulder caress her fleetingly through the cloth of her gown. She had almost served up *herself* with the breakfast. Yet ultimately, she had known she mustn't do that. She could tease, but *he* must make the first move.

Later that morning, when it was time for Hannah's riding lesson, Amy joined Matt outside near the corral. "All right, little miss, you can ride out from the house by yourself today if you'll promise to be careful," Matt acquiesced as he adjusted the girth on the pony's saddle. Amy laughed when she heard Hannah's corresponding shout of joy and watched her throw her arms around Matt's neck, pulling his head downward to plant a sound kiss on his cheek. Amy felt warmed by Matt's delighted grin as he hugged Hannah back, then helped her mount the palomino. "Mind you, stay within sight at all times," he warned Hannah as the impatient pony stamped the ground. "And remember—no more than a canter, just like we practiced. The colt's gentled right good, but I don't trust him in a gallop yet."

''Yes sir! Giddyap, Sundance!'' The colt pranced off with Hannah perched on his back, the child laughing exuberantly, her curls, along with the animal's tail, waving in the breeze. Matt watched her, and Amy observed him, touched by his proud, tender expression. After a moment, he turned to look at his wife almost shyly. As part of her plan to win Matt over, Amy had worn her most enticing dress today—a red gingham, with low boat neckline. She now let her wool shawl slip down about her shoulders a bit, and she heard Matt's corresponding wince as he caught an alluring hint of cleavage. She smiled at him guilelessly, pleased by the perceptible darkening in his eyes that told her in no uncertain terms that he desired her.

Matt blinked rapidly, then sighed in obvious frustration, drawing closer to his wife and wrapping the shawl securely about her neck and shoulders. ''Woman, you'll catch your death with your wrap slippin' down that way,'' he scolded. But when he finished draping the wool about Amy, he couldn't quite seem to take his hands off her shoulders. His fingertips remained there, his gaze poured down passionately into hers and his fingertips began softly kneading the tender flesh of her shoulders. ''There—warmer now?'' he asked huskily.

''Oh, yes. Did you enjoy—um—your breakfast this morning, Mr. Kendall?''

He fought a smile and lost. ''It was right fine. But if I were you, Mrs. Kendall, I wouldn't make a habit of doing that.''

His fingertips felt wonderful! ''Of doing what?'' she bantered back.

He drew her a bit closer. ''Of bringing me my grub dressed like you ain't aiming to get out of bed all day.''

She feigned a scandalized look. ''Heavens! Is that what I looked like?''

''Sure as sunshine.''

''And why shouldn't I attend you so attired, Mr. Kendall?'' she went on innocently, her dark eyes aglow with mischief.

His smile became a lazy grin. ''You'll just get me spoiled somethin' shameful. And expecting more. And more.''

"Is that a fact?" she asked, sensuously running her tongue over her lower lip and watching him swallow hard in response.

He leaned over toward her then, and, for an exquisite moment, she was sure he was going to kiss her. Her heart pounded in her chest, welcoming the moment, but then his eyes darted to the west and he cursed under his breath, abruptly releasing her. "Hannah!" he shouted to the little girl who was wildly galloping her pony down the trail a couple hundred yards beyond them. "I told you not to run that pony yet! Damnation, child, are you trying to break your fool neck? Do that again, little miss, and there'll be no more riding for you for the rest of the week! Now get on back here—*slow* like."

Down the road, Hannah had halted her pony and was looking back contritely toward Matt. "Yessir!" she called out guiltily, turning the spirited animal and nudging him into a trot back toward the couple. "I'm sorry, Matt," the child told her teacher breathlessly moments later, halting the colt before them.

Not half as sorry as I am, Amy thought to herself ruefully, feeling bereft now that her husband was no longer touching her.

Fifteen

++

For the next few days, Amy continued to try to entice Matt, but with not nearly her initial success. He was on his guard now, and did his best to dodge her overtures. Amy took special pains with her appearance and never missed an opportunity to toss her husband a flirtatious smile or maneuver her body close to his, but he often reacted grumpily, as if annoyed. She was not afforded another opportunity to bring him breakfast in bed, since he now arose each day before anyone else; more than once, as Amy trudged into the kitchen in the predawn light, she half gasped as she found him already sitting at the table, fully dressed, sipping coffee. He'd often be out the door, mumbling something about some chore or the other, before she could even offer a "Good morning." Amy was not deterred from her plan, but she soon began to feel dismayed when she coupled her lack of success in winning over Matt with the fact that her little sister would be leaving in a few more days' time.

Matt privately felt every bit as frustrated as Amy did. He didn't know how to interpret his wife's sudden and seemingly illogical advances. He was dying to make passionate love to her, but the memory of the fear in her eyes when he touched her before put him off. Would that terror return if he pushed one of their romantic interludes to its natural conclusion? What if she wanted to stop, and he couldn't? Now that Matt knew he loved her, the thought that he might lose control and possibly meet her resistance with force was intolerable.

The hell of it was, Amy was so young, so innocent and naive that he just couldn't be sure she was fully aware of the consequences she might heap upon herself by teasing him so recklessly. To her, flirting with him might be just a new game to pass the time—or even a way to let him know she was feeling kindly disposed toward him for bringing Hannah to the farm. But to him—Christ, the things that girl was doing to him! Images of her in that sexy gown danced through his head at night, tormenting him. He'd wake up sweating even in the cold, aching to hold her, to plant himself so deep inside her there'd be no separating them. During the day, when he caught the aroma of her rosewater, it was all he could do not to drag her off and make those coy, teasing eyes of hers dilate with violent passion. If he were a religious man, she'd have him losing his religion, he was sure. For he simply couldn't risk taking her until he was sure she was completely ready to follow through.

He was also, like Amy, very sad about Hannah's imminent departure. He'd grown quite attached to the child, and it worried him, her having to go back and live with that crazy woman who was her mother. Bless the child's heart, Hannah had brought joy to their home and created a bridge between him and Amy, their first really smooth period together. Would the atmosphere grow chilly again as soon as she left?

All too quickly, Hannah's last full day at the farm arrived, and both Amy and Matt tried to hide their sagging spirits and make her final day with them as pleasurable as possible. The morning dawned cool and balmy for early December, and Matt decided to take the day off. He hitched Sampson up to the wagon, filled the bed with hay, and took the two girls out into the countryside for a picnic. The three had a wonderful time, eating fried chicken and potato salad and pickles until they thought they would burst. In the afternoon, they explored the woods together and found a delightful cove where a waterfall cascaded into a lovely, deep spring. They all stood silently awed, watching the dappled light play on the cold emerald pond, as the wind softly rustled the late-autumn trees surrounding them. It was a magical moment for each of them, as if they were sealed up in their own private little world. On the way back to the wagon the three held hands, Hannah between the two adults, each comforted by the bond that distance could never break. . . .

Their mood lightened up as they rattled home in the wagon, loudly singing folk songs in the nippy twilight, laughing and showering each other with hay. . . .

Back at the house Matt lit a fire in the parlor grate, and Hannah swiftly fell asleep on the settee. Amy sat down next to her sister, stroking her golden curls. She knew there was no delaying Hannah's departure, for the Chandlers would be coming back through Rolla on the train late the next morning.

Across from the sisters, Matt, sitting in a wing chair, looked equally disheartened. He leaned forward toward the girls, his elbows on his knees, his tight jaw resting on laced fingers. The fire snapped in the grate, but even the homey crackle and the fragrant smell of hickory smoke was lost on the preoccupied couple tonight.

Finally, Amy cleared her voice to speak and looked up at Matt. She saw his troubled expression. "Matt, I want to thank you again—for bringing Hannah out here," she ventured at last. "And—it was so good of you to buy the pony, to teach her to ride—"

"Amy, I don't want your gratitude," Matt cut in abruptly, straightening in his chair. His eyes were bright and fervent. As she flinched, he quickly added, "I'm sorry. I mean, I lo—I care for Hannah, too. Thanking me is not necessary."

Amy nodded, smiling weakly. "I guess it makes me feel better, though."

Silence fell between them again. The fire hissed, and a log slipped in the grate, sending a shower of sparks spiraling up the dark chimney. At last, Matt clenched his fists and gritted out, "Amy, I only wish the child could stay permanent. But you know how your ma is."

"Yes, I know." The hot, bitter tears were getting harder for Amy to restrain. Matt's sharing her concern for Hannah brought her own emotions even closer to the surface. Bless his heart, Matt did look enmeshed in turmoil as his dark eyes now shifted with anguished tenderness to the sleeping child on the settee. Hannah herself looked so small and vulnerable as she slumbered, her delicate hands pressed close to her face in an attitude of prayer. To think that Esther Harris would soon have complete power over this adorable little girl!

"We'll find a way to get her out here for keeps, Amy," Matt continued hoarsely. "I vow it."

She looked at him in wonder. He appeared on the verge of tears now himself, the emotion raw on his face, and it was her undoing. "Oh, Matt. You're so dear. . . ."

Her tears could no longer be restrained. To her horror, she began to shake with sobs. Embarrassed, she stood and stumbled from the room. There was so much welling inside her heart at that moment. Certainly Amy grieved over Hannah's departure. But she also throbbed with the love she felt for this dear, caring man who was her husband—

But it was a love she couldn't express to him. She felt a prisoner of her own emotions.

Matt caught up with her near the stairs, his hand on her shoulder. "Amy, what is it?"

She fell into his arms then with a low cry, pressing her face against his shoulder. "You're—so—dear," she repeated brokenly, "so good to me, so good to Hannah. You—you said you don't want my gratitude. But I don't think you'll ever want me, either!"

"Not want you?" he demanded, his eyes wildly incredulous as he drew back to look down at her face. "Are you funning me, woman? I've been going insane with wanting you!"

She stared up at him aghast, the tears frozen on her cheeks. "You have? But every time I come near you, you get so—so riled—"

"You bet I do!" he interjected, scowling. "Woman, you're enough temptation to make an angel turn in his wings and take to hard liquor."

"B-but"—now she found herself insanely fighting a laugh—"but why do you keep—"

He grasped her face with his strong hands and looked down at her fiercely. "Amy, you must understand. You can tease, but with a man it's different. With a man, there's a point of no return. That's why I pull back. I don't want you to start something I can't stop. I don't want to hurt you, frighten you."

"Matt, I'm not frightened anymore," she said simply, looking up at him with her heart in her eyes.

He released her. "Amy, are you sure? Have you truly thought about what you're saying?"

"I'm not frightened anymore."

He gripped her by the shoulders. "Oh, God, woman! Mean it! If you're going to say it, for Christ's sake, mean it!"

Her eyes were glowing with tears of joy. "I mean it. I'm not afraid. I'm ready to be your wife now. To have your children, too."

"Oh, God." He lost control then. With an anguished cry, he crushed her against him, kissing her ravenously, until she could not think or breathe. He seemed hard as steel against her. Yet she ached for him and welcomed his ravishing strength. Matt's hands gripped her buttocks, lifting her to press her hard against the swollen length of his manhood. Amy felt dizzy with passion, aching, hurting to become one with him, thinking how right he felt.

Right! Yes, right, like Matt's strong arms that now swept her up, carried her possessively up the stairs and into his room.

It was dark and cold in Matt's room, silvery shadows strewn about. He put her on her feet near the head of his bed and kissed her again, holding her in his arms. "Oh, sweet wife! I want you so badly!"

His impatient fingers pulled at the tiny buttons on Amy's wool dress and she automatically tensed. He pulled back.

"Amy!" he scolded in a tortured tone. "Are you sure, love?"

She embraced him, her arms quivering about him, and whispered in a small, almost childlike tone, "Matt, this is all so new to me, and I won't deny it's bewildering in its way. But please be patient with me."

He studied her with a look of grave concern. "Amy—do you know . . . ?" His voice trembled and his face colored in a miserable combination of desire and embarrassment. "I mean, you mentioned children just now. Did your ma or . . . or someone explain to you what's going to happen?"

She hung her head to hide her sudden blush. "Yes. Vida did, a few years back. Please, Matt," she continued breathlessly, hugging him to her, "I just want us to be together."

"Oh, Amy!" he whispered hoarsely, kissing her. He pulled her down to sit beside him on the bed, his mouth still passionately locked on hers. Slowly, gently, he began unbuttoning her dress, inwardly reminding himself that he must go slowly, woo his lovely virgin wife, not frighten her. It was pure devilment for him, for she was so very lovely. As his fingers slipped inside her bodice, caressing a lush, firm breast through the thin covering of her chemise, he thought he would lose his mind, for touching her aroused him mightily. He reached for the already tautened nipple, twisting it between his fingertips and the tenuous cloth, and he had to smile to himself as he heard the muffled, gasping response come from deep within her throat. His fingertips then moved to the center of her chest, and he felt her heart palpitating wildly, like that of a bird. He kissed her more deeply, tasting every honeyed recess of her mouth, and after a moment, he thought he would explode if he could not feel her soft naked flesh next to his.

He drew her to her feet and finished undressing her hastily, whispering endearments in her ear, telling her with husky, soothing words that he must dispense with her clothes quickly, get her into bed before she caught a chill. Indeed, she shivered before him as he pulled off her dress and quickly untied her chemise. He hoped her tremblings were with desire for him, for when he at last had removed her underclothes and stockings, when he saw her standing naked and glorious before him in the moonlight, he thought he had died and gone to heaven. She was passionately beautiful—her hair like spun gold about her angelic face and slender neck, her breasts full and firm, her belly flat, her hips lusciously curved, the dark valley between her legs beckoning him to taste deeply of her womanly secrets. Her skin was baby-soft and glowed like satin in the silvery light. With a groan he swept her naked body up into his arms, lifted her onto the bed, then covered her with the counter-pane. Quickly he dispensed with his own clothes.

Amy watched Matt from the bed with love in her eyes. Her man was beautiful, his hard muscles rippling in the moonlight, and just the sight of his large swollen manhood made the core of her hunger exquisitely to be filled by him. He joined her on the bed at last, pulling her into his strong embrace and kissing her. The sensation of their naked bodies melding was so intense that it took her breath away. For long moments they kissed and caressed. With wonder she stroked his muscular chest, touching the matted hair with her fingertips. His hands reached downward to cup her bare bottom, pulling her against his hard readiness. She tensed again, as much with excitement as with apprehension, as his bold hard instrument pressed into the tender flesh of her belly. He groaned and said, "My darling, sweet wife. I want so much to be patient. But you're so beautiful—so very desirable."

With a low moan, he drew his head lower and latched his mouth upon her breast. Amy cried out in wild pleasure as his tongue, his teeth, his lips, sent fierce currents of passion streaking through her. "Yes, yes," he encouraged, feeling her respond as he planted hot, moist kisses on her breasts, her stomach. "You'll be ready—I want you so ready, love."

His arms clenched about her, and he nuzzled a breast again, flicking his tongue sensuously over the swollen nipple. She squirmed ecstatically, the provocative movements of her supple body exciting him even more. Boldly his hand reached downward, seeking the cleft between her legs.

Again, she stiffened momentarily, but he made no attempt to force her. Instead, he slowly insinuated his hand between her thighs, until she relaxed and let his fingers slip inside. With his mouth still firmly suckling her breasts, his fingertips teased the bud of her womanhood so gently that she moaned and lost consciousness of all except her overpowering obsession to join herself with him. Amy breathed in gasps, writhing in rampant need as his mouth moved upward to kiss her possessively again, while his fingers now teased the small opening he would soon penetrate. Slowly, but firmly, he slid a finger inside her. She gasped, and he pulled back to look down into her eyes. The pressure from his probing was intense, yet the pleasure he brought her was so exquisite she forgot the discomfort. Being touched by her husband so intimately made her feel closer to him not just physically, but emotionally and spiritually. She only knew she had to have more . . . all. She curled her arms around Matt's neck and moaned unabashedly, "Please. . . ."

Something electric and wildly passionate flashed in his dark eyes as he heard Amy's soft plea and observed her feverishly flushed face beneath him. His fingers left her, replaced by the hard, burrowing tip of his manhood. She lay panting beneath him as he firmly hooked his elbows beneath her knees, and she willingly opened herself to the vulnerable position that would allow him greatest intimacy. He continued to observe her in fascination, his own expression intense, turbulent, as his hard instrument pushed against her delicate maidenhead, soon with hurtful pressure. She experienced a moment of unease, not knowing how such a large implement could penetrate the small crevice that had resisted even his gentle fingers. Yet ultimately she put her trust in him. This was not at all like what had happened with her mother and father. If there were pain involved, then it was meant only to bond them more deeply as husband and wife. At his desperately questioning look, she whispered, "Yes, Matt! Oh, yes!"

"Love . . ." She could hear the tears in his voice as he prepared to make her his wife in every way. He pushed against her forcefully, and she bit her lip to keep from

wincing aloud, determined not to discourage him. Meeting
her resistance, he slipped his hands beneath her and tilted
her hips upward. His mouth then clamped down hard on
hers to help smother away the moments of pain that must
come before the pleasure. At last he pierced the fragile
membrane, and hot tears stung her eyes. His mouth ground
passionately into hers, smothering her soft sobs as his
manhood plunged fully inside her, forging an exquisitely
deep path, where seemingly none had been before. It
hurt, splitting her apart and bringing new tears. But the
tension created by the plundering instrument was unbearably
wonderful!

"Amy! Oh, love . . . it will be better now." Matt's lips had
left her bruised mouth, and he comforted her for a moment
in his trembling arms, letting her adjust to the unyielding
pressure of his penetration. When at last he felt her begin to
relax, he drew back and slowly began to move in and out of
her tender flesh. "God, you feel so good, love."

"You, too," Amy gasped back, her hands reaching upward to grasp his face. Despite the searing friction of his
possession, it did feel so wonderful to be joined with him
this way, so deeply and intimately. Never had she felt so
close to him. She brought his mouth down to her ravenous
lips, plunging her tongue into his mouth.

Matt lost all control then, thrusting into her deeply, fully,
again and again. She cried out, but had her cries reached his
foggy brain, he would have realized that they were more
whimpers of pleasure than sobs of pain. Yet he didn't hear
her at all—he was a man totally beyond reach now. He rode
her wildly, powerfully, until he felt the glorious explosion
inside himself and fell limply against her.

At that very moment, Amy knew the first, quivering
stirrings of what it was like to soften to a man, her husband.
It was her first vision of the sensual wonders her man would
unlock for her in their marriage. She lay beneath Matt in
tears. She had never known loving would be this beautiful,
that the touch of his heat could melt her beyond words.
Now, even the ache felt glorious.

* * *

"Amy, did I hurt you?" Matt asked tensely.

Sometime later, Amy awakened to see her husband standing by the bed, wearing his denim trousers. She reached out and took his strong, wonderful hand. With a lilt of humor in her voice, she replied, "In the best possible way."

He chuckled, looking relieved, as he shrugged on his shirt. "Amen, woman."

"Don't tell me I've given you religion now, Mr. Kendall," she went on to taunt.

He looked down into her eyes, his expression deadly earnest as he buttoned his shirt. "Woman, you've given me more pleasure than a man deserves on this earth." He winked at her. "But you haven't given me religion. You're my religion from now on, Mrs. Kendall."

His words excited her wildly, but she managed to go on teasing, "Oh? If I'm your religion now, then why are you so impatient to leave my bed? I'm fearing I disappointed you."

"Tailfeathers!" he scoffed, adding, "You've forgotten about Hannah, my dear."

"Hannah!" Amy threw off the counterpane. "She's still downstairs."

Matt's eyes darkened with passion as Amy's movements unwittingly gave him a stirring glimpse of her luscious, full breasts. "You'd best cover yourself, woman," he scolded huskily, "or baby sister will be spending the rest of the night down there."

Amy chuckled, covering herself. Matt planted a quick, possessive kiss on her lips and left the room. With him safely out of sight, she moved to hop out of bed, then fell back, wincing, as unexpected soreness clenched her thighs. She had to smile to herself, even at the discomfort, for it was almost as if Matt's passion had branded her. She could feel his imprint even when he wasn't there. She liked that; it made her feel his in every way, and also made her wonder if his flesh remembered *her*, as well.

Amy sat up, more gingerly this time, and reached for her gown and wrapper on the floor. She was dressed and had gone into the bedroom she shared with Hannah by the time Matt came upstairs carrying the sleeping child.

Hannah did not even awaken as Amy removed the child's dress and shoes. The couple put the little girl to bed in her underclothes, covering her with heavy quilts. Afterward, Amy offered Matt a shy smile, murmuring, "Should I stay . . . I mean, in here with her?"

"No way in hell, woman!" he informed her in a hoarse whisper, grabbing her hand and pulling her out of the room.

Back in his bedroom, Matt astonished Amy by whisking off her gown and wrapper, then pulling her trembling, naked body against his hard, fully-clothed frame. "No fair!" she taunted him. "You still have clothes on."

"My God!" He laughed incredulously. "I've unleashed a siren." Stroking her bare hip with titillating fingers, he went on huskily, "If I do take off my clothes, what's that going to get you, woman?"

"What I want," she whispered.

"Oh, God."

He didn't make her wait. He stripped quickly and took her with him to the bed. Long preliminaries were not necessary this time, since even the pressure of their touching bodies was agonizing arousal to them both after the long hours they had spent in bed earlier. Several ravenous kisses brought them both to a level of unendurable desire. Matt was impatient, but Amy was ready, opening to him as he thrust quickly and deeply, moving with him to a pounding rhythm that forever increased in intensity. "Oh, woman," he panted above her, his eyes glazed in an agony of need, "I know I must have made you sore somethin' frightful before. But I just can't get enough of you. . . ."

"It's all right," she soothed back, encouraging him to have his way, to give free rein to his passions. When he still held back, she made a small movement with her body that pushed him over the edge. He bruised her with kisses and ravished her with his rapacious need. Half frightened by the turbulence of his movements, she nonetheless forbade herself to tense against him. She wanted what he was leading her to, needed so desperately the complete, searing pleasure that had just eluded her the first time. And she knew that to attain this new height, she would have to let him touch her with his body as he never had with words. . . .

He did just this. His hands slipped beneath her and he pounded into her as if to join them for all eternity, filling her with a cutting ache of rapture that forever built, until it demanded that she arch into his thrusting, meet him, soften, melt, and urge him to plunder even deeper. All this she did, and he went wild then, riding faster and harder until she gripped him into herself with a convulsive cry and knew what it was like to share her soul with a man. . . .

He came to rest inside her at that same, glorious moment, which left them both in tears. "Amy . . . my sweet love," he breathed, collapsing against her.

Sixteen

‡‡

Matt and Amy exchanged shy smiles over the breakfast table. They saw each other on a new basis this morning—as lover to lover, two people who had shared long, incredibly intimate hours together. Amy had a special glow about her as she sipped coffee across from Matt, and his fervid glances made her ache with remembered ecstasies.

After a moment, Matt nodded at Hannah's vacant place and asked, "Hadn't you better awaken your sister? We'll need to leave within the hour to take her to the train. Reverend Chandler told me they'll be coming back through from Springfield this morning at eleven sharp."

Amy sighed, her spirits sagging. She had been trying hard since she got up not to think of the fact that Hannah must leave them today. "Hannah's up and finishing her packing," she told Matt dully. "She should be down any moment now. I checked on her while you were feeding the stock."

"How's she taking it—going home today?" Matt asked with concern.

"She's trying her best to keep up a cheerful front—but I know her, and she can't hide the sadness in her eyes."

Matt nodded. With a shy smile, he added, "Did she say anything about you being gone last night?"

Amy blushed. "She never knew. I was in the room dressing by the time she awakened."

Matt reached across the table and tenderly took his wife's hand. "Well, Mrs. Kendall, you'll be wanting to move all your clothes into my—*our*—bedroom before sundown, now won't you?"

Amy's heart fluttered at the dark ardor in Matt's eyes. She also had to smile to herself as she recalled the list of chores he had informed her she'd be "wanting" to do back on her first day at the farm. "Yes, Mr. Kendall, that I *will* be wanting to do," she now quipped back.

"Good morning."

Matt and Amy unclasped hands and uttered cheerful greetings as Hannah stepped into the room. The child looked lovely this morning. She wore one of the frocks Matt had purchased for her in St. Louis, a navy wool garment with white lace collar and matching gauzy apron. The dress was midcalf length, complemented by dark stockings and the high-topped leather-and-cloth walking shoes Matt had also bought the child. Hannah's hair fell in thick, shiny blond curls about her neck and shoulders, and a brave smile crinkled her young face. But, just as Amy had said, there was no mistaking the dark sadness in her soulful brown eyes.

Amy served Hannah a steaming, succulent breakfast of grits, sausage, biscuits with gravy and fresh milk, but the child merely picked at the fare. Matt tried to cheer the little girl up by saying, "Amy and I were just talking about trying to get you out for a visit again next spring."

"I'll have school," Hannah said dully. "I've missed two weeks as it is."

"But don't they sometimes turn out school for Easter time?" Matt questioned.

"Sometimes," Hannah replied with equally lacking spirit.

Amy felt extremely sorry for the child. The idea of being in Hannah's shoes was tremendously depressing. She was sure she could not even begin to imagine her sister's despair. The child was so young, and totally at Esther's mercies. "Hannah," Amy said with forced cheerfulness. "You'll get to see your friend Gracie at church when you get back. Haven't you missed her?"

Hannah looked up at Amy quickly, her lower lip trembling. Obviously, the child was trying hard not to cry. "I'll miss you and Matt."

Amy's heart sank, and Matt, too, looked miserable. "I know, darling," Amy whispered, trying to console the child, "we'll miss you, too."

"Then why can't I stay?" the little girl demanded, her heart in her voice.

Amy and Matt exchanged anguished glances. Finally, Matt said to his wife sternly, "Amy, we're gonna have to tell her the truth," and Amy mutely nodded. Turning to the little girl, Matt explained gently, "Honey, your sister and I want you to stay here permanent, but your ma won't allow it."

"I hate her!" Hannah blurted, pounding a fist on the table.

Amy was stunned by her vehemence. Luckily, Matt went on with soothing patience, "I know it's hard on you, Hannah, but look at your ma's point of view. No one likes to be left alone—"

"She deserves it!" Hannah cried, tears bright in her young eyes.

"You're right," Matt agreed. "But still, someone has to care for your ma. Looks like it's up to you, for now, honey. I know that's a big burden, but before you know it, you'll be grown and your ma won't be able to boss you around ever again. In the meantime, I swear to you that your sister and I will do everything in our power to change your mother's mind and get you back out here."

Matt's words were so sincere that Hannah's forlorn countenance grew hopeful again. Seizing the advantage, Amy jumped in, determined to help the child face going home with a better attitude. "Things weren't always that awful at home, honey," she pointed out bravely. "We had some good times, too. Like sitting with Vida in the evenings—I know you're welcome there any time. And we had church, and going to the store, and taking walks—''

"Well, I did like it when Gracie Stallings's father took Gracie and me to the fair," Hannah admitted, catching a little of her sister's spirit.

"And remember how much you loved it when the revival came to town?"

Now Hannah giggled, successfully distracted from her misery. "That preacher was so funny, Amy," she said, her curls bobbing up and down. "The way he screamed and pounded the pulpit—the way his eyes bulged out . . . I was just waiting for them to pop out into the collection plate!"

"And just think, with Christmas coming, you'll get to go caroling with the churchfolk, and you'll be invited to parties, too." Amy paused for a moment, depressed at her own mention of Christmas, the realization that Hannah would not be there to share the occasion with her and Matt. But she steadied herself, changing the subject before Hannah could make the same realization. "And even work can be fun, if you make it a game, like we used to."

"Oh, yes!" Hannah agreed gleefully. "Remember the time we had to scrub floorboards, and we gave them each a name?"

As Matt listened in wonder to this enchanting exchange, Amy answered, "Yes. 'That one looks strong and straight— we'll call him Buck.' ''

" 'And that one looks splintery and rough—we'll call him Harry,' '' Hannah added, clapping her hands. Riding a crest of excitement, the child went on, "Remember the time a skunk got into Vida's chicken coop, and the whole neighborhood smelled for weeks?"

"Do I ever!" Amy laughed. "Remember the time the possum got in our attic and we had to listen to him running around at night for weeks? Then his wife and children, too!"

"Oh, yes! And remember the time Lacy got tipsy and

threw pebbles at Ma's window in the middle of the night,
thinking it was yours?''

Hannah's last damning remark was interspersed so casually in the conversation that at first, no one seemed to
notice. Then, as the child's words finally registered upon all
three people sitting at the kitchen table, a horrible silence
ensued. Young Hannah's hand flew to her mouth as she
realized the terrible slip she had made. Amy felt her heart
thud in desolation, and a hard twinge of guilt gripped her at
this blatant reminder that she had married Matt without ever
telling him of her former fiancé.

Swallowing hard, Amy dared to turn and look at her
husband. He was scowling murderously, obviously brooding
over Hannah's statement. As he caught her glance, his gaze
fastened on her reprovingly and he demanded, ''Who's
Lacy, Mrs. Kendall?''

Amy's heart raced at her husband's harsh query. She
simply could not address this with him now and ruin
Hannah's final moments with them! ''Matt,'' she said with
all the firmness she could muster, ''I think we'd best get
Hannah to the station. We can discuss this later.'' Her eyes
added a silent plea.

For a moment, Matt's features twisted in a terrible war of
emotion. Then he grunted his assent, his jaw tight with
resentment as he stood and stalked out the back door to go
ready the buggy. The minute he was out of earshot, Hannah
burst out with, ''Oh, Amy, I'm so sorry!''

''It's all right, honey,'' Amy reassured the child. ''I'm
sure Matt would have found out about Lacy sooner or later.
I don't want you to worry about it, not for one second.
Now, let's go upstairs and make sure you haven't forgotten
anything.''

Amy maintained a cheerful facade as she and Hannah
went up to the bedroom together. She was determined
that Hannah should not fret about her slip at the breakfast table. The child had enough to contend with as it
was.

But Amy was worried. Very worried.

* * *

The three were quiet as they waited in the late-morning coldness outside the Rolla station house for the train from Springfield. Hannah stood solemnly between Matt and Amy, her portmanteau at her feet. Promptly at eleven A.M., the big iron horse of the Atlantic and Pacific Railroad chugged into the yard. As the tender was refilled with water from the tower, Reverend and Mrs. Chandler disembarked from the passenger car, both dressed in traditional black traveling clothes and looking exuberantly happy as they approached the Kendall couple and Hannah.

"My dear, it's so good to see you!" Mrs. Chandler greeted Amy, embracing the bride warmly as the reverend, nearby, shook hands with Matt. The little woman smiled down at Hannah. "Ready to go home, honey?"

"Yes, ma'am," Hannah answered dully, watching with resentful eyes as the conductor picked up her portmanteau and loaded it in the baggage compartment.

"It's very kind of you and Reverend Chandler to escort my sister out here and back," Amy told the minister's wife.

The woman waved Amy off with a flourish of a black-gloved hand. "Dear, it's been our pleasure."

The Chandlers chatted with Amy and Matt briefly about their visit with their married daughter in Springfield. It turned out Mrs. Chandler had won the argument with her husband concerning their grandson's age; the baby boy was nine months old, not eight, as the reverend had previously insisted. As Mrs. Chandler gloated over her small victory, the reverend admonished his wife, "Just remember, Mildred. Pride always cometh before a fall."

Even as the reverend spoke, the train whistle blew its own warning, and the silver-haired minister added sternly to his wife, "My dear, it is time for us and young Miss Harris to board."

Time for good-byes, Amy added to herself in silent misery. She turned to her sister with tears in her eyes, and the two girls embraced as if they'd never let each other go. Finally, when Reverend Chandler cleared his throat nervously, when the conductor shouted, "All aboard!", Matt gently put his hand on his wife's shoulder and said, "Amy, you've got to let her go."

Amy nodded, releasing the child, who quickly hugged Matt, then tearfully said to the two, "Good-bye, Amy, Matt—I love you both!" In a flurry of blue skirts and dark cloak, Hannah dashed up the steps into the passenger car ahead of the Chandlers. Amy and Matt voiced their thanks to the minister and his wife, and the Chandlers waved back as they also hurried to board. Then Matt and Amy stood helplessly waiting for the train to leave.

Moments later, the A. & P. Flyer pulled out, and Hannah waved to them from the window, hanging on to her blue straw hat, her curls and the hat's ribbon streamers tangling in the breeze. Tears rolled down her vulnerable young face, and the stark emotion gripping her features was soul-rending to Amy and Matt. Watching Hannah depart, Matt clenched his fists and blinked rapidly to mask smarting eyes. Amy wept openly, waving and calling out to the child over the roar of the engine, "We love you, too, darling!"

The couple stood there, not touching, each enmeshed in private grief, until the train was but a smoking black blur on the distant landscape. Amy ached for Matt's comfort, but knew he would not offer it, not after the events earlier that morning. She and Matt had been like two strangers with each other ever since breakfast. Their glorious intimacies of the previous night might never have occurred.

Finally, Matt cleared his throat and said to his wife, "At least we know Hannah's in good hands on the journey back. Come on, let's go."

The two had a quick dinner at the Grant Hotel, then started back for the farm. Sitting next to her husband in the buggy, Amy drew her cloak tightly about her and shivered in the chilliness. It was a blue, misty early-winter afternoon, and the cold dreariness of the weather as well as the drabness of the countryside seemed ironically appropriate to her. Hannah's departure had brought a dark cloud down upon them, in more ways than one. Both she and Matt were tremendously saddened that the child had left. But Amy also knew that Matt hadn't forgotten Hannah's unwitting mention of Lacy, and she dreaded the confrontation she knew must occur when they got home. For now, Matt was concentrating on his driving, his immutable eyes fixed on the road ahead.

Back at the house, Amy sat down in the parlor with a cup of tea, trying to calm her nerves and warm herself, while Matt unloaded the supplies. The house was so lonely, she reflected, so silent with Hannah gone, and now there was such a terrible distance between her and Matt, too. Amy couldn't blame her sister for making the slip about Lacy— Hannah was but a child, and Lacy had always been an important part of Hannah's life, as well as Amy's. The fact that Hannah had not mentioned Lacy over two long weeks was in itself miraculous. Sooner or later, a misstep by the child was inevitable. Yet, despite Hannah's innocent motivation in making her remark, her describing Lacy Garrett's midnight rendezvous with Amy left the older sister in quite a pickle. The situation rang of illicitness. How would she explain this to Matt? He might well think that she and Lacy had—

"So tell me, now, Mrs. Kendall. Who is Lacy?"

Amy jumped, her teacup clattering into its saucer as she spotted her husband standing in the archway to the parlor, regarding her sternly. Even though his words had been deceptively soft, there was not a hint of mercy in his dark eyes. He looked quite formidable, his arms akimbo, his denim trousers and dark twill jacket outlining the taut muscles of his body. Amy swallowed with great effort. Again she wondered how Matt, so ardent and tender last night, could have turned into the cold stranger who now stared at her so dispassionately.

"Matt, would you come sit down, please, and I'll try to explain," Amy said, struggling to sound calm but betraying her uneasiness through a telltale quiver in her voice.

Grudgingly, he crossed the room toward the wing chair, and as he sat down across from her, Amy automatically observed the rippling strength in his magnificent frame and remembered that hard male body driving into her flesh the night before. His strength could be gentle, but it also could be brutal, she feared. There was so much that she didn't know about this man, so much that remained locked inside his head, and if he wanted to, he could do . . . anything with her.

From his seat, he stared at her in steady challenge, and hesitantly, she began. "Matt, Lacy was—has always been—a friend of mine."

"I see. Do your friends normally come a'courtin' you in the middle of the night?"

Amy's spirits sank. There was no fooling this man, not at all. "All right," she muttered, twisting her hands miserably as she burned beneath the scrutiny of his dark eyes, "Lacy was my sweetheart—for a time."

"For what time?" Each word was enunciated with the punch of a bullet.

"W-we were supposed to marry," she stammered at last, in a barely audible whisper.

He tensed visibly. "When?"

"Matt, does it matter?" she cried.

"Yes."

"R-right before you came," she admitted wretchedly.

He was silent for a moment, scowling at her. Finally, he repeated, "Right before I came. What happened, then?"

"He . . ." Miserably, she lowered her head. "Lacy was gone on a trip—he's a peddler, you see—and he promised me we'd marry when he returned, but . . . he never showed up."

"And I did?" Matt challenged.

"No! No!" Amy cried. "That wasn't it at all!"

"Wasn't it?" Angrily, Matt got to his feet and went to the window. His broad, rigid back to her, he demanded, "What was his last name?"

"He?"

"Your sweetheart, Lacy," came Matt's growling reply. "The one who did his courtin' in the middle of the night at your bedroom window. What was his last name?"

Amy was appalled. Matt's voice was filled with barely controlled fury. In a trembling voice, she answered, "Garrett."

He turned on her, his dark eyes gleaming with outrage. "Garrett?" he cried. "Lacy Garrett! You were going to marry that low-down snake?"

"You know him?" Amy whispered incredulously.

Matt's features were blood-red as he stood glaring at his wife with eyelids blinking rapidly. His mouth twisted as if he were about to say something, then he cursed savagely and stalked out of the room.

Stunned, Amy followed him. She caught up with him in the hallway, clutching his sleeve. "Matt, please—"

He pivoted hard, shaking off her grasp. "You married me under false pretenses, girl," he ground out, shaking a finger at her. "Then you had the gall to say it was me doing the trickin', just because I had a woman's picture in my coat, someone I ain't never even met! Well, I sure as hell wasn't engaged to no one else when I come a'courtin' you! All the time it was you—you doing the lying and deceiving! You in love with that no-account!"

Amy shook her head in horror and disbelief, unable to comprehend the stark rage gripping her husband's features. It struck her violently that she didn't know this man at all, even as her voice rose to say, "No, Matt, that wasn't true when I met you. I felt—"

"Betrayed?" He laughed bitterly. "So you used me to get your revenge on Garrett." In a fierce whisper, he continued, "Oh, I know how it feels to be betrayed, woman. But I fight my own battles. I don't use nobody else to get even with those that wronged me."

"Matt, no, that wasn't it, not at all!" Amy argued desperately, feeling hot tears sting her eyes at the injustice of his accusations.

"Wasn't it?" His hands gripped her shoulders. "Why'd you come to my bed last night, woman? So you could lie there in the dark, moaning beneath me, and pretend I was your peddler man?"

With these cruel words, he pivoted and stormed out the front door, slamming it violently behind him, leaving Amy behind, broken and in tears.

* * *

Amy sat in the bedroom she had shared with Hannah, numb after her exchange with Matt. Moments earlier she had spotted him through the window galloping off on Ginger to parts unknown. She was now trying her best to recover from their explosive argument. She had figured Matt would become angered when she told him about her former engagement to Lacy, but her husband's unmitigated rage had bewildered her. She only half understood some of the things he had said. What did he mean, for instance, when he said he knew how it felt to be betrayed, yet he used no one else to gain his revenge? And what was the connection between him and Lacy? Why was the mere mention of Lacy Garrett's name enough motivation to turn Matt Kendall into a savage stranger?

Amy got up and began to pace, her fists clenched, hot tears rolling down her cheeks. Matt's accusations were so cruel and unfair! Of course, she had felt betrayed when Lacy stood her up in St. Louis, but she never would have married for that reason alone. She had felt attracted to Matt, had felt warmed and drawn by his many fine qualities. Yet all those fine qualities now seemed buried beneath his wrath, an uncontrolled fury that threatened explosive consequences.

Amy glanced at the wardrobe, filled with her clothes. That morning, Matt had asked her to move her things into his room. She laughed to herself bitterly. She was sure he wouldn't want her there, not now. He had made it clear that she disgusted him. He had even accused her of pretending he was Lacy at the very moment she had surrendered her virginity to him! Oh! How could she live with a man who held her in such low regard? She wished she had left with Hannah and the Chandlers! She wished she could leave now, right this minute!

Maybe she could! Maybe she just would! she thought angrily, resuming her pacing, pride clenching her features. She smiled with bitter triumph as she remembered the ten-dollar gold piece Vida had given her on her wedding day. The coin was still safely tucked away in her reticule. Thank God for dear Vida! Amy realized that if she could just get to Rolla, she could take the next train back to St.

Louis . . . whenever that might be. Anyway, the first step, the most important step, was getting to Rolla.

Yet even as her wounded pride conjured the mutinous scheme, her softer side intervened. After all, she loved Matt—shouldn't she stay and try to make him understand her side of the story, try to work things out?

The question made tears spring to her eyes. She had come to Matt Kendall's bed last night with her maidenhead intact; she had given him no reason to doubt her fidelity. Yet the mere mention of her prior engagement to Lacy had just about driven him over the edge. His reaction was disproportionate, baffling, frightening. How could she live with a man who was filled with such repressed violence? No, she had thought she had known Matt, but obviously she had made a fatal error in judgment. The sooner she got away from here, from him, the better. Otherwise, she feared what he would do to her when he returned.

Yet the problem remained, how to get to Rolla. Amy snapped her fingers as she realized she could take Hannah's pony to town. The colt was almost fully grown and could bear her weight.

But wouldn't that be horse thievery?

No, she quickly amended to herself, recalling how Matt had told her that the pony would be hers once it was grown. Taking the animal to town would not be stealing, then. Besides, she could leave Matt a note to pick up the pony at the livery in Rolla. She really didn't want to keep anything of his.

Amy hurriedly packed, wiping tears as she worked. She almost had her portmanteau filled, when a tense male voice inquired from behind her, "Where do you think you're going, Mrs. Kendall?"

Amy jumped and whirled, her hand flying to her heart. Matt stood in the doorway. While he still looked angry, he seemed more in control that he'd been earlier. His imposing presence was far from innocuous, however, and his dark gaze steadily impaled her. Heavens, she had been so immersed in her own troubles, so busy slamming drawers and the wardrobe doors that she hadn't heard him return or come up the stairs! Now, with all the courage she could muster, she faced him and said, "I'm going home. You don't want me here."

"Is that a fact?" He strode into the room, still regarding her sternly. "I believe I remember the preacher saying something about us sticking together come better or worse."

Amy lowered her eyes. "You think I married you under false pretenses."

"Well, you did, didn't you?" he demanded. "But that don't mean I'm throwing you out."

She bristled at his arrogance, glaring up at him mutinously. "How generous of you, Mr. Kendall. But maybe I'll just leave, then."

"Maybe you just won't," he growled back.

They glowered at each other in a fierce battle of wills. Amy knew she had to get past him to leave the room, and she was frightened by visions of what he might do to restrain her. It wasn't in her to back down, however, not under these circumstances. After a moment she quickly turned to the bed, fastened her portmanteau and took it in hand. Squaring her shoulders, she bravely headed for the door.

At the archway, Matt's hand on her arm restrained her, even as his other hand grabbed the bag from her fingers and tossed it aside almost negligently. "You ain't going anywhere."

"Aren't I?" she challenged, her face gleaming with defiance. She was determined to stand there and face him down until hell froze over.

Surprisingly, after a moment, he cursed softly under his breath and released her arm. Then something even more curious happened. For a brief, telling instant, she watched a glimpse of pain cross Matt's dark features; for a flicker of time, his broad shoulders sagged and he looked entirely defeated, almost on the verge of tears. And in that moment, before the fierce facade of his pride returned to tighten his face and body, she saw his vulnerability and understood. She had been thinking only of herself, she realized, not of him. He was hurt, too, he was scared, he needed reassurance after learning about her previous engagement. But he was a man, and proud, and couldn't ask that of a woman, his wife. Then, too, Lacy must have really hurt him in the past, she mused. Whatever Lacy had done to Matt, it must make the idea of her supposed betrayal even more hurtful to him now.

Yes, Matt's accusations had been outrageous and unfair, she thought. But hurt knew no logic, she well knew that herself. All at once, she was filled with the realization that Matt was her husband and she loved him and didn't want to leave him. As much as she was frightened by the violence in him, she knew she must reach out and accept the rage in him, reassure him until the hurts inside him were healed.

She reached out and touched his sleeve gently, gaining strength when he didn't immediately wrench away from her touch. "Matt, I want you to know that when I married you, it was you I was marrying. You alone. In God's name, I swear it."

His expression softened somewhat, but he still looked hurt and unconvinced. "Don't try to deny that you wanted to get back at Garrett when you wed me!"

"All right—I won't deny it, not totally," she acknowledged bravely. Watching dark anger flash in his eyes, she hastily went on, "But Matt, I—I was really drawn to you when I met you in St. Louis. And since then—since last night . . ." She blushed, biting her lip miserably, then forced herself to look up at him and say with heartfelt sincerity, "If marrying you was my revenge, then I never knew vengeance would be this sweet."

His features wavered once more, and his eyes grew glazed, as if stinging with tears. "But you were going to leave me just now—that's how much you value what you feel for me, the vows you took in the presence of your God."

"No, Matt," she denied calmly. "That's not why I was packing. I was going to leave you only because I thought you didn't want me anymore."

His expression broke. "Oh, God, Amy, I do want you—I do!" He crushed against her. "Now!"

Amy didn't fight the desperate desire in him as he kissed

her so hard her teeth hurt. She felt his tears intermingle with
hers as he pulled her down onto the sunswept bed with him.
His impatient hands sent the buttons on her dress flying and
ripped open her chemise. She gasped as his mouth fastened
greedily on her breast.

"I have to be inside you," he growled.

Amy was at once horrified and shamelessly aroused as
Matt rolled her beneath him on the bed, pulling down her
chemise and nipping at her breasts, her body, with his teeth.
He was insatiable, and his hands, his mouth, seemed to be
everywhere on her soft flesh at once—biting, sucking,
kneading and probing. She panted and writhed beneath him
in near-painful, total arousal. He hiked her skirt up around
her middle and thrust into her with his hugeness, and she
cried out at the explosive, wondrous ache surging straight to
the core of her. Her flesh softened to him, accepting him,
and he kissed her ravenously as he plundered her deeply and
thoroughly.

She felt herself losing all control then, moaning convulsively
as she arched into his shattering possession. The climax he
brought her was quick and blindingly intense, and left her
breathlessly clinging to him, tears of ecstasy on her cheeks. . . .

For a long moment afterward, all that could be heard was
the labored breathing of their mutual release. Then Matt
gently rolled off her and looked with dismay at her torn
frock. He swallowed very hard as his anguished eyes met
hers. He looked like a man just recovering from a crazed
state. "Are you all right, love? Did I hurt—"

"No," she said simply.

He pulled her into his arms. "Oh, Amy!" He rained her
face and throat with kisses. "I'll buy you a new dress—ten
new dresses."

She tried to reply, but his mouth clamped down on hers,
still wet, still desperately needing her. They trembled together, holding each other close. The intensity of their
coupling had turned Amy inside out, both physically and
emotionally. But it was a distinct comfort to her now to
know that her uninhibited surrender to his needs had somehow quenched the fearful violence in him, that her body's

abandonment had reassured him as no words could. She also knew that he felt badly that they had fought regarding Lacy. She even sensed that he wanted to apologize in full measure, but that his pride wouldn't let him.

His loving arms were the only apology she needed.

Seventeen

✦✦

D uring the next weeks, Amy and Matt explored all
the nuances of ecstasy between a man and a woman. Winter had arrived, so the chores were considerably lessened, and they spent long, languorous hours in bed
together, loving each other beneath downy quilts. The intimacy of marriage was both startling and heavenly to Amy
after the misery of her upbringing, the years of deprivation
and loneliness. Matt's hunger for her was insatiable. She
loved it.

Lacy Garrett was not again mentioned—neither Matt nor
Amy wanted to spoil this beautiful period between them.
Amy felt grateful that their lovemaking had made the rage
subside in Matt, that he was like his old self again. There
remained a slight, barely discernible barrier between them,
one that allowed them to love each other with indescribable
passion, but not to put that love into words. When Amy was
in bed with Matt, with him deeply inside her, she did want
so badly to tell him how she truly felt about him. Yet she
feared he might still not believe her, considering that she
was betrothed to another when she met him. And the idea of
losing this exquisite intimacy was too painful to be borne.

They drew closer each day nonetheless. The morning
after their argument, Matt pinned Amy to the bed and said

with a husky chuckle, "I don't want you to think I'm always going to love you like a madman." Keeping his word, he aroused every inch of her to unendurable readiness with his wonderful mouth, even the very bud of her desire. She resisted this last at first, but he scolded gently, "You're my woman now, and there's nothing wrong between us." Indeed, as she lay writhing beneath him, there seemed nothing wrong at all, except that if he didn't soon fill her, she would scream and tear her hair. Later, she did scream, but with rapture, when his hard heat drove her to a seizure of pleasure she could not endure. Much later, when she begged to be taught how to pleasure him—just that much— he taught her.

Their days passed in constant togetherness. The two did chores together, chatting about little things. They went to town together on Saturdays, having dinner at the hotel. On Saturday nights, Matt made it his custom to bring the tin bathtub into the kitchen from the back porch. After helping Amy fill it, he would announce with a lascivious gleam in his eyes that he would assist his wife with her bath. Amy invariably reacted with mortification, laughing and dodging her lustfully advancing husband. But Matt was merciless, chasing his shrieking wife around the kitchen until he wrestled her into submission. Inevitably they wound up in the tub together, deeply coupled and rocking until the water grew quite cold. She wondered why she ever fought him— even if just for fun.

Christmas drew near, and the days beforehand became extra special. Matt took Amy into town shopping; at the general store, he bought a doll for Hannah and fine wool shawls for both Esther and Vida; he then paid the store's owner, Mr. Salter, to box up the items and ship them to St. Louis. Amy was very touched by Matt's thoughtfulness, and knew the doll would help make Christmas more bearable for her young sister, whom she missed dearly.

When Christmas day came, Amy cooked a huge meal, including the wild turkey Matt had once again provided, and set the table with their best dishes and linens. Almost shyly, she and Matt exchanged presents before sharing the festive repast. Matt gave Amy several lovely bolts of material, including handkerchief linen and dainty ribbons for new undergarments. "You'd best be doing a lot of sewing," he teased, " 'cause I'm planning to do a lot of ripping."

Amy was delighted with the expensive fabrics, the imported linens, the wonderful-smelling, sturdy wools. In return, she presented Matt with a large, ribbon-graced box. She spotted a tear in his eye when he opened the present and pulled out a new pair of everyday boots. She had known he needed the boots, had noticed how worn his other pair was. She watched him gently stroke the fine tooling on the expensive tan leather. "Oh, Amy . . . you shouldn't have. Where'd you get the money for these?"

Amy smiled secretly but didn't reply. She had used most of her ten-dollar gold piece to buy the boots in town. She had realized long ago that Vida would never accept the money back, and, to her, spending the gold piece was her way of cheerfully burning her bridges, giving her heart away. Matt seemed to sense this, for he bestowed upon his wife's lips a beautifully tender kiss before they started their meal.

After Christmas dinner, the two tidied up the kitchen, then went upstairs to take a nap. Despite their full stomachs, they found themselves making love with great hunger. Afterward, Amy fell deeply asleep. She awakened late in the afternoon to find that Matt was gone. But she heard an enormous ruckus downstairs, as if someone were moving the furniture around!

Amy quickly freshened up, dressed and went down into the parlor, only to find all four of the Stocktons in the room with Matt! The five were laughing, happily gathered about a small piano that had miraculously appeared against the wall flanking the fireplace! The instrument, which looked to be about fifty years old, was carved of rosewood, complete with graceful gold-leaf etchings in a fleur de lis pattern. Amy was stunned, and instantly fell in love with the elegant old instrument.

Nell Stockton was the first one to notice the young bride's presence in the room. "Merry Christmas, honey!" the matron greeted, rushing over to embrace her friend. "Why, we've all been just a'waitin' for you to come down and play us some purty Christmas songs on your new pianer."

While Amy remained too flabbergasted to speak, Matt came over and kissed his wife's flushed cheek, saying warmly, "Happy Christmas, honey."

"You—you're giving me that piano?" she managed to stammer to him at last, her eyes huge and bright.

"Sure am," he assured her, grinning.

"But—you've already given me too many presents!" she protested.

"This present is for me, too," Matt responded warmly. "I love your music."

"But—but where did it come from, and how on earth did you get it out here?" Amy burst out.

Everyone laughed as Matt answered, "Why don't you ask Nell about that?"

"I'm the one who put the bug in Mathew's ear," Nell admitted to Amy. "I knew you was a'missin' your music, girl. Then one day I was sittin' next to Widow Weaver at church, turnin' the pages of the hymnal for that poor old soul, and I thought to myself, that dear little granny is too far gone with the rheumatiz to enjoy her pianer at home no more. So the next time I come by here, I mentioned the idear to Mathew. And wouldn't you know, it turned out Berta Weaver was plum tickled to have that pianer took off her hands—plus she had plenty of use for the cash money, too."

"I bought the piano a couple weeks back," Matt told Amy, "and then this afternoon Lyle helped me haul it out from town." He strode to the coffee table and picked up a large stack of sheet music that had been sitting there. Returning to his wife's side, he placed the music in her hands and announced proudly, "All of this came with it."

Amy glanced from the music to Matt and back to the piano. She was hard-pressed not to burst out crying. All of this was so dear of Matt—and of the Stocktons! She was holding in her hands more sheet music than she had ever seen in her life; and the piano itself was exquisite, delicate and intricately carved, definitely the instrument of a lady!

"Now, I'll have you know, Amy Kendall, that your husband here invited us out this afternoon for a singin'!" Nell put in stoutly from the girl's side. "Surely you ain't gonna let us down. Why, these boys here is bustin' to troll a carol or two!"

"Yes, ma'am, let's have us a singin'!" Nell's youngest son put in exuberantly to Amy, his eyes bright with the magic of Christmas.

"Ma brought fruitcake and cookies—kin we have some a'that, too?" the older boy chimed in, looking at Amy expectantly.

"Oh, of course you can! Forgive me for being so rude!" Amy flashed the boys a conciliatory smile as she finally recovered her full composure. She winked at Nell's smallest son. "I've plum pudding and pie in the kitchen. Of course, we'll have a singing, and plenty of refreshments, too!"

As the boys let out a simultaneous whoop of glee, Amy turned to Mr. Stockton, who had been standing off to the side grinning as he observed the others. Extending her hand to the farmer, she said sincerely, "Mr. Stockton, thank you so much for helping my husband bring the piano out to the farm today."

"Twarn't nothin', ma'am," Stockton assured Amy with his usual modesty as he shook her hand.

Thus, the Kendalls and the Stocktons had a party, singing carols, eating homemade delights and sampling leftover turkey. Amy adored her new piano—it resembled her cabinet grand at home, but was much smaller and more finely detailed. Though it was an older instrument with a range of only five octaves, it had a full, rich tone and was in remarkably good tune considering its age.

It was dark by the time the Stocktons happily left to return to their own farm. Alone with her husband in the parlor, Amy embraced Matt warmly. "Thanks for the piano, Matt," she said with tears of happiness shining in her eyes. "I just love it. You're too good to me, you know."

"I love to hear you play," he responded.

"And it was good of you to invite all the Stocktons over," she added.

"Well, it's only seemly that I thank them for the help," he returned a bit stiffly. Then he smiled. "And I thought it might make Christmas a little more special for you."

"How about for you?" she asked.

"You make Christmas special for me."

"Oh, Matt!" She kissed him warmly, then, after their lips parted, she abruptly giggled. "I bet—"

"What?" he demanded, scowling down at her, even though his eyes twinkled.

"Oh, it's nothing," she hastened to add, embarrassed.

"Tell me," he ordered.

She tossed him an impish look. "I'll just bet you wore me out this afternoon, Mr. Kendall, so you could sneak off and make the piano a surprise."

Matt threw back his head and laughed. "Wore you out? Why, Mrs. Kendall! What a wicked little mind you have." He touched the tip of her nose with his index finger, in a mock gesture of admonishment. "You're right that I wanted the piano to be a surprise. But I ain't through wearing you out, woman. Not yet!"

And she laughed with pure delight as he hefted her over his shoulder like a sack of grain and carried her up the stairs. . . .

Thus flowed their days, their nights. Amy adored the intensity of it, of losing herself and being totally possessed by this passionate man. Even when they were simply sitting at the kitchen table and exchanging small talk—just to hold Matt's hand and look at him and know everything they did was right . . . her joy was indescribable. Indeed, all Matt had to do was to touch her, or to look into her eyes in that special, yearning way, and she would ache, throb, melt. . .

She wondered how anyone could be this happy.

Eighteen

✦✦

St. Louis, Missouri

O n a cold, blue December afternoon in St. Louis, a
tall, slim man paced in front of the Harris home,
nervously smoking a cheroot. Lacy Garrett's boots
pounded a restless cadence on the sidewalk as he struggled
to screw up the courage to go knock on his sweetheart's
door. In the street nearby was parked his peddler's wagon,
the pots and pans rattling in the wind, the tired old horse
harnessed to the conveyance neighing his protest as wet
autumn leaves swirled down upon his back.

Lacy was oblivious to the animal's distress. He had
finally gotten up the nerve to come see Amy Harris again,
and he wasn't at all sure what kind of reception he would
receive from his beautiful young fiancée. For that very
reason, he had taken his time working his way from the
Boothill Country northward to the booming metropolis of
St. Louis. He feared that this time Amy might reject him
entirely. Hell—he'd missed the girl. There was still that
hankering inside him for her that time wouldn't satisfy. . . .

Lacy's gaze now darted nervously to the house. Still no
sign of life. Damn, he had been hoping Amy might come
out on the porch, shake a rug or something so he wouldn't
have to deal with that scorpion of a mother of hers. No such
luck, though—he'd been pacing for the better part of an

hour, yet the house looked shut up, tight as a tomb, with only the sound of the wind howling about it. Finally, he got up his nerve, ground out his cheroot, entered the yard and climbed the steps to the house, rapping on the front door of the weather-beaten cottage.

Silence. He tried again, but still no response. Where the devil was she? In a last, desperate attempt, he went around to the back of the house. Miraculously, there he found young Hannah, stooped over, diligently working in the winter root garden, a ratty shawl about her young shoulders. "Hannah!" he shouted cheerfully.

The little girl straightened, watching the peddler approach. Hannah had always liked Lacy; he had invariably been kind to her, and kindness was quite a luxury in her benighted young existence. She couldn't help feeling some resentment toward him for breaking his promise to Amy, but it was hard for her to act angry now, in her overpowering joy at seeing a friendly, familiar face. "Lacy!" she called back.

"Hello, kitten," he said, using her pet name as he moved nearer. He shivered slightly, pulling his black jacket closer about him.

Studying the peddler, Hannah noted that Lacy wore his traditional black suit and hat, a crimson satin vest and matching bow tie accenting his ruffled white shirt. Despite Lacy's snappy clothing, she knew he must be quite cold without a greatcoat. He was closer now, close enough that she could look beneath the wide brim of his hat and see his startlingly bright blue eyes and sharply honed features. He looked tall, thin, and quite handsome to her. Yet not nearly as handsome or wonderful as Matt, a small voice added.

Matt! The thought of her new brother-in-law brought Hannah up short, making her drop her garden trowel as she finally realized why the peddler must have come. All the things Lacy couldn't possibly know . . . Oh, Lord. Of course Lacy would demand to know where Amy was! And what could she tell him? Would she make another horrendous blunder, like the one she'd made out at the farm? She clutched her shawl tightly about her and stared at him warily.

Her changed attitude was not lost on Lacy. His handsome brow furrowed, he asked the child, "What is it, honey? Where's Amy? Where's your ma? There's no sign of life at the house."

"Ma has the ague," Hannah hedged. "She's been sleeping most the day for weeks now."

"Where's Amy?" the man pursued tensely.

"She's . . ." Hannah sighed helplessly. He was bound to find out sooner or later. "She's gone."

"Gone? Where?" The peddler looked like a sleek black panther, ready to spring.

"Lacy, where have you been?" the child demanded, hoping to distract him.

"I—I been ailing, too," he lied. "Now, tell me where Amy went."

"Lacy, I don't think I'm supposed to tell you!" Hannah cried miserably.

"Hannah, I'm your sister's fiancé!" Lacy half barked. More gently, he reasoned, "Don't you think I have a right to know where she is?"

The child twisted the matted fringe of her shawl fretfully. "But you broke your promise to my sister. You didn't come back when you were supposed to marry her."

"That weren't my fault—I told you I was sickly," he retorted gruffly. Watching the child back away a step at the tension in his voice, he cajoled, "But I'm here, now, ain't I, kitten?"

Hannah wavered. "Well—yes—but—"

"And I just want to know for sure that you and Amy are safe. You know how much I care for you both, kitten, don't you?" He moved closer and protectively wrapped Hannah's shawl more securely about her young shoulders.

His charm was dangerous, and Hannah floundered even more. "Yes, I know, but—"

"Do you really think Amy wouldn't want me to know where she is?"

"I don't know!" Hannah cried wretchedly, clenching her fists.

"Come on, kitten, tell me," he said in a smooth voice that nonetheless brooked no challenge.

The struggle on Hannah's vulnerable young face was intense. Yet the peddler was too strong for her, and at last, she whispered, "Amy's married."

"Married!" he exclaimed. "Married? Well, I'll be danged! Just like that?" His eyes narrowed suspiciously. "Who'd she marry?"

"Lacy, I'm not supposed to—"

He gripped her young shoulders with insistent fingers. "Tell me, Hannah!"

Miserably, the child blurted, "His name's Matt Kendall, and he owns a farm down near Rolla—"

But Hannah's voice froze as Lacy abruptly released her and uttered a stream of invective that made her ears burn. Finally, he turned and again grasped the upper part of her arms. "Matt Kendall? Are you sure that's who she married?"

"Y-yes. Matt came here to find Pa. Then he met Amy, and they decided to marry right sudden—"

"I'll bet," Lacy retorted cynically, realizing at once what proud young Amy's motive must have been. "Damnation! She just went and—You say Kendall owns a farm near Rolla?"

"Y-yes," the child stammered. Frantically, she begged, "Lacy, you're not going to do anything, are you?"

"Nothing that ain't deserved," came the bitter reply.

"Lacy, please!" Hannah begged, near tears.

Yet the child's plea was lost on Lacy as he turned and left her, consumed by his own feelings of anger and betrayal. Matt Kendall was back—back with a vengeance. And his precious Amy had given herself to that bastard! Would he let her treason go unpunished? And would he let that thieving scoundrel keep the woman who was supposed to be his?

Never!

BOOK

TWO

BOOK

TWO

Nineteen

✦✦

January came to the Kendall farm, and hard freezes were regular. Before dawn each morning, Matt left the bed he and Amy shared and went outside to feed the stock and break ice off the water troughs. In these cold winter months, he had taken over her outdoor chores, which she greatly appreciated. She realized that he had only asked for her help before because he needed her assistance in getting the farm ready for winter. In the spring, when he was busy with the planting from sunup to sundown, the chores would doubtless fall back to her again. She didn't mind at all, now that she understood.

Now that she loved him.

Things were going quite smoothly between them—they lived in their own private, perfect little world here on the farm. While Amy occasionally missed the church and community activities she had known in the city, all she had to do was look at Matt's ardent face and those longings would immediately vanish. He was her world for now, and she prayed it would last forever.

Of course, Amy missed Hannah, but her worries regarding her sister were partially allayed when she received a cheerful note from Vida telling Amy how much both she and Hannah appreciated the presents the Kendalls had sent to St. Louis. Amy now had her music to help fill her free hours, and she and Matt weren't totally isolated—Nell Stockton came by for an occasional visit on a mild day. Amy reciprocated whenever possible. Matt made no objection to his wife's jaunts; in fact, he chuckled each time she wanted to go to Nell's, recalling Amy's first visit to the Stocktons' on the old plow horse. Now, he hitched up the buggy for her each time, promising her he'd teach her to ride the palomino in the spring.

On a Saturday night in mid-January, the Stocktons invited Amy and Matt over for supper and a candy pull. After the meal, Lyle and Matt sipped corn liquor in the large kitchen as the women boiled down syrup and later added soda. Then everyone laughed as the Stocktons' two boys, their hands generously larded, pulled the sticky concoction into long yellow strips. Watching the two strapping boys, Matt gave his wife a secret smile, and she blushed, catching his meaning and hoping no one would notice. He wanted to have a child with her—she knew this and she felt exactly the same way. She had long since cast aside her fears that Matt might want to make her pregnant simply to begin producing a new generation of farmhands. She somehow knew that, like her, he hungered for the ultimate, bonding experience of creating new life together. Indeed, at home later that night, Matt's lovemaking was especially passionate and especially long. They slept in late the next morning, until the racket of their indignant barnyard friends awakened them.

The only thing missing in this idyllic world were the words of love, and Matt and Amy grew closer to this revelation each day. Amy longed to tell Matt of her feelings, and she dearly hoped they were returned. She'd tell herself that the special way he looked at her, with his eyes glazed and full of yearning, with his mouth tilted in that special, sensual way, had to be love. Yet what if she were wrong? What if she were mistaking desire for a much more profound emotion? She could envision nothing more humiliating than laying her heart on the line, telling Matt she loved him, and having him look at her with surprise—or, worse yet, pity—and say nothing. What if he were still secretly bitter, and answered with something like, "Are you sure that's what you're feeling for me? Or have you still got me mixed up with Garrett?" She knew he hadn't forgotten about Lacy—his doubts and fears came out in subtle ways, in secret, assessing, half-suspicious glances, in the intensity of his lovemaking, which sometimes bordered on ravishment.

So she waited for him to make the first move, but when it came, it was not at all in the direction she wanted.

On a mild, late-January day, Matt announced that they must go to Rolla for supplies. "We're most out of chicken feed," he told his wife. "And I want to get my order for seed in early, since spring planting's just around the corner."

They dressed warmly and drove into town in the wagon. At the general store in Rolla, a collection of farmers was gathered about the potbellied stove. No sooner had Amy and Matt gotten inside the door than they heard the startling news—the A. & P. Flyer had been robbed twenty miles southwest of Rolla the previous week! The couple stopped in their tracks to listen, as a thin, older fellow, wearing a homemade flannel shirt and suspendered trousers, rocked on his bootheels and dramatically informed the others regarding the incident. "My friend Gopher Woodson over to Waynesville was aridin' on the Flyer when he heard them bushwhackers a'firin'. The train stopped right dead, and then four of them fellers sashayed up bold as brass. Two a'them blew out the safe in the express car, while the others robbed the passenger car. Them varmints snatched rings offen the ladies' fangers without a 'by yer leave,' nossir."

"Was anyone kilt?" a robust man with tobacco-stained teeth inquired.

"Nope, them fellers was sly and quick as a fox in a henhouse—gone a'fore most folks was through havin' their apoplexy on account of it."

"Silas, do you 'spose them fellers was the James and Younger brothers?" a thin, grizzled middle-aged man inquired.

"Dunno, Henry," the one called Silas replied, thoughtfully stroking his pointed beard. "Could be the James boys, or the Youngers. Could be someone's copycatting 'em."

A hush fell over the throng of men, amid much chin scratching and the exchange of worried glances. Finally, a younger man with a high-pitched voice said, "I'll wager you fellers my shiniest ten-dollar piece that Rolla's bound to be hit. I've read about them bushwhackers out to the border region. Them boys never did quit hell-raisin' after ridin' with Quantrill back during the war. I heard tell how they robbed the bank out at Gallatin, the train at Council Bluffs. I reckoned sooner or later they'd be wearin' out their welcome out west a'here and scoutin' for new territory."

Nods and mumblings of assent rumbled through the group of men. "Well, if'n you boys is worried, I'd suggest you all come to the next Grange meeting," Silas went on. "I've invited Banker Whitcomb to come discuss them thievin' rascals with us. If them fellers is aiming to hit Rolla National Bank, we'll give 'em a howdy-do they won't soon fergit! Right, boys?"

A rush of zealous resolve spewed forth as one of the farmers, a short, stocky man who hadn't as yet spoken, took note of Matt and Amy. "Well, hello, Kendall." The shyly smiling man with carrot-colored hair shook hands with Matt, then nodded at Amy. "Howdy, ma'am."

Amy and Matt said their hellos to the group. They knew the men vaguely, since the collection of farmers was frequently gathered about the stove when they came in to town for supplies. Amy recognized the man who had greeted Matt as Charlie Moss, the distant neighbor Matt had bought the palomino pony from. Now, Charlie asked Matt, "Well, Kendall, will you be joinin' us at our next Grange meeting? Second Saturday in February, you know."

Matt awkwardly shifted from foot to foot. "Maybe so, Charlie. Thanks for the invite." To the one named Silas, he added rather tensely, "So them bushwhackers just popped up out of the blue and ambushed the Flyer, eh?"

Silas proudly hooked his thumbs in his bib overalls, preening like a rooster to have the undivided attention of all the menfolk assembled. He expectorated a generous mouthful of tobacco juice into a nearby spittoon, then settled himself in to recount the story in even more vivid detail.

"Yessir, bob. Gopher said one of them fellers had purely black eyes, like he'd just as soon kill a feller as spit on him. That black-eyed devil snatched Gopher's pocket watch so fast it broke the chain, then . . ."

Amy left the men to their animated discussion at the front of the store and walked toward the back to hunt for needed kitchen supplies. It surprised her that Matt had shown so much interest in the men's discussion, for he normally spent their every moment in town by her side. Amy remembered that he had shown a similar interest in activities of the outlaw gangs when he spoke with the U.S. marshal on the train coming out from St. Louis.

Maybe he was just concerned that the gangs were hitting so close to home, she reflected. The outlaws might even threaten whatever funds Matt had deposited in the Rolla bank. She reasoned that Matt's knowledge of the gangs had probably come like that of most folks, through reading newspapers or dime novels.

As Amy continued toward the back of the store, she perused the array of supplies and smiled her greeting to several other housewives who were browsing. The wares were varied, but plain and unvarnished by St. Louis standards—tools, grinders, mills, scales, canned goods, yard goods, spices, lamps and candle makers. Amy adored the potpourri of smells permeating the building—tobacco, leather, pickles, jerky. This simple collection of stores supplied all the rudiments of daily life, without frills. Even the selection of "ready-made" garments was geared more toward practicality than style: for the women, straight-lined, high-necked frocks of calico or muslin, along with enormous "slat bonnets" for protection from the sun; for the men, simple, sometimes subtly striped trousers, plain shirts, dark vests and jackets and broad-brimmed hats. Missing were the more fashionable items Amy remembered from St. Louis, the new, high-bustled dresses for the ladies, the long sack coats, broadly striped trousers and derby hats for the gentlemen. The more fashionably dressed citizens of Rolla, she figured, must do their shopping in the distant city.

At the back counter, the merchant, Mr. Salter, was

conversing with a heavyset young woman dressed in dark wool. "Ain't you wanting no coffee today, Edna?" Mr. Salter asked the woman as he placed sacks of flour and sugar, along with a small tin of allspice, on the countertop.

Amy smiled at the question she overheard. "Salter" was a good name for him—he was sharp in feature and action and never missed an opportunity to make a penny. He looked very merchantlike today in his shiny bow spectacles, white shirt with flowing, gartered sleeves, and bibbed canvas apron.

"Don't need me no coffee beans today, W. B.," the woman was now replying in a teasing tone. "A peddler stopped by the house the other day and solt me the freshest Brazilian beans—honey, ain't no beehive smelled sweeter. Not to mention, he solt me one of them newfangled coffee grinders I been after you to stock fer nigh onto a millennium, W. B."

At the mention of the word "peddler," Amy stopped in her tracks. Surely, it wasn't . . . ? Oh, don't be silly, she scolded herself. There were doubtless hundreds of drummers peddling their wares in rural Missouri. Why should this woman be referring to Lacy Garrett? Nevertheless, Amy continued to listen to the exchange intently. She ensconced herself a few feet away, fingering cloth bolts on a tabletop to mask her interest.

Merchant Salter now stood with arms akimbo and chin tilted, obviously insulted by Edna's taunts. "Well, if that there feller was so dad-burned accommodatin', I don't suppose you'll be needin' flour today, neither."

"Oh, he was right low on flour, sugar, too," Edna went on casually, unperturbed by the ire she had inspired in the merchant. "In fact, he was plum near sold outten everythin'." In a low, smug voice, she added, "Seems some folks in these parts 'preciate his prices."

The merchant drew himself up with dignity, his mouth screwed up as though he'd just bit into a persimmon. "Why, sure, woman, that drummer kin undercut my prices. He don't got no store to run—no shop girls to pay, only his dad-burned wagon to pull."

"I wouldn't be quite so sure, if I were you, W. B.," Edna said casually.

"What do you mean?"

"Well, when I told the drummer man what things was like hereabouts, how folks are kinder at your mercy, if you know what I mean, he said he might just settle down here in Rolla and give you a run fer your trade."

The merchant's eyes narrowed, while Amy, nearby, listened in increasing distress. Surely, *surely*, she prayed, the woman wasn't referring to Lacy! But what if she were? As if reading Amy's thoughts, the merchant now demanded, "What's that there peddler feller's name?"

Edna scratched her dark head. "Don't rightly recall, W. B., but seems like it were something common..." Suddenly, she snapped her fingers, smiling to reveal a wide mouth filled with crooked teeth. "Lacy—that were it—Lacy something or 'tother."

At this stunning announcement, Amy turned violently, throwing a hand over her palpitating heart. Then she gulped miserably as she spotted Matt standing just a few feet beyond her, staring at her intently, his eyes filled with suspicion and distrust.

Oh, Lord. How long had he been listening?

Long enough, Amy realized ruefully as they headed home in the wagon filled with supplies. The afternoon had turned colder, but Amy and Matt nonetheless sat stiffly apart on the seat, a cold breeze carving its way between their two bodies. Matt was staring moodily ahead as he worked the reins, the tenderness in his expression completely gone now, Amy noted with dismay. As they passed a stand of bare-branched trees along the curving road, she noted a group of blackbirds feeding on the orange pods of the bittersweet vine, which snaked up trees and coiled about branches. The vine seemed like her relationship with Matt at the moment—entangled and blooming bittersweet.

Why, *why* did Lacy have to be coming this way? she asked herself angrily. Why—horror of horrors—did he have to be thinking of settling down in Rolla? The very thought of Lacy's establishing a business in the town was ludicrous, unless—

Unless Lacy knew she was here! Unless he had decided to show up just to cause trouble between her and Matt!

But how could he know she had settled here with Matt? Surely her mother, who hated Lacy, would never reveal her eldest daughter's whereabouts to the peddler.

Hannah! Oh, Lord, what if Lacy had somehow gotten to Hannah? It all made sense, Amy realized grimly. Hannah had always looked up to Lacy and was too sweet-natured to resist the clever, handsome drummer for long. What if the child had simply made another slip, like the one she'd made her last day at the farm . . . this time, to Lacy?

Yes, it had to be Hannah who had told her erstwhile fiancé where she was, Amy mused. Still, Lacy's showing up in the area was odd. He had obviously gone to great lengths not to marry her before. Why should he exert even greater effort—establishing a business in Rolla, no less—in order to reenter her life now?

Then she remembered that there was bad blood between Lacy and Matt. She still didn't know what the nature of the conflict between the two men was, since she hadn't yet dared broach the subject with Matt. But she did know it would be too much for Lacy's pride to let a rival have the woman who was supposed to be his—never mind that he'd neglected his own duties there. Oh, heavens, this was terrible!

Everything made sense, she realized. Lacy, by all appearances, was charming and carefree, yet Amy also knew he had a vindictive side to his nature that only rarely emerged. She recalled a day many months ago back in St. Louis, when she had run off to meet Lacy and he had taken her on a long drive in the country, much like Amy's drive with Matt today. Amy and Lacy had been ascending a glade in his rented buggy when a rabbit skittered into their path, unwittingly spooking the horse, a rather high-strung black stallion. Lacy calmed the animal readily enough, and no harm was done. But to Amy's astonishment, he had then set the brake on the conveyance, had jumped out and grabbed his rifle from the boot. As the rabbit hopped toward the summit of the rise ahead of them, Lacy calmly, cold-bloodedly picked the animal off with his gun. The doomed cottontail flew into the air with the force of the bullet, then fell dead at the side of the road. Afterward, Lacy had replaced his rifle, climbed back into the buggy and cheerfully proceeded with their drive, whistling under his breath.

Amy had been appalled. Lacy had shot the defenseless rabbit not for meat but out of a lust for vengeance, out of a bully's desire to exercise power over something smaller and helpless. How could he heartlessly kill the animal, then blithely proceed with their drive?

At the time, Amy had pushed the incident to the back of her mind, since Lacy was her best friend and she needed him—not to mention the fact that living with Esther's cruelties made the shooting of a cottontail pale by comparison! But now, the incident reemerged to fester and grow in Amy's mind. . . .

One thing she did know: her husband, Matt Kendall, might be temperamental, baffling and exasperating at times, but Amy knew she had made the right decision in marrying him.

At home, the tense silence continued between Amy and Matt as they unloaded their supplies. Though it was difficult for Amy to concentrate on her household duties, she stewed a chicken for supper, heated up a jar of turnip greens and boiled some potatoes.

"This is right good," Matt said later, during the meal, surprising her with the compliment.

Matt's words were stiffly polite, and he was unsmiling as he sat across from her, but at least he was talking to her, Amy thought. "Thank you," she murmured back.

"It's something about those outlaws robbing the train," he went on, sipping his coffee.

She hastened to encourage his unexpected overture. "Are you going to the Grange meeting to discuss the outlaw threat with the other farmers?"

"Maybe."

"It's odd that they'd want to discuss train robberies at a

Grange meeting," Amy continued with a shy laugh. "I thought Grangers discussed crop rotations, things like that."

"They do," Matt replied. "But there ain't much point in a man taking his crop to market if the money he gets paid for it ain't safe at the bank."

"You've got a point there. I hadn't thought of it that way. I suppose there is a connection, after all," Amy replied. "More biscuits?"

"No, thanks."

Amy restrained a sigh. Things were awkward as hell between them, but at least she and Matt were communicating on some level. She may as well find out how shaky things truly were. Looking up at him with her chin tilted, she remarked, "Nell invited me over tomorrow. She's going to teach me how to make molasses bread. Do you have any objections to my going?"

Matt's jaw tightened as he put down his earthenware cup. "As a matter of fact, I do. With bushwhackers in the area now, I don't think you should be gallivanting off alone."

Amy's lower lip trembled as she bravely argued, "But Matt, the train was robbed many miles to the southwest—"

"Don't you think them fellers can ride?" he demanded with much more vehemence than was necessary, glowering at her from across the table.

Amy bit her lip to stop its quivering. What was left unsaid here was every bit as critical as what was actually being said, and they both knew it. Desperately, she asked him, "Matt, will everything change now?"

His expression hardened, and the fierceness in his eyes told her that he knew she was referring to much more than the outlaws. "You tell me, Mrs. Kendall."

She shut her eyes and entreated, "Matt, you take me to Nell's, then."

"Can't," he muttered, his expression remaining immutable as she opened her eyes to look at him. "That heifer in the barn is bound to drop her calf any day now. That's how come I wanted to get stocked up on supplies. I'll have to be sticking around the place for a while."

"I see." She stood, and wordlessly began cleaning up,

emptying food into the slop jar, then slamming dishes onto the dry sink, heedless of the noise. Matt left the room.

Amy had to pause to wipe an angry tear or two as she tidied up the kitchen. Everything had changed, and there seemed no reaching Matt now. It was obvious that he was planning to keep her his prisoner here once again, and she knew the reason had nothing to do with train robberies. It was so unfair. She'd done nothing to merit this lack of trust—she was but the innocent victim of Lacy Garrett's machinations!

Was there no reaching Matt? She thought of how beautiful things had been between them lately, and was hard-pressed not to break down and succumb to sobbing. They'd drawn so much closer, it was true. Yet their lovemaking was not enough by itself to build an enduring marriage. Amy wasn't sure their budding, fragile relationship could stand a test like Lacy Garrett's appearance in the area. Heavens, the peddler had not even arrived in town yet, and already he'd created a terrible schism between her and Matt. Damn Lacy!

Most devastating of all, Amy knew that things would indeed become hopeless between her and Matt if this distance couldn't somehow be bridged. Couldn't she go to him and—

Blast it! She banged the cast-iron skillet as she replaced it in the drawer of the stove. *He* should be the one who should come to her and apologize, on his knees! She was the one who had been doubted, for no good reason.

But then her softer nature intervened, reminding her of the glimpse of vulnerability she had seen in his eyes when he first discovered her prior engagement to Lacy. It must be hard for a man to realize his wife had once been the sweetheart of his rival, his enemy. Perhaps, again, he simply needed her reassurance; perhaps, as before, he feared losing her.

Yet how many times would she be expected to do this, to go to him, to level her pride, when she'd done absolutely nothing to deserve his mistrust? Then she remembered the Bible speaking of God forgiving "seventy times seven..."

Couldn't she bring herself to set her own ego aside for a mere second time, rather than lose the man she had married?

Amy finished the dishes, hung her apron and went in search of Matt. She found him in the parlor, smoking his corncob pipe in the rocking chair near the hearth, his dark gaze fixed upon the fire. She went to him and put her arm on his sleeve. He glanced up at her, and she studied his brooding face, the turmoil in his eyes. . . . At that moment, she knew he was suffering every bit as much as she was.

"Matt . . ." Her fingers on his shirt trembled, and she had to swallow the thick lump in her throat before she could continue. "Matt . . . if he is around, I want you to know I've no plans to see him."

Her husband stood so suddenly and violently that Amy took a quick step backward, her hand recoiling from his sleeve. "You damn well better believe it, woman," he said in a dangerous hiss, his dark eyes gleaming as he tossed his pipe down on the hearth. Before Amy could react, Matt grabbed her by the shoulders and continued in an explosive burst, "What the hell is Garrett doing around Rolla? Did the two of you arrange this? I should have known it was all too good to be true—the way you snapped up my offer of marriage! Were you planning a bit of entertainment on the side, Mrs. Kendall? Well, woman, I'll have you know a bargain is a bargain. You're *my* wife now, and I'll be seeing to it that you honor your promise to *me*—in full!"

With that, he savagely ripped a row of buttons from the bodice of her dress. She slapped him hard across the face.

Matt backed off, looking stunned, staring at his wife's trembling hand, then at her, as if he couldn't believe what she'd just done—or what *he'd* just done.

"What's wrong with you?" Amy cried, her fists now clenched, trembling at her sides as she faced the stranger who was her husband. "I had nothing to do with Lacy's being around Rolla—nothing! I—he—we never planned anything together—that's insane! I only wish to God Lacy Garrett were a thousand miles away from here!"

Matt gulped hard, his expression wavering.

"It's the truth, Matt!" Amy half screamed.

At last the tortured honesty of her words, her expression, penetrated the crazed fog of jealousy in his mind. "Amy... God, what have I done? I'm sorry." He ran a hand through his hair, then gestured at her frock. "Can the dress be repaired?"

"Yes." Boldly, she met his gaze. "What makes you think you have to force me into your bed, Matt?"

He looked very taken aback, blinking rapidly at her unabashed query. "Amy... Christ, just the thought of you with another man..." A vein throbbed in his temple as he whispered plaintively, "Try to understand, love. I lose control."

"Matt, you know I haven't had another man." Their eyes met and locked in shared memory, mutual anguish; after the night they consummated their marriage, neither could doubt the truth of her statement.

Matt nodded, looking miserably resigned as he turned to stare at the dying embers in the grate. "Do you want me to leave you alone tonight, love? I'll sleep in the other room, if you want me to."

She should send him away, she knew that. He deserved it. But she couldn't. "No," she said.

He turned to her with eyes gleaming fiercely. "Then take my hand, Amy."

She slipped her trembling fingers into his.

Sometime later, Amy awakened in the bed where she had given herself unreservedly to Matt. He was gone. In the dark coldness, she donned her gown and wrapper and then went searching for him.

She found him downstairs in the parlor, cleaning his shotgun as he sat on the settee. He wore a flannel dressing gown and slippers, and his blond hair gleamed with the light of the kerosene lanterns he'd lit on both end tables. "Matt?"

"Hello." He looked up at her.

Amy's heart fluttered. Just watching those dark eyes thoroughly peruse her body, she found herself throbbing with potent memories of his insatiable possession an hour earlier. Then she noted his restrained smile, and her heart sank. He had not held back one iota when he devoured her in bed, but he was pulling away from her again now; she just knew it.

Cautiously, she moved closer to him. "Why are you cleaning your shotgun at this hour?"

He didn't reply. The stock of the gun slammed shut with an ominous click, and he raised the weapon to gaze through the sight at an unseen object somewhere in space beyond them both.

"You're not—you're not afraid of outlaws coming here, are you?" Amy ventured at last.

Matt lowered the shotgun, laying it across his lap and staring at his wife meaningfully. "No sense taking chances. Besides, woman, it's purely winter now. Every fox and skunk in these parts will be itching to carry off one of my laying hens." He continued to stare at her in an odd, intense way. "And I don't let nothin' take what's mine."

Helplessly, she watched him raise the weapon again, aim at the fireplace, then test the trigger with a heart-stopping click. "I—I see," Amy finally stammered, leaving the room, fleeing his mistrust and his inexplicable hatreds.

Fool that she was, she had thought things had changed.

Twenty

+ +

During the next few weeks, the strain between Matt and Amy continued. February arrived. Wild watercress bloomed near the spring, and icicles hung in glassy tentacles from the house and all the outbuildings. Amy and Matt made two more trips into town, but no further mention of Lacy Garrett was heard. Surprisingly, Matt attended the February Grange meeting, at which volunteers from among the farmers were organized to take turns guarding the Rolla bank. Matt went in to town and dutifully worked his shift at guard duty, but the weeks passed without further word of outlaw activities in the region.

Amy and Matt's relationship was stiffly polite, except when they were in bed together. There, Matt became wildly erotic. To Amy, he seemed tense almost all the time, like a wary animal awaiting its attacker, and she consoled herself that at least he seemed to find some release in his demanding lovemaking. Yet she also missed the more tender times they'd once shared.

During this bewildering period, Amy turned whenever possible to Nell's friendship. Amy decided, as well, that it was high time she began attending church regularly in Rolla. When she told Matt that he must either start taking her in on Sundays or let her attend with the Stocktons, her husband brooded for a time. But, come Sunday, he grudgingly hitched up the buggy and drove her in. Amy knew Matt was attending services with her essentially because he didn't trust her around Reverend Fulton. But at least he was there with her. On Tuesdays, he even let her out the door alone to attend Circle with Nell. Amy reveled in this bit of social interaction, and soon became friends with a few of the women in the church.

With spring coming, the ladies were planning a bazaar to help finance a new roof for the church, and Amy offered to do her part by making several aprons and potholders to sell at the event. On a Saturday in mid-February, she asked Matt to take her into town to buy material for the craft items. "I also need cloth to make new kitchen curtains," she told her husband. "When I laundered the gingham panels last fall, most of the color stayed in the washtub."

Matt agreed readily enough to drive Amy in, since he was low on several medicines he used from time to time on his animals. By just being around Matt, Amy had picked up that hogs had to be wormed periodically, cattle made to vomit if they got into wild laurel or ivy, and that horses sometimes took colic. But, beyond these snippets of information she garnered incidentally, Amy took little active interest in the physiology of barnyard life, her session in hog butchering having been enough of an animal anatomy lesson to last her a lifetime!

The couple took the buggy into town, since they would be fetching home only a light load of supplies. The weather was chilly as they entered Rolla and headed for Salter's General Store. About a block away from their destination, Amy suddenly exclaimed to Matt, "Look! There's a new dry-goods store."

"Whoa!" Matt called to his horse, bringing the conveyance to a halt in front of a store whose freshly painted shingle creaked in the wind, proudly announcing, "Fancy Dry Goods." "Looks like you're right," Matt told his wife as both of them glanced through the large front window of the shop at its beckoning, brightly lit interior, where several women browsed among bolts of cloth and ready-made garments.

"Matt, could I . . . ?" Amy asked wistfully.

"Sure, why not?" he replied with unexpected cheerfulness. "I'll get what I need at Salter's, then pick you up here." He reached into his breast pocket, extracted his wallet, then stuffed several bills into her hand, an overgenerous amount. "Get whatever you need—cloth for curtains, church goods, dresses, anything you want."

Beaming, Amy tucked the bills inside her reticule. As Matt hopped down into the dirt street and went around to the other side of the buggy to help his wife alight, she reflected that her man could be wonderfully generous and thoughtful in so many ways, yet so possessive and distrustful in others. "Thank you, Matt," she said breathlessly as he helped her down into his arms, holding her against his hard body a bit longer than necessary.

"Don't be thanking me too much, missus, 'cause you'll be paying me back for every red cent," he teased back, a wicked, endearing twinkle in his eye.

Amy was warmed, feeling closer to Matt than she had in weeks. He had been so intense lately, she had feared the playful side of his nature was dead and buried. Now she rejoiced at this new evidence that things might, at last, lighten up between them a bit. Impulsively, she hugged him and whispered back, "It will be my pleasure, Mr. Kendall."

Releasing Matt, Amy crossed the street and entered the small shop. Warmth from a potbellied stove greeted her as she shut the door with its rattling bell and turned to look back through the window, waving at Matt as he drove off. Then she turned to examine the stores. Amy's already heightened spirits soared as she examined the stylish, quality goods. As she fingered the edge of a shimmering bolt of royal-blue velvet, a comely redheaded girl, whom Amy recognized from church, came over to help her.

"Why, hello, Sally," Amy said, greeting the girl, whom she knew was the eldest daughter of the town's sheriff. "So you're working here, now?"

"Howdy right back at you, Amy," the tall, slim girl

replied. "Yes, I'm working here. What else is there for an old maid to do in this town?"

Amy laughed. "Old maid? Why, you're no older than I am." Amy felt a rush of sympathy for the girl, who had an ordinary sort of face, but was attractive in a wholesome way, with her wide mouth, smooth, straight forehead and the sprinkling of freckles across her upturned nose.

"Betcha I am older than you," the girl replied. "I'm nineteen since October."

"Then you're not that much older, since I'll be nineteen in five months myself," Amy scolded. She glanced about at shelves stocked with brightly printed fabrics, at racks of fashionable ready-made garments. The smell of new cloth was exhilarating. "How long has this store been open?" Amy asked the girl. "Mr. Kendall and I only spotted it today."

"We've been open three weeks, but with a husband like yours, it's no wonder you haven't spied us," Sally replied, smiling with a mixture of humor and wistfulness. "I saw him out there wishing you good-by. . . . Law! He's a honey, is all I can say. He don't have a twin, now does he?"

Amy giggled, but inside, she was filled with empathy for Sally, well understanding the deep yearnings behind the girl's teasing words. Obviously, Sally had no beau of her own as yet. Amy remembered when she used to live at home, when a couple would be married at their church, or have a baby baptized—the rituals painful reminders of how Lacy was, at the time, toying with her affections. Sometimes back then, she couldn't control the tears of bitterness that welled up. Yet Lacy was all she had at the time, and she couldn't quite let him go, either. Her mother's reputation as a sharp-tempered, religious fanatic had been enough to scare off most eligible young men in their neighborhood. So Amy could well understand Sally's longings, her feelings of isolation, since having Lacy Garrett for a beau had often been no better than being left entirely alone. Now, Amy placed a hand on the girl's wool sleeve and said earnestly, "Sally, believe me, your time will come. I never thought mine would. Then one day, the most wonderful man just stepped into my life.''

"Oh, I hope so, Amy," the girl replied. Forcing a smile, she went on, "Well, I'd best get you served before my new boss comes checking up on me."

Excitedly, the two girls went through the yard goods, and by the time Amy had selected a bolt of gingham and a length of bright calico, along with threads, cotton batting and eyelet lace, she felt she had a new friend. Amy had paid for her purchases, and Sally was wrapping them in brown paper, when abruptly, the curtains at the back of the store parted, and a tall, black-haired, stylishly dressed man emerged.

Amy tried to restrain an audible gasp, but couldn't. She was staring eyeball to eyeball at none other than Lacy Garrett!

For a stunned moment, the two merely continued to look at each other—Lacy grinning on one side of the counter, Amy trembling in horror on the other side. For Amy, seeing Lacy Garrett at this point in her life was like a nightmare come true. She was tempted to run, fleeing, from the store, but fear momentarily rooted her to the spot.

Suddenly, with a shout of laughter, Lacy rushed forward through an opening in the counter. "Amy! Amy Harris!"

Mercifully, Amy at last found her voice. "It's Kendall now!" she retorted tersely, her heart hammering as she backed away warily from the arms that reached out to embrace her.

Lacy stopped in his tracks, looking momentarily abashed. "So I hear," he muttered. Then, decisively, he stepped forward and pumped Amy's resisting hand with his own. "Well, it's right good to see you, girl."

Amy was far from pleased. Hastily she snatched her hand from Lacy's, as if burned by his touch. Still reeling from his shocking presence, she hissed, "Lacy, what on earth are you doing here?"

Undaunted, Lacy indolently hooked his thumbs in the pockets of his red brocaded vest, replying proudly, "Why I've gone respectable, darlin', just like you always wanted me to. I just up and decided to set up store in this charming

little town." He gave her a devilish wink. "Too bad you
didn't wait for me, sugar."

"Is that a fact?" Amy snapped, glancing wildly over her
shoulder and praying that Matt would not come bursting
through the front door any second now. This was terrible!
She must grab her package and leave at once! Frantically,
Amy glanced at Sally, who was wrapping her bundle behind
the counter. "Sally, please, don't bother with that," she
called out fretfully, stepping forward. "I'm really in quite a
rush—"

"What's the hurry, darlin'?" Lacy interjected solicitously,
taking a step forward and effectively cutting off Amy's path.

She stopped in her tracks and glowered at Lacy. They were
hung at an impasse as he blocked her from her package. He
seemed to be enjoying it, too. His eyes gleamed with
cynical humor as he grinned down at her, yet there was also
a veiled menace there that almost dared her to try to get past
him. She seethed in frustration. Blast Lacy to the devil for
doing this to her, for coming here like this! The situation
was potentially lethal, especially if Matt—oh, Lord, if
Matt. . .

Amy shuddered, biting her lip until she tasted blood. She
struggled to control herself and dispassionately assessed her
adversary. Lacy looked—well, dangerous, there was no
other word for it. Tall, lean, he seemed to possess all the
deadly reserved strength of a coiled snake. His sharply
handsome features, his snappy dress in black suit and red
vest could not conceal from her what he was up to. His eyes
gave him away—deeply set and cold as sapphire ice, they
fixed on her now with implacable resolve. Lacy was obviously furious that she hadn't waited for him in St. Louis,
and he was here strictly to stir up trouble. Damn him!

Even as Amy made these horrible realizations, she also
became aware that Lacy's presence filled her with no joy
and no desire—only fear. Now that she knew what it was
like to live with a man who honored his commitments, she
could fully recognize that her infatuation with Lacy had
been a childish dependency. What mattered now was that

she mustn't let Lacy's vindictive machinations spoil things between her and Matt. She *must* get out of here.

Amy gritted her teeth and squared her shoulders. Quickly and decisively, she sidestepped Lacy and approached the girl at the counter. "Sally, are you finished yet?"

"Um—just about, Amy," Sally muttered back, her expression puzzled as she glanced from Amy to Lacy, then reached for string.

Meanwhile, Lacy drew closer to Amy again. "Now, darlin', why do you want to run off like this, when we've just now said our howdys?" He pivoted to wink at Sally. "Here she is boltin' on me, when I ain't even seen her since October."

"For that, you've no one to thank but yourself!" Amy interjected hotly. Then, at Lacy's chuckle, she mentally kicked herself. Why, *why* had she been so foolish as to give this man the impression she was at all dismayed that he'd stood her up?

Unfortunately, the damage was done. Lacy continued to grin maddeningly as he studied Amy's indignant, trembling visage. "Why, darlin', I think you actually missed me." Before Amy could hurl a rejoinder at him, he confidentially went on to Sally, "Nothin' like a backtalking woman to warm a fella's heart on a cold day. Are you that feisty and full of sass, Sally, girl?"

"N-no, sir," Sally stammered, blinking rapidly and blushing.

Watching Sally, Amy was stunned. For the shopgirl seemed to undergo a transformation as she absorbed her employer's attentions. The redhead's eyes now glowed with unmistakable ardor, and her cheeks gleamed with high color as she smiled at her boss. Lacy's smug grin as he ogled the girl back filled Amy with outrage. Lacy was toying with the shopgirl's affections, and his petty purpose could not be more obvious. How dare he use Sally in a cheap maneuver to arouse her own jealousies!

To the obviously smitten redhead, Amy now said insistently, "Sally, *please*. My package."

"Oh—oh, yes ma'am!" the embarrassed girl replied,

turning her attention to the bundle and tying the strings with trembling fingers.

"I must meet my husband at the general store," Amy added, her defiant eyes locking with Lacy's.

At last Amy scored a retaliatory barb. A spark of anger flickered in Lacy's bright blue eyes. "Your husband—that would be the *noble* Matt Kendall, now wouldn't it?"

Before Amy could contemplate Lacy's odd remark, the door at the front of the store blew open, and Amy knew, even as a chill tenaciously gripped her back, that her husband had entered the shop.

Amy gasped and turned, helplessly watching Matt approach, his boots pounding out an ominous cadence. Her husband looked formidable as he stormed across the store in his sheepskin coat and tight denim trousers that gripped the hard muscles of his legs. Amy mentally winced as she observed his tense face and tightly clenched jaw. At first, she couldn't see his eyes, not until he tore off his hat with a savage, impatient hand. Then she died inside. First his gaze was fixed murderously on Lacy, then flicked to her with bone-chilling menace. By the time he reached the back of the store, his eyes were dilated, black with anger as he glowered at both his wife and Lacy.

Once Matt arrived at her side, Amy tried to speak to him, but her throat felt paralyzed. Matt looked like a stick of dynamite with a very short fuse. She glanced helplessly from her scowling husband to Sally and Lacy. Sally shared Amy's mortified expression, while Lacy observed the newcomer in studied contempt.

It was Matt who broke the silence. "Lacy Garrett!" he hissed to the peddler. "What the hell are you doing in Rolla?"

Lacy grinned and said the worst possible thing under the circumstances. "Why, I'm flirting with your lovely wife, Kendall."

Amy and Sally gasped in unison at Lacy's provoking words. Meanwhile, Matt blew, lunging at Lacy. "Matt, no!" Amy screamed, struggling to restrain her husband even as Lacy leapt back to dodge the other man.

"Sir, please—" Sally interjected frantically from the sidelines.

Fortunately, Matt seemed to absorb the near-hysterical pleas of the two women and grudgingly retreated. Yet he still looked like his blood was boiling as he glared at Lacy. Matt's chest was heaving, his teeth were savagely clenched, and one of his tightly clenched hands was literally pulverizing the rim of his felt hat. "Weasel," he growled to Lacy under his breath. "I forgot, Garrett. You're damn good at squirming out of a fight, aren't you?"

"Matt, please, can't we go?" Amy begged, clutching the sleeve of Matt's coat.

Matt threw off Amy's grasp and gave her a look so quelling that she shrank away from him. Once again, he fixed his ferocious gaze on Lacy. "I repeat, Garrett, what the hell are you doing in Rolla?"

At a safe distance from Matt, Lacy grinned indolently and replied, "Like I was telling your wife, Kendall, I got me a hankering to settle down here." He glanced from the red-faced Sally to the furious Amy. "Got some mighty fine women in these parts."

Matt drew himself up in burgeoning fury. "Look, you lily-livered no-account," he growled, shaking a gloved finger at Lacy, "you look twice—no, once—at any female in these parts and I swear you'll be ground up into blood sausage before you can spit. This one"—he jerked his head curtly toward Amy—"is *my wife*, and this one"—now he nodded toward Sally—"got the sheriff for her pa. If you so much as touch either of them, you'll be eating dust for breakfast, mister!"

Amy shuddered at Matt's bloodcurdling speech, but Lacy merely whistled, ruefully shaking his head. "Danged if you didn't always have a temper, Kendall! Is it still getting you in just as much trouble as it used to?"

For a moment, the two men merely glared at each other, Matt's expression savage, Lacy's eyes glowing with a secret, lethal meaning. Then Matt snapped to Amy, "We're leaving, Mrs. Kendall."

Matt grabbed Amy's hand with steely fingers and dragged

her toward the front of the store, even as she gasped, "Matt—please—my package!"

"You wait here!" he barked, pivoting hard and heading for the back of the store.

Before Matt had taken two steps, Lacy tossed him the wrapped bundle. "We aim to please, folks," he crooned in a voice designed to infuriate his rival. "You folks come back, now."

In wordless rage, Matt turned back to his wife and tugged her, stumbling after him, out of the shop.

Amy exploded at Matt in the buggy going home. "Matt, how could you?" she demanded as they jolted along through the cold countryside just outside town.

"How could *you*, Mrs. Kendall?" Matt countered furiously, snapping the reins so suddenly that Ginger bolted forward with a high-pitched neigh.

"How could I what? Buy cloth?"

"You know what the hell I'm talking about, girl!"

"Matt, I only saw him for a minute!" she pleaded.

"You were in that store—*with him*—for a goddamned half hour, so you can just quite your lying, woman!" he roared back.

"I'm not lying!" she half screamed. "I didn't even know he was in town and—and he only came into the room a minute or two before you did. If you don't believe me, ask Sally, for heaven's sake!"

"Woman, if you think I'm ever going back to that store—if you think I'll allow you within three hundred yards of it—you're crazy!"

He snapped the reins again, and Amy fell into seething silence. She knew there was no reaching Matt now, not while he was in this black rage. He scared her when he was like this. Sitting next to her now, he looked like a cold-blooded stranger. His features were rigid and implacable, passion boiled in his dark eyes, and his hands gripped the reins with murderous strength. What on earth had Lacy Garrett done to her husband that incited him to such violence? she asked herself wildly. There *had* to be some vendetta between the two men, for nothing else made sense. The two men were both from St. Louis had both fought for the South during the Civil War, she recalled. Perhaps *that* was the connection. . . .

How could she find out for sure? Approaching Lacy, giving her former fiancé even the slightest hint of encouragement, was of course out of the question. That meant she would have to ask Matt about the source of the enmity between him and Lacy. She shivered, envisioning Matt's probable reaction if she even broached the subject. Amy would have to bide her time and try to select the right moment, which now clearly wasn't. . . .

Back at the house, Amy was eager to put as much distance between her and Matt as possible, to give him a chance to cool off. In the downstairs hallway, she rushed for the staircase with her package of fabric, but Matt restrained her by gripping the sleeve of her cloak. "I'll have a word with you, Mrs. Kendall."

Amy turned to face the stranger who was her husband, the man who now stood before her with arms akimbo, with eyes glittering ominously. "Yes?" she inquired, her chin tilted bravely.

"I believe it's time to clip your wings, woman."

Her eyes narrowed. "What do you mean?"

He shifted to an insolent stance. "I'll be seein' to our business in town from now on, and you'll be stayin' right here, where you belong."

Amy's mouth dropped open. Finally, she hissed in a disbelieving voice, "Are you forbidding that I leave this farm, Mr. Kendall?"

"Yes."

"Not for church, not for anything?"

"Not for nothin'."

"Why, Matt?" she entreated desperately.

He was unmoved, his dark eyes blazing back at her. "You know damn well why, girl. It's time for you to quit flirtin' with half the countryside and see to your husband's satisfaction, like a dutiful wife."

"Why—why you scoundrel!" she retorted, fists clenched at his arrogance.

He took a menacing step closer, shaking a finger at her. "Don't you be calling me names, girl—or I'll have a few for you that fit a mite better."

Matt's words infuriated Amy, but she wisely resisted retaliative namecalling. Still, her eyes gleamed with outrage as she inquired, "And what if I choose not to obey your dictate, Mr. Kendall?"

His hand moved inside his sheepskin coat, touching his belt with brazen menace. "You wouldn't be the first wife in these parts to be taken behind the woodshed for a good blistering."

"I see," she gritted. Amy hurled her package onto the floor and held up her joined hands to Matt, defiance oozing from every pore as she asked, "And why don't you just shackle my wrists while you're at it, Mr. Kendall?"

He cursed under his breath, turned on his bootheel and walked out on her.

That night, Amy went to bed in her old room, weeping herself to sleep. Things had gone too far this time. Matt was sure she had deliberately betrayed him, simply because she had accidentally run into Lacy, and it would be like moving mountains to get her husband to change his mind. It would take an apology on her part, as well—and by God, she wasn't groveling before him on account of something she hadn't even done! She'd swallowed her pride twice in order to soothe his outrageous jealousies, and look what it had gotten her. Locked up at this farm again and threatened with a thrashing! Well, let him apologize for *that*! Let him give a little this time!

So Amy wept, and ached for Matt, and slept very little. . . .

Though she didn't know it, Matt felt equally tortured as he lay in the next room. He could hear Amy's soft sobs through the wall, and he hurt to go to her. Yet his own injured pride restrained him. Seeing Garrett again, watching the peddler flirt with Amy, had filled Matt with such jealousy and rage that he couldn't even trust himself around his wife right now.

Rationally, he realized that Amy was not responsible for bringing Lacy Garrett to Rolla. Oh, no, he knew exactly what that slimy bastard was up to in settling hereabouts. Garrett was out for blood—*his* blood. The peddler had brought with him to Rolla all the ugliness and antagonism of their shared, shameful past, had brought to Matt's mind all the wartime horrors he'd struggled so hard to forget.

Why did that lowlife have to know Amy before he did? Why'd Garrett have to show up in Rolla, obviously bent on stirring up trouble? Matt's world had been near-perfect up until now, with Amy as the center of his life here at the farm. Now Garrett had threatened the very bedrock of his existence by appearing on the scene.

In fairness to Amy, he felt almost certain that she planned to honor her commitment to him, Matt. Yet he couldn't banish from his mind the fact that Garrett knew his wife first and that Amy had never told him of the prior engagement. And blast the girl, why had she stayed with Garrett at his store, even if only for a moment? She should have walked flat out of there, should have gone straight to Salter's to find her husband. Instead Amy had stayed with that no-account, and that he could not ignore. The girl should own up that he was right about this at least, should face her medicine for flirting with Lacy Garrett.

Thus, neither slept. The night grew longer, the cold wind howled, and the very walls themselves seemed to ache with the anguish of the lovers' separation.

Twenty-one

++

The next few days brought no improvement in Amy and Matt's relationship. At night the two continued to sleep in separate bedrooms, during the day were, at best, only stiffly polite with each other.

By Sunday, Amy had had enough of Matt's arbitrary imprisonment. She decided it was time to break free. It was the last Sunday of the month, traditionally "Foot-washing Sunday" at Rolla Presbyterian, and there was to be a covered-dish dinner following the service. Amy had promised the other ladies that she would fry up two chickens and bring them along as her contribution to the occasion, and she wasn't about to break her word. Thus, although she generally did not cook on the Sabbath, Amy got up in the frigid predawn, butchered, plucked and cleaned the chickens, then set about to fry them up.

By the time Matt came down into the kitchen, the room was filled with the aroma of succulent frying fowl. "Ain't that a bit much for the two of us?" he inquired, staring at the sizzling poultry crammed in the cast-iron skillet, and the already-fried pieces draining nearby.

Amy turned defiantly to her husband, a wooden fork in her hand. Matt looked a force to contend with this morning, wearing his snugly fitting denim trousers and dark flannel shirt, and sporting a heavy line of whiskers on his scowling face. Despite her husband's all-too-apparent displeasure, Amy was determined to face him down on this issue. If Matt Kendall wanted to remain a distrustful old recluse, fine; but, by thunder, she would not join him in his antisocial behavior. She was going to church today! And if he attempted to lift a finger against her—tried to belt her backside as he'd threatened—well, Amy would bite him a good one in the shin. Let him see how he liked that! She continued to stare at Matt bravely while she announced, "I'm going to church, Mr. Kendall. I promised the other ladies I'd fry up two chickens and bring them along. There's a covered-dish dinner after the service today."

Matt's eyes narrowed dangerously, and he crossed muscular arms over his broad chest. "I see. And just how are you planning to get in to town, Mrs. Kendall?"

Amy clenched her jaw at Matt's sarcastic tone. "I was hoping you'd hitch up the buggy for me. But if I have to, I'll ride the plow horse."

Amy turned back to the cast-iron stove to tend and turn the chicken pieces. Matt glared at the back of his wife's housedress, his mind wavering. He wasn't a religious man, but nevertheless, it didn't sit well with him, his forbidding that his wife attend church. Not knowing what else to do, he turned and stalked out of the room.

Matt paced the length of the hallway, glowering, as he brooded about Amy's defiance. Why had he married such a stubborn little spitfire? Seemed to him that no well-brought-up woman would sass her husband the way she was doing.

But Matt hadn't wanted a well-brought-up woman, he realized with a rueful smile. He paused to run a hand through his hair. He'd wanted her, Amy. Then he scowled again, resuming his pacing. That didn't change the fact that if he let her go in to town this time, his authority would be broken. Worse, if she started gallivanting about again, sooner or later she would run into that lowlife Garrett. And the very thought made Matt's blood boil.

Hang it all. On one hand, he feared losing Amy if he let her go, but on the other hand, he sure as blazes was going to lose her if he continued to try to tie her down here. His wife obviously had some needs Matt couldn't satisfy—for womenfolk, socials, that sort of thing. Couldn't he let her go . . . just this once?

Blast it, the girl hadn't even given him the apology she owed him for flirting with Garrett! He should take her out back and give her that good blistering he'd threatened. He should—

All at once, Matt sighed, and leaned against the wall feeling limp and defeated. He didn't want the girl hating him. He wanted her loving him. He groaned audibly as memories of Amy bombarded his senses—Amy in his arms, Amy smiling up at him as he drove into her sweet body. The beautiful lovemaking the two of them had shared over the past few months had been his salvation. Despite everything, he needed her so! One of them had to make a move. Their marriage couldn't survive with so much anger and distance between them.

Matt squared his shoulders, then strode back into the kitchen and stopped near Amy. He threw open a drawer on the cast-iron stove and began noisily rummaging for a tin bowl. Amy watched in amazed silence. Matt slammed the drawer shut and then, bowl in hand, dipped shaving water from the large pot that sat simmering on the back of the stove each morning. He strode from the room with the steaming bowl, calling over his shoulder to his wife, "Well, you ain't goin' alone, that's for damn sure."

Matt half smiled as he went upstairs, imagining Amy's shocked expression when she heard his terse announcement. So he'd given in this time. But he didn't have to be gracious about it—and that was a fact!

It was a crisp, cold day, and there was a fine blanket of snow on the ground around the Presbyterian Church. Amy and Matt had come early to drop off Amy's chicken before the service began. As the two crossed the churchyard together with Amy's filled basket, headed for the fellowship hall, she studied the myriad icicles hanging from the bare-branched trees above. Winter had finally arrived in full force, and her relationship with Matt had grown almost as chilly. But at least he'd taken her to church today, she thought. Perhaps there was some hope after all.

The ladies bustling about in the fellowship hall were delighted to see the young couple and graciously received their contribution. Seeing friendly, smiling faces buoyed Amy's spirits. Her step was sprightly as she and Matt left the hall, yet her joyful mood abruptly disintegrated as the two approached the main church building. There standing on the steps, visiting with several merchants from the community, was none other than Lacy Garrett.

Amy glanced quickly at Matt. She surmised from viewing her husband's tight jaw and dangerously glinting eyes that he had spotted Lacy, too. Her spirits sagged even further. She half expected Matt to drag her posthaste back to the buggy and drive them both straight home. But surprisingly, he didn't. His face remained rigid, but instead of insisting that they leave, he gripped Amy's elbow and led her up the steps.

The group of men in greatcoats and hats uttered greetings as the couple passed, the salutations spewing forth like so many puffs of steam on the frigid air. Lacy, in contrast, was quite direct, tipping his hat to Amy and addressing her and Matt with a smug smile. "Well, good morning, neighbors." Lacy's bright blue eyes sparkled with vindictive pleasure.

Amy just gritted her teeth. She glanced warily from Lacy to her scowling husband, not sure what to say or do. Yet even as she floundered, Matt ended the awkward moment by simply turning without a word and walking on, tugging his wife behind him into the church. As they entered the foyer together, she heard the shocked murmurings of the men at their backs. Amy was embarrassed by Matt's abrupt behavior, yet she was relieved that no full-scale confrontation had erupted.

Inside the sanctuary, Amy and Matt sat down on a hard bench near the front. She considered saying something to her husband to reassure him, yet he appeared unreachable. He sat beside her, his features adamantine, his hands clenched on a hymnal. Amy sighed. Matt would simply have to get used to Lacy's being in the community. It wasn't her fault!

Unfortunately, during the service Lacy Garrett commanded center stage by being baptized into the flock by Reverend Fulton. The congregation grew hushed as he came forward at the appropriate time, accepting Christ as his savior and repeating Fulton as he read the baptismal litany. Since it was a cold day, going to a nearby stream for an immersion ritual was impossible, so the reverend merely sprinkled holy water on Lacy's dark locks while he pronounced, "I baptize you in the name of the Father, the Son and the Holy Ghost." Matt scowled fiercely throughout the ceremony while the churchfolk regarded the same scene in smiling approval.

After the service, Amy and Matt headed out of the sanctuary. Everyone else was rushing down to the front of the church to greet the new convert, Lacy. Amy turned quickly and covertly, observing Lacy with the others. He was pumping the hand of his chief competitor Merchant Salter, and both were grinning. Amy reflected dismally that the peddler had already entrenched himself, indeed, well ingratiated himself, into this community. Lacy still had that slick, deadly charm, Amy reflected ruefully. . . . Then she caught Matt's glare and quickly turned to leave the building with him.

In the fellowship hall, all was in readiness for the covered-dish dinner. Picnic tables, normally kept outside under a thatched-roof pavilion, had been brought inside and draped with oilcloth, and the benches were cleaned and lined up beside them. Amy and Matt loaded their plates from the dishes of fried chicken, ham, hot German potato salad, assorted root vegetables, corn fritters, soda biscuits with homemade preserves, and desserts ranging from cakes and puddings to sweet potato pie available on the central serving table.

They sat down next to Sally Freeman and her father, the Rolla sheriff. Everything was proceeding pleasantly enough until Lacy Garrett sauntered over to plunk himself down next to Sally. Amy restrained an urge to curse aloud as he lifted his fork and flashed the Kendall couple a cynical smile.

As Amy fearfully turned to eye Matt, she found him staring directly at her, his hand tensely gripping his coffee cup. Their eyes locked for a charged moment, then Amy, stunned, noticed her husband's features softening somewhat. She would have given her eye teeth to know what he was thinking—

Matt was realizing that she, too, was scared, and in a way, this astonished him. It had never occurred to him before that Garrett's presence in Rolla might actually frighten Amy. Yet just now he'd seen the stark fear in her eyes as she glanced from Garrett to him. Could it be that this was all way beyond her control—that the man's presence was as much a threat to her as it was to him?

Lacy addressed Sheriff Freeman. "Hear anything more about the bank robbery over to Jefferson City?" he inquired.

Matt grew instantly alert, his blond head shooting up. "Robbery? There's been another robbery?" He addressed the question to the gray-haired sheriff.

"Yessir, the bank was hit over to Jefferson City on Monday," Freeman replied as he spread orange marmalade on a soda biscuit. "Sheriff Clark telegraphed me to have an extry watch out."

Merchant Salter, who had just joined the group at the long table, now asked Freeman, "Did Clark have any luck tracking them varmints?"

"Nope. As usual, them boys just hit and vanished." Stroking his handlebar mustache, the sheriff went on thoughtfully, "Sounds like the James and Younger brothers to me."

"Where do you suppose them bushwhackers is hiding?" Salter pursued.

The sheriff shrugged, while Amy spied Lacy and Matt exchange veiled, suspicious glances. That was odd, she reflected. Did the two men know something about the situation that they weren't telling?

A grizzled old farmer wearing a well-worn brown suit put in, "They's caves 'round Jefferson City, as I recollect. If'n it's the James and Younger boys doin' the robbin', you can bet they're crawlin' in an holin' up like snakes afterwards."

Mumblings of agreement echoed down the table. Still, Lacy and Matt stared at each other in a private, tense confrontation, as the sheriff replied, "Whatever them boys is doin', it's working right fine for 'em so far. We'd best double up on you boys doing the guardin' at the bank."

A plump old woman sitting next to the grizzled farmer now put in, "I heard tell the James and Younger brothers kilt a girl child nary ten year old when they robbed the fair at Kansas City last year."

"And I heard old Jesse shot the cashier dead at the bank in Gallatin back in 'sixty-nine—fer no reason, neither," a middle-aged man put in.

"Before we know it, hit's gonna be just like the war again, when Quantrill and Bloody Bill Anderson wuz laying waste to the land," came a disgruntled male voice from far down the table.

Rumblings of apprehension filled the room as Merchant Salter said, "Well, one thing's for certain, with the James boys robbin' in these parts, ain't gonna be no time before them Pinkerton boys show up here, just like they did out to Kearney."

Several people voiced their agreement and went on to recount some of the alleged exploits of the James and Younger boys. Amy again glanced at Matt and Lacy, noting that the two men had since quit glowering at each other and were listening avidly.

The storytelling lasted throughout the meal, and the rest of the afternoon passed without notice.

On the way home, Amy asked Matt, "Do you suppose Rolla will be hit by the outlaws?"

"Dunno," her husband said stiffly, his eyes glued straight ahead as he worked the reins.

"Matt . . ." Amy swallowed hard and braced herself as the buggy rattled over a rock. "About you and Lacy . . ." She watched the color rise in her husband's face, but nonetheless pressed on. "Do you two know something about the outlaws?"

"What do you mean, do we know something?" Matt half barked, shooting her a resentful glance.

Amy bit her lip and fretfully twisted her gloved fingers. "Well, everyone knows that the outlaw gangs got their start during the war. What I mean is, weren't you and Lacy together—back then?"

With a mighty tug on the reins and a harsh, chilling "Whoa!" Matt halted the conveyance. He turned to Amy and snapped, "Woman, don't you think you've pushed me enough for one day?"

Despite her frustration, Amy realized she wouldn't be able to tug an answer from him. "Perhaps you're right," she conceded. As Matt turned to whistle at the horse and reapply the reins, she added, "Thanks for taking me to church, Matt. And thanks for staying."

Back at the farm, Amy and Matt passed the balance of the day in strained silence. Several times, Amy caught Matt staring at her. She spent the next few hours practicing her piano in the parlor, as she often did on Sundays. When she started playing a fiery rhapsody by Liszt, she heard Matt come into the room. She paused and shot him a glance where he stood near the archway, but he said firmly, "No, don't stop." Amy obediently continued with her playing, as Matt sat down in a chair flanking the piano. As she concluded the Liszt and launched into a Chopin waltz, it was impossible not to absorb the heat of Matt's focused gaze. The intensity, the turbulence in his dark eyes unsettled her greatly.

After a few minutes, Matt quietly left the room. He took his pipe and tobacco, donned his coat, and went out onto the front porch to smoke. It was a frigid afternoon, but the aromatic smoke warmed him as he rocked to and fro on the swing, still able to hear his wife's lovely music filtering out through the planked walls. She was playing some sweet, sad song now—a favorite of his, though he couldn't remember the name—and its haunting melody tugged at his conscience.

Matt felt badly about his shortness with Amy on the ride home from church. But he'd been scared—especially when she'd hit on the connection between the robbers and the war a decade earlier.

He simply couldn't share what he knew with her. It would be like ripping open a fresh wound, and Amy might well think low of him for the shameful things he would reveal. But Matt was also sure that she would never fully understand the hatred between him and Garrett unless he told her all about those painful days.

Why not try, then? He reckoned he knew enough about Lacy Garrett to change Amy's opinion of that low-down skunk forever.

His pride argued that he shouldn't have to win Amy's trust that way; she should stand by her man and believe in him already.

Did she believe in him? And just as important, was he trying to believe in her? Sure, it had been an enormous blow to Matt's pride when he'd found out she had been engaged to Garrett before. But there had undeniably been stark fear in her eyes today every time she looked at Garrett.

That he understood. He was damn frightened, too. . . .

When it was time to go to bed, Amy went to sleep alone in the guest room, as she had been doing all week. She dreamed that Matt was loving her again. She awakened with a start to find her husband's hard, naked body pressed against her backside, his arms possessively about her middle. "You can tell me no if you want to, Amy," Matt whispered to her in the darkness, his voice hoarse with his anguish, his need. His breath scorched her ear as his hand slid up a silky leg, possessively clutching her bottom.

"Oh, Matt!" Amy's eyes filled with tears of joy at his presence. "I don't want you to leave. I just want you to trust me. I mean, I never—"

"I know," he said simply.

"Oh, Matt—I'm so glad you're here."

She tried to twist around to kiss him, but his hard arm clenched about her middle, restraining her. "No, don't turn," he whispered, raising her gown. "I love the way you feel against me."

She obeyed him and didn't turn, though her mouth ached to devour his. He kissed and caressed the sensitive flesh of her back and neck, his hands kneading her buttocks, making exquisite pangs of desire shoot through her. By the time his hands reached around to her front, to her breasts, her belly, and lower, she was struggling to breathe, consumed with fire. All the time she could feel him growing hard and large against her backside, and she hungered to be filled with that wonderful, plundering proof of his need. When his fingers sought and caressed the aching bud of her longing as his teeth nipped the sensitive back of her neck, Amy actually cried out and bucked, the arousal becoming so acute.

Abruptly she was turned and rolled beneath him. Above her, Matt's eyes glittered intensely in the moonlight and his breathing was quick and fierce as he surged into her powerfully, filling her womanhood to bursting with his heat. She cried out at the rapturous, rending pressure of him sheathed so tightly inside her, and each hard thrust that followed seemed to bring a riotous climax of its own. The last was the best, when he sought his own release with quickened, pounding fury, then drove home with a force that melded them as one. . . .

When he gently withdrew, Amy flung her arms around his neck. "Matt, I didn't get to kiss you," she gasped. "I must—"

"Kiss me," he growled, pulling her on top of him and raking his hands through her moonlight-drenched hair. "Kiss me."

He pulled her trembling lips down to his.

Twenty-two

++

Chicago, Illinois

O n a dreary March morning in the winter-worn city of Chicago, Allan Pinkerton, founder and principal of the Pinkerton National Detective Agency, sat at his cluttered desk staring drearily at the telegram he'd just received from one of his operatives in Monegaw Springs, Missouri. Pinkerton was a large, imposing Scotsman with deeply set, intelligent eyes, blunt features, and a full dark beard and head streaked with gray. The silver in it had been dramatically increasing its insidious path of late.

Staring at the telegram, Pinkerton steadily tapped a clenched fist upon his desk. Two more of his agents were now dead, murdered in cold blood, according to this dispatch. The operative and two associates had been trying to track down the Younger brothers in rural Missouri when the three were ambushed by John and Jim Younger near Monegaw Springs. Two were killed, while the one who had wired managed to escape. That brought the death toll among Pinkerton's Missouri operatives to three, all within the same week! Mere days earlier, another of Pinkerton's agents had been murdered near Kearney while attempting to make his way to the James family farm.

Never had Allan Pinkerton known such frustration. Success had been the rule, not the exception, of his existence in the United States ever since he arrived back in 1843. Pinkerton was vehemently opposed to slavery, and during his first years in America, he was able to smuggle countless runaway slaves into Canada. Next, he'd gotten a job as the first detective on the Chicago police force, effecting several triumphs with them. His detective agency developed as an outgrowth of his work there.

His achievements for business and government clients were legion, and he now had offices in several northern cities.

Pinkerton was most feared by outlaws due to the successful and innovative tracking methods of his agency. In 1856, when a bank hired him to track the murderer of one of its tellers, Pinkerton craftily assigned a detective to the case who resembled the murdered man. His operative followed the prime suspect, haunting him day and night, and in no time the murderer, named Drysdale, cracked under the pressure and confessed. And since then, those on the other side of the law had dubbed Pinkerton "The Eye."

And now, after all these successes, to meet with failure at the hands of an itinerant group of outlaws in frontier Missouri! The James and Younger boys seemed to be on a rampage—audaciously robbing trains and banks all over Missouri, then sending news releases to local papers that both arrogantly flaunted their exploits and denied their own personal involvement. When Missouri bankers first got together and hired Pinkerton's agency to track the gangs, it was assumed that justice would be imminently forthcoming, considering the agency's reputation as well as the gang's cocky exploits.

It was assumed wrong, by all involved, including Pinkerton himself. The Scotsman hadn't realized the citizens of rural Missouri often viewed the gangs as folk heroes. The gang members had had their origin in Quantrill's raiders back during the Civil War, and sentiment regarding the War Between the States still ran high in Missouri, especially in the border region. That was where most of the Missouri slaveowners had lived. Most damning, though, was the fact that even the citizens of Missouri who were opposed to slavery or had never even taken a stand on the issue, were nonetheless quite suspicious of northerners. Thus Pinkerton's operatives had been thwarted at every turn. Try to question one Missourian regarding another Missourian and the ranks often closed decisively. Worst of all, no one even seemed to know what the James and Younger brothers looked like. Although their names were now well known, likenesses were unavailable, and again, the Missourians themselves were highly reticent—

"Sir?" The voice of Pinkerton's young assistant pulled him from his troubled thoughts, and he turned in his swivel chair to face his clerk standing in the archway holding a sheaf of papers.

"What is it, Ben?" Pinkerton inquired wearily.

"Sir, there are several men outside answering our newspaper notice for new operatives. Do you wish to see the gentlemen this morning?"

Pinkerton sighed. "Should I be sending them all to their maker, like these two?" Angrily, he crumpled up the telegram he was holding.

"Sir, I'm sorry. . . . This is doubtless a bad day for you, and perhaps I should send them all away. It's just that there's one man here who says he's from Missouri, and I thought . . ."

Pinkerton's bushy brows shot up, and he drew himself up in his chair. "From whereabouts in Missouri?"

"St. Louis, sir. But he says he rode with Quantrill's Raiders during the war."

By now, every muscle in Pinkerton's large body was tensely alert. "Send the Missourian in," he ordered, "and unless the others look especially promising, ask them to come back tomorrow."

"Yes, sir."

The young man left to go fetch in the Missourian, and Allan Pinkerton straightened his black wool cravat and buttoned a button on his frock coat, his spirits improving considerably. So a Missourian who actually rode with Quantrill was applying for a position at his agency! It seemed a godsend—

Yet would this man be any more trustworthy than other

Missourians had proven to be? What if the man had actually been sent by one of the Missouri outlaw gangs to infiltrate Pinkerton's organization and foil his activities?

Yet as soon as he stepped into the room, Allan Pinkerton sensed that this was a man he could trust. The Scotsman was a true master at judging character, and he instinctively knew that the tall, spare, middle-aged man in threadbare suit had come to him with sincere motives.

Pinkerton stood and strode over to greet the applicant. "Allan Pinkerton," he said, offering a broad hand. "And you, sir?"

"Abel Harris," the man replied in a steady, soft-spoken voice.

"Please, Mr. Harris, have a seat."

"Thank you."

The two men sat down, Pinkerton behind his desk, Harris in a straight chair across from him. For a moment they assessed each other intently. Harris looked like he was a man of limited means. His callused hands testified that he had labored hard to earn his existence: his finely honed features, the telltale lines of sadness radiating outward from his eyes and mouth, bespoke that he was a man stamped by experience, not all of it pleasant by any means. A complex man, perhaps even a haunted man, Pinkerton deduced. But an honest man nonetheless.

"So, Mr. Harris, you would like to become an operative in my organization?" Pinkerton began.

"Yes, I would." Harris met Pinkerton's direct, speculative gaze, his own expression unwavering.

"Could you tell me a little about your background, then?" the Scotsman pursued.

"Well, I was born and raised in St. Louis, and fought for the South during the war. After the war, I was foreman for a section crew that repaired railways in Georgia and Virginia. Eventually, I got a job as conductor on the Illinois Central line, and that brought me here to Chicago."

"I see," Pinkerton murmured, leaning back in his chair. "So tell me, if you're currently employed by the railroad, what made you become interested in applying for this position? Did you read our newspaper notice, like the others?''

There Harris smiled wryly. ''Actually, I must admit that I'm here on something of a whim. You see, last night as I sat in a nearby grogshop, I heard two men discussing your current openings. I asked them a few questions, which they kindly answered for me, and today I decided to come see about the job myself.'' Harris ruefully shook his head. ''I can tell you that my companions of last night gave me rather baleful glances just now, when I was asked to come in here and they were asked to leave.''

Now Pinkerton grinned, too. ''I'll admit that you intrigue me, Harris. My assistant tells me you rode with Quantrill during the war.''

Harris crossed his long legs and replied carefully, ''That's right.''

Pinkerton struggled to control his building excitement. ''Then you must know what the James brothers and the Younger brothers look like.''

''I do, indeed,'' Harris admitted calmly.

''Then tell me, sir, if indeed you rode with the Raiders, why are you now willing to track your former comrades in arms?'' Pinkerton inquired incisively.

Harris hesitated for a moment, frowning thoughtfully. Then, slowly, he replied, ''Because of what I saw when I rode with Quantrill.''

Pinkerton leaned forward, his expression intent. ''Please elucidate.''

The thin, graying Harris nodded solemnly. ''Mr. Pinkerton, I won't lie to you,'' he began. ''As I told you, I did side with the South during the war. You see, two of my best friends were killed by abolitionists down in St Louis in 'sixty-one.''

''I'm sorry,'' Pinkerton said gravely. ''I was on the other side, of course, but I readily admit that the wrong went both ways.''

''Aye, it did,'' Harris agreed. ''Anyway, I did give my allegiance to Quantrill back when I first rode with him. But what I subsequently saw drove me away.'' Harris' features twisted with disgust as he went on, "Quantrill's brigade turned into little more than a gang of thieving cutthroats. I left the Raiders after Lawrence, Kansas. I don't hold with killing innocent civilians, sir."

"I see," Pinkerton replied. Both men were well familiar with Quantrill's massacre at Lawrence, Kansas, when his Raiders shot every man and boy in sight, then burned the town. "So this is why you're willing to track down the James and Younger brothers now?"

Harris leaned tensely forward in his chair. "I once watched Cole Younger line up a group of Yankee prisoners and fire into their backs, just to see how many men he could kill with one bullet."

Pinkerton shook his head, shuddering. "This has become something of a moral issue for you, hasn't it, Harris?"

"In a manner of speaking, yes."

"You do believe, then, that the gang deserves to be brought to justice?"

"I do indeed."

Pinkerton smiled with both amazement and admiration. "A quite singular attitude on your part, sir. Amazing, for a Missourian."

"I learned some important lessons during the war," the thin man admitted ruefully.

Pinkerton nodded. "Harris, I like you."

Harris smiled expectantly. "Then I have the job?"

Pinkerton was not a man to belabor a decision. "Yes, man, you do. And I must tell you I'm tremendously excited to have found you. You're the first man I've hired who actually knows what the outlaws look like."

Harris nodded. "I'll do my best to help you track them down and bring them to justice."

"I believe you will, man."

Harris glanced about the cluttered office. "So what would you have me do first, sir?" he said with a smile.

"First, I'll get my assistant to orient you on our procedures. Once we feel you're sufficiently trained, we'll send you on to Missouri. I'll give you the names of our client bankers, as well as our operatives in the area. You'll need to garner as much information as possible when you get down there, before you even begin tracking. You may wish to check with the governor's office in Jefferson City, too. The legislature recently appropriated funds for a strike force of secret agents, and they may be able to provide you with leads, also."

"I'll do everything you say."

The two men stood and shook hands on their agreement, then Harris awkwardly added, "Sir, there is one thing . . ."

Pinkerton eyed the other man skeptically. "Be out with it, Harris. If you've any misgivings, now is the time to voice them."

"It's not a misgiving," Harris hastily corrected. "I was wondering if you'd allow me some extra travel time when I head down to Missouri. I'd like to stop off in St. Louis for a few days and visit my family. I haven't seen them since the war."

"Why, of course, Harris," Pinkerton said, looking relieved, and wisely not asking the man why he hadn't seen his kinfolk for such a long time. Harris was his best bet at the moment for capturing the outlaws, and he wanted to treat him with as much deference as possible. "Do take some extra time. Be with your family."

"Thank you, sir," Harris said graciously as Pinkerton led him to the office door. "You won't be sorry for hiring me."

"I'm sure I won't," Allan Pinkerton replied.

Two hours later, after talking at length with Pinkerton's assistant about his new duties, Abel Harris donned his ancient bowler hat, pulled his worn greatcoat tightly about him and left the Pinkerton building. A harsh blast of winter wind assaulted him as he entered the cold, snowy streets of downtown Chicago.

Despite the discomfort of traversing the bitterly windy, slushy streets, Abel felt a great sense of satisfaction. He also felt a stab of guilt. He would do his best by Mr. Pinkerton, for he did feel that Jesse James, as well as the Youngers, should be brought to justice. The elder James brother, Frank, had always struck him as being far more honorable, perhaps even worthy of redemption—but Jesse and the others were, in Abel's view, no more than savage animals who deserved the full brunt of justice under the law.

Thus he would try his damnedest for the agency, yet he also had a strong ulterior motive in accepting the position, a motive he hadn't dared reveal to Allan Pinkerton. Taking this job had at last given Abel the opportunity to return to St. Louis without losing face. Abel had a daughter there, a daughter he hadn't seen for eleven long years, and while his conscience had tortured him endlessly for not being there while Amy grew up, circumstance had forbidden his return, until now.

Turning a corner, Abel was hit by a new jolt of wind coming from Lake Michigan. But icy tentacles of memory chilled him even deeper, clenching about his very heart as he remembered the last time he'd been home.

It was his first leave after the war began, and no man had ever been more eager than Abel to get back to a waiting wife and child. Yet when Abel arrived home, he discovered that Esther, his wife, had radically changed. Esther had always been a devoutly Christian woman, but he now found the vengeful fire of fanaticism in her eyes as she quoted scripture endlessly to him, mostly Old Testament passages about sin and death and the destruction of Sodom and Gomorrah. While he had been gone, his wife had apparently come to the bizarre conclusion that the marriage act was depraved, that men were no better than lusting animals. He recalled his own exasperation when she had even accused him of drinking and being unfaithful while he was off soldiering.

Of course, Abel fought with Esther bitterly over her unjust accusations. Things reached a crescendo that night when young Amy was in bed. He drank too much—something he rarely did—and when Esther's taunts pushed him beyond endurance, Abel had picked her up, carried her off, and did something he had regretted every day, every second, since then—

He had asserted his husbandly rights by force. In his crazed, love-starved state, he had deluded himself, reasoning that if only he and Esther could truly be man and wife again, then he could reach her, penetrate her barriers of sanctimonious religion. He had been wrong, deadly wrong, for his violence had solved nothing. It had only made things much worse. Indeed, he awoke the next morning to see Esther standing above him with murder in her eyes, with a knife at his very throat!

She'd cut him before he could get the knife away from her, and he still bore the small diagonal scar near the base of his neck. After he'd taken the knife away from Esther, he knew it was over; there was no salvaging their relationship, not now that they'd both descended to such depths. It broke his heart to leave his daughter, but he knew Amy would be safe with Esther, who had been a good mother, aside from her peculiar religious leanings.

Once Abel returned to his company, the violence of war made it easy to forget. When peace came, he knew he couldn't return home; so he procured a job as foreman of a section gang, repairing war-damaged railways in the South. It required much travel, and, of course, being a father to Amy was impossible then, just as it had been when he was a soldier. Finally, he had gotten the position as conductor on the Illinois Central line, and that led him to where he was today.

The timing of the opening with the agency could not have been more perfect. He would return to Missouri and see his daughter! Amy would be eighteen now, he mused, and she would be old enough to make her own decisions. Even though reconciling with Esther might prove impossible, his wife could not now deny him a relationship with the girl. In an uncanny way, he felt Amy needed him now. He knew he had to make her understand the reasons that he had left, and he would have to pray that she would forgive him for not being there while she grew up.

Abel passed the post office and paused, catching his worried reflection in the glass. He saw a pale man with a troubled face, looking older than his years. Should he write his family and let them know he was coming? Maybe that would ease the blow somewhat. After all, he had changed greatly over the years. Perhaps Esther had changed, too.

He headed for the boarding house then, to get out writing supplies, and prayed that the right words would come to him. He sighed, catching a ragged breath of frigid air. The thought of returning to that shabby, noisy brownstone house where he had let a room filled him with depression. It had been so long since he'd known what home was like—he'd even forgotten how to dream about it. . . .

Twenty-three

⁂

E arly on a morning in mid-March, Lacy Garrett showed up on Amy Kendall's doorstep.

It had started as an ordinary day, a bit milder than usual, and Matt had left early by horseback to survey their fields for the coming spring planting. Amy was just finishing tidying up the kitchen when she heard a knock at the front door. Hanging her apron on a peg, she rushed for the front of the house, wondering who would come calling at this early hour.

"Lacy Garrett!" Amy exclaimed as she opened the door and saw the peddler on her porch. "What on earth are you doing here?"

"May I come in, Amy?" he asked cordially, unruffled.

"Certainly not!" she snapped. She took a moment to assess him. Lacy was dressed in a fashionable, double-breasted redingote of dark brown, his fawn-colored trousers tucked into black boots. A gold satin vest, high-collared white shirt, black cravat and broad-brimmed hat completed the outfit. From the shine on his boots to the odor of bay rum emanating from his hair, Lacy projected the aura of the gentleman come courting. And his audacity infuriated Amy. "If you think I'm asking you into this house, you're insane," she snapped.

"Oh?" he bantered back. "Afraid I'll come in and disturb your husband, Mrs. Kendall?"

Exasperated, Amy stepped out onto the porch and shut the door. "My husband is out riding in the fields. And may the devil take pity on you if Matt comes back and finds you here!"

Undaunted, Lacy grinned, baring even, white teeth as he dramatically removed his hat. "You know you look uncommonly pretty this morning, my dear, especially with your brown eyes snapping such sweet fire. Quite a fetching frock, too," he added, his bright blue eyes boldly roving her figure.

Amy blushed, drawing her white wool shawl tightly about her shoulders. She felt a discomforting flush spread in the wake of Lacy's errant eyes, and her cheeks, neck and bodice burned with the heat of her embarrassment. "Lacy, damn it, what game are you playing with me?" she demanded.

"Game?" he echoed innocently.

"I'm a married woman, for heaven's sake!" she railed. "You had to have known this, yet you came here, to Rolla, and settled. Now you're at my very door—"

"Such ingratitude," Lacy cut in with a chuckle, not the least bit perturbed by her outburst. He shook his dark head with a grin. "And after I came all the way out here to bring you a letter from St. Louis, purely as a favor to the postmaster. Tsk, tsk, my dear."

Suddenly, Amy was all attention. "A letter? What letter?"

"Aren't you going to ask me in?" Lacy taunted.

"Damn it, Lacy, don't bait me! Give me the letter!" Amy extended an insistent hand.

He sighed. "You're a hard woman, darlin'." Reaching into his breast pocket, he extracted a parchment envelope.

Amy snapped up the letter greedily, her worried gaze darting to the return address. "It's from Vida!" She ripped the letter open. "It must be about Hannah."

Amy hurriedly read the terse communication, her expression growing crestfallen. She finished reading it with a groan. The letter slipped from her fingers, and she numbly collapsed on the steps.

Lacy picked up the letter from the porch floorboards. "What is it, darlin'? You look like you've seen a ghost." He read the note, then whistled under his breath, plopping himself down beside Amy on the steps. "By Jesus, it looks like your ma has really wigged out this time, sugar," he remarked sympathetically.

Amy nodded desolately, a huge lump of pain in her throat. In this moment of crisis, of sick fear, her resentment of Lacy was pushed into the background and she found herself returning to a former, familiar role with her ex-fiancé. "Oh, Lord, Lacy," she said, glancing up at the peddler with her heart in her eyes, "Vida is sure she has heard Hannah's screams coming from our house. Ma must be beating her. What am I to do?"

"Go home, darlin'," Lacy quickly responded. "I'll take you."

Amy shook her head vehemently. "I can't just up and leave. And certainly not with you! There's Matt—"

"What can he give you that I can't?" the peddler interjected hotly.

"He's given me his name!" Amy snapped, now angry herself.

"That can be remedied," Lacy said hoarsely.

Amy's brown eyes widened luminously. "That sounds like a threat to me."

"It's a promise."

Amy got to her feet, snatching the letter from Lacy's fingers. "Lacy, I think you'd better go."

He bolted up, too. "Maybe I'll wait and have a word with your husband first."

"Lacy, why are you doing this to me?" she asked with a flabbergasted gesture.

His bright eyes narrowed. "Has it occurred to you that I might be hurt by what you did, Amy?"

"What I did? What *I* did?" she ranted, with great restraint resisting an urge to stamp her foot at his arrogance. "What about what you did to me? It seems to me that I was the wronged party in this."

"Amy, I'm not Matt Kendall," Lacy pointed out rather

heatedly. "I'm not dogged and dependable like a plow horse. But I would have come back for you, darlin', if only you'd waited." Abruptly, his mood shifted and he grinned down at her, his eyes sparkling with deadly charm. "I may not be predictable, but I sure was fun, wasn't I, sugar?"

Despite her frustration, Amy had to fight a smile at Lacy's devilish remark. It was true—she and Lacy had had some good times together. On more than one occasion, she had even climbed out her bedroom window to go riding with him in the moonlight. They had laughed and sipped apple cider while sitting beneath moss-hung, spectral trees. Later, she had fought off his artless kisses . . .

Amy's countenance darkened at the memory. She and Lacy had had fun, yes—but as two children, as boy and girl, not as man and woman. That time was gone forever—and Amy knew now that she owed her loyalty to her husband.

Still, it gave her pause, realizing that Lacy had felt disappointed that she hadn't waited for him. He had been a very good friend to her at one time. Cautiously, she told him, "Lacy, I'm sure that from your perspective, you were hurt that I married Matt. But that doesn't change the fact that you broke your word to me—three times."

"I know, Amy," he admitted abashedly, running a hand through his dark locks.

She put her hands on her hips. "Well, fair is fair, Lacy Garrett. You stood me up and I accepted another's suit, which I had every right to do. So why are you still coming around, trying to ruin my life?"

His eyes narrowed with a fierce intent. "Have you thought that perhaps rather than trying to ruin your life, I might actually have your welfare in mind?"

"No!" she snapped. "How could you possibly have my welfare in mind? The only thing you seem to have in mind is wrecking my marriage!"

"That's not true, Amy," he insisted. "It's just that—you have no idea what manner of man you married."

At his words, Amy felt a chill streak up her spine, especially as she recalled the tense looks Lacy and Matt had exchanged at the recent covered-dish dinner. "Just what do you mean by that comment?"

"I'll tell you, if you'll ask me in," he cajoled, his face bearing the smug expression of a fisherman about to pull in a big catch.

"No, absolutely not," Amy retorted. "Matt could come home at any moment."

"Then meet me somewhere," Lacy insisted. When she bit her lip and didn't immediately reply, he pointed to a glade to the north of the house and said, "Meet me on the other side of that rise, this same time tomorrow. When you come, I'll tell you all about the honorable gentleman you married."

The words "honorable gentleman" were delivered with great cynicism, making Amy swallow hard. She was getting a bad feeling from this conversation. "Look, Lacy, I—"

"You'd best come, Amy," he insisted, his mouth grimly set as he shook a tanned finger at her, "or I swear, I'll come straight to this house again tomorrow and lay my cards on the table, whether that noble husband of yours is around or not."

"Lacy, that's blackmail!" Amy cried.

"You gave away your future with me, darlin', so you at least owe me a hearing," he argued. "Besides, maybe we can figure out some way to help Hannah."

"Oh, all right, I'll come," she agreed with exasperation. "But for now, will you just leave?"

"Of course, darlin'," he returned graciously, donning his hat and turning to stride down the steps toward his waiting buggy.

But his taunting grin would not leave her.

The rest of the day, Amy fretted about Hannah, and about her forthcoming meeting with Lacy. She felt trapped and apprehensive. There was no way she could tell Matt about the episode this morning without inciting his rage, and if she didn't go to the meeting with Lacy, she was sure he would follow through on his threat and audaciously come straight back to their home. Thus, she figured the only way she could avoid a violent confrontation between the two men was to keep her mouth shut and do what Lacy asked. Besides, she was starved for information regarding her husband. Why was Matt so distrustful of people, so reluctant to share his feelings, even with his own wife? What was the source of the bad blood between him and Lacy? Although she knew Lacy might well color the facts to suit his own purpose, he might at least provide some insight into her husband's baffling behavior.

If Matt noticed Amy's preoccupation regarding these matters, he made no comment. Things were still awkward and tense between them, but at least they were sleeping together, making love, at night. Indeed, when Matt came to Amy that night, drawing her into his arms, she breathed a sigh of relief, realizing that he suspected nothing, at least not so far. . . .

Toward morning, Amy had a nightmare in which Esther savagely beat Hannah with a briar switch. Hannah's screams echoed through the dark passages of Amy's dream, and she vividly saw small, savage tears in the child's bloomers, blotches of blood soaking the pristine white across the back of Hannah's legs. . . .

Amy jerked awake in the frigid half-light, gasping for breath. Her body was covered with cold sweat, and her heart was hammering so savagely she feared it would burst from her chest. The nightmare had been so real: she was choked with tears of alarm and frustration.

She glanced at Matt, still sleeping peacefully beside her. How she longed to tell him of Hannah's current peril! But how could she do so, without spilling it all out—without telling Matt of Lacy's visit yesterday and their planned meeting again today? If she told her husband the truth, he would doubtless be enraged, and might never trust her again simply because she had planned to meet Lacy at all.

Of course, Amy rationalized, she could tell Matt someone else brought her the letter yesterday—Nell, for instance. But what excuse could she give her husband for waiting until now to tell him about Hannah? And what if Matt later thanked Nell for bringing the letter by, or even mentioned the matter to the postmaster? She shuddered at the very thought. No, for the time being, Amy was caught in her own intrigue—Lacy's intrigue, rather.

"Amy, why are you crying?"

Amy started as she realized Matt was now awake, staring up at her while he wiped sand from his dark eyes. He looked very sexy lying next to her, with his golden hair tousled, his chest bare above the covers. She struggled for control at his question. Yet this proved impossible, as all the things she couldn't share with him and all the things he couldn't share with her seemed to burst inside her. She succumbed to heartbroken weeping.

"Amy, what *is* it?" he demanded, sitting up, looking alarmed as he pulled her upright beside him and wrapped an arm possessively about her shoulders.

Amy knew she had to tell him something. "You just seem—so angry at me lately," she choked.

"Angry? Did I seem angry at you last night?" he teased gently.

She shook her head, coloring miserably. "But—but even when we're . . . like that . . . it just seems like there's something gnawing at you, that you're unhappy with me."

"Oh, love!" He drew her close, and his breath was hot against her neck. "Don't you have any idea how much you please me?"

She drew back to look up at him with tear-filled eyes. "I just wish we could be . . . closer. I wish we could talk about . . . things."

A shadow of pain crossed his dark eyes. "There you must be patient, Amy. All that will come in time."

"Matt, I don't think—"

"It will come in time," he repeated hoarsely, drawing her closer against his warm chest. "In the meantime, I've a remedy for those tears."

Amy started to protest, but Matt's rough hands gripped her face and he smothered her resistance with tender yet insistent lips. She had been on the verge of telling him that *this* wasn't the kind of closeness she meant—but then she realized it *was* what she meant. For his body communicated to her with warmth and concern what neither of them was ready to say. It had been weeks since they had loved so sweetly, and the wrenching feeling of alienation, of being apart even when they were together, was absent this time. Matt réclined on the bed and pulled Amy on top of him, soothing her with slow, sensuous kisses and gentle words, his fingertips teasing the aching, taut nipples of her breasts. Feeling hot pangs of arousal at his touch, she caressed his chest with its enticing matting of hair, kneaded his muscular shoulders and returned his kisses fully, her tongue engaging his in provocative interplay. The closeness of their melding bodies, their devouring lips and tongues, soon became unendurable to both. The lovers pulled apart just to breathe, their passion-bruised lips throbbing, their eyes locking in a torment of need in the stillness.

Abruptly, Matt tossed off the covers and brought Amy astride him.

Breathing became painful for Amy, and she felt her entire body breaking out in a flush. There was something very bonding about giving herself to him this way, both of them totally naked, vulnerable, in the streaming sunshine. Matt's eyes were everywhere, devouring her flesh, her breasts, the silken joining of her thighs. She eased herself downward and felt the hard tip of him pierce her with demanding pressure. . . .

Tasting her flesh, Matt groaned as if in pain. His eyes were dilated, dark with need as he gripped her buttocks in his strong hands. Their eyes locked passionately as he pulled her downward, impaling her with a force that was intensely pleasurable. Amy cried out in ecstasy and Matt tightened his grip on her bottom, settling her even deeper onto his vast hardness. She gasped, looking down into his possessive, burning gaze. She was on fire with him, her insides throbbing, her lungs bursting. When she whispered, "Matt," in a breathless whimper that was half a plea, he smiled back in the secret way he reserved just for her. "I'm going to drive you crazy," he whispered.

He did. With his hands kneading her hips, he rotated her slowly upon his swelling organ, and she bit her lip to keep from screaming out her delight. Never would she have dreamed that such a gentle motion could be such divine torture. When she began to move with him, the rapture was total and mind-shattering. She rode him freely, wildly, her golden hair streaming down about his face. He smiled back in transport, his hands boldly gripping and squeezing her soft bottom, then her breasts. When her movements grew more wanton, he drew himself upright with her, deepening the already unbearable friction and tension of his possession. She moaned aloud, tossing her head from side to side as his teeth nipped her rigid nipples, as his loins beat out a hard, rhythmic tattoo against the very core of her. They rocked together on the brink of madness, clinging to each other and moving forever closer, deeper, soul merging with soul. Finally, when Amy begged him with her eyes to give her release, he rolled her beneath him, kissing her with great tenderness even as his manhood brought them both to an explosive climax.

Afterward, they clung together breathlessly, still joined, their bodies damp even in the coolness. There was an air of desperation about their soft shudders and warm, wet kisses. It was as if each instinctively knew that the world was plotting to pull them apart again; each struggled to protect the other from the outside forces that sought to destroy them. The dearness of it all brought Amy to tears once more. . . .

Amy felt guilty an hour later, going fresh from her electrifying encounter with Matt to her secret meeting with Lacy. Even though she had washed and dressed, she still felt stamped with her husband's imprint. With each step, her womanhood twinged with a slight soreness that was a sensual reminder of their passionate coupling at dawn. But Amy welcomed the sensation. She wanted to remember the entire time she was talking to Lacy that she was Matt's woman now, that Lacy no longer had any place in her life. In fact, the only reason she was going to see the peddler today was to better understand her husband.

As Amy climbed the rocky, cedar-studded glade that Lacy

had chosen for their meeting, she glanced back at the sun-dappled farmhouse in the hollow below. Matt was nowhere in sight. Soon after breakfast, he had left with the horse and plow to go cultivate one of their western fields. He probably wouldn't be back until nooning, she reasoned.

Amy crested the rise, drawing her shawl tightly about her as the crisp, cedar-scented breeze snapped at her clothing. She spotted Lacy just downhill from her, sitting on an outcropping of rock, dressed in black. He was scowling and smoking a cheroot. As she drew near, he sprang up, removed his hat and smiled, stamping out his cheroot. "Mornin', sugar."

"Good morning," she replied stiffly.

Lacy eyed her speculatively, taking in her modest pale-blue wool dress, the white shawl protecting her shoulders, her blond hair pinned in a comely bun beneath her dark bonnet. His gaze came to rest upon her flushed, defiantly tilted face. "Quite a bloom on your cheeks this morning, my dear," he remarked. "Dare I hope it's your excitement at seeing me again?"

Amy gave him a quelling look and didn't answer his question. But curiosity forced her to ask one of her own, a question that had gnawed at her ever since Lacy had come to Rolla. "Lacy, why didn't you come back for me in St. Louis when you promised?" she inquired tensely.

A maddening smile spread across his dark face. "Why, darlin', I do believe you're sorry you didn't wait for me."

"I'm not in the least bit sorry!" she snapped. With stiff courtesy, she added, "But I'd like an answer to my question, please."

Still, he grinned that infuriating grin. "Well, actually, darlin', I ran into some friends who were in a bit of trouble—"

"You were gambling again," Amy cut in angrily.

He shook his head in incredulity. "Why, sugar, whatever makes you say that?"

"Don't lie to me, Lacy," she ordered through clenched teeth.

He offered her a sheepish smile and a gesture of contrition. "Truth was, darlin', I was kinda down on my luck for a few months there. I even spent a long miserable night in a jail cell in some little burg down in the Boothill Country—"

"Were you cheating at cards again?" she asked him nastily.

"Why, Amy. You are a suspicious woman," he rejoined with a grin.

"Were you?"

"Yes," he admitted at last. "Though they never could prove it," he added with self-satisfaction.

"I see. You always were quite adept at dealing from the bottom of the deck, weren't you?" Not waiting for a reply, Amy went on bitterly, "So you didn't show up to marry me because you were too busy carousing with your friends and cheating at cards, rather than traveling back to St. Louis, as you promised." She shook her head in disgust. "Too bad you escaped the hangman's noose, as well."

He scowled. "Why, darlin'! That sounds downright unforgivin'."

"And it's exactly what you deserve!" she finished with a nasty smile. "Now, can we please get down to business?"

"Business?" he inquired innocently.

"Whatever it is you wish to tell me about my husband," she retorted.

"Why, sure, darlin'." He grinned and gestured at the rocky ledge nearby. "Won't you have a seat?"

Grudgingly, Amy stepped forward and seated herself on a boulder, smoothing her wool skirts about her. "All right, Lacy. What is it you feel I should know about my husband?"

He sat down next to her, too close for comfort. But Amy couldn't move away, since she was already seated near the edge of the rock, and she feared that if she got up, it would really put Lacy off and he might not tell her what she wanted to know. Meanwhile, Lacy turned to stare straight into Amy's eyes and replied ominously, "Matt Kendall is not at all the man you think he is. You made a big mistake in marrying him, sugar."

Amy's heart hammered, but outwardly her features remained impassive. "Oh? Explain that, pray tell."

"Have you heard of Quantrill's Raiders?" Lacy pursued.

Amy scowled. No Missourian had not heard of Anderson and Quantrill, raiders of border communities in Kansas and Missouri during the war. "Yes," Amy replied. "Didn't Quantrill head up a brigade during the war that later turned outlaw?"

"Yes," Lacy concurred. Carefully, he asked, "Were you aware that your own father was a member of Quantrill's guerrilla band?"

"No!" she cried. "You mean—"

"Abel was a member, and so was your husband Matt Kendall, and so was I."

Amy tried to digest these astounding revelations, swallowing hard. "Good heavens, Lacy! Why didn't you tell me about this before?"

He shrugged. "Well, darlin', an association with William Quantrill is hardly a banner of pride for any southerner. Besides, I didn't even see your pa that much."

"But you saw Matt?"

"Oh, yes, I saw Kendall."

Amy's eyes narrowed. She didn't like the turn of conversation, but curiosity spurred her on. "Tell me what happened when the three of you rode with Quantrill."

"Well, at first, I admired Quantrill and obeyed his orders. We all did. But after Lawrence, Kansas, I left the guerrillas."

"That was the site of a massacre of Free-Staters, wasn't it?" Amy asked, scowling.

"Yes."

"Was my father involved?"

"He was there, but he wasn't involved in any of the actual killing."

"Thank heaven!" Amy replied with a heavy sigh. "Do you know what happened to my father afterward?"

"After I left the Raiders, I'm assuming your father stayed on with Quantrill, though I can't be sure."

"And Matt?"

Lacy laughed bitterly. "Oh, I'm sure he stayed on with

the guerrilla band. Wild horses couldn't have dragged Matt Kendall away.''

Amy felt the skin at the back of her neck prickling. ''What are you saying? What did Matt do?''

Lacy shook his head. ''I hate to disillusion you, my dear, but I've never known a man to be more filled with bloodlust than was your darling husband.''

Amy was horrified. ''That's a lie!''

''Is it?'' Lacy stared at her savagely, his blue eyes gleaming with bright vehemence. ''Do you know that right before I left the brigade, I watched your husband cold-bloodedly kill a Kansas woman, for no reason other than blood sport?''

''No, that can't be true!'' Amy cried.

''It's true!'' Lacy exclaimed. ''I know, because I'm the man who tried to stop Matt. And I got savagely cracked over the head with Kendall's pistol for my troubles.''

Amy stared at Lacy, thunderstruck. What he was saying simply couldn't be true—

Yet if it were true, wouldn't this explain the violence in Matt?

No, no, a voice in her head screamed, she could not believe this of her husband! She simply could not be married to a cold-blooded murderer!

''Well, Amy, what have you got to say about it?'' Lacy now challenged.

''I don't believe you,'' she exclaimed. ''And I also think you have plenty of reasons to lie to me—revenge, for one.''

''Is that so?'' he countered. ''Well, if what I'm saying isn't true, then why hasn't your husband stepped forward to tell you of his past? Don't try to convince me you haven't asked him about it!''

Amy bit her lip miserably; Lacy had her to rights there. Finally, she asked him, ''But what reason would Matt have to remain with such a gang of cutthroats?''

''That's easy,'' Lacy replied, seizing his advantage. ''Both Matt's pa and his uncle were killed by pro-Unionists in St. Louis at the start of the war. Then his ma died of the grief of it.''

"I see," Amy murmured woodenly, remembering the things Vida had told her about Matt's background.

"There's more, Amy," Lacy went on meaningfully.

"Very well—be out with it!"

"Both Frank James and the Younger brothers belonged to Quantrill's Raiders."

"Oh, my God." Realizations splintered Amy's brain at Lacy's words. She remembered snatches of newspaper articles regarding the Missouri outlaws and their background, comments made by the townfolk regarding the possible connection between Quantrill's Raiders and the outlaws active in the region now and her own questions to Matt—unanswered! Heavens! The implications of what Lacy was saying were horrible! What if . . .

Before Amy could put her thoughts into words, Lacy announced dramatically, "And now, my dear, I very much fear that your husband may have rejoined his former partners in crime."

Lacy's last comment brought Amy forcefully to her feet. "Lacy Garrett, you're a three-horned liar!" she shouted, shaking a fist at the peddler. "Matt would never join up with an outlaw band!"

"Wouldn't he?" Unruffled, Lacy joined her in a standing position. "Then why don't you go ask your darling husband to defend himself?"

"He doesn't have to defend himself to me!"

"You're scared to ask him, aren't you?" Lacy taunted. "Afraid of what you'll learn—"

"I am not!"

"Do you know where he is all the time?"

"Yes!"

"Do you keep him in sight?"

"I—well—I know where he is, and that's enough!"

"How do you know he didn't sneak off to meet his cronies this morning before you even awakened?"

"Because he was with me!" she screamed, then immediately blushed crimson, realizing she had made it clear to Lacy what she and Matt had been doing earlier this morning.

Lacy took a menacing step closer, his blue eyes gleaming,

his corded body tense with outrage. For a moment, the two merely glared at each other, and there was only the sound of the wind howling through the glades, tugging at their clothing. Then Lacy demanded, "You came to me from his bed, didn't you?"

"Yes!" Amy cried, not caring that her face was burning.

"Damn you!" Lacy growled, and crushed her to him for a savage kiss.

Amy was horrified to have Lacy's insulting mouth so brazenly clamped on hers. She struggled to push him away, beating at his back with her fists. But he seemed to take no note as he held her fiercely against him and continued to kiss her with punishing force. As his bruising lips tried to part her own, she was revolted by the mingled taste of stale tobacco and lust. When his tongue audaciously attempted to slip between her teeth, her rage spurred her to act. She drew up her foot, then brought it down forcefully on his instep.

Lacy howled with pain and released her. Before he could even contemplate taking any action, Amy had spun away from him and was tearing over the rise and back down the hillside. "You stay away from me, Lacy Garrett—you lying no-good!" she screamed back at him, not even breaking her stride as she fled as if for her life.

Yet his enraged words followed her, haunted her. "You can run away from me, Amy, but you can't run from the truth!" he shouted down the glade. "I know that animal you married, girl! And he'll break you with his bare hands!"

Twenty-four

++

St. Louis, Missouri

On a crisp morning in late March, young Hannah
Harris hurried along the bustling streets of St. Louis.
The child had already completed her first errand in
picking up Esther Harris's patent medicine at Ferguson's
Apothecary, and now she was on her way to the post office
to check for mail.

Hannah fervently hoped a letter from Amy would be in
their box. Amy had written her sister three times since she
went to Rolla, and Hannah had been aching to write back.
Yet her mother had forbidden this, stating that they had no
money to waste on postage. Well, they seemed to have
plenty of coin to spend on the liquorlike medicine her
mother gulped down each day! Hannah mused bitterly. Why
couldn't they spare mere pennies for postage stamps? Only
once had Hannah dared to point out this fact to her mother.
When she had, her mother had viciously slapped her face,
again and again, until Hannah could barely see straight. So,
for the most part these days, the little girl kept her silence
around her hateful, temperamental mother, and kept herself
busy with the laundry and sewing they took in. The chores
had doubled for Hannah since Amy left, and the child was
far from equal to the increased burden. Worse yet, in past
months, Hannah had received more than one switching from

her mother on account of her "laziness." Esther Harris was determined to use her younger daughter for every penny the child was worth, and Hannah found her mother's greed really rankled, especially since Matt Kendall had already given them enough money to provide for their basic needs.

Hannah hurried into the small, dark neighborhood post office and rushed toward their box; if she dawdled at all, it would mean a sure beating when she got home. She uttered a cry of delight as she glimpsed an envelope through the window. Hastily, she stuffed the bottle of Doctor Hammond's Stomach Bitters into her cloak pocket, then dialed the combination to their box and swung open the tiny door, extracting the envelope.

The child felt a quick twinge of disappointment as she noted the masculine handwriting and realized that the letter, addressed to her mother, could not possibly be from Amy. But then, Hannah's depression quickly changed to elation as she noted the return address: the name "Abel Harris," and the city, Chicago Illinois!

Her father had written to them!

Hannah was so exhilarated at this wonderful news, she literally jumped up and down. Finally, catching her breath, she studied the envelope with mingled awe and anticipation. The correspondence was addressed to her mother, it was true. Yet going all the way home with the letter unopened was too much temptation for the love-starved child. No matter what punishment awaited her at home as a result, she had to read this letter! She was dying to learn news of her father. Amy had spoken so often of him—how kind and gentle he was. She assured Hannah that their father had left only because their mother drove him away. Living with Esther Harris day in and day out, Hannah could well understand her father's sense of despair.

Hannah sought an isolated corner of the building, took a deep breath, then with trembling fingers ripped open the parchment. The letter's contents filled her heart with joy. Her father was coming home! Abel Harris had missed his family, and he was sorry he had ever left them! Oh, surely this would make all things right with her mother!

When she finished reading, Hannah literally skipped out of the building, her treasure clutched in hand. In her glee, she almost collided with a stylishly dressed man and his wife who were entering the edifice. "Sorry, sir, ma'am!" Hannah called out with a bright smile, and the couple laughed as the exuberant girl raced past them.

Hannah raced down Twenty-fifth Street, then tore up the steps to their weather-beaten cottage, her excitement so intense that she took no note of the carriage and team sitting in the street in front of the house. She burst in the front door, breathing hard as she hung her cloak and bonnet on a peg, then hurried into the parlor.

Inside the small, drab room, the sound of voices stopped her in her tracks. Hannah paused just inside the doorway to see Reverend Chandler sitting in the room with her mother. Both adults were sipping tea and eating rice cakes. Hannah took in the scene warily and automatically stuffed the letter behind her back.

Yet Esther had already noted her daughter's abrupt entry into the room. The old woman fixed a ferocious scowl upon her. Dressed in black, Esther appeared all the more formidable to the child. "Hannah, what is the meaning of this intrusion?"

While Hannah swallowed hard, struggling to think of a reply, the silver-haired parson turned to smile at the cowering girl. "Hello, dear. How good to see you again." He added to her mother, "Now, Esther. You know, the Good Lord could use some of that child's zeal in His work."

"Hmmph—the child's zeal, as you call it, is misdirected," Esther snorted back to her guest. To Hannah, she added harshly, "Now, sit down and behave like a lady, missy."

"Yes, Ma." Looking quite mollified, Hannah sat down in the rocking chair, secreting the precious letter beneath her.

"As I was saying, Reverend Chandler," Hannah's mother went on, "do thank the Women's Society for sending us the canned goods. It's so hard for me to support my child, me a poor widow lady. I work my fingers to the bone, but, alas. . . ." Esther concluded her lies with a melodramatic sigh, drawing a withered hand over her eyes.

Observing her mother's histrionics, Hannah burned with resentment and shame. She glanced at the crate of lovingly filled, ribbon-graced mason jars sitting on the floor near the reverend's chair. How dare her mother lie in order to steal the generosity of others, when there were poor folk in St. Louis much more deserving of the church's charity! Had her mother no pride? Well, when her father came home, he would take charge of things, and change all that!

The reverend stood up, running his hand down his jacket to smooth wrinkles and straightening his clerical collar. "Well, Esther, I've several shut-ins to visit before supper, so I'll be on my way." He smiled at Hannah. "Good day, my dear."

Cane in hand, Esther escorted the preacher out. Then she hobbled back into the parlor, fixing her venomous gaze on her daughter. Extending a threatening hand, Esther demanded, "Now, show me what you were hiding behind your skirts, missy!"

Hannah stood up, and with trembling fingers, extended the letter to her mother. "It's from Pa," she said in a small voice.

In reply, Esther hissed a stream of invective that made the child's ears burn. The woman's features were twisted in fury as she tossed her cane aside and pounced forward to tear the communication from her daughter's hands. "Why, that bastard! What the tarnation does he think he's . . ."

Esther scanned the letter quickly, her face contorting in a malice so fierce that Hannah trembled at the mere sight of it. At last the child could stand no more, and, in a choked voice, she asked, "Aren't you glad Daddy's coming home?"

Esther's gleaming yellow gaze flashed to Hannah, her eyes oozing rabid hatred. "This has been opened!" the old woman shrieked, shaking the envelope as she took a menacing step toward the little girl. "How dare you read my mail, you misbegotten, ugly little runt!"

"Ma!" Hannah cried helplessly, backing off in tears. Never had her mother directed such fierce hatred toward her. But worse horrors awaited her as Esther Harris smiled with pure malice, then tore the letter into a hundred shreds in front of her daughter's eyes. Before Hannah could react, the old woman tore across the room and tossed the remnants in the fire.

"No! No!" Hannah screamed, racing to the grate, frantically trying to snatch the blackened pieces from the coals, burning her tender hands.

Esther grabbed the back of Hannah's dress and yanked the child away. Holding Hannah just out of reach of the burning remnants, she hissed, "Watch your father's letter burn, child, just as his evil soul will burn in hell!"

"No. No," Hannah cried, tears rolling down her young, tortured face. For once, her mother's cruelties were more than she could bear, and Hannah twisted around to rail at the old woman, "You can burn his letter, but you can't stop him from coming here! And you can't stop me from seeing him, either! I'll see him. I will!"

"Brat!" Esther screamed, her eyes gleaming with brutal menace. One hand tightened on the child's pinafore, while the other savagely grabbed the child's mane of blond hair. "Defy me, will you, you stinking little snippet? I'll remedy that, missy!"

Twenty-five

❖

At the Kendall farm, the cold days of March gave way to April, heralding the advent of spring in the foothills of the Ozarks. The trees grew knotted with buds, grasses and the first sproutings of wildflowers peeked up from the glades, and life, so long held dormant, prepared itself for a full surge of energy.

Amy and Matt occupied themselves in the seasonal rush at the farm. Matt worked sunup to sundown, planting a new crop of corn, and Amy took over the yard duties he had assumed for her during the winter. She also kept the fires tended in the smokehouse, where the now-cured slabs of meat were hung to absorb a smoky flavor. Amy knew she definitely was having the easier time of it—sometimes she ached for Matt as she watched him in the distance, guiding the plow horse endlessly back and forth across a field. Once the plowing was done, Matt still had to repeat the process, this time dragging a harrow over the furrows to finish preparing the seedbed.

Lacy's accusations had been hard to forget. Sometimes when Matt wasn't in sight for hours on end, Amy fretted, remembering Lacy's charge that perhaps Matt sneaked off during the day to rejoin his outlaw friends. At such times, she would immediately scold herself for her traitorous

274

thoughts, reminding herself of what an honorable and dependable man she married.

The Kendalls went into town for supplies twice during this period, and Amy was relieved that she heard no further news of robberies in the immediate vicinity. However, she was dismayed to hear of the murders, weeks earlier, of three Pinkerton agents who had been tracking the outlaw gangs in western Missouri. The James and Younger brothers were thought to be responsible for the slayings, and it was rumored that John Younger had died following one of the shoot-outs between gang members and Pinkerton's operatives. The consensus among the farmers at Salter's Store was that the James and Younger brothers might well become even more active in the Rolla region now, as they tried to elude the extensive manhunt out west.

Thus, the subject of the outlaws and Matt's past never really left Amy's thoughts. Suspicions continued to plague her, even as she valiantly fought them and vowed to believe in her husband. She and Matt were still close physically, yet sometimes in the obscurity of the night, she couldn't help but wonder if she might actually be sleeping in the same bed with a murderer. Sometimes when Matt reached for her, she saw instead a horrible image of him with a gun against the forehead of that poor Kansas woman Lacy had told her about. Inevitably at these disquieting moments, Matt would warm her with his kisses, making the terrifying visions recede. Yet Amy's feelings were often in turmoil, and she slept fitfully, at best. When morning came and the uncertainties of the night fled, she would ask herself how the fine man she married could possibly be a cold-blooded killer. Surely Lacy had lied to her for his own selfish purposes, she would tell herself. It was Matt Amy loved, Matt she owed her loyalty to.

Despite all this, Amy still felt impelled to hear a denial of Lacy's terrible charges from Matt's own lips, and a true accounting of what had happened between him and Lacy during the war, as well. Only then, she realized, could she lay all her doubts to rest.

Amy finally gathered her nerve to approach the subject

with her husband on an early April evening, as they sat across from each other at dinner, eating ham and beans with "sock eye" gravy, a traditional Ozarks dish Nell had given her the recipe to. "I'll have to go to town to Emmett's tomorrow," Matt was remarking to Amy as he cut his ham. "Sampson's harness broke clean through while we were plowing today, and I can't get the rest of the crop in till it's fixed."

"I see," Amy murmured. "May I go with you? I need some trim for the bedroom curtains I'm making—"

"Do you, now?" Matt's head shot up, and the handsome contours of his face grew rigid at her words. Amy realized he was no doubt remembering the time weeks earlier when she unwittingly ventured into Lacy Garrett's new store.

"I—I'll get everything at Salter's, of course," she hastened to elucidate.

"Everything?" he challenged, his dark eyes regarding her sternly.

She kept her voice calm, despite her racing heart. "Yes, everything."

"I reckon you can go, then," Matt conceded, taking a sip of his coffee.

Amy bristled at Matt's arrogance, his lack of trust, but decided not to pursue those matters now. If she did, a horrible row would surely result, and she couldn't afford to divert herself, at present, from her more critical purpose. Of course, questioning her husband regarding his background might prove equally dangerous—but assuaging her doubts was well worth the risk, she decided. "Matt," she began awkwardly, "do you ever think about . . . the war?"

Her husband's eyes narrowed, and she watched his fingers tighten about his coffee cup. "That's a right peculiar question, woman. The war was ten years ago. Why are you so all-fired interested now?"

"Well, you did go off with my father, you know."

"I did."

"And you never told me much about your experiences together."

Matt shifted in his chair but said nothing.

Amy nervously played with the lace trim on her checked napkin. "You know, my neighbor back home, Vida, once told me that some of the men from St. Louis who fought for the Confederacy later joined up with Quantrill's Raiders." Finishing the bold statement, Amy quickly glanced up at Matt. Her words to her husband had been an audacious lie, since it was Lacy, not Vida, who had told Amy about the connection between Matt and Quantrill's Raiders. Yet she had to broach the subject with Matt somehow, and she couldn't dare mention Lacy's name.

Unfortunately, Matt didn't rise to her bait. His features remained impassive as he drawled, "Is that a fact?"

Amy bit her lip. Matt was obviously intent upon subverting her at every turn. "What about you, Matt?"

"What about me?"

"Did you and my father hook up with William Quantrill?"

Now Matt's countenance darkened, his expression fierce and threatening as he leaned forward. "Woman, I don't think you want to know the answer to that."

Amy's heart hammered. "But I do want to know, Matt. Please tell me."

That brought vivid color to his face. He cursed under his breath, and shook a finger at her. "Listen well, 'cause I'm not telling you this again," he scolded. "There were things that went on during that war that no decent man would discuss with his wife—and I'm not just talking about Quantrill's guerrillas, either."

"Does that mean you were involved in some of those . . . terrible things?" Amy asked anxiously.

Matt bolted to his feet, his features explosive. "Woman, you're asking questions no loyal wife would ever ask of her husband!"

And he stormed out of the room.

Amy was crushed, biting her lip as she heard his footsteps stomp off. She stared down at her half-eaten dinner, a sickening thought gripping her: if there were no truth in

Lacy's charges, why did Matt act like a man with something to hide?

During the following days, Amy did not dare again bring up the subject of Matt's past. Unfortunately, though, Lacy Garrett soon brought things to a head.

On an early-April Saturday night, Nell Stockton had invited the Kendalls, as well as half the community, to a "bran" dance to celebrate early spring and the successful planting. The event got its name from the custom of throwing bran husks on unplaned barn floors where the dancing was held. Folks journeyed from miles around to attend Nell's gathering, bringing happy spirits and covered dishes.

Since Amy's best friend was hostessing this social event, Matt knew better than to try to keep his wife home, and dutifully hitched up the buggy that crisp evening. He even smiled when Amy came down the porch steps to join him in the yard, for she looked quite lovely in the new green-and-white flower-printed frock she had sewn, the puffed sleeves and lace-trimmed boat neckline showing off her willowy torso and creamy coloring to perfection. She wore her golden hair down, the way Matt liked it, and she had spent much extra time heating a curling iron inside the chimney of a lamp, then laboriously coiling ringlets of shiny hair about her face and shoulders. Matt whistled as he glimpsed the dramatic effect, and Amy smiled back at him and said, "You look quite elegant yourself, Mr. Kendall." Matt did look quite fine in the black suit he had worn on their wedding day, his pleated linen shirt and black string cravat adding flair to the ensemble.

When the couple arrived at the Stocktons' farm, almost all the guests had already gathered in and about the large barn. As Matt parked their buggy beneath a tree, the sounds of laughter and the delicious smells of country dishes filtered out toward them. They approached the large building. Numerous colored lanterns were strung from the eaves of the barn and the outbuildings. Most of the folk were gathered in the barnyard, visiting and keeping an eye on the horde of rambunctious children darting about. At the edges of the yard, boards had been laid across sawhorses for makeshift eating tables.

Matt and Amy located Nell near the central serving table, where she was overseeing the placement of the covered dishes. "It's so good of you to invite us, Nell," Amy told her friend warmly as she placed her dish of chicken and dumplings on the oilcloth-draped table. "Seems like we haven't gotten together in ages. And you've gone to such trouble readying everything," she added with an appreciative glance at the colorful scene.

"Twarn't nothin'," Nell insisted self-deprecatingly, a twinkle in her green eyes. She looked quite comely tonight in a cheerful red-checked, full-skirted dress with long fitted sleeves and a colorful ribbon bow on the high neck. "You two kids just have a good time." Leaning toward Matt, Nell added, "Lyle and some of the others'd be right pleasured if you'd join 'em behind the barn to wet your whistle, Matt."

Matt favored the two women with a smile. "Thanks for the invite, Nell. Believe I would like to have a word with Lyle about that hog cholera I've heard they got over to Jeff City. If you'll excuse me, ladies . . ."

Matt sauntered off cheerfully, only to stop in his tracks. Amy frowned, seeking the source of her husband's resentful gaze. In the distance, she spotted a knot of pretty girls in swirling frocks, all gathered about her nemesis, Lacy Garrett! For a terrible moment, Amy was sure Matt would spin about and drag her back to their buggy. The expression on her husband's face was murderous, and his fists were tightly clenched at his sides. Yet in a moment, Matt seemed to gain control of himself. Turning to give his wife a stern, meaningful glance, he muttered, "I won't be long," then strode off toward the back of the barn.

Amy sighed heavily as Matt went off. Meanwhile, Nell exclaimed, "Whew! I never seen a man act so riled!"

"He has cause," Amy muttered.

Nell slanted a quizzical look at her friend. "You mind

explaining that to me, honey? You don't seem like the type who'd flirt with someone yer not wed to."

Amy laughed mirthlessly, touching Nell's sleeve. Although Nell was aware that Amy had been engaged previously, the two women hadn't had an opportunity for a truly intimate chat since Lacy Garrett had settled in Rolla. "I'm sorry, Nell. I didn't realize how that must have sounded," Amy explained. Taking a deep breath, she blurted, "You see, Lacy Garrett's the one I was engaged to before, back in St. Louis."

"Law's a mercy! Well, I'll be hanged!" Nell exclaimed. "You mean, he's the fella you told me about, the one that stood you up three times?"

"He is, indeed."

Nell braced balled fists on her hips. "Well, what the tarnation do you suppose that snake in the grass is doin' showin' up here in Rolla?" When Amy merely shook her head ruefully, the older woman's eyes narrowed. She inquired, "Do you reckon he's come here out of pure-dee meanness, just to stir up trouble between you and your Matt?"

"Looks that way," Amy replied drearily.

"No wonder your man's so riled!" Nell exclaimed, whistling. "Honey, I wish I'd known that before. I thought of not invitin' Mr. Garrett tonight, since I seen him and Matt givin' each other the evil eye at church. But Lyle said it wouldn't be seemly, Garrett being the only one left out—"

"Of course I understand, Nell," Amy said, squeezing her friend's hand affectionately.

"I'll tell you one thing, honey," Nell put in. "He's only actin' that ornery 'cause he's crazy in love with you."

"He? You mean Matt?"

Nell laughed, elbowing the younger woman. "Why, of course I mean Matt! You didn't think I meant slick old Garrett, did you?"

Amy smiled. "Well, I hoped not." Lacy might have

almost the entire town fooled, Amy reflected, but Nell Stockton was an astute judge of character.

"You'd better watch that 'un," Nell now went on confidentially, inclining her head toward Lacy and his throng of giggling admirers. "He's still got a yen for you, a body can see it plain as the stripes on a polecat. Though it weren't your fault, of course," the matron hastily added. "Too bad yer man don't see it that way."

"I know," Amy agreed. With forlorn hope, she asked her friend, "Did you really mean what you said just now? That you're sure Matt's"—here she paused and blushed—"crazy in love with me?"

"Honey, ever met a dog that don't like to suck eggs?" Nell chortled, slapping her thin, bony hands on her aproned skirts.

Amy laughed good-naturedly along with Nell, although inside she was still worried. "Crazy in love," Nell had said. . . . Seeing Matt's eyes moments before, she could almost believe the crazy part.

The love part she still doubted somehow.

Amy soon forgot her worries in the excitement of the occasion. Thankfully, Lacy pretty much left her alone at first, merely tipping his hat to her when she walked past him and his bevy of girls to fetch a cup of tea from one of the tables. Amy didn't doubt that Lacy was flirting with the other females in order to rouse her jealousies—and if he were waiting for her to descend like a spitting cat, he was going to have one hell of a long wait.

True to his word, Matt didn't remain long with the men behind the barn. He came back to join his wife, looking slightly flushed, his breath heavy with alcohol. As he wrapped an arm about Amy's waist and kissed her, smacking her quickly and audaciously right there in public, she prayed there wouldn't be an altercation between him and Lacy later on. Already Matt was acting arrogant and possessive, his eyes gleaming with potential menace.

At dinner, he seemed to calm down somewhat. The luscious country fare evidently had a sobering effect on him.

They sat next to a wiry old couple they knew from church. The man's hands shook with palsy and his wife cared for him with motherly concern. She said, "Here, Father, let me blow and saucer this coffee for you," preparing and handing her husband a saucerful of the steamy brew. Amy and Matt exchanged amused glances. They watched the farmer lift the saucer and swallow the coffee. Then he began to talk in a loud, discordant voice, instructing Matt regarding his farm. "Now, the next time that boar hog of yourn gets feisty and breaks down yer pen," he told the younger man, "you just come borry me castrater, son, and that'll learn that wind splitter to stay outten yer root garden."

Amy giggled at the crude rhetoric, even as Father's wife said, "Mr. Biggham, have a care! You're in the company of womenfolk now, and us having our vittles, too!"

The guests visited and ate, while a teenaged youth played haunting melodies on a homemade mountain dulcimer. After the guests had had their fill of the chicken, ham, beans and vegetables, and the last dribbling of homemade apple pie was wiped from the corner of the last mouth, everyone gathered in the barn to get down to the serious business of square dancing. Pete Sweeney, a wiry, quick-talking man who called all the dances thereabouts, took the stage on a makeshift platform at one end of the barn. He was joined by three musicians, playing the fiddle, harmonica and banjo. Thus the picking and calling began, and Amy and Matt watched from the sidelines as the townfolk hurriedly grabbed partners and rushed for the center of the well-lit enclosure. Their folk dancing had a stomping, fiercely rhythmic quality that Amy loved, and she found herself tapping her foot in time as Sweeney's nasal twang called out the first reel, "Rye Whiskey":

"I'll eat when I'm hungry, I'll drink when I'm dry;
If the hard times don't kill me, I'll live till I die."

Amy desperately wanted to join the others in the center of the barn, and glanced at Matt. Then, unfortunately, she spotted Lacy Garrett coming toward them from across the barn, a meaningful gleam in his eyes. Oh, Lord, surely Lacy wouldn't be foolish enough to ask her to dance! Before she could really contemplāte this distressing question, she heard Matt curse at her side, then abruptly her husband pulled her out into the throng.

At first, they were like two lost children out in the middle of the lively fracas, neither of them knowing what to do as booted feet and swirling skirts swept by. But soon enough, they merely started imitating the others, joining arms and stomping around in the circular pattern, singing out the chorus loudly with the rest. By the time they had started the second dance, "The Ground Hog," Amy was surprised and pleased to see Matt laughing and thoroughly enjoying himself with the others.

After five exhausting reels, the panting couple sat down on a bench at the side of the barn to rest and have some punch. Matt was laughing to Amy about one of "Father's" crusty comments at dinner, when the Rolla banker, Mr. Whitcomb, came up to them. The tall, hatless man in double-breasted sack coat and stylishly striped trousers greeted them courteously. "Evenin', Mrs. Kendall, Mathew. May I have a word with you, Kendall?"

"Of course," Matt returned politely, setting his punch aside and getting to his feet. "Pardon me a moment, dear," he told his wife.

Amy watched the two men go off to a corner of the barn. For some reason, the banker seemed quite angry with her husband now— Whitcomb's dark brow was knitted in a fierce scowl, and he was gesticulating vividly with each word. Yet Amy had little time to fret over this curious situation; she jumped as a warm hand clutched her shoulder.

"Evening, Amy," Lacy Garrett said.

Amy gasped and looked up at Lacy's flushed face. His eyes had a droopy quality that testified he had imbibed heavily this evening. His black jacket was unbuttoned, his cravat askew, and the smile he sported at her was more of a leer. He looked like the very devil lurking above her, with the lamplight gleaming in his black hair and casting sinister shadows across his angular features. Fuming at his sudden,

unwelcome presence, she wrenched herself away from his
touch, set down her punch, and stood. "Lacy, please go
away! My husband's just over there talking to the banker,
and any second now, I'm sure he will spot you."

"Then we'd best go outside, my dear," he drawled back
with a crooked grin.

"Absolutely not!" Amy hissed.

Despite Amy's protest, Lacy grabbed her hand in his
surprisingly strong grip and half dragged her out into the
cool night air. "What is it you want, Lacy?" Amy snapped,
finally managing to jerk free of him as they stood alone in
the moonlight. She might as well try to find out what this
was about, see if she could get rid of him, she told herself.

He stood across from her. "Have you thought about what
I told you?" Lacy demanded, tottering slightly.

"You mean about Matt," she said warily.

"Yes, of course about Kendall—the outlaw you married."

Amy drew herself up to her full height. "I find your
accusations . . . very difficult to believe, Lacy." Angrily, she
added, "And how do I know you're not covering up for your
own sins?"

"I'm the one who's made a clean breast of things, who's
told you everything," he pointed out nastily. "Why would I
do that if I had something to hide? I'll bet your sainted
husband hasn't told you one thing about his past—even if
you've gotten up the nerve to ask him."

Amy bit her lip. Lacy was rubbing salt in a wound now.
He used the moment to close in, both physically and
emotionally. "Amy, I've told you once and I'll tell you
again. You're not safe with that man. Perhaps considering
the robberies that have been going on in these parts, I
should inform the authorities of your husband's past activities—
for your own protection, of course."

"You do that and I'll never speak to you again!" Amy
vowed, her teeth clenched.

Lacy cursed. "Amy, don't you think you're taking wifely
loyalty to extremes, considering that you're risking your
own life in doing so?" Fiercely, he gripped her shoulders.

"I tell you, Amy, you can't trust Matt Kendall. Come away with me. I'll take care of you. . . ."

Lacy leaned closer to Amy, and, unfortunately, that was the exact moment when Matt emerged from the barn and saw the two of them. Lacy wasn't kissing Amy, but he was close to doing so, and Matt mistook the confusion on his wife's face for trembling eagerness. With a savage cry, Matt hurled himself at Lacy.

Amy gasped with alarm as she watched her husband tackle Lacy and throw him to the ground. Then she looked down in horror, watching her husband pin Lacy down, his hands at the other man's throat. Lacy's face was blood-red as he struggled futilely to disengage Matt's tenacious hands.

"No, Matt, you'll kill him!" Amy screamed. She collapsed on her knees in the dirt beside the two struggling men, frantically trying to pry Matt's fingers from Lacy's throat. But it was useless—her husband appeared possessed as he eagerly strangled his adversary, his fingers like steel tentacles on Lacy's neck. Amy's screams and pleas had no effect on Matt whatever.

Desperately, she sprang to her feet and ran into the brightly lit barn. For now, wifely loyalty had to be abandoned—in fact, she could think of nothing more disloyal than letting her husband hang for Lacy's murder! "Please, come help!" she shrieked to the dancing throng, her eyes wild, tears rolling down her cheeks. When there was no immediate reaction inside the noisy building, she screamed at the top of her lungs, "Please! My husband is killing Mr. Garrett!"

At once, the dancing ceased, amid startled gasps and thunderstruck expressions. Several men, including the sheriff, rushed outside with Amy. Matt was still on Lacy, and Lacy's legs were kicking out wildly now, testifying that he still fought for his life. Freeman and the others went straight to work, tackling Matt and trying to pull him off. Ultimately, it took four strong men, including the sheriff, to drag Matt away from Lacy. Afterward, he still struggled savagely against the restraining hands that kept him from Lacy until Sheriff Freeman pulled his Colt Peacemaker from its holster and pointed the gun at Matt's head. Amy gasped in horror, fearing for her husband's life. But thankfully, Matt at last quit fighting, though he still looked murder at everyone. Most of the townfolk had now left the barn and were gathered about the site, their shocked murmurings filling the cool night air. Lacy Garrett was still on the ground, gasping and sputtering for air.

"Mind telling me what's going on here, Kendall?" the sheriff demanded of Matt.

"That bastard was touching my wife!" Matt hissed.

"Is that so, Garrett?" Freeman questioned the fallen man.

Lacy sat up, grimacing as he gingerly stroked his bruised neck. "Yes," came his hoarse reply to Freeman.

The sheriff replaced his Colt in its holster and nodded to the other men to release Matt. "Ain't no point making charges, then, since the wrong cuts both ways. But I'm remindin' you boys to mind your manners from now on." He eyed Matt sternly. "I think you'd better gather your missus, Kendall, and head home."

"Yes, sir," Matt said.

Meanwhile, Amy approached Lacy. She had to be sure he was all right; it was a matter of principle to her. At the moment, she didn't care whether Matt was a witness to her concern or not—in fact, she was so furious at her husband right now that she was trembling. Sure, she had been outside with Lacy, but her husband's lethal reaction was totally unjustified, disproportionate. She knelt by the still-gasping man, and while she wisely didn't touch him, she inquired solicitously, "Are you all right, Lacy?"

In reply, Lacy nodded tersely toward Matt and hissed back to her, "Do you believe me now, Amy?"

Amy swallowed hard but did not reply. Her blood ran cold at his words.

"Are you coming or not, Mrs. Kendall?" Matt now barked out from above, his dark eyes gleaming with rage as he observed his wife.

Amy stood, slowly brushing dirt from her skirts as her eyes locked defiantly with her husband's. "I'm coming."

Matt strode forward, grabbed Amy's hand and tugged her

away. She exploded at him as soon as they were in the buggy going home. "Matt, how dare you! You almost murdered a man back there, not to mention humiliating me in front of the whole town!"

"You brought it on yourself, Amy," he said menacingly.

"I did not. I was just talking to the man!"

"That's not how it looked to me," he snapped.

"Well, that's how it was!" she screamed. "What on earth got into you, anyway? My God, Matt! If I hadn't gotten the sheriff, you would have killed Lacy!"

"A pity that I didn't," he snarled. Suspiciously, he demanded, "Why are you defending that skunk, anyhow? And what were you doing with him outside in the first place?"

"He—he pulled me out there to talk—"

"And you just went along, like a docile little lamb?" Matt cut in sarcastically, snapping the reins. "Too bad you're not that obedient around your husband, Mrs. Kendall."

Amy bit her lower lip in savage fury. "Matt, the fact remains that you nearly strangled him!"

"Next time there won't be a nearly."

"Do you kill men so easily?" she demanded.

"When my wife's meetin' them on the sly, I do."

"I wasn't meeting him on the sly!"

"Then why were you speaking to him at all?"

Amy drew a steadying breath. She might as well confront her husband now—things were showing no signs of improvement between them. "Matt," she began carefully, "Lacy told me some things—about your past and his, about the war. Would you please tell me what went on then?"

Matt clenched his jaw at his wife's question, and he turned rage-blackened eyes toward her. "Looks like Garrett already filled you in. Why didn't you just stay back there with your fancy man, Amy?"

His hurtful words stung, but she refused to be put off. "Because I'm married to you, Matt. And I want *you* to tell me the truth."

"Sure," he flung at her bitterly, "just as soon as you tell me the truth about what you and Garrett were doing tonight!"

"Matt, I have told you the truth! We weren't doing anything!"

"Then it looks like you and me got nothin' more to discuss, don't it, woman?"

At home, Amy wiped tears from her cheeks as she undressed for bed in her old room. There was no way she was sleeping with Matt until he gave her an apology—and an explanation. She paced miserably, endlessly reliving the nightmare at the Stocktons' farm, remembering Matt's savagery, and Lacy's horrifying words, "Do you believe me now . . . ?"

She didn't want to believe Lacy—oh, Lord, how she didn't want to believe him! Yet her suspicions remained: if there were no truth in Lacy's charges, why wouldn't Matt defend himself and tell her what had really happened in his past?

There was no more turning from her doubts and fears. Not after tonight. And one central fact jolted her the most: sometimes Matt Kendall scared her to death.

Downstairs, Matt was pacing, his boots thudding a restless cadence on the braided rug in the parlor.

Never had he lost control as he had tonight. Never had he wanted to kill a man as much as he had wanted to kill Garrett! Now, he ached to go to Amy; he knew his violence had appalled and frightened her, and he wanted to reassure her. But he was tortured by doubts. After their argument on the way home from the Stocktons, she had turned away from him, and he had watched her shoulders shake with silent sobs. He had been mightily tempted to stop the damn buggy then, haul her roughly into his arms and kiss her with all the pent-up passion in his body. Yet his suspicions held him back. Had she cried for him because of the rift Garrett had created between them, or had she cried because of the harm he had done her fancy man?

The hell of it was, he just didn't know! He strongly suspected Garrett had filled Amy's mind with lies concerning him and his past. He should set her straight; yet it wounded his pride that she would doubt him and side with Garrett instead. Watching her kneel anxiously beside that no-account had hurt and angered him beyond reason. What loyal wife would shame her husband that way, insulting him in front of scores of witnesses?

No, he'd be damned if he'd humble himself to her now. Whose side was she on, anyway?

Twenty-six

♦♦

Southern Illinois

Abel Harris sat in the passenger car of the Chicago, Rock Island and Pacific Railroad, which was heading southward from Illinois toward Missouri. As the train rattled along in the coolness of morning, Abel stared out the window, watching the blooming wildflowers and farmers out plowing. Evidence of burgeoning spring was everywhere.

He was seated next to a consumptive young man who coughed frequently, spasms racking his frail body. Abel realized many passengers would have avoided the compartment, but after having witnessed widespread suffering during the war due to consumption, dysentery and ague, Abel had no fear of becoming infected himself—indeed, he felt nothing but sympathy for those afflicted.

His thoughts turned to the past couple of weeks he'd spent in Chicago, preparing himself for his new job and the journey home. He spent a number of hours with Allan Pinkerton's young assistant, acquainting himself with the history of the detective agency, as well as with the tracking procedures followed by Pinkerton's operatives. Abel had also visited the Chicago Public Library, reading everything he could get his hands on concerning the James and Younger brothers' activities in Missouri. He would do his best now to help Mr. Pinkerton make some progress in the stalemated case.

But first he would see his family, which filled him with both anticipation and dread. Abel had sent a letter on to Esther informing her of his plans, and he had prayed his correspondence was well received. In another day, he would find out for sure. He would also find out whether his daughter would forgive him. . . .

The man sitting next to Abel now became gripped by a severe spasm, and Abel turned to pat his fellow passenger's shuddering back, noting with dismay that the poor man was coughing blood into his handkerchief. "Sir, may I get you some water?" Abel inquired with concern. "Or perhaps there's a physician on board—"

"No, no," came the weak protest as the man finally managed to catch his breath. He straightened, flashing Abel a weak smile and looking at him with listless, vacant eyes. "It's good of you to be concerned, sir. But don't mind me. There's not much folks can do for me no more. This last winter in Chicago like to kilt me."

"Aye, the winter was bitter," Abel concurred. "What is your destination, if I may ask?"

"Kansas City," came the rasping reply. "I've been visitin' with my Aunt Edna up in Chicago for the last year. But the family decided I might fare better with Cousin Betsy out in Kansas City. It's a mite warmer there, you know."

"I see," Abel murmured. He did see that the man was one of those unfortunates in life, a poor relation who could not administer to his own needs and was therefore shuttled from relative to relative.

"It don't matter where I'm heading," the man now went on in a resigned tone, almost as if he'd guessed Abel's thoughts. "I've had me this misery in my chest ever since the war. I reckon I won't last another winter, anyhow—no matter where they send me."

Abel knew better than to try to cheer the young man out of his gloomy but no doubt accurate prediction. "Aye, the war hurt so many," he murmured thoughtfully.

A silence settled between them, interrupted only by the

clickety-clack of the train on the tracks. "And you, sir," the young man finally ventured, forcing a smile. "Where are you heading?"

"To St. Louis—my home," Abel replied. "I've not seen my family since the war," he admitted.

The young man nodded, and silence descended between the two once more. No further words were necessary. Each man well knew that over the past ten years there had been so many divisions to heal—not just in the country itself, but among families, friends. . . .

Abruptly, the other man began to hack again, and Abel Harris, feeling helpless, turned to stare out the window.

And what of those that he, Abel, had left behind in St. Louis? Was Amy alive? Was she healthy? Time passed, changes occurred . . . What were things truly like at home?

"There, dear, that doesn't look bad at all," Vida Peterson said bravely to Hannah Harris, smoothing down the child's hair.

In St. Louis, the young girl sat at the dressing table in Vida's spare bedroom, staring dismally at her reflection in the mirror. Behind her, Vida forced a smile as she laid the last rag roller on the dresser tray. She then picked up the hairbrush and began to brush out the curly wisps of hair remaining on Hannah's head.

But as she worked on the girl's closely cropped locks, Vida found it hard not to succumb to the sick feeling in her heart, and burst out weeping.

Damn Esther Harris! she thought angrily. Damn the old shrew straight to hell! Vida Peterson was a devoutly Christian woman and knew it was wrong to judge others. Vengeance should be left to the Almighty's hand alone. Yet during the past two days, she had condemned Esther Harris's wicked soul to perdition at least a thousand times.

What she had done to the girl was depraved!

Two days earlier, Vida had heard Hannah's screams coming from the Harris house again. This time, she had gone over with her broom to investigate. What she saw when she stepped inside the living room had sickened her beyond belief.

Esther Harris had been going at Hannah's beautiful hair wildly with scissors, slashing off the child's locks close to the scalp. The crazed old woman was shrieking obscenities mixed with misquoted Bible passages all the while.

Vida acted at once, getting a terrified Hannah away from Esther and threatening the ranting, advancing old woman with her broom. Somehow, she managed to get Hannah out of the Harris house, and took the child home with her. She then locked the doors and comforted the hysterical girl as best she could.

Hannah was basically unharmed—but her hair was ruined. Once she calmed Hannah down, Vida had taken out her own scissors and had tried to even out Esther's butcher job. Just as Hannah was finally beginning to quiet down and breathe a bit easier, Esther Harris had appeared at Vida's door, screaming curses that would have burned a sailor's ears. As the widow and child listened in horror, Esther threatened to go to the police if Vida didn't return her daughter. The widow had of course refused to move. As soon as Esther finally left, Vida immediately dispatched a letter to Amy in Rolla telling her of the situation and begging that the young woman return to St. Louis at once.

For Esther's threat of going to the authorities was worrisome. She had come to Vida's front porch several times in the past two days to repeat her threats. Now, Vida wondered what she would do if Esther sobered up long enough to talk to the authorities. And what if, horror of horrors, Esther somehow managed to win the police over to her side? The widow could only pray that Amy received the letter right away and would come straight on to St. Louis. . . .

"My hair looks terrible," young Hannah now commented to Vida. The child was still staring morosely into the mirror, her eyes wet with tears, her lower lip trembling. "It's so short—I look like a boy!"

"No, you don't," Vida assured the child stoutly, fluffing up the child's wispy blond curls as best she could. "Why, you're the prettiest little girl I've ever seen—your hair is all gold, just like angel fluff.'' The woman squeezed Hannah's frail young shoulders. ''And it will grow, child.'' The widow's voice broke on the words. ''It will grow.''

''If Ma doesn't go at me with the scissors again,'' Hannah interjected in a trembling voice, tears now rolling down her pale cheeks again.

Vida pulled the child up from her seat and into her strong arms. ''I swear to the Almighty, child, that that woman will never lay a hurting hand on you again! Not while there's breath in my body.''

''But how am I going to face Daddy when he comes, looking as I do?'' Hannah sobbed.

''He'll love you to death, child, just as I do,'' the widow reassured her.

Hannah's trembling at last began to subside, only to begin again with desperate force as the child and her protector heard the sudden sound of wild screaming coming from the front of the house! ''It's Ma again!'' Hannah whispered to Vida in a frantic tone, her young eyes wide with terror. ''She's out on your porch rattling the screen door again! I can hear her!''

''Don't listen, child!'' Vida ordered, placing her hands over the little girl's ears. Esther's foul shrieks pierced the very walls of the house. ''Your ma will go away when she figures out we're not coming.''

''But she'll come back,'' Hannah sobbed. ''She'll come back, until—''

''Hush, now,'' Vida admonished softly, patting the little girl's back. ''Your sister is coming, miss, and she'll take care of your ma. In the meantime, mark my word, you have Vida Peterson to depend on.''

''And there's Daddy,'' Hannah reminded, looking up at Vida with new hope shining in her brown eyes. ''When he comes, I bet he'll give Ma her comeuppance.''

Vida nodded, embracing the child warmly. ''Aye, Hannah. That your pa will do, I'm sure.''

Twenty-seven

✦✦

Just before noon a few days later, Amy was outside sweeping the front porch when Lyle Stockton came galloping up on a red horse and halted in a cloud of dust. "Morning, Amy," the overall-clad man called out tensely, tipping his straw hat as he held his snorting horse in rein. The ruddy-faced farmer glanced about the landscape worriedly. "Matt around?"

"He's plowing the south field, on the other side of that rise," Amy replied, pointing in the direction Matt had taken when he left at sunup with the plow horse. "Is something wrong?" she added to Stockton.

"'Fraid so, ma'am," Stockton informed Amy grimly. "The bank's been robbed at Rolla."

"Oh, no!" Amy cried, turning white.

"At least one of the Grangers guards was kilt, too, I heard tell," Stockton went on.

"How horrible!"

"Yes, ma'am, it looks right bad. Cleaned out the safe, them fellers did."

"Was it—the James gang?"

Stockton shrugged. "Could be. They's organizing a posse in town to track them bushwhackers, and when Jeb

Bennett came by to give me the word, I reckoned your husband would want to join up, too.''

''I'm sure he'll want to help,'' Amy replied, biting her lip as she thought of Matt exposing himself to such danger.

''Yes, ma'am.'' Again, Stockton tipped his hat. ''Reckon I'll just go hunt up Mathew, then.''

Stockton turned his horse and rode off in a new flurry of dust. Amy quickly finished sweeping the porch, then sat down on the swing, nervously waiting for the two men to return. She didn't have long to fret. Soon afterward, Stockton rode back up, this time with Matt beside him, riding bareback on Sampson. Matt must have left the plow in the field in his haste, Amy reasoned.

As the men halted and dismounted in the yard, Stockton told Matt, ''I'll take the draft horse to the barn and saddle your mount, Kendall. You'd best be fetching your firin' irons.''

''Thanks, neighbor,'' Matt muttered grimly, whipping off his hat and wiping sweat from his brow as he headed for the front porch. Meanwhile, Amy still stood uncertainly by the swing. ''Amy, come here,'' Matt called as he opened the front door. ''I've got to have a word with you, and we don't have much time.''

Nodding, Amy followed him inside. In the front hallway, he hung his hat, then told her solemnly, ''Come upstairs with me for a moment.''

Again she followed her husband, wondering why he was taking her off alone this way. Things had been extremely strained between them since the night of Nell's party. Yet their marriage problems seemed petty and inconsequential now, compared with the peril Matt was facing—indeed, the entire town was facing!

Upstairs in Matt's bedroom, he opened a drawer and pulled out a leather box. Amy's brown eyes widened as Matt placed the case on his bed, opened it and drew out a pistol in leather holster attached to a handsomely tooled gunbelt studded with bullets. Putting on the belt, Matt said to her, ''Amy, the bank in Rolla's been robbed and—''

''I know.''

"I'm going to join the posse with Lyle, but I don't like the idea of you being here alone."

"I'll be all right."

Securing the holster strap about his thigh, Matt asked impatiently, "What if the outlaws head this way? With you here alone—"

"Matt, this is our home. I'll be fine."

He drew closer, a world of emotion in his eyes as he placed his hands on her shoulders. She could smell the sweat of his labors this morning, and see the tracings of dirt and fatigue on his handsome face—all of it endearing him to her. He drew a ragged breath and said, "Amy, if anything should happen to you . . . Oh, hell!" Abruptly, he pulled her into his arms, kissing her possessively.

Amy responded warmly, tears filling her eyes at the joy of being in her husband's embrace again. She wrapped her arms about him and stroked the sinewy muscles of his back. He groaned as his kiss deepened.

Yet the tender moment was short-lived, as the sound of voices arguing outside made both of them stiffen and pull apart. Amy and Matt exchanged perplexed glances. They hurried out of the room and down the stairs. Matt grabbed his hat from a peg and disappeared into the parlor to fetch his shotgun. Then he and Amy went outside to investigate.

In the front yard, they found Nell Stockton sitting in a wagon, one overall-clad boy on either side of her. Lyle was beside the wagon, his features red and clenched as he shook a finger at his wife. "If you aren't the orneriest woman, setting off by your lonesome this way—"

"I ain't by my lonesome," Nell denied stoutly. "In case you haven't noticed, Mr. Stockton, I got me two strapping boys sittin' right here beside me that say I didn't come by my lonesome, neither."

The two boys giggled, while Stockton cajoled, "Now, Nell—"

"Don't you 'Now, Nell' me, Mr. Stockton!" Nell retorted. Spotting Amy and Matt on the porch, she paused to offer the two a gracious smile. "Well, howdy, folks." As Amy and Matt grinned back and waved, Nell unceremoniously lit into her husband again. "See here, Mr. Stockton. Ain't no way I'm letting you two menfolk go off a'posse'in' and leave poor Amy here all by herself." Nell raised a Winchester rifle that had been wedged, barrel down, between her and one son. Winking toward Amy, Nell informed the men, "Why should you menfolk grab all the glory? Amy and I might just catch us a varmint or two ourselves, if'n those outlaws is nervy enough to head this way!"

Amy and Matt laughed. Stockton threw up his hands. Matt called from the porch, "Nell, I'm really glad you've come. I didn't like the idea of Amy being here all alone."

"See, Mr. Stockton?" Nell goaded her husband triumphantly.

Stockton shook his head as he helped his wife and sons down from the buckboard. "Guess we'd best ride for town, Kendall, before these womenfolk show us up good and capture the whole gang theirselves."

As the Stocktons were bidding each other farewell, Amy turned to Matt. She glanced at the Colt strapped to his hip, then back up into his troubled dark eyes. Despite her doubts, despite the distance between them these past days, the thought of him becoming hurt was unbearable. She moved closer and buttoned a button that had come undone on his red-checked shirt. "Matt, please take care," she told him breathlessly.

He smiled at her words, leaning his shotgun against the house. Donning his hat, he pulled his wife into his arms for a quick kiss. "You, too, love," he said gruffly.

While Amy and Nell settled into the kitchen and fixed dinner for the boys, Lyle and Matt rode hard for town. The scene that greeted them at the Rolla National Bank was grisly—all the front windows had been blown out when the outlaws dynamited the bank vault. The unfortunate teller who had refused to open the vault had been shot in the chest for his troubles, along with the farmer doing guard duty that morning—though Charlie Moss had gotten off one shot, grazing one of the bandits. He had given his life in the exchange, though, and it looked like three of the robbers had opened fire on him. The clerk, now at the doctor's office, was not expected to live, either, and the blood-splattered bank lobby gave mute testimony to the siege of fatal violence.

Observing the terrible scene, Matt found anger and outrage welling inside him. Charlie Moss had been a fine man, a good neighbor, and it was such a waste that he had died this way. It reminded Matt all too painfully of another time when good men had died needlessly. Yet this time, he vowed to himself, the culprits would be brought to justice.

As Matt moved with Lyle through the still-smoky building, sidestepping large shards of glass and splintered wood, he spotted half a dozen angry farmers gathered near the empty vault, confronting the sheriff and the bank president. "A pretty pass we've come to now," one irate Granger was telling the bank president. "You told us guardin' the bank would prevent this sort of thing, and now Charlie Moss is dead as a coffin nail and all our money gone, to boot!"

"Where were you when all this was going on?" another demanded of the sheriff.

Matt, observing all this, decided enough was enough. To Stockton's surprise, the young farmer went straight into the middle of the fracas. "Look, men, why should we stand around here steamin', blaming these two men who were doing their best for us, when the outlaws are getting away?"

Matt's question was met by silence. Then one of the men put in deprecatingly, "Their trail is cold by now, Kendall."

"Not so," Matt contradicted vehemently. "We can still track them, but not if we keep wasting valuable time here."

"Kendall's right," the gray-haired sheriff put in, looking extremely relieved that Matt had arrived on the scene. "This is not the time for us to fight among ourselves, men. We're going to have to pull together if we're going to capture those thieving varmints."

"All right, then, let's be about it," a bearded older man put in, shaking his fist. "I got me a good length of rope on my horse—mebbe we can git them bushwhackers strung up before sundown."

At this pronouncement, a whoop of bloodlust went up

from the enraged townsmen, and Sheriff Freeman instantly raised a broad hand to silence the throng. "Let's get one thing straight, men. If you're coming with me, it's as my posse, not as a bunch of vigilantes. There'll be no lynchings in my town. Is that clear?"

The men mumbled grudging consent, and the sheriff ordered, "All right, then. Raise your right hands, men, and I'll deputize you."

The sheriff recited the oath of deputation, which the group solemnly repeated. As the duly sworn posse headed for the door, with Matt and the sheriff leading the way, Lacy Garrett abruptly burst into the glass-strewn lobby.

Matt eyed his adversary with contempt. Lacy's face was covered with an uncharacteristic gloss of sweat, his fashionable jacket was askew and he was breathing hard. "Am I too late to join the posse, Sheriff?" the black-haired Lacy inquired of Freeman. Then Lacy spotted Matt, and the two men glowered at each other in a secretive, suspicious way.

Before the sheriff could answer, Matt growled out, "If Garrett's going, Freeman, count me out."

"Now, Kendall," the sheriff scolded, "we'll need all the help we can get with the trackin'. Cain't you boys lay aside your differences for one afternoon?"

The two rivals continued to glare at each other. Matt sized up Lacy contemptuously, his gaze darkening with surprise and suspicion as he noted a loose bandage on the peddler's right hand. "Cut yourself on a piece of glass, did you, Garrett?" he drawled meaningfully.

Lacy colored hotly and hastily stuffed his wounded hand into his trouser pocket. "Not that it's any of your goddamned business, Kendall, but as a matter of fact, I scratched myself on a nail while unpacking crates at my store."

Matt snorted his disdain, shouldered past Lacy and strode out of the building. The sheriff and the other posse members followed him, exchanging confused glances among themselves. Lacy left the building last, keeping to the rear, a vengeful expression on his dark face. . . .

*   *   *

The posse had little information to go on other than the snippets provided by the bank teller: that seven masked men had robbed the bank and they had fled to the west with their loot.

It wasn't much of a lead, but fortunately for the posse, Matt was an expert tracker. Starting at the bank, he carefully followed the tracks of the fleeing robbers down the city streets and out of the community. Just on the outskirts of town where the road narrowed into a trail winding off between closely grouped hills, Matt halted the group and dismounted. Pointing at the collection of hoofmarks in the dirt, he announced to the others, "One of the outlaws doubled back here and headed back for town. There's only six sets of hoofmarks going out into the hills."

Confused mutterings rose from the men as Sheriff Freeman also dismounted, studying the tracks. "You're right, Kendall. Looks like one of the outlaws did double back for town here." He removed his hat and scratched his graying head. "Do you suppose they split up to set us off the trail? The one who doubled back might have all the money, you know."

"I doubt that," Matt replied. "Six ain't gonna trust one with all that loot. Looks to me like the money's hightailed it out into those hills somewheres. As for the one who doubled back . . ." Matt glanced meaningfully at Lacy, who was still at the back of the group. "Maybe he headed back for town 'cause he lives right there among us in Rolla."

As shocked murmurings filtered through the gathering at Matt's astonishing accusation, Lacy Garrett spurred his horse and galloped toward the front of the posse. "I heard that comment, Kendall!" he snarled, halting his horse near Matt and the sheriff. "And I've a word or two for you, mister. Before you start pointing a finger at the rest of us, why don't you explain to us what you were doing this morning while the bank was being robbed?"

"I don't got to explain nothin' to nobody," Matt hissed back to Lacy, enraged by the man's gall.

Off to the side, the banker Whitcomb called out resentfully to Matt, "Then why are you so quick to try to lay the blame on Garrett, Kendall? First in town, and now here. I tell you, it won't wash. We all know what a fine contribution Lacy has made to our community. And he lost money in the robbery today, too—which is more than I can say for some folks I know of," the banker concluded meaningfully, staring straight at Matt.

While the other farmers nodded their agreement one to another and voiced their support for Lacy, Matt ground his teeth. The men were acting like fools, but there was little more he could say at the moment. Ignoring the cynical triumph in Lacy's gaze, Matt muttered, "You men want to track these desperadoes or not?"

He mounted his horse and headed down the trail. Shrugging to themselves, the others followed.

As the afternoon progressed, Matt earned the grudging respect of the men of the posse as he followed the bushwhackers' trail through the hilly countryside into the tortuous woods beyond. Matt discovered that the outlaws had tried every trick in the book to cover their tracks: hoofmarks that streaked for a hundred yards down a stream bank, an attempt to obscure the fact that the group had crossed over earlier; the deliberately rumpled bushes and flowers on the rocky outcroppings of the glades, attempts to trick the posse off the true trail. Matt ignored the false signals and ruthlessly followed the barely discernible markings of the outlaws' actual trail—not even a bent twig or an overturned rock in a creekbed was lost upon his practiced eye.

The robbers had had better than an hour's start on them, but Matt and the other townsmen were determined to catch up with them before nightfall. This proved extremely difficult— the day had turned misty, and the undergrowth became denser with each step the men took. Riding became impossible and the men were forced to proceed on foot, leading their horses deeper into the tangled wilderness west of town. The sprouting grasses and blooming flowers of spring served only to snarl their footsteps; even the lushly blooming dogwood, usually a feast for the eye, seemed only to further cloud the path. They sweated as they followed Matt's lead, hacking at brambles and vines with their knives and growing increasingly depressed and irritable.

The posse's break finally came about two hours after they'd left the trail and started cross-country. Matt smelled the smoke before the others did. He halted the men, and, after conferring briefly with the sheriff, he went on ahead to scout. It wasn't easy to make his way soundlessly through the brush; but finally, he came to the top of a ledge. He peered out through a camouflaging bush to note a group of six men nestled in the hollow below. The valley was filled with smoky mist, and the men were shadowy figures at best. But Matt could discern that one of them was tending a fire while several others made camp. Another member of the group, who walked with a noticeable limp, was removing two heavy white bags from one of the horses! ''Well, I'll be damned,'' Matt muttered under his breath.

The men below him were murderers and thieves, that he knew for a fact. They were part of his past, and now they had invaded his present, perhaps even his future—

No! He would put a stop to it, here and now!

He glanced about him, grimacing. It was a bad place for an ambush. The hollow was surrounded by hills, and the outlaws could choose from a number of exits into nearly impenetrable undergrowth and trees. Matt shook his head ruefully. The desperadoes had chosen their hideout well. A posse of nine could not possibly cover every avenue of escape from the small valley.

But they must try, for this might be their only chance to nab these criminals. Matt had a personal stake in seeing that these desperadoes were brought to justice, it was true; but it also didn't sit well with him that these men had robbed the folk of Rolla of all their resources. Even though he didn't feel really close to the townfolk, he admired their spirit and self-sufficiency; the citizens deserved to reap the fruits of their labors, not have them unjustly snatched away.

He quickly made his way back to the posse. ''There's six of them, just like I thought,'' he told the men tensely. ''They're in a hollow half a mile west of here. The north side is thick as a bale of hay, but maybe we could run 'em from the southern ridge. We'll need to leave our horses here and advance on foot.''

The men grunted their assent, tethered their mounts to nearby trees and checked their guns, stuffing extra ammunition into their vest pockets. The group headed out single file through the dense growth, Matt leading them off, tension and excitement rising in the breast of each man.

Soon, the men were positioned along the rocky ridge, looking down at the outlaws in the hollow below. Visibility was poorer than ever, the haze much denser now. Matt reflected dismally that considering the distance to the bottom of the hollow and the fog that had settled there like an earth-bound cloud, it would be most difficult for even an expert marksman to get off an accurate shot.

Then, disastrously, the unexpected happened. From along the ledge came a scraping sound, like a boot being dragged along a boulder. Then a rock came flying off the hillside, tumbling into the valley below.

Matt cursed under his breath as he watched the outlaws' immediate and fierce reaction. In unison, they grabbed guns and dived for cover behind boulders and shrubs. Then, as if on cue, they opened fire in a deafening blast at the ledge above them.

The men of the posse, mouthing their frustration, fired back, and for a few moments there was only the sound of gunfire pelting back and forth. Then, gradually, the men from Rolla began to notice that the answering fire was diminishing. And they realized soon after that there was no one left down in the hollow to return their fire.

''Damn!'' Matt Kendall hissed under his breath. Turning to the sheriff, he said grimly, ''We'd best investigate, Freeman.''

The sheriff nodded, informing the other members of the posse to remain where they were and hold their fire while he and Matt went down to have a look.

The two men literally crawled down into the hollow, keeping their bodies close to the rough, rocky incline, in case the outlaws had decided to turn the tables on them and pull an ambush.

When the two men arrived down in the misty valley, all signs of life were gone save for the still-glowing fire. "What do you make of this, Kendall?" the sheriff asked his companion. "They vanished like a bunch of haints or something."

Matt nodded grimly. "We'll never track 'em, not in this fog, with nightfall here in two hours or less." He gestured toward the north. "I'll wager they camped here because they've got a dozen secret paths through that thicket yonder. They're probably holed up in a cave right now, maybe within a hundred yards of us. We'll never find 'em, though."

The sheriff nodded gloomily. "Guess we'd better tell the men and head back for town. This won't sit well with them, I'm afraid."

"I know," Matt said soberly as a melancholy rain began to fall, reinforcing his feeling of impending doom.

Twenty-eight

✦✦

Toward evening, Matt and Lyle Stockton rode up through the mist to the Kendall farmhouse, tired, damp, and dispirited. Amy and Nell rushed outside to greet them. "Any luck?" Nell asked her husband anxiously. Amy knew from her discussion with Nell this afternoon that the Stocktons' meager savings had been housed at the Rolla bank. Amy assumed Matt's money was there, too, although her husband never discussed finances with her.

Stockton shook his head dismally as he dismounted. "Matt tracked 'em for us. We even found the robbers' camp and got off a shot or two. But then them outlaws gophered up somewhere in the hills west of town."

"That area is honeycombed with caves," Nell put in morosely.

The men nodded but did not speak. Further words were unnecessary. Everyone knew the outlaws were now safely hidden away.

"You men come in and have some hot coffee before you catch your death," Amy scolded.

Matt smiled down at his wife as he dismounted, and it warmed her.

Inside the cozy Kendall kitchen, the four adults sipped coffee and discussed the events of the day, while the two

Stockton boys were sequestered out in the parlor playing checkers. "Folks is in a panic in town," Lyle told the women. "There's going to be a town meeting tonight at the courthouse to discuss what should be done."

"You folks going?" Matt asked the Stocktons.

"Yessir," Stockton replied.

"Why don't you stay on for supper, then, and we'll pile everyone in the wagon and go in together," Matt suggested to his neighbors, surprising Amy. He turned to his wife. "That is, if it's all right with Amy—the extra cooking and all."

"It's fine with me," Amy responded cheerfully.

With Nell's help, Amy prepared a supper of ham, beans, corn dodgers and strong coffee. It was nearing twilight when Amy piled quilts in the back of the farm wagon and everyone boarded—the men up front driving, Amy and Nell in the back with the boys. Fortunately, the weather had cleared, and the rising stars guided their path. The women struggled to keep everyone's spirits up as they headed for town. Amy and Nell led folk songs for the boys—"Wait for the Wagon" and "Nelly Bly"—as the wagon rattled over rolling hills in the deepening chill.

In Rolla, several dozen buggies and wagons were parked around the courthouse, a tall reddish brick building on the town square. Amy glanced about at the array of conveyances, guessing that the whole community was out for the meeting.

The courtroom was overheated and crowded, and the two families barely got seats toward the back of the paneled room. Most of the attendees were plainly dressed farm folk, with the exception of several stylishly attired merchants. The feel of the room was animated and tense, the seating area humming with anxious, subdued voices.

Finally, Sheriff Freeman came forward to the podium and pounded the gavel on it. A hush fell over the room, save for complaints from a couple of small babies. The tall, gray-haired sheriff thoughtfully stroked his handlebar mustache and began. "Folks, we're gathered here tonight to discuss what happened at the bank this morning—"

"Where were you when them outlaws blew the safe and stole our money?" an angry citizen demanded, standing and interrupting the sheriff.

"Yes, where were you, Freeman?" another man cried, and a roar of assent rose from the throng of people. Amy glanced at Matt worriedly—there was an undercurrent of hysteria in the room, which was frightening her.

Luckily, Sheriff Freeman took the complaints in stride, raising a hand to quiet the throng. "Now, Hiram," the lawman told his accuser calmly, "you know right well I was minding the jail this morning. Someone had to watch them cattle rustlers I caught out near St. James last week."

The crowd hushed somewhat at this evidence that their lawman had indeed been doing his part in keeping the peace. The man named Hiram grudgingly seated himself. Freeman went on sympathetically, "Now, I know you good folks lost most of your savings today. Hell, folks, I lost every nickel I have to my name, and think of poor Henry Clark and Charlie Moss, who gave their lives for us."

Amy gasped under her breath at the mention of Charlie Moss's name. Evidently, the townfolk were also affected, for as she looked around, the citizens looked mollified, some even ashamed, their heads bowed at Freeman's words.

"There's no point hashing over what's already done, folks," the sheriff continued. "I've alerted the authorities in all the neighboring towns to keep a watch out for the robbers, and we're taking the posse out at first light to start tracking them varmints again. What we need to do now is to figure how to keep this from happening again. We need to line up more men to stand guard here in Rolla, in case those desperadoes decide to pay us a return visit."

While the townfolk listened to the sheriff attentively, Lacy Garrett abruptly stood. Amy restrained another gasp, for she hadn't even realized that he was in the room tonight. Lacy looked dashing in a black frock coat, gold satin vest and black-and-white striped taffeta cravat. Dramatically, he addressed the sheriff. "Don't you think, sir, that before we go tearing off after those outlaws again, we should clean things up right here at home?"

"What do you mean, sir?" Sheriff Freeman demanded of Lacy.

"May I address the group, Sheriff?" Lacy requested.

"Very well, Garrett, but be quick about it," the sheriff replied.

The crowd waited in hushed anticipation as Lacy slowly walked up to the front. Meanwhile, his ominous words had produced a gnawing fear in Amy. She glanced at Matt, noting that his features were gripped in a murderous scowl. Oh, dear! What was going on here?

The sheriff had now relinquished his place at the podium. Lacy cleared his throat and smiled, his white teeth flashing like those of a predator. "Folks," he began in a confidential tone, "I feel duty-bound to tell you that the way that bank job was pulled off today, ain't no doubt that it was the work of the James and Younger brothers." Lacy paused for dramatic emphasis, and a hum of frantic whispering filled the room. When the noise abated, Lacy hooked his thumbs in his vest pockets and went on with confidence, "And there ain't no doubt in my mind either that them bushwhackers had an informant right here in Rolla."

Now the buzz of worried excitement grew to an angry roar. Heads bobbed back and forth as everyone in the room questioned his or her neighbor regarding the possibilities raised by his statement. "Who is it, Garrett?" one man demanded. "Who is the lily-livered weasel?" came another insistent male voice.

Lacy Garrett's blue eyes sparkled with vengeful pleasure as he calmly raised a hand to quiet the crowd. "Just ask yourself this, folks. How did them outlaws know that our bank was guarded? I tell you, folks, Charlie Moss and Henry Clark never had a chance. I say one of our very own citizens tipped the robbers off!"

"Yes! Yes! Who was it, Garrett?" came the cries from the audience. Amy looked around until she felt Matt, next to her, grow rigid with suppressed fury. She tried to catch his eye to reassure him, but he was staring stonily ahead. She did catch the worried glance of Nell, who sat on the other side of Matt. The two women shook their heads, both

knowing of the enmity between Lacy and Matt and realizing
this situation was potentially lethal. Lacy had the all mes-
merizing charisma of a tent revivalist! Every man in the
room was now sitting on the edge of his seat, absorbing
every word the smooth-talking peddler said. "Who is the
traitor, Garrett?" a barrel-chested farmer now demanded,
even as another man called out, "We'll string up the
backstabbing coward!"

Grinning his triumph, Lacy pointed straight ahead and
said, "It's Matt Kendall!"

The crowd, well primed by Lacy, let up a roar of
bloodlust. Men sprang to their feet with fists waving. "Wait
a minute! Wait a minute!" Sheriff Freeman shouted, rushing
forward and summarily shoving Lacy away from the podium. "Hush, everyone! Sit down! Hold on, folks!" Freeman
ordered, pounding the gavel. As the crowd grudgingly
obeyed the lawman, Freeman whirled toward Lacy, saying
nastily, "Garrett, you got no call to make charges like that!
Not without proof!"

"I got proof! Kendall there rode with Frank James and
William Quantrill during the war—just like he rode with the
James brothers today!" he shouted triumphantly.

An enraged outcry spewed forth from the crowd as all
eyes in the room turned suspiciously toward Matt, sitting in
stony silence. Meanwhile Freeman called out, "Is it true,
Kendall? Did you ride with Quantrill during the war?"

Abruptly, Matt stood, the expression on his face so fierce
that a hush fell over the crowd. "Yes," he said simply.

"String him up!" someone screamed as pandemonium
erupted in the room, all the men springing out of their seats
once again.

"No! No!" Amy cried, now terrified, bolting to her feet
to defend her husband.

"You sit down," Matt growled to his wife, even as
several angry men who had been sitting nearby moved
menacingly toward him.

"Hold it, boys!" Lyle Stockton shouted, also on his feet
now, his broad, sunburned face livid with outrage. As the
advancing men paused, Stockton argued, "Kendall here is

my neighbor, and a finer man I've never known. Tell me, if he's one of the gang members, then how come he helped us track them outlaws today?''

Stockton's words made the men back off slightly, exchanging puzzled glances. Amy heaved a sigh of relief as the din in the room died down, as she heard several murmurings of agreement filter through the assemblage. Lyle Stockton had spoken up not a moment too soon, she realized, for mere seconds earlier she had spotted her husband's fingers moving treacherously close to the gun he still wore strapped to his thigh!

Yet Amy's relief was short-lived, as Lacy Garrett, still at the front of the room, ruthlessly pointed out, ''Sure Kendall helped us track 'em today, to cover his own guilt. Just remember that he's the one who let 'em give us the slip, too.''

A collective gasp went up from the throng as the fashionably dressed banker Whitcomb bolted to his feet. ''I think Garrett's right.'' Turning to Matt and giving the younger man a resentful look, Whitcomb demanded, ''Tell me, Kendall, if you didn't know about the robbery, then why did you withdraw all your funds from Rolla National Bank two weeks ago?''

At Whitcomb's words, the crowd lost all control, turning into a yelling, fist-waving mob. Amy's hand flew to her mouth in horror as things began happening so fast she could hardly keep track. Her husband still stood in murderous silence, refusing to say one word to defend himself, as several screams of ''Let's hang him!'' shrilled forth. Several men moved closer to Matt, then stopped abruptly when the sheriff suddenly shouted, ''I'll shoot the first man who tries to harm Kendall!''

A deathly silence fell over the room. All eyes turned to Sheriff Freeman, who stood at the front of the room with his Colt Peacemaker drawn and cocked. But then, disastrously, Lacy Garrett lunged at the sheriff and grabbed the lawman's pistol, yelling to his supporters in the crowd, ''Get Kendall, boys!''

Amy screamed as the men once again rushed toward

Matt. She saw her husband grab for his gun. But then Matt looked down, thunderstruck, at his empty holster. At that very moment, an angry shot rang out in the building.

The silence that followed was unearthly. Everybody in the room seemed frozen in place as every eye in the room cautiously turned toward the back, where a puff of black smoke slowly wafted toward the ceiling. When the smoke cleared, Nell Stockton calmly blew on the pistol in her hand, recocked it, and stepped out into the aisle. Pointing the gun squarely at the middle of one of the men who had come after Matt, she asked calmly, "Care to come any closer, Claude McGowan, you old toad?"

The fleshy man in tattered overalls actually blushed, shaking his head and backing away from the deadly earnest woman who held a gun on him.

"All of you, git in your seats!" Nell barked to the throng, heading purposefully toward the front of the room. As she strode down the aisle, pistol in hand, the white-faced men dived for their chairs. Meanwhile, at the podium, Sheriff Freeman had grabbed his gun away from a very stunned looking Lacy Garrett.

Nell laid her gun on the podium and took up the gavel. "You folks should be ashamed of yourselves," Nell scolded to the crowd, "believing this here lyin' mesmerizer." With a threatening wave of the gavel at the much sobered peddler, Nell continued, "You folks well know there's bad blood between Garrett here and Matt Kendall. Yet just because Mathew's on the quiet side, not always flappin' off at the mouth like the peddler man here, you have to go believe this no-account tumbleweed. Hell, folks, Garrett ain't even been in our town two months, and already you trust him more'n the Good Book." Shaking the gavel, Nell went on, "By thunder, we might just as well say one of the robbers was you, Dave Ugghams, or you, Wily Finch, or you, Silas Evans!" Nell made appropriate gestures toward the men mentioned, and there was many a shamed male face out in the crowd.

"Now, I know you folks is purt near wrung out over losing your savings," Nell went on placatingly. "Lyle and I lost everythin', too. But just 'cause Matt Kendall here was smart enough to see it coming and move his money somewheres else don't give you no call to lynch this fine man.''

"But he rode with Frank James during the war!" came one still-indignant male voice.

"There's many a Missourian rode with Anderson or Quantrill back then," Nell retorted to the angry citizen. "Just 'cause a man lives in the woods don't make him a polecat."

Mumblings of assent rose from the crowd as Nell went on, "But let's ask Mathew, anyhow. Let the man speak for himself." Grinning, Nell called out to Matt, "Kendall, did you rob our bank today?"

Matt stood, a smile actually pulling at his tight mouth. "No, Nell."

Several people laughed, and the tension in the room lessened. "See, there you have it—straight from the horse's mouth." Nell pounded the gavel for emphasis. "Case closed."

With those words, Nell laid down the gavel, picked up Matt's gun and retreated. A very relieved-looking Sheriff Freeman took the podium. "Folks, I'm calling a brief recess. Then we'll get on with the rest of our business."

As the people milled about during the recess, Nell rejoined her husband, sons, and the Kendalls, replacing Matt's gun in his holster. "Ma! You were great!" the boys chimed in in unison.

"You always got to show me up, don't you, woman?" Lyle Stockton demanded, but he grinned and affectionately wrapped an arm about his wife.

"Nell, how did you learn to shoot like that?" Amy asked.

"I told you, honey, when Lyle and I was first married, I had to chase many a skunk out of the house."

Everyone laughed, except for Matt, who remained thoughtfully watching Nell. Meanwhile, Sheriff Freeman walked up. "Sorry, Kendall," the lawman told Matt sincerely, giving the younger man a sheepish look and shaking his hand. Clearing his throat awkwardly, the sheriff added,

"Say, would you folks mind going on home before we resume?"

"You're damn tooting we'd mind!" Nell put in, hands on her hips.

"Please, folks," the sheriff reasoned. "Nell's got things pretty well calmed down for now, but I'm still afraid there could be more trouble later on this evening. These folks are really hurting," he finished lamely.

"Then why don't you make that snake Garrett leave?" Lyle Stockton demanded.

"I am making Garrett leave," the sheriff explained simply.

"You orta slam that three-horned liar straight in the poke, the way he pulled rank on you tonight," Nell pointed out to the lawman.

Freeman shook his head ruefully. "That won't solve nothin', Nell, only put a new burr in the britches of most every man here tonight." He gave the two families an openhanded gesture. "It's best we let it lay, folks."

Nell nodded. "Much as I hate to admit it, I think you're right, Walter." She glanced speculatively at Matt. "What do you say, Matt?"

He grunted. "I don't know why we came here in the first place." Looking thoroughly disgusted, he turned and strode out of the room.

Amy and Nell exchanged sympathetic glances as Matt walked out. The sheriff tactfully retreated. As the two women hastily gathered their shawls and reticules, Lacy Garrett passed by. Amy didn't see him at first, as he placed his hand on her shoulder and said, "Amy, I—"

She whirled, spotted Lacy and, without even thinking, slapped him so hard across the face that he actually recoiled. Without a backward glance at her former fiancé, Amy grabbed her things, pivoted hard and left the room.

The Stocktons followed her. "Wish Mathew coulda seen that!" Nell called out to Amy, whistling under her breath.

"I doubt it would have made any difference," Amy muttered back.

Moments later, the two families were somberly quiet as the Kendall wagon rattled out of the dark town. Nell had insisted that Amy and Matt sit up front together on the return trip, while she and Lyle sat in the back with the boys. Yet Amy found her closeness to Matt to be of little help, since he did not so much as glance in her direction.

As they clattered down Springfield Road in the moonlight, Amy finally gathered the nerve to speak. "Oh, Matt, I'm so sorry! That was so scary back there."

Her husband said nothing, working the reins, his features grim in the wavering yellow lantern light.

"Matt, the people didn't mean it," Amy cajoled. "It's just like the sheriff said. They lost everything . . ."

He said nothing.

"Matt . . ."

"What?" he finally snapped.

Amy took a deep breath. "Why didn't you defend yourself tonight?"

"Defend myself?"

"I mean, when Lacy said those horrible things, you just stood there, saying nothing. You wouldn't even let me say something in your behalf."

For a moment, he was silent, his jaw savagely clenched. Then he turned to her with eyes blazing and roared out, "I don't need to defend myself, woman—not to you or to anyone! And I don't need you doing it for me, either!"

"Matt! Please!" Amy begged, embarrassed by his outburst, which she was sure the Stocktons heard. "I just mean . . . When are you going to tell me the truth about your past—the grudge between you and Lacy?"

"You seem to have it all figured out—you and the rest," he retorted bitterly.

Amy mentally flinched at his cruel tone, realizing at last how hurt he was by what happened. But it wasn't fair that he try to lump her with the hysterical lynch mob back at town, just because she'd asked him to tell her the truth about his background! It wasn't as if she were accusing him of being involved in the bank robbery—indeed, she found Lacy's accusations tonight absurd and contemptible. Matt would never turn on his own community that way, betraying fine people like the Stocktons! Patiently, she told her husband, "Matt—you're being unfair. I'm not like the others. And just like I told you, I really am sorry about what happened tonight."

He turned toward her almost violently. "Are you? I saw you staring at Garrett tonight! Couldn't take your eyes off him, could you? Oh, I'm sure you're sorry—damned sorry you didn't wait for your fancy man in the first place!"

"Matt!" she cried, crestfallen, feeling as if she were conversing with an utter stranger as she glimpsed the wild violence in her husband's dark eyes. Merciful heavens, what had happened? Had Matt somehow mistaken her horror and amazement at Lacy's behavior for some kind of perverse fascination? Well, it wasn't true, and it wasn't fair! She opened her mouth to defend herself, then clamped her lips shut, realizing that it was useless.

When he halted the wagon in front of the farmhouse, Matt shocked Amy by turning to address Nell. "Would you mind taking Amy home with you for a couple nights?"

"Matt!" Amy cried.

Still ignoring Amy and looking at Nell, Matt went on, "I'm going to track the outlaws, and I don't want Amy sleeping here alone."

"You're going tracking at night, Mathew?" Nell questioned sternly.

Matt shrugged. "It's a clear night, and the moon is full."

"Hold up a bit, son, and I'll go with you," Lyle Stockton offered.

"No, Lyle, someone needs to stay with the women and your boys during the night. Besides, tomorrow you can tell the posse I'm out tracking and maybe"—he smiled ruefully— "they won't shoot at me if they spot me."

"But Mathew, you can't capture those outlaws alone," Stockton reasoned.

"I can locate them and double back for help, if necessary," Matt maintained. He jumped to the ground and offered an assisting hand to Amy. To Stockton, he added, "Sooner or later they'll have to come out of their hole in those hills, and when they do, I'll be waiting."

"Matt, please don't go!" Amy cried as her husband helped her to the ground.

Matt grabbed one of the two lit kerosene lanterns that were hanging from the wagon. "You go home with Nell," he scolded her, summarily turning and walking off toward the barn.

Amy stood in tears as Nell came up to wrap a motherly arm about her shoulders. "Let him cool down, honey," she advised. "He'll be home before you know it."

"No," she protested. "I can't let him go—not like this."

Amy hurried after Matt into the barn. She found him in one of the stalls, putting a blanket on Ginger's back. "Matt, please don't go," she repeated breathlessly as she approached him. "You could be killed!"

She paused a few feet away from him and he turned to look at her, his features softening somewhat as he glimpsed the fear in her eyes. "I'll be careful," he said rather gruffly. "Anyhow, it's high time you found out you've been distrusting the wrong man."

Amy quickly stepped closer, placing her hand on Matt's sleeve. "Matt, you're wrong," she insisted. "If I was staring at Lacy tonight, it was only because I was totally horrified and stunned by what he did. I'll never forgive him for putting you in such danger. And—and you have no idea how badly I feel about all this," she continued in an emotional tone. "If I hadn't known Lacy before, he never would have said those things about you tonight. I'm sure now that Lacy only made those terrible charges to force a wedge between us. And it's worked like a charm, hasn't it?" she concluded bitterly.

By now, Matt looked both amazed and moved by his wife's perceptive words. "Maybe so," he conceded. "But I still got to—"

"You don't have to go off half-cocked in the middle of the night to prove anything to me, Matt Kendall," she cut in fervently, her hand tightening on his arm, her eyes bright with vehemence. "Why won't you believe me?"

He stood scowling at her for a long moment, obviously at war with himself. Finally, he gently disengaged her fingers from his arm. "Amy, you've got to understand. This thing between Garrett and me—it's gone too far this time. It's not just about you anymore, it's about the whole damn town. I do have something I've got to prove—to all of them this time." He turned away decisively to pick up the saddle, then hoisted it onto Ginger's blanketed back.

Amy helplessly watched him tighten the girth on Ginger's saddle. She knew there was nothing she could say to change his mind. Still, when he clutched the leads on Ginger's bridle and turned to lead the horse from the barn, she pleaded, "Matt, please don't go."

He turned, and they stared at each other for a long, anguished moment. Then, abruptly, he dropped the leads and pulled her to him for a crushing kiss, his arms trembling about her with the intensity of his need. "Promise me you'll go home with Nell," he scolded softly, his eyes dark and deeply troubled above her.

"I promise," she whispered back.

"When I get back, we'll talk," he vowed in return. "And I *will* be back," he added, brushing a tear from her cheek with his thumb.

Amy nodded. For her, at that moment, it had to be enough.

Twenty-nine

†

Amy spent a fitful night at Nell's, worrying about Matt. Early the next morning, she asked Lyle Stockton to take her back to the Kendall farm. She wanted to be there when Matt returned, even though he probably wouldn't come home for another day or two. She felt a bit guilty about going back after promising Matt the night before that she'd go home with Nell. But she rationalized that she did not promise her husband how long she'd stay with the Stocktons. Besides, Matt's farm was her home now, the place she belonged.

Lyle Stockton reluctantly agreed to escort her home, and, after breakfast, the worried young wife hugged Nell goodbye and left with Lyle. Back at the cold, deserted farmhouse, Amy lit a fire in the grate, then puttered around doing chores, trying to keep her mind off her apprehensions regarding Matt. She comforted herself by remembering his promise to her the previous night, that when he returned, they'd at last talk. Amy was sure she and Matt were finally within range of getting things worked out between them. If something happened to him— She couldn't even think about it. Amy cursed Lacy Garrett for the thousandth time—for exposing her husband to near-death, and for making Matt feel he had to go out and prove his innocence to the town!

Amy's spirits soared at midmorning when she heard the sound of a horse approaching. She put down her mending and rushed out onto the front porch, only to watch Lacy Garrett gallop up in a cloud of dust. She seethed, her fists balled on her hips. If only Matt hadn't taken their guns— Amy would give Lacy a worse scare than Nell had given him last night! That is, if she could figure out how to fire a gun at all.

"Lacy Garrett, you get out of here!" Amy cried before Lacy had even stopped his horse. "How dare you come to this farm after what you did last night!"

Undaunted, Lacy dismounted and headed for the porch. He doffed his handsome black felt hat and casually flicked dust from his elegant brown frock coat and buff-colored trousers. "Where's your husband this morning, Mrs. Kendall?" he inquired with blue eyes gleaming.

"Not that it's any of your damn business, but he's out tracking the outlaws, thanks to your lies last night!" Amy snapped back, fuming. "Now, get off our land, Lacy Garrett!"

Garrett whistled at the venom in Amy's tone. "But darlin'," he cajoled, "I've brought you another letter from Mrs. Peterson. Don't you want to see it?" Grinning, Lacy pulled an envelope from his breast pocket and approached Amy, the letter extended like a peace offering.

Biting her lip, Amy snatched the envelope from Lacy's fingers and tore it open. She hated having to tolerate his presence, but, for the moment, she had little choice. "Oh, Lord, it's probably about Hannah," she muttered under her breath.

As soon as Amy spotted the uncharacteristically rushed handwriting in Vida Peterson's brief note, she knew something was terribly amiss. She quickly read the note, her mouth falling open in horror. "My God!" she gasped. "I must go home at once. Ma went on a rampage, cutting off Hannah's hair, and threatening to kill my little sister!"

"Let me see that!" Lacy cut in, grabbing the letter from Amy, his dark brow knitted in a fierce scowl. He scanned the correspondence hastily, then whistled under his breath. "Good Lord! Mrs. Peterson says here that she's keeping Hannah at her house for now, but she doesn't know how much longer she can hold your ma off." Lacy shook his head. "Poor Mrs. Peterson. She says your ma has threatened to go to the police to get Hannah returned."

Amy fought back tears at this disastrous turn of events. Esther had obviously gone totally insane, and poor Hannah was in terrible danger! "Surely the police would realize Ma's in no shape to care for Hannah," she said, thinking aloud.

But Lacy shook his head grimly. "Don't delude yourself, Amy. Your ma can put on quite a respectable act when she wants to."

Amy nodded dismally, remembering how her mother had manipulated the Methodist minister into giving the Harrises much more than their fair share of church resources for the needy. "Why do you suppose Ma cut off Hannah's hair?" she asked Lacy, still bewildered by the turn of events.

"Who knows?" he replied, shrugging. "Maybe the poor child spilled the soup or something." He studied the letter again. "All we can do is to return to St. Louis at once, just as Mrs. Peterson asks."

"We?" Amy asked, her voice rising as she again remembered Lacy's treason the previous night.

"Amy, you can't go to St. Louis alone," he scolded.

"And why not?"

"You—you'll need protection, with outlaws in the region and all," he reasoned, shifting his weight rather awkwardly. "And besides, what if your ma gets violent? You and Mrs. Peterson won't be able to hold off that madwoman by yourselves. You'll need a man."

Amy bit her lip—Lacy had a point, though she seriously doubted his motives were noble. "Well, I'm sure as Sunday not going anywhere with you," she told him adamantly. "I'll wait for Matt."

Lacy snorted, glancing around impatiently. "You'll likely

have a long wait. Your saintly husband has no doubt joined up with his bushwhacker friends again.''

That did it! Amy's blood boiled. ''Lacy Garrett, that's a bald-faced lie, and you can get the hell off our property!''

''Are you sure it's a lie?'' he taunted.

''Yes—you scheming liar!''

Garrett took a menacing step closer, his expression immutable. ''Look, Amy, I said what I said last night to protect you and this community.''

''Hah! You said what you said because you hate Matt Kendall. And the feeling is mutual—from his wife, too!''

Lacy might not have heard her, for all he noted her outburst. ''Come on, Amy, you're wasting time. Pack your bag and I'll take you to St. Louis.''

Still seething, breathing hard, Amy studied Lacy incredulously. It occurred to her that he seemed rather nervous, very antsy to leave for St. Louis himself. Several times during their conversation, he had glanced furtively over his shoulder, and he kept shifting from foot to foot as if ready to spring off the porch. ''Tell me, Lacy, why are you in such an all-fired hurry to leave Rolla?'' she demanded. ''Could it be you're the one with something to run away from?''

Lacy's blue eyes gleamed with resentment at her words. ''Blast it, Amy, I'm offering to take you to St. Louis because I still care about you—and your sister. But my patience is not limitless. I don't have to stand here and be insulted by you.''

''Does that mean that you're finally leaving?'' Amy inquired nastily.

''So be it, woman.'' Lacy stuffed Vida's letter into Amy's hand, clapped on his hat, then turned on his heel and strode down the steps.

Amy watched Lacy ride off with a gleam of bitter triumph in her eyes. Then her thoughts quickly turned back to her sister. What was she to do?

She would have to go to St. Louis, she decided. But the question was, when? She could wait for Matt, of course.

But he would likely be gone at least another day or two. Could she afford to wait that long?

She scanned Vida's letter once more, noting the desperation revealed by the widow's tone. She shook her head grimly. Amy feared for Hannah's life. She was doubly alarmed by the fact that several days had passed since the letter had been posted. No, she could not afford to wait another minute before leaving. She would have to go to Rolla and take the next train back to St. Louis.

Amy rushed inside the house, her mind a maze of confusion and apprehension as she tried to plot her course of action. First, she would need money. She rushed into the kitchen and hurried to the sugar bowl, grabbing several dollars in coin that she'd managed to save from the grocery money Matt had given her over recent months. She'd been setting aside the coin a little at a time in order to buy him a birthday present next summer, and now she thanked God that there was enough there to secure her ticket home.

Amy went upstairs, packed a bag, then dressed in the bustled traveling outfit she had worn on the train coming out from St. Louis several months before. She decided she would ride Hannah's pony, Sundance, into town; the colt was almost fully grown now, and easily bore her weight.

Just before she left, Amy rushed into the parlor, grabbed a pen and paper, and scribbled Matt a hasty note: "Have gone to St. Louis. Hannah in terrible danger. Will explain later. Love, Amy."

Though it was awkward for Amy to ride Sundance into town, trying to balance both herself and her portmanteau on the saddle, the journey proceeded without incident. In Rolla, Amy boarded her horse at Emmett Teague's livery; then she hurried for the railroad station. She discovered to her immense relief that a train would be coming through Rolla within a quarter of an hour bound for St. Louis. She bought her ticket and left the depot just as the smoke-billowing engine chugged into the yard.

The train was making a brief stop, and thus Amy boarded

just as the other passengers were leaving to stretch their legs on the nearby wooden ramp. She sat stiffly in a seat near the window, watching the passengers mill about outside and worrying about her sister and husband. What would happen when Matt came home and found her note? Would he leave to come join her in St. Louis? Perhaps she should have suggested he do so in her note. But she had been so frantically rushed back at the house.

Amy began to feel somewhat better as the passengers started to reboard the car and the engineer blew the whistle. Then her momentary relief was shattered as a familiar male voice addressed her from the aisle. "Afternoon, darlin'."

Amy turned, horrified, to see Lacy Garrett slip into the seat beside her. "Lacy Garrett, what do you think you're doing here?" she demanded, appalled.

"Why, escorting you to St. Louis, sugar," he replied with an infuriating grin. "Surely you didn't think I'd really let you go off traveling all by your lonesome, a respectable little lady like you?" He winked at her. "Even good old Mathew wouldn't approve of that."

"How did you know I was taking the train?" she snapped.

"How else would you get to St. Louis?" he replied with a laugh. "I figured you'd grab the next Flyer out of here. But I did ask the ticket agent if you'd boarded yet, and he was right helpful."

"Well, you can just jolly well ask him for your ticket money back! Get out of this seat!" she hissed through clenched teeth.

"Can't, darlin'," he replied, flicking a speck of lint from one of his stylish velvet lapels. "It is a public train, you know, and I got as much right to be here as you do. As to where I'm sittin' "—he grinned that maddening grin again—"in case you ain't noticed, this car is plum full up, sugar."

Amy glanced around, noting with intense frustration that he had spoken the truth. The car was unusually crowded. Damn him! Lacy had her boxed in at every turn. She decided her only recourse was to ignore him, so she turned to stare moodily out the window as the train pulled out.

Amy continued to seethe as the train left town and

chugged through the countryside. It infuriated her that, after all he'd done, Lacy was still blithely assuming he could somehow break up her marriage with Matt. How she hated him at this moment! She knew she must keep her wits about her, and she tried to calm herself by studying the countryside they were passing through. The glades were quite lovely, with their rainbow assortment of blooming flowers, the sweet scent of nectar and fresh cedar sweeping in the window. Yet even the beauty of spring could not cool the ire boiling in Amy's veins.

"Should be in St. Louis well before sundown," Lacy remarked conversationally after a while.

"Good—I can't wait to be rid of you," Amy couldn't resist replying.

"Look, Amy, how long are you going to keep up this wounded-deer act of yours?" he demanded irritably.

"It's not an act!" she retorted.

"You know you're being damn foolish," he informed her resentfully. "You'll never be able to handle that ma of yours alone. And have you forgot the bushwhackers hittin' every train and bank in these parts?" Hooking his thumbs in his satin vest, Lacy concluded self-righteously, "I should think you'd be grateful to have me along."

"Grateful?" she cried. "After what you did to Matt last night?"

Too angry to say another word, Amy turned away from him and again moodily studied the landscape. Lacy glowered at her for a moment, then turned resignedly to start a conversation with a man across the aisle from them, a bullwhacker who had spent a number of years taking supplies to railroad crews in the west, before the transcontinental lines sealed up the continent.

Half an hour later, as they were approaching the town of Sullivan, Amy heard gunfire coming from somewhere in the distance ahead of them. She gasped, straining to see outside her window. But since their car was near the end of the train, and they were just navigating a rise, she could see nothing but the car ahead of them.

She turned to Lacy with alarm. "Are those guns I hear?"

Lacy nodded grimly, his features white. He stood, leaning over her to peer tensely out the window. By now, most of the other men in the car were doing the same thing, and harsh whispers of concern filled the air. "Blast it, someone's firing at the engine," Lacy told Amy over his shoulder. "I can see them now, up at the next curve. Damnation, they're masked! It must be bushwhackers!"

Before Amy could react, she heard the ear-splitting screech of the train's brakes, and she was forced to hang on to the seat in front of her for dear life as the heavy car lurched to a stop. Despite the jostling, she somehow managed to stay in her seat as Lacy fell back into place beside her. Once the train had come to a complete halt, the passengers waited in tense fear. After several seconds, they heard the ominous jingle of spurs, and a collective, hysterical gasp went up from the group. Three men wearing bandanna masks and brandishing pistols burst in through the back door of the car. At Amy's side, Lacy said quickly and harshly, "Don't move, and do exactly what they say!"

The three gun-wielding bandits quickly strode to the center of the car. All were dressed in nondescript dark jackets and trousers and wore black, wide-brimmed hats. Two of the outlaws were of medium height and appeared fair, with blue eyes, whereas the third man was much taller, dark and menacing with crafty eyes that peered out, cold and black, over his red and white bandanna. They were a deadly-looking lot, Amy reflected sinkingly, her heart thumping with wild fear. As the frantic whisperings of terrified passengers filled the car, the shortest member of the trio of bandits announced in a near-friendly, nasal twang, "All right, folks. As I'm sure you've conjured, this here's a robbery. Don't none of you get smart, now—just toss yer valuables friendly like into my partner's hat, and we'll be on our way."

While the two shorter bandits guarded the passengers, the man with the black eyes went down the aisle with hat extended. By now, several women were crying as they removed rings and other jewelry, while the male passengers grumbled their outrage but complied. Then, suddenly, there was a deafening explosion somewhere in the train ahead of them, and the entire car rocked! The car righted itself quickly enough, yet in the resulting confusion an enraged older gentleman at the back of the car surged to his feet with derringer in hand and shouted to the robbers, "I'll learn you a lesson, you blackguards!"

Gunfire erupted inside the passenger car. There were four or five shots in all. Lacy literally dived on top of Amy as soon as the first bullet flew, pressing her body close to the seat to shield her from harm as additional gunblasts spewed forth, loud and horrible amid the shrieks of the passengers. Finally, there was a sickening silence, interrupted only by one woman's hysterical sobbing.

"Now, just look what you made me do," one of the bandits said disgustedly.

At last, Amy and Lacy dared to look up through the acrid, eye-stinging smoke. At the back of the car was the old gentleman who had dared to defy the outlaws. He was sprawled on the floor, in his wife's arms, a look of blank shock on his pallid face as he watched his lifeblood spread quickly and remorselessly over his brocaded suit vest. Meanwhile, his wife shrieked at the robbers, "Bastards! Bastards!"

Ignoring the woman, the bandit leader gestured threateningly to the crowd with his pistol and drawled, "All right, folks. Fork over. We ain't got all day. And if you don't want to end up like Dad over here, no more funny stuff, you hear?"

There was ominous silence in the car as the tall, black-eyed bandit continued down the aisle with hat extended. For a few moments, all that could be heard were the muted sobs of the women, the grating jingle of the desperado's spurs and the clink of watches and jewelry being tossed into his hat. Amy dared to lean toward Lacy and whisper in his ear, "Why did we hear an explosion a minute ago?"

He whispered back, "They doubtless blew the safe in the express car. We must be carrying a gold shipment bound for St. Louis."

Amy shuddered as the bandit collecting the valuables strode closer to them. Would he be angered that she had no money to give him? She had her wedding ring, which she would give up only if there were a gun at her head—which there might well be, soon. She prayed the robbers would be satisfied with whatever cash and jewelry Lacy had.

But just as the dark-eyed outlaw paused by their seat and Lacy reached inside his breast pocket to withdraw currency, the outlaw shook his head. "Afternoon, Garrett," he muttered simply, and went on his way.

Amy was astounded. Quickly and fearfully, she glanced about the car, feeling relieved to note that at least none of the passengers nearby had seemed to note their good fortune. As soon as the bandit was out of earshot, she hissed to Lacy, "Why did that man pass us by?"

Lacy replied in a terse whisper, "That was Charlie Pitts. The ones standing guard yonder are two of the Younger boys. Didn't I tell you I knew them during the war, just like your darling Matt did?"

Amy bit her lip, too frightened of the bandits to further pursue the matter at the moment.

At last the men left the train car, and looking out the window, Amy watched six men ride off with bulging moneybags slung across their saddles, firing their guns into the blue skies and whooping their delight.

Within minutes, the conductor and the engineer burst into the passenger car to check on everyone. The unfortunate old man who had defied the outlaws was now dead at the back of the car, his gray eyes open but unseeing. The passengers were informed that the guard in the express car, who had tried to defend the gold, had also been killed by the outlaws. The conductor appointed half a dozen men to remove the corpses to a freight car, even as several of the women huddled about the sobbing, red-faced elderly matron widowed by the desperadoes.

The conductor explained that the outlaws had stopped the train through a combination of firing at the engine and pulling a rail out of line up ahead. "Folks, the danger is over now," the wiry man assured the still-shaky passengers. "I know it's been right rough. But if several of you men will kindly come help me set the rail back in place ahead of us, we'll be on our way to Sullivan to inform the authorities."

Several men, including Lacy, left the car to assist the conductor in straightening the tracks. Within thirty minutes, the train was chugging on eastward with its much-sobered group of passengers.

They stopped at the station in Sullivan. The conductor told the passengers to stretch their legs but be back in ten minutes, since he was going to fetch the sheriff.

When everyone assembled in the station house ten minutes later, the sheriff of Sullivan arrived and questioned the passengers regarding the robbery. "Does anyone here know who the bandits were?" asked the tall, balding man in dark trousers and white shirt with leather vest.

Lacy, standing near Amy at the back of the crowded room, was grimly silent. As one of the passengers informed the sheriff that all of the robbers had worn masks, Amy glanced at Lacy resentfully and hissed, "Lacy, tell the man what you know!"

Lacy didn't look at her, staring cautiously at the lawman at the front of the room as he said under his breath to Amy, "Do you want to get us killed? The Younger boys don't hold with squealers, and neither do the James brothers."

"Were the James brothers there, too?" she whispered incredulously.

He nodded grimly. "I'm pretty sure they're the ones who blew the safe."

"Then tell the sheriff what you know!" she insisted through gritted teeth. "Or I will!"

Lacy turned on her savagely and said in a hoarse whisper, "Amy, do you want to go to St. Louis and rescue your sister or not?"

Her eyes narrowed. "What do you mean? That sounds like a threat!"

"It's not a threat at all," he informed her in an urgent tone. "Just a fact. Think, Amy. If I say I know something, we'll be detained here for God knows how long."

Amy bit her lip. "*We're* not together. You'd be the one detained," she pointed out.

"Not if I tell them you know something, too," he countered ruthlessly, moving closer to her, his stance threatening, his cold, determined blue eyes mere inches from her own.

Amy ground her teeth in frustration and backed away from Lacy. It was obvious that if she pointed the finger at him, he intended to do the same with her, whether it was fair or not.

"I didn't hear no complaints out of you when I saved your little hide back there," Lacy now snapped, relentlessly driving his point home. "Tell me, Amy—you want to handle your ma alone? You want to risk not getting to St. Louis at all?"

Wretchedly, Amy shook her head, as the sheriff's final plea for information regarding the bandits was again met with head-shaking silence from the crowd. . . .

Amy felt miserably torn as they and the other passengers trudged out of the station house and reboarded the train. She was virtually certain now that Lacy was connected with the outlaw gangs. Why else would Charlie Pitts have recognized Lacy so readily? Indeed, why else would the outlaws have passed them up during the robbery? The fearsome thoughts made a chill grip her heart, even as pangs of guilt needled her belly. She couldn't turn Lacy in to the authorities. She had to get to Hannah, and, just as Lacy had said, she could not risk being detained with him by the sheriff.

They took their seats glumly with the other passengers. As the train chugged out of the station, Lacy pulled an ornate pocket watch from his vest, opened it and glanced at the dial ruefully. "Damn, we've no chance of getting to St. Louis before nightfall now."

Studying Lacy with the watch in his hand, Amy was immediately struck by two oddities. First, she noted a jagged wound across the back of his right hand that she was sure hadn't been there before. It looked as if he'd recently cut himself quite badly on a piece of glass. Second, and even more distressing, she noticed that there was something wrong with the watch he held in his hand. The chain was foreshortened, obviously broken off, the fob missing. All at once she was filled with a sickening feeling of déjà vu as she recalled the grizzled farmer at Salter's store telling them of a recent train robbery, saying, "That black-eyed devil snatched Gopher's pocket watch so fast it broke the chain, then..."

Amy stared horrified at the broken chain as Garrett snapped the watch shut with a cold click.

Thirty

+⊢

It was dark by the time the train pulled into the St. Louis station. Amy and Lacy were both exhausted and hungry, running on nervous energy as they quickly disembarked and gathered their luggage. Lacy had steadfastly insisted that he would accompany Amy to Vida's house, and by now Amy was too tired and overwrought to fight him. On Poplar Street in front of the passenger terminal, they were lucky enough to catch one of the day's last horse-drawn trolley cars, which took them rattling through the gaslit streets toward the quiet residential Harris neighborhood.

They disembarked on Cass Avenue and hurried around the dark corner to Twenty-fifth Street. The night air was heavy with the scent of earth and honeysuckle, but its sweetness was lost on Amy. Actually, now that darkness had fallen, she couldn't help but feel slightly grateful that Lacy was with her, for it was unthinkable that a lady should venture out on the St. Louis streets alone at night. Those females who were brave enough to strike forth unescorted after sundown were usually not ladies—and were often treated accordingly.

As Amy and Lacy drew closer to Vida's well-lit cottage, Amy noted with relief that the Harris house next door was dark. Evidently, her mother had already drunk her fill for the day and had passed out, she thought to herself grimly.

Lacy squeaked open the picket gate to Vida's yard, and the two hurried for the front steps of the widow's home. Their knock was promptly answered by a worried-looking Vida Peterson, who wore a dark dress and wool shawl. "Amy!" the widow cried. "Thank God you're here. Come in here. Get yourself out of the night air."

Amy and Lacy entered the front room of Vida's home, setting down their luggage and blinking at the brightness after their moonlit walk. Amy warmly embraced Vida, then asked anxiously, "Hannah?"

"Safely asleep in my guest room, thank God," she assured Amy, squeezing the younger woman's hand. The handsome dark-haired woman turned to eye Lacy suspiciously and coolly. Lacy stood by Amy's side, awkwardly shifting his hat from hand to hand. "Evening, Mr. Garrett," the widow finally acknowledged stiffly.

"Evening, Mrs. Peterson," Lacy muttered back.

Now Vida slanted a reproachful glance at Amy, and the younger woman restrained a sigh. The widow had never approved of the ne'er-do-well peddler who had once been Amy's fiancé, and Amy knew her friend must now be wondering why she had come to St. Louis in his company, instead of having her husband escort her. Well, she'd simply have to explain the circumstances to the widow later, in private. It wasn't her fault that Lacy had imposed his presence on her!

Garrett and Vida continued to eye each other distrustfully for an uncomfortable moment. Then their hostess said with strained courtesy, "Well, you two, do have a seat."

Once the three were seated in the parlor, Amy and Vida on the settee, Lacy across from them in a Windsor chair near the piano, Amy quickly told her friend, "I'm glad Hannah's sleeping right now. Can you explain to us what happened?"

She nodded, and Amy spotted tears in her eyes. "That poor child. Heaven knows what possessed your ma. It was a week ago when I heard Hannah's screams—much worse this time than before. I told myself, 'Vida Peterson, you've got to put a stop to this. If you don't, Esther Harris is going to kill that poor girl.' So I fetched my broom and went over there.'' The widow paused to pull an embroidered handkerchief from her housedress pocket, wiping several tears before she continued in a choked voice. ''I'll never forget the sight of it, Amy—it has haunted my dreams every night since. Your ma, with that lunatic gleam in her eye, choking that poor girl by the collar of her dress as she went at her wildly with the scissors! All the while Esther was screaming some Bible passage about Delilah cutting off Samson's hair.''

''Oh, my God!'' Amy cried, her stomach knotting so violently she feared she would vomit. Things were so much worse than she had feared!

Vida went on shakily, ''That's when I shouted at her, 'Esther, you release that poor child, or by God, I'll have my broom to you!' '' The widow shook her head and dabbed at new tears. ''Do you know what your ma said then? She said, 'You come a step closer, Vida Peterson, and I'll slit this brat's throat!' ''

''No!'' Amy exclaimed, horrified, even as across from her, Lacy pounded a fist on a tea table and said hoarsely, ''Christ!''

''Luckily, at that point,'' Vida continued, ''Hannah bolted out of your ma's grasp and rushed to my side. I guess I must have distracted Esther enough that she slackened her grip a bit. Anyway, as soon as Hannah was in my arms, Esther started shrieking obscenities and came at us with the scissors—''

Her words abruptly halted as Amy broke down completely and began sobbing. The pain and shame of these dreadful revelations regarding her mother was more than Amy could bear.

Vida placed a comforting arm around Amy's heaving shoulders. ''There, dear. It's all over now,'' the widow soothed. ''Hannah is safe here.''

Even as Vida spoke the comforting words, Lacy Garrett came over and awkwardly stuffed his handkerchief into

Amy's fist. She mouthed a stiff "Thank you" to him and wiped her eyes. Once the peddler was again seated and Amy had calmed herself somewhat, the widow asked the girl gently, "Do you want to hear the rest, dear?"

"Yes! Yes, please," Amy insisted, the words ragged with her tears.

"Very well, then. When your ma started coming at us with the scissors, I told Hannah to get behind me. Then I drew my broom back like I was fixing to fight a freight train. Your ma must have seen the fire in my eyes, for she backed off right quick. That's when Hannah and I left and came over here."

"Oh, Mrs. Peterson, thank God for you!" Amy exclaimed, embracing her friend with trembling arms. For a moment, the two women comforted each other. Then Amy drew back and asked, "What has happened since then?"

Vida shook her head, giving Amy a resigned gesture. "Dear, there's no delicate way to put this."

"Tell me!" Amy demanded.

"I'm afraid your ma's been on a five-day drunk," she informed the younger woman. "At least once a day, she comes up to the porch, ranting and screaming that she'll have her child back. That broom of mine still gives your ma pause, but I've been frantically worried nonetheless, just like I told you in my letter. Esther's been threatening to go to the police to get Hannah returned. She hasn't done so yet, thank God. Even in her demented state, I think she realizes she won't be able to get action from the authorities until she sobers up and puts on a respectable air. But I've been fearing she might try it any day. Thank God you're here, Amy," the widow concluded with feeling.

Amy nodded, blinking back new tears. "And Hannah? How has she been? Emotionally, I mean."

Vida bit her lip, fighting fresh tears of her own. "Such a sweet little soul," she choked. "I cry into my pillow each night that that depraved woman would hurt her!"

Suddenly, Lacy burst up from his chair, an enraged gleam in his blue eyes, every muscle in his lean body rigid with fury. "Maybe I'll just go next door and teach that woman a lesson or two!"

Amy turned to Lacy, stunned by his outburst. He did care about her sister, or so it seemed.

Meanwhile, Vida Peterson scolded the peddler, "Oh, no, Mr. Garrett! I assure you that confronting Esther Harris now would accomplish nothing—except to tip her off to Amy's presence here. Esther has doubtless passed out for the day, so let's leave her be. Besides, we'll need the time to plan what's to be done about the child."

"I suppose you're right," Lacy replied grudgingly, taking his seat. His features were still tight with frustrated anger, his eyes blinking rapidly. Amy studied him with continuing astonishment, frowning thoughtfully to herself.

"Now, as for Hannah," Vida continued to Amy, "the child seems to be snapping back well enough, I must say. We tried our best to even out her hair, and she's so excited that your pa is coming—"

"I beg your pardon?" Amy cut in, stunned, her brown eyes enormous at this revelation.

Vida Peterson's hands flew to her face. "Oh, my dear, my dear! How could I have forgotten to tell you? I meant to mention it in my letter to you, but I was so frantic to get it posted...." Quickly she informed Amy, "You see, this whole thing started when Hannah brought home a letter from your father saying that he's planning to return to St. Louis."

Amy was speechless. Her father was returning to St. Louis, after eleven long years! Abel Harris was alive, after all! It was almost too much to absorb at once.

But before Amy could even consider the full implications of this news, a child with boyishly short hair, wearing a long white nightgown, burst into the room. "Amy!"

Amy's face was consumed with anguish as she viewed her younger sister. She struggled to her feet, fearing her knees would buckle beneath her as she held out her arms. "Oh, Hannah!"

The child flew into Amy's arms, and both sisters burst into heartbroken weeping.

* * *

Once the emotion of the moment receded a bit, Amy drew back, dabbing at tears on her little sister's face and saying hoarsely, "Oh, Hannah, darling. Let me have a look at you."

Amy studied the child carefully. Hannah looked basically healthy and unharmed, except for the loss of her long blond hair. Seeing the visible proof of her mother's cruelty hurt Amy so badly, her throat ached and her stomach burned with nausea. But Vida had done a good job of evening out the butcher job Esther had committed on the child. At least there were no signs that Esther had cut Hannah with the scissors, and that in itself was a miracle, considering her mother's demented state when she attacked the child. Fortunately, Hannah's hair was naturally fluffy and curly, and with the right ribbons and perhaps a few pins at the back, an effect could be lent that she had more hair. She touched the short wavy curls on the little girl's head, then her hand fell away as her eyes again began to sting and blur.

Hannah immediately noted the agonized pain in the older girl's expression. "Amy, please don't fret," she pleaded breathlessly, looking up at her sister with brown eyes wide and earnest. "My hair will grow back, and I'm just so glad you're here. I'm never going back to Ma again—never!"

Amy hugged the child fiercely to her breast. "You're absolutely right there, darling. I'm here now, and I'll see to it that you *never* go back to Ma. I vow it, my love! Now, let's sit down and talk."

As the two sisters joined Vida on the settee, Hannah asked with eager excitement, "Did Mrs. Peterson tell you Daddy is coming back to St. Louis?"

"Yes, darling!" Amy replied, smiling back and shaking her head in wonder. "I'm tremendously excited that he's coming. What did he say in his letter?"

Hannah's mouth began to quiver. "Ma burned his letter, Amy. But don't worry, I read it first. Daddy said he's sorry he left us and he's coming home. He's got a job, sister, with the Pink—with some detective agency. And he's coming to Missouri to capture Jesse James!"

Amy raised an eyebrow at this astonishing news, while Lacy, across the room, whistled under his breath. Frowning as she studied her former fiancé, Amy noted he had turned quite pale and was nervously loosening his cravat.

For the first time, Hannah noticed that Lacy was in the room. Turning to the black-haired man, she muttered rather confusedly, "Well, hello, Lacy." Scowling, she glanced back at Amy. "Why didn't Matt bring you here?"

Amy bit her lip, finally saying, "Sweetheart, that's a long story, and I think you'd best get back to bed. We can talk about it in the morning—"

"Is Matt all right?" Hannah demanded, looking extremely concerned now.

Amy placed her hand over Hannah's. "Darling, he's fine. It's just that he's very busy with the planting right now, and—and it turned out Lacy was heading this way, too."

Hannah frowned but said nothing. Amy knew that an adult would never believe her story, that even Hannah might find it farfetched. Fortunately, at this point, Vida intervened by gently scolding the child, "Your sister's right, young woman. Off to bed with you. You'll have plenty of time to visit with Amy tomorrow. Come on, I'll tuck you in."

"All right." Hannah kissed Amy good night, nodded to Lacy, then let Vida lead her back to bed.

Once the widow and child were out of earshot, Lacy inquired, "Amy, do you really think we should be hanging around here? I mean, with your ma wigged out and threatening Hannah and all?"

Again, Amy noted how nervous Lacy was, how he kept rapping his fingertips on an end table. "I can't take Hannah anywhere at this time of night," she pointed out.

"I don't like it," he gritted back.

For a moment, they stared at each other in tense silence, then Vida reentered the room, saying, "Of course, you folks are staying the night? And mercy, I didn't even think to ask you if you've had your supper." She sat down next to Amy and patted the girl's hand. "My dear, you look so pale. Don't you think the child is recovering well?"

"Oh, yes, but—"

"Mrs. Peterson, we've had quite a day of it," Lacy interjected from across the room, leaning tensely forward in his chair. "You see, the train we took was robbed out near Sullivan, and I'm afraid Amy saw a passenger being killed—"

"Forevermore!" Vida gasped, her hand flying to her heart. "How terrible! Why didn't you two say something before?"

"The most important thing was seeing about Hannah," Amy explained. "I didn't want to alarm her—or you." Briefly, Amy provided Vida with details of the robbery; then she added with a fierce sigh, "I'm afraid the same desperadoes who ransacked the train robbed the bank in Rolla the other day. In fact, that's why Matt couldn't bring me here—he's out tracking the robbers."

"My kingdom!" she cried. Purposefully, Vida got to her feet. "Well, in that case . . . Will you folks excuse me for a minute?"

Exchanging confused glances, Amy and Lacy said in unison, "Yes, of course."

Moments later, Vida reentered the room with a tray bearing a bottle of whiskey and two glasses. "Now, I'm a good Christian woman who doesn't believe in imbibing spirits," the widow began, "but I think even the Good Lord knows that sometimes a body can only stand so much." Setting the tray down on the coffee table, she poured two shots of whiskey, handed one glass to Amy and the other to Lacy. With a wry smile, she informed her guests, "I've been saving Mr. Peterson's last bottle for an emergency such as this. You two take this to calm your nerves, and I'll stir you up some supper."

Amy and Lacy murmured their thanks, and Vida left for the kitchen. Lacy quickly gulped down his shot of whiskey, then went to the coffee table, grabbed the bottle and poured himself another one. Amy merely stared at the amber liquid in her own glass. "Drink it, Amy," Lacy urged, returning to his chair with his drink. "You'll feel better afterward."

Amy had never drunk a drop of alcohol in her life, but she knew that if there were ever a time to tipple, tonight was the night. She seemed to have lived a lifetime in a single short day. She took a small sip and almost choked. The whiskey tasted fiery and bitter, making her eyes burn. At least she didn't have to worry about acquiring a taste or an addiction for alcohol, as her ma had! Grimacing, she quickly gulped down the rest of the shot, then leaned back, letting the liquor work its magic, loosening her veins.

Meanwhile, Lacy was back at the coffee table pouring himself a third glassful. "Amy, we've got to get out of here," he repeated tensely.

Amy eyed Lacy skeptically as he downed the liquor. This time, he didn't even bother to return to his chair, but stood by the coffee table with bottle still in hand. He looked quite overwrought, his face flushed, his bright eyes forever darting toward the door. She noted that his nervousness had accelerated dramatically since Hannah had mentioned that their father was returning to St. Louis, and she mused about the connection. "If Hannah and I leave now, we will miss being reunited with our father," she informed Lacy. Giving him a hard, assessing look, she added, "Tell me—does my father's coming to St. Louis threaten you in some way?"

At Amy's incisive question, Lacy ground his jaw and started to pour himself another drink. Then, spotting the bright suspicion in Amy's eyes, he slammed the bottle and his glass down on the coffee table and spun about to leave the room, muttering under his breath that he was going outside for a smoke.

He returned a few minutes later, acting calmer but rather sullen and taciturn. During supper, Amy supplied Vida with additional details of their journey and the train robbery, wisely leaving out the fact that Lacy knew who the bandits were.

Of course, part of her wanted to hurl accusations at him, to find out the exact nature of his connection to the outlaws and to make him admit to the wrong he'd done Matt. Yet she feared Lacy's reaction if she tipped his hand that way in front of their hostess. Considering the telling events on the train today, Amy felt bound and determined to find a way to help clear Matt of Lacy's charges. She knew that gaining more information about Lacy's involvement with the bush-whackers would definitely help. But she would have to bide her time carefully before making her move.

Vida filled Amy in on some of the activities she and Hannah had undertaken during the last few days; how they'd gone to church together, to the library and museums, even down to the levee for a showboat performance. Amy thanked her profusely for treating her little sister to such richness, and the widow waved her off, assuring the younger woman that she had been in her glory to have the little girl all to herself for a week.

When bedtime came, Vida told Amy she could share Hannah's bed in the guest room. To Lacy, she added, "There's a cot on the back porch, Mr. Garrett. You're welcome to fetch it into the kitchen and sleep there tonight. I'm sorry, but that's the best I can do."

Lacy nodded. "That's fine, ma'am. I'm much obliged."

Vida proceeded to help Lacy make up his cot in the kitchen. Afterward he excused himself to go outside and have another smoke before retiring. As soon as the peddler was out the front door, Vida Peterson took Amy aside in the parlor. "Want to tell me what's really going on here, dear? You look beside yourself tonight, and I could tell all evening that there's much tension between you and Mr. Garrett."

"Yes, there is," Amy admitted readily. "You're very perceptive, Mrs. Peterson, and I do need to talk to you. Is there some place where we can speak privately?"

"Yes, dear, let's go to my bedroom."

In the widow's small, lamplit bedroom, Amy sat down on the bed while Vida seated herself in a small tufted chair across from the girl. "You've had quite a day of it, haven't you, dear?" she asked sympathetically, studying Amy's weary, distraught countenance.

"Oh, yes!" Amy replied with a fierce sigh. "First I got your letter, then the train was robbed on the way here, then I saw Hannah and learned my father is coming home . . . ." Her voice trailing off, Amy shook her head in amazement.

"I know it's a great deal to absorb at once," Vida

comforted. "But there's even more troubling you, isn't there?"

"Yes."

"And it has to do with Mr. Garrett?"

"Yes."

"Tell me, girl—why did he bring you here? How did he even know you were in Rolla in the first place?"

Amy expelled a ragged breath. "It's a long story, Mrs. Peterson. Are you sure you want to hear it?"

"Every word," the widow said firmly.

Amy went back and explained to the older woman how Lacy had come to Rolla in the first place and had begun stirring up trouble between her and Matt. She told of Lacy's despicable behavior at the town meeting, of how Matt was out tracking the outlaws even now because of Lacy's lies. Then she explained how Lacy brought her the letter this morning, how he'd later joined her on the train, against her will. "And the worst part is, Mrs. Peterson, I am convinced Lacy is guilty of committing the very treason he accused my husband of at the town meeting."

Amy explained how the two of them were passed up during the train robbery today, how he'd threatened her when she'd urged him to give information to the authorities, how she'd later seen him pull out a watch that strongly resembled one she'd heard the outlaws had stolen previously.

"Oh, my dear!" Vida gasped when Amy had finished. "Bless your heart—it's unspeakable, what you've had to contend with! That scoundrel Mr. Garrett!" Her brow deeply furrowed, the widow went on, "So you think Garrett's definitely hooked up with these outlaws?"

"Yes, I do, although I can't be sure of the exact connection. He could have been paid for information, or to keep silent, or it could be—"

"Something much worse," Vida finished ominously.

Amy nodded grimly, then got to her feet and began to pace. "But the point is, what am I to do, Mrs. Peterson? If I don't take some kind of action, Lacy may get off scot free. Tonight he kept saying we must get out of here. I really think he's on the run from his troubles. And I think hearing that my father is now a Pinkerton agent was just about the last straw for him."

"You mean, you think Mr. Garrett will run off again, rather than risk being here when your father comes?"

Amy nodded. "Or when Matt comes, for that matter. I'm sure Lacy won't risk facing either of them now—especially not considering what I can tell them about the robbery. And if Lacy leaves, I'll lose my chance to help prove Matt is innocent." She stared at her friend intently. "Should I arise before Lacy in the morning and sneak off to the authorities here?"

Vida scowled pensively for a moment. "Perhaps. But wouldn't they question your not coming forward at Sullivan today?"

Amy brushed an errant gold lock from her eyes and nodded soberly. "They might. And, Lord knows, I don't need to get into any trouble myself, not with Hannah in such peril."

"I think, Amy Louise, that you should wait till your husband gets here," Vida put in wisely. "Matt Kendall will know what's to be done with that blackguard."

Amy gestured helplessly. "But I don't know when Matt's coming—or if he's coming."

"He'll come, dear." Vida Peterson stood and walked over to Amy, patting the girl's hand reassuringly. "Amy Louise, there's nothing to be accomplished at this time of night. You're overwrought, and with all you've been through, I'm surprised you can think at all. Get some rest now, and the answers will come. If Mr. Garrett tries to leave in the morning—well, we'll cross that bridge when we come to it. For now, go join your sister in bed, before Mr. Garrett comes back and hears us talking."

"You're right, Mrs. Peterson. Oh, thank you so much." Amy embraced her friend warmly, then departed for the guest room, quietly slipping inside. Just as her friend had said, she found she was so bone-weary that her knees felt weak. She undressed in the darkness and slid into bed beside Hannah.

Amy thought of Matt as she drifted off to sleep. How she

missed him and prayed that he was all right! Was he returning to the farm even now? Would he come to St. Louis soon to join her, as Vida had assured he would?

And would her father come to St. Louis soon, too, astonishing as it was? Would the two men help her protect Hannah against Esther Harris and help her bring Lacy Garrett to justice?

The questions were too much for Amy's teeming, confused mind. First, she knew she must rest, let sleep clear her frazzled thoughts. Then, whether Matt or her father came or not, she must find a way of ensuring Hannah's safety. And, somehow, she'd also find a way to make Lacy Garrett pay for the wrong he'd done to her husband!

Thirty-one

⊷

Early the next morning, the household was awakened by a fierce banging at the front door. Amy grabbed her wrapper from the foot of the bed and quickly got up, noting that Hannah was still asleep on the other side of the mattress. Hastily she tiptoed out of the room, shutting the door behind her, then hurried for the front of the house, where she found Vida confronting her mother across the latched screen door.

Amy gasped as she viewed her haggard, crazed-looking mother out on the porch. Esther Harris's features had yellowed considerably in Amy's absence. The old woman's hair was down, wildly tangled and clinging greasily to her shoulders. Her dress was torn and filthy, and the wind at the old woman's back swept inward the nauseating odor of soured liquor and human excreta exuding from her dissipated body. While Amy hung back a few feet, reeling at the odious visage her parent presented, Esther fixed venomously gleaming eyes on Vida Peterson and hissed through the door, "You give me my child back, you black-haired scarecrow, or I'm fetching the police, I am!"

"You'll get that darling girl back over my dead body!" Vida snapped back at her neighbor, fists balled on her hips. The widow looked formidable this morning, even wearing her blue flannel wrapper and white lace nightcap, her black hair hanging in a long plait down her back.

Amy edged closer to the altercation, tying the ribbons on her wrapper and struggling not to shudder as she viewed the wreck of humanity that was her mother. "Ma—Ma, please," she finally begged.

Esther at last noted her older daughter's presence, turning rabidly glittering eyes on the younger woman. "You! So you're back, are you?"

"Yes, Ma. I'm here because—I only want what's best for Hannah—"

"You lying hussy!" Esther shrieked, waving a fist at her daughter. The old woman grabbed the handle on the screened door, wildly yanking at it, trying to break the latch. "Let me in, you scheming she-devils!"

On the inside, Vida frantically hung on to the door, trying to keep Esther from breaking in. Then a determined male voice interjected from behind the widow, "I think you'd better go, Mrs. Harris."

Amy gasped, whirling to see that Lacy Garrett had joined the two women near the door. He stood scowling behind them, wearing a black velvet dressing gown, his hair still ruffled from sleep.

Immediately, Esther jumped to the wrong conclusion, her eyes flashing with malicious pleasure as she viewed Lacy. She turned her contemptuous gaze on her daughter. "You're back—with him?" the old woman scoffed. "So your husband threw you out, did he? You filthy little whore! Doubtless, Matt Kendall got tired of you spreading your legs for this no-account!"

"Mrs. Harris, you'd better leave!" Lacy roared, stepping forward between the two women to face Esther down.

"I'll leave!" Esther cried back with a deranged cackle, shaking a fist at the threesome across from her. "I'll leave and fetch the police, I will! I'll have them throw the lot of you in jail for kidnapping, I will! You filthy, thieving fornicators!" With a maniacal laugh, she added, " 'The wages of sin are death!' "

Esther whirled and hurried off down the stairs, her gait

wild and rambling, her filthy hair trailing behind her in a crazed tangle as she shrieked with vengeful laughter. "Oh, my God!" Amy gasped, feeling faint.

As Amy tottered, Vida wrapped a reassuring arm around the girl. The three adults numbly seated themselves in the front room, heedless of the fact that they weren't properly dressed to be conversing.

"Ma looks horrible," Amy told Vida, who sat by her side on the settee. "I had no idea she had degenerated to this degree."

"Honey, I hate to say this, but you're looking at her on one of her better days," Vida replied morosely.

"Oh, Lord! What are we to do?" Amy cried. "Surely if Ma does go to the police, they won't take her seriously."

Yet Vida shook her head doubtfully. "I wouldn't bet Hannah's life on it, dear. Your ma is crazy as a loon, but she is sober this morning, and if she thinks to clean herself up before she goes to the authorities, they might attribute her state to a concerned mother's hysterics."

Amy nodded grimly. No doubt the widow was right. Even as she furiously tried to plot a course of action, Lacy announced from across the room, "Amy, I think we'd best get out of here as quickly as possible."

Amy frowned at his words, glancing perplexedly at Vida. She quickly suggested to Amy, "Maybe you and Hannah could hide out at a hotel for a few days. I'll give you some money—"

"That won't work," Lacy cut in impatiently. "Not with Amy's ma notifying the police." Lacy turned to Amy and announced vehemently, "We must leave St. Louis entirely."

Amy's mind was teeming as she listened to Lacy. He certainly had a point. But if she left St. Louis with Hannah, she wouldn't be here when Matt came, or when her father came. Yet could she stick around and endanger Hannah's life? Amy glanced at Vida for guidance, but the woman merely shook her head sadly, obviously stumped herself.

Amy realized she would have to leave with Hannah; she couldn't take any chances with the child's safety. She had no way of knowing for sure when Matt or her father might appear. Yet she also hated to give up on her plan to make Lacy pay for his wrongs, to turn him over to one or both of the men when they came!

Decisively, Amy turned to him. "Lacy, will you take me and Hannah back to Rolla?"

His reaction was one of sheer incredulity. "Amy, have you lost your mind? If I do that, that husband of yours will put a bullet through my head, and you know it!"

Vida gasped at Lacy's words, and Amy ground her teeth. Obviously, manipulating him to suit her purpose would not be easy. "Well, if you won't take us, maybe I'll just take Hannah back myself," she told him defiantly, hoping to goad him into relenting.

Yet instead, Lacy sprang to his feet, wildly gesturing his exasperation. "You're going to take that child back to the farm alone? With outlaws loose all over the region? And just how in blue blazes are you planning to get there? Are you takin' the train the bushwhackers hit yesterday? Or are you aiming to walk all ninety miles? You're talkin' plum crazy, woman!"

"Then what do you propose?" she half shouted back, standing herself to face him down.

Lacy glanced meaningfully from Amy to Vida Peterson, but said nothing. Taking the hint, their hostess rose. "Think I'll let you folks discuss this while I check on breakfast."

Once Vida was out of earshot, Lacy announced to Amy, "Amy, I'm leaving Missouri."

"What?" she cried, stunned. "But—what about your business in Rolla?"

He shrugged. "The store is only rented. I'll drop Sally a note and tell her she can have the stock."

"My, that's generous!" Amy snapped, eyes narrowed suspiciously. "Mind telling me why you're in such an all-fired hurry to get out of this state?"

"I just told you—your husband will—"

"I think there's much more to it than that, and we both know it."

An electric silence settled between them. Finally, Lacy

swallowed hard, stepping forward and saying earnestly, "Amy, I want to go to Texas and buy some land, maybe raise cattle. And I want you to come with me."

She was flabbergasted. "Lacy, that's insane! *You*, a rancher? And—and you're asked me to—? How can you even suggest such a thing? I'm a married woman, for heaven's sake!"

"Amy, please—"

"No. Absolutely not."

"Amy, think," he pleaded, moving a step closer, a glimmer of desperation in his eyes. "You know you've got to leave here or your ma may take Hannah back."

"I know," she conceded miserably, her shoulders slumping.

"I don't want you to risk going back to Rolla alone," he reasoned. "Like I said, there's simply too much outlaw activity in that area."

Amy scowled, distractedly brushing tangled locks from her brow and wracking her brain for what to do. She was torn between her desire to get Hannah to safety and her determination to bring Lacy to justice. She knew she needed to get Hannah out of St. Louis—but to leave with Lacy for Texas? That seemed a bit extreme, to say the least!

Before Amy could fully contemplate her unhappy choices, Vida burst back into the room. "I hate to alarm you, Amy Louise," the widow began to the girl, "but I was setting the table in the dining room just now, when I saw your ma pass." The older woman shook her head grimly. "Never saw anyone get cleaned up so quick. Esther Harris looked respectable, if I do say so myself. And heading straight for the Cass Avenue trolley, she was."

"Oh, Lord!" Amy gasped, her brain seeming to splinter with the force of this new revelation. "Ma's on her way to the police right now—I'm sure of it!"

"Come on, Amy, let's get Hannah and get out of here!" Lacy ordered.

"But you won't take us to Rolla!" she cried back, her fists balled at her sides, her eyes wild with desperation.

"Look, Amy," Lacy gritted, "I'm leaving St. Louis this morning—whether you come with me or not."

At his implacable words, Amy thought frantically. Lacy was leaving, and with him was going her only real chance to help clear Matt. Should she head south with him and hope Matt would come tracking them? No, no, she couldn't take off with Hannah that way, with no real destination in mind! She couldn't simply flee to the south, across country, in the direction of—

Then, suddenly, she remembered! There might be a workable solution after all! "Cousin Josie!" she cried.

"I beg your pardon?" Vida asked from Amy's side.

Amy turned with excitement to the widow. "My father has a first cousin who lives in Steelville, to the south of here. We went to a family reunion there when I was a child. In fact, I recently wrote to Cousin Josie, and she wrote back asking me to come for a visit anytime." She turned to Lacy. "Will you take Hannah and me to Steelville? You'll have to head that way anyway if you're leaving the state."

He scowled and didn't immediately reply, while Vida gave Amy a stern look. "Amy Louise, are you *sure* that's what you and Hannah should be doing?"

"Yes," Amy told her friend adamantly, adding a pleading glance that said, *Please trust me on this*. When the widow sighed and grudgingly nodded back, Amy again turned to Lacy. "Lacy, will you take us to Cousin Josie's?"

He again hesitated, then said with a scowl, "Yes, I'll take you there."

"Thank you very much," Amy said dryly.

Listening to the two, Vida still looked skeptical. She said to Amy, "Well, if that's what you folks think you should be doing, then I'd best grab the muffins from the oven before they catch fire. I'll leave you two to your packing. In any event, I'd advise you to step lively, before Esther returns with the authorities."

Vida left the room. Taking her friend's warning seriously, Amy was about to dash off herself, when Lacy grabbed her arm. "I wish you would come with me all the way to Texas," he told her.

Amy struggled to hang on to her patience. "Lacy, that's

out of the question," she replied, disengaging his fingers from her arm.

"But you'll use me to get you as far as Steelville, won't you?" he countered darkly.

Amy bit her lip, fearing he was trying to back out of his promise. At the moment, he was her best hope for getting Hannah to safety, and she wasn't about to let him out of her sight while she still had a chance to help Matt! "Lacy, it's on your way," she reminded. "And going to Cousin Josie's is the only real solution for Hannah and me right now. There's been no outlaw activity spotted that far south. It's the perfect place for the two of us to stay until we can get back to Rolla."

"So, that's it! You can't wait to get back to your precious Mathew, can you?" he demanded.

Amy shook her head in bewilderment. "I wasn't aware that I'd ever left my husband. I only came here to see about my sister. It was always my intention to go home to Matt."

"Maybe I'll change your mind before we get to Steelville," he retorted.

"You can try, but you won't be successful," she informed him. With a pleading gesture, she finished, "Lacy, please, think of Hannah."

"All right, I'll take you there," he half growled back. "Believe it or not, I'm as concerned about getting Hannah out of here as you are."

With these terse words, Lacy turned and strode out of the room. After taking a couple of deep, steadying breaths, Amy followed him, desperately hoping she'd made the right decision.

In the kitchen, she found Vida alone frying bacon in a cast-iron skillet. Spotting Amy, the woman called out over her shoulder, "I'll just throw your breakfast and some sandwiches into a knapsack, if that's all right, honey."

"That's fine, thank you," Amy replied. She glanced about the homey room. "Where's Lacy?"

"Out back at the convenience," came Vida's reply.

Amy stepped forward, glad to have a private moment with the widow before she left. "Mrs. Peterson, when my father comes—when Matt comes—tell them where we've gone, will you?''

The widow turned to the girl, frowning. ''I will. But Amy Louise, are you certain you're doing the right thing, leaving with that scoundrel?''

''I'm only going with him as far as Cousin Josie's,'' Amy reasoned back. ''With luck we might even get there today. Anyway, I've got to get Hannah to safety, and maybe I can find out more about Lacy's activities on the way, find out what his exact destination is and let the authorities know in Steelville. I must help Matt if I can.''

The widow nodded. ''I suppose you know what you're doing, dear. Just take care, now, will you?''

''I will. And try to make Matt understand the reasons I'm leaving with Lacy, will you?''

''Of course, dear. With any luck, Mr. Kendall will be joining you soon.''

With any luck! As Amy hurried from the room to go awaken Hannah, she had a feeling she might be needing quite a lot of luck!

Thirty-two

+ +

As Amy and Lacy were preparing to leave St. Louis, Matt Kendall was heading for Rolla, searching for news of his wife. Earlier that morning, before day-break, he'd ridden to the Stockton farm to get Amy, exhausted and frustrated after a day and a half in the hills fruitlessly tracking the outlaws. Yet Matt arrived at the Stocktons' farmhouse only to discover that Amy had gone home more than twenty-four hours earlier. He'd raced back to his own farm, where he had found her note. A quick check upstairs confirmed that Amy's portmanteau, along with several changes of clothing, were missing. He hurried down to the barn and discovered that Sundance was gone as well.

Matt gave all his animals water and double portions of feed, then stuffed a change of clothing in his saddlebags and rode hard for town, his mind a maze of fear and disturbing questions. What time had she left? Was it day or night—yesterday, or today before sunup? The thought of her ventur-ing forth unescorted, with outlaws loose in the region, terrified him. And how had she learned the news about Hannah in the first place? he wondered. What terrible danger was she in?

In Rolla, the pieces of the puzzle began to fall in place for Matt. He got his first break at the livery stable. Emmett

Teague, who was just opening up, informed him that the young farmer's wife had indeed been there around noon the previous day, and she had left Sundance to be boarded there. "I recollect your missus mentioned she was goin' to St. Louie," Teague remarked, scratching his scruffy head. "Reckon she caught the afternoon Flyer, don't you?"

Matt left his horse in Emmett's care and hurried to the train station. The inside of the station house was deserted except for the ticket agent, Stan Murray, who stood behind the counter sorting ticket stubs. Striding quickly across the room, Matt asked Murray anxiously, "You seen my wife, Stan?"

"Er—yessir," the thin, spectacled man replied, nervously glancing up at Matt. "Your missus left for St. Louie on the Flyer yesterday afternoon."

"She say anything to you about why she was goin' there?"

"Er—nossir," Murray stammered. Watching a scowl spread across Matt's face, the ticket agent added appeasingly, "Mr. Kendall, I'm right sorry your wife run off on you that way."

"What do you mean, run off?" he snapped back.

Murray dropped the ticket stubs he was trying to sort and swallowed hard. "Nothin', sir. I was just assumin' you knew—"

"Knew what?" Matt barked.

Murray eyed Matt warily as he adjusted his spectacles. "I just figured you knew your wife didn't go to St. Louie by her lonesome."

"What are you saying?" the farmer demanded.

The thin man swallowed hard, then announced, "Well, sir, I hate to be the one to be makin' trouble between a man and his missus. Like I said, I was assumin' you knew—"

"Spill it out!" Matt growled.

"Yessir." In a hesitant voice, Murray explained, "Well, sir, just a few minutes after your wife boarded yesterday, Mr. Lacy Garrett came in here and bought a ticket for St. Louie." Watching the young husband's features turn blood-red at this pronouncement, Murray rushed on, "Garrett wanted to know if your wife was on the train yet. Said the two of them was plannin' to meet and go off to St. Louie together. Said it with a grin, Garrett did.''

Matt lunged forward and grabbed the slim man by the lapels of his vest. ''Murray, are you funning me?'' he demanded furiously. Matt well knew that at Salter's store, Stan Murray had a reputation for being as much of a gossip as some of the local dowagers.

''No, sir!'' the frightened clerk said, shaking his head vigorously. ''I'm tellin' you the God's truth, Mr. Kendall! Garrett knew your wife was on that train, and he told me they was plannin' to meet—*sly* like—and go off together!''

''Damnation!'' Matt growled, releasing the clerk and turning away to try to make sense of his raging thoughts. He gnashed his teeth and clenched his fists, his chest heaving with the force of his emotions.

So Amy had gone off to St. Louis with Lacy Garrett! The two of them had planned to meet on the train. Was Hannah in trouble at all, then? Or was the note merely a ruse to cover their tracks? The very idea made him mad enough to rip this station house apart, board by board.

But then his conscience intervened. What if something terrible truly had happened to Hannah? Amy *had* departed for St. Louis, he reminded himself, just as she said she would in her note . . . .

Yet nothing made sense. He still didn't know how Amy could have learned Hannah was in danger in the first place. And if the child truly was in peril, why hadn't Amy gone to the Stocktons for help, to anyone but to that low-down skunk Garrett?

Face it, Kendall, he chided himself bitterly. The girl still has feelings for the man. They've pulled the wool over your eyes, and you've acted like a blame fool! She only used you until her fancy man came back.

Well, Amy was his wife, by damn! It would be a cold day in hell before he'd let her sashay off with another man and get away with it.

In this murderous frame of mind, Matt turned back to the ticket agent. ''Murray, when's the next train for St. Louis?''

Murray nervously glanced at a schedule posted behind

him. "Couple hours from now. But—Mr. Kendall, I'm afraid there's something else you gotta know," the man added in a miserably squeaky tone.

"What is it this time?" Matt demanded, banging his fist on the counter.

Murray literally jumped backward, looking about as happy as a man about to be hanged. "Well, Mr. Kendall, I'm afraid the Flyer your wife took yesterday was held up just west a' Sullivan, by a gang of bushwhackers. Got word late last evenin'."

"Hellfire!" Matt banged his fist on the counter again, his fury now transformed to desperate concern. "Was my wife hurt?"

The ticket agent shook his head. "Two men was kilt, according to the telegraph."

"Was one of them Garrett, I hope?" Matt inquired nastily.

"Er—nossir. One of them was the guard in the express car, and the other was an elderly gent who tried to stop the robbers. Neither of 'em was from Rolla."

"Were the bandits . . . successful?"

"Oh, yessir. They dynamited the safe and kiped all the passengers' valuables."

"Son of a bitch! What happened to the train then?"

"Went on to St. Louie afterward. Weren't no point in hanging 'round Sullivan, once the sheriff was notified."

"Blast!" Matt shook his head grimly. "At least Amy's safe."

"Looks that way," Murray replied cautiously.

"What do you mean, looks that way?" Matt roared.

The ticket agent nervously loosened his cravat. "Well, sir, there ain't no other report of casualties, that's all I'm saying."

Consumed by new fears, Matt glowered at Murray. Amy obviously hadn't been shot, he knew that much, thank God. But he also grasped what Murray was hinting at, which was that his wife might have been roughed up or otherwise hurt by the outlaws. He had been the worst kind of fool to leave Amy alone that way. Damn! He'd had no luck tracking them, doubtless because they had moved farther east to rob the train. Matt's thoughts were whirling. His suspicions about why Lacy Garrett really tried to frame him for the Rolla bank robbery were being confirmed—Garrett was at the scene of another robbery, this time involving his wife . . . .

Matt's thoughts were suddenly interrupted as, across the building, the door opened. "Morning, sir," Stan Murray called out.

Matt pivoted as a tall man dressed entirely in black, sporting long sideburns and a handlebar mustache and wearing a black hat with snakeskin band, strode toward them. He nodded briefly at Matt before he addressed the ticket agent at the counter. "You Murray?"

"Yessir."

The stranger extended a hand over the polished counter top. "I'm Jack Adams, agent of Governor Silas Woodson. I just rode in from Jefferson City."

Instantly, the ticket agent straightened his shoulders, accepting the other man's handshake solemnly. "What can I do for you, sir?"

"I was wonderin' if you could tell me 'bout the passengers who boarded the train here at Rolla yesterday afternoon."

"You're talking about the Flyer that was bushwhacked near Sullivan?"

"Yessir. How many folks boarded here?"

Murray glanced cautiously at Matt, then cleared his throat before he haltingly answered Adams's question. "Well, sir, the only passengers who boarded here yesterday were—er—the wife of Mr. Kendall here, and"—Murray miserably colored—"and a friend of the lady's."

"I see," Adams replied thoughtfully, glancing wryly at Matt, who glowered back at the newcomer. "Guess they was the folks that was passed up during the robbery, then."

"What?" Matt and the ticket agent exclaimed in unison.

Heedless of the shocked expressions of at least one of his companions, the coolly laconic stranger slowly pulled a thin cheroot from the breast pocket of his handsomely tailored black jacket. As he fished for a match in his satiny inner pockets, Matt caught a glimpse of a deadly-looking Colt .45

with an ivory handle strapped to his narrow hips. Adams was obviously a hired gun, Matt thought with distaste. He'd heard of how the state legislature had appropriated funds to hire professional gunmen to track down the James and Younger brothers. It all fit, for there was something quite cold and calculating about this lean, soft-spoken stranger; even the man's slow movements seemed deliberately orchestrated to mask a whiplash-quick energy, a lethal readiness, concealed beneath. As Adams located a match and indolently lit his smoke, Matt asked in an explosive burst, "What's this about my wife and . . . her companion . . . being passed up during the robbery?"

Adams tossed his spent match on the floor and took a slow drag on the cheroot. Unperturbed by Matt's demanding tone of voice, he drawled, "One of the passengers saw a couple board here at Rolla yesterday, the lady first, and the gent soon afterward. Then later, during the robbery, the bushwhackers passed them two by like they was kinfolk or somethin'. Kinda strange, ain't it? Anyhow, our informant told the stationmaster all about it once the Flyer got to St. Louis. Seems our man was afraid to speak up back at Sullivan, since the sheriff questioned everyone together." Adams chuckled. "That poor bastard was sure if'n he spoke up in front of that couple, they'd'a pumped some lead in his drawers right quick—the little lady, or her companion." Blowing out a puff of smoke, Adams again glanced meaningfully at Matt.

Matt burned with resentment at Adams's accusation. Shaking a fist at the gunfighter, he snapped, "See here, you smart-mouthed upstart! My wife had nothin' to do with that train robbery yesterday! Do you understand? Nothin'!"

Adams shrugged, and a ghost of a smile pulled at his thin mouth. "Sure, mister. Whatever you say. If'n that's the case, then I reckon you won't mind telling me where your missus—and her boyfriend—was heading yesterday, now will you?" Adams's dark eyes shone with cynicism and his insolent stance exuded challenge as he carelessly flicked an ash on the planked station-house floor.

Matt was boiling with rage. He glowered back at the

gunslinger. He was struggling between his desire to protect Amy and his thirst to kill this arrogant bounty hunter who dared to stand there mocking him. But he knew now that he needed Adams on his side if he was to save Amy. And save her he would, if only to have the satisfaction of beating the mischief out of her cheating little hide! With monumental effort, he finally took hold of himself, informing Adams through clenched teeth, "Adams, I think you and me had best cut a deal."

Adams took a slow drag on his smoke and shrugged. "What do you have in mind?"

Matt bit down his rising fury. "If you give me your solemn word you'll leave my wife out of it, I'll lead you to the man you're looking for." Eyes gleaming with cool contempt, he added, "Do I have your attention now, you cocky bastard?"

Adams actually grinned as he stamped out his smoke. "You do."

At the moment Matt Kendall and Jack Adams struck their deal in Rolla, a stranger strode down Twenty-fifth Street in St. Louis. His excitement mingled with trepidation, Abel Harris approached the familiar, now weather-beaten cottage where he used to live.

Harris looked handsome in his new, store-bought brown suit and a snappy derby hat; he was clean-shaven and his gray-brown hair was smartly trimmed. A crisp spring breeze tugged at his coattails as he came alongside the ancient picket fence that now so desperately needed whitewashing. He creaked open the old gate on its single remaining hinge.

Inside the yard, he paused. His heart was pounding fiercely. The house looked winter-worn and deserted, several pieces of broken furniture strewn on the porch, cracked mason jars and filthy rags scattered about the yard. He knew a moment of terrible hesitation. What would he do if his family had moved elsewhere, if there was no one left at home to greet him? He steeled himself against a rising panic and forced himself onward into the yard. He had come this far; he simply couldn't give up now.

The path beneath his feet was thick and spongy with last fall's rotted crop of leaves. Near the porch a single, scrawny marigold peeked out through winter's debris. Seeing the flower gave Abel new courage. Hell, he had promised Mr. Pinkerton that he would tackle Jesse James and company. Surely he could handle Esther Harris! Bravely, he climbed mottled, grayish steps that groaned beneath his shiny black shoes.

On the porch, Abel rapped on the door, waiting seemingly in vain for an answer. Sighing, he tried again. Still the same ominous silence. Finally, in desperation, he tried the door, finding to his surprise that it was unlocked. The cracked oaken panel groaned on its hinges as it opened, casting a wide beam of light into the nightmare world beyond.

Inside, the house appeared deserted and nothing like Abel remembered it. Just beyond the door, he stumbled on a filthy, bunched-up rug as his nostrils were violently assailed by the putrid smells of rotting food and human excrement. The air was so foul, he actually fought nausea, and a fat gray rat skittered across the hallway into the sitting room beyond. He glanced from the dreary parlor on his left to the the unlit dining room on his right. Everywhere was clutter—yellowed newspapers on chairs, dirty dishes on every table, mice attacking crumbs on the floor. Wallpaper hung in tatters from the ceiling of the central hallway, and water-marks mottled the walls. The house was literally falling apart! He swallowed a painful lump in his throat, then cautiously started down the hallway, calling, "Esther? Amy? Anyone home?"

Suddenly, a thin voice called out, "Be gone, you friggin' blackguard, or I'll brain you one good!"

"Esther? Is that you?" Abel called out, perplexed.

Suddenly, an old woman crept out of the doorway to one of the bedrooms, a long black umbrella in her trembling, liver-spotted hand. "I don't know who you are, you thieving riffraff, but you'd best leave my house while you still can!" she spat in a hostile tone. The umbrella quivered as the old woman held it, and her eyes burned, yellow and crazed.

Abel Harris was appalled. Could this filthy old crone who stood trembling before him in a dirty nightgown, her greasy hair standing on end about her head, her skin like leather, be the Christian woman he had married twenty years previous? Sweet Jesus, what had become of her that she did not even recognize him?

"Esther—Esther, it's me," he said at last. "Abel Harris. Your husband."

At that, the woman's jaundiced eyes glowed with a light that could only be described as rabid. "You!" she shrieked, shaking in her fury. "You!" Then a vacant stare replaced the rage. "No, it can't be you. My husband, Abel Harris, is dead." Esther's laugh was a cackle of vengeful pleasure as she added triumphantly, "My Lord smite him with His sword . . ."

Abel swallowed hard again, revulsion creeping up his throat like bile. The woman was babbling like a lunatic! "Esther—where's our daughter?" he demanded, growing more distressed every second.

"Daughter?" Esther repeated, now staring back at him blankly.

"Yes. Amy Louise."

"Amy Louise!" the old woman shrieked, all at once springing back to life again. "Amy Louise! That whore!" The old woman took a step closer, her malevolent eyes shooting poison as she angrily studied Abel. "By God, it *is* you, Abel Harris! You fornicating old bastard!"

Harris shook his head in horror and disbelief. "Esther! For heaven's sake, get hold of yourself! And tell me where our daughter is!"

Esther's response was a shriek of cruel laughter. "Your daughter Amy Louise left with the brat you fathered on your last visit!" she hissed, her eyes bright with malice.

"Brat?" Abel repeated, looking stunned. "Esther, what are you saying—"

"Get out of here!" the woman suddenly screamed, stepping forward and wielding her umbrella, snarling doglike and baring brown-stained teeth at her husband.

Abel restrained a shudder at the vision steadily approaching him. "Esther, please, you must—you must let me explain—"

"Get out of here, you bastard, or I'll ram this through your stinking heart!" the old woman screeched, her eyes wild.

"Esther!" He could not believe the obscenities he heard spewing from his wife's mouth. "Please, you must—"

It was too late. The insane old woman lunged for her estranged husband, umbrella poised to strike. He quickly sidestepped her, then gasped aloud as she abruptly stopped in her tracks, a look of stunned pain on her face. She looked as if she'd just received a massive blow from a giant, unseen hand. With an awful cry of agony, she dropped the umbrella, grasped her chest, then fell in a heap at Abel's feet . . . .

When Matt Kendall and Jack Adams arrived at the Harris home in St. Louis late that afternoon, Matt was shocked when his old friend Abel Harris opened the door.

"Harris!" Matt exclaimed, smiling incredulously as he offered the older man his hand. "What are you doing here?"

Abel accepted the handshake with a sad smile. "Hello, Mathew. Good to see you. It's been far too long, son. As to what I'm doing here—well, I came here with the same purpose you must have, according to the neighbor lady. I'm here looking for my daughter, Amy—who I understand is now your wife."

Matt nodded, half smiling. "That she is." The smile faded as he added, "I take it she's not here, then?"

Harris shook his head regretfully and glanced with curiosity toward Matt's companion. Jack Adams stood off to the side, his arms akimbo, his expression shuttered beneath the brim of his black hat. Following the direction of Abel's gaze, Matt hastily explained, "Oh, sorry, Abel. This here's Jack Adams, an agent of Governor Woodson. Adams is hunting the James gang."

Abel laughed ruefully and shook Adams's hand as the bounty hunter stepped forward. "Excuse me for laughing, sir, but I do find meeting you rather ironic. You see, I've come to Missouri on an identical mission for the Pinkertons."

"Is that so?" Adams asked the older man with interest.

"Look, gentlemen, come in," Abel urged. "Mrs. Peterson is in the parlor straightening things up. Vida has told me some disturbing things this afternoon, which I think I should share with you. Aside from which—well, there's another matter I must fill you in on."

The three men trooped into the parlor, where Adams was introduced to Vida Peterson. Thankfully, Vida had made some order of the room and opened windows, and the stench in the house had abated considerably. Once everyone was seated, Harris announced, "The first thing I must tell you gentlemen is that when I arrived here earlier today, Amy, as well as my other daughter, Hannah—whom I never even knew I had—were gone. When I tried to question Esther regarding my children, she went into some kind of state, and . . ." Abel's voice trailed off and he shook his head helplessly, turning away.

Vida at once took up the slack. "Esther Harris is dead, gentlemen," the handsome widow woman announced bluntly. "It happened late this morning. Massive heart attack, according to the doctor."

Matt Kendall whistled. "Wish I could say I'm sorry," he stated flatly.

Glancing at Matt, Abel Harris nodded grimly. "From what Vida here has told me about the way Esther treated my girls, I must say, too, that her death was a blessing."

"I'm sorry about all this, folks," Jack Adams put in tersely from across the room, shifting uncomfortably in his chair. "But I do need to be about my business, and I fail to see what any of this has to do with the outlaws."

"Hold your horses a bit, Adams," Matt cautioned, giving the bounty hunter a quelling look. His conversation with Adams on the train coming out from Rolla had only confirmed his initial impression of the gunslinger as a cold-blooded killer who was concerned only with the gold he would ultimately collect for the James and Younger brothers. Now, Adams seemed to take the hint from Matt's threatening stare and leaned back in his chair, shrugging. Satisfied, Matt glanced from Harris to Vida. "Where's Amy gone? And what's this trouble concerning Hannah? My wife left me a note saying that the child was in some kind of danger."

She nodded somberly. "That's right, sir." Briefly, Vida explained to Matt why Amy had to come to St. Louis to rescue Hannah in the first place. The widow told the farmer of the letter she had written Amy regarding Hannah's peril. She then explained what Amy had later told her—that Lacy had taken Amy the letter and had later joined her on the train to St. Louis, against her will.

"Damnation!" Matt exclaimed when Vida had finished, his fists clenched. "You mean that scoundrel imposed his presence on my wife?"

"Yessir."

"Why that low-down, lying snake!" Recalling Garrett's falsehoods to Stan Murray, Matt was enraged about the peddler's latest bit of chicanery; but he was even more concerned about Amy and Hannah. "So that's why Amy had to leave Rolla." Matt glanced at Harris.

"I flew into a rage myself when Vida here told me what my wife did to that poor child," Abel added. Blinking back tears, he smiled bravely at Vida, who sat near him on the horsehair settee. A look of intense compassion passed between the couple. Matt noted this with a thoughtful smile. He was glad his old friend Abel had found a new and much needed friend on this very distressing day in his life.

After a moment, Matt asked Vida gently, "Where is Amy now?"

Vida Peterson turned to the worried young husband. "As I explained to Mr. Harris here, early this morning, before Abel arrived and before Esther's—er—death, Amy and Hannah left with Mr. Garrett, who promised to take the girls to the home of their father's cousin in Steelville." At Matt's menacing scowl, she went on scoldingly, "Now, they had to leave, sir. You see, minutes before they departed, Esther had threatened to go to the police to get Hannah returned. Your wife felt she and the child would be safe in Steelville until you could join her there."

"I see," Matt replied, still frowning. He could certainly comprehend the desperate state Amy must have been in when her mother threatened to go to the authorities to get Hannah back. He glanced at Vida. "Was Mrs. Harris successful in getting help from the police?"

She shook her head. "They never came, but an hour after your wife left, Esther came home looking mad as a wet hen. I thought I was hearing an earthquake when she slammed the door to this house. I guess the police saw through her crazed ravings."

"Too bad Amy didn't wait," Matt couldn't help but comment.

Vida saw the hurt expression on Matt's face turning to anger. She guessed he was thinking about Lacy Garrett. She added to Matt, "I believe that Amy asked Mr. Garrett to escort her and her sister so you would be able to straighten matters out with him when you caught up with them." Vida threw Matt a conspiratorial look.

Matt was confused by Amy's actions. She must have realized along the way that Garrett was an outlaw himself.

"Steelville . . ." Matt muttered. He again glanced at Harris. "Abel, can you take us there?"

Harris nodded. "Sure, son." He leaned tensely forward. "But I'm disturbed about something else. You see, Vida here also told me about the train from Rolla being robbed yesterday. Amy Louise told Vida that she and Garrett were passed up by the outlaws. It seems my daughter now suspects Garrett is linked in with these desperadoes."

"What?"

Vida quickly explained, "Your wife wanted me to tell you that she's going to try to gain more information from Mr. Garrett concerning his illegal activities. And she also suspects he's on the run from his troubles. She wants to find out Mr. Garrett's exact destination after he drops her and Hannah off at Steelville. I believe Amy intends to help clear your name back in Rolla, Mr. Kendall,'' Vida finished with some pride.

"Christ!'' Matt groaned, his head in his hands.

Meanwhile, Abel Harris shifted on the settee uneasily. "Mathew, do you think Garrett's hooked up with the outlaws again? Just remembering what he did during the war...'' Abel's voice trailed off, and he shook his head ominously.

Matt looked up at his old friend with fear and angry desperation in his eyes. "I think Garrett's up to his neck in it. All our troubles began in Rolla when he appeared. I'll lay odds he's planning to rejoin his cronies shortly, to collect his share of the take.''

"Oh, my gracious!'' Vida gasped. "That possibility never occurred to Amy Louise or me.''

"Oh?'' Matt asked. Abruptly, he banged his fist on the coffee table. "Damnation! Amy and Hannah could be in terrible danger, and they don't even know it. How can we be sure Garrett will take them to Steelville at all?''

"Oh, dear!'' Vida cried, now looking genuinely alarmed herself. "You don't think that Mr. Garrett would... I must say that he seemed quite concerned about getting Hannah safely away from here this morning.''

Matt laughed bitterly. "Lacy Garrett is concerned about *himself*, that and nothing more.''

"I agree,'' Abel Harris put in. "Gentlemen, I think we should ride south immediately.''

"Count me in, gents,'' added Jack Adams, lighting his smoke.

As Matt voiced his own concurrence with the plan, Abel turned to smile briefly at Vida Peterson. "Vida, I can't thank you enough for everything you've done today— helping me with Esther, with the house and all. I hate to ask this, but would you mind doing me one more favor?''

"Of course. You just name it, Abel,'' the widow replied, her dark eyes aglow with sincerity.

Abel nervously cleared his throat, then asked, "Would you see that my wife gets laid to rest proper-like? I mean, I already paid the undertaker for the burying when he came to fetch her. But maybe you could get aholt of the preacher, and—"

"Of course I'll do it, Abel," Vida replied, patting Harris's hand. "I'll take care of everything for you. What are neighbors for?" She glanced worriedly from Harris to Matt. "You men just take care now and bring Amy and Hannah back safely, you hear?"

"We'll do our best," Matt Kendall vowed.

Thirty-three

◆◆

By the time Matt, Abel and Jack Adams had bought horses and rifles and were preparing to leave St. Louis, Amy, Lacy and Hannah were well into the countryside south of the city. Lacy was driving the buggy at a reckless pace over the crude, twisting road. He wouldn't even stop to water the horse in the small villages of House Springs and Hillsboro that they passed through. By early afternoon, Amy could feel her very bones rattling as she and Hannah were jostled endlessly on the uncomfortable, thinly padded seat. Her nerves were rapidly fraying!

Convincing Hannah that they had to leave St. Louis had been frustrating for Amy, as well, since the child had been determined to remain in the city until her father arrived. "I don't want to miss Daddy. He should be here any time now," Hannah had argued, tears in her bright brown eyes. "And when he does come, Ma won't dare raise a hand against either of us."

Through laborious persuasion, Amy had finally gotten across to the child that they could not afford to wait until Abel Harris came home, since their mother had already gone to seek help from the police. When Vida promised Hannah that she'd direct Abel Harris straight on to Steelville the minute he arrived in St. Louis, Hannah finally relented.

Still, she kept up her worrying on the trip: "Amy, we're going so very far away. Daddy will never know where to find us!" "Don't be silly," Amy would admonish back. "It's Daddy's Cousin Josie we'll be staying with. Of course he'll know where to find us."

Yet inwardly, Amy was praying that everything would work out as she had planned. She disliked having to rely on Lacy to get Hannah and herself to Steelville; but at least this way, maybe she could glean some information from him regarding his connection to the outlaws, and perhaps learn of his exact destination in Texas. She hadn't really had an opportunity to interrogate Lacy yet; it was difficult enough just holding on during the bone-jolting ride. But she resolved to question him as soon as they took their first break, which they would have to do before long.

Amy turned her thoughts to Matt. Mulling over the events of the past couple of days, she reasoned to herself that her husband was probably all right. After all, the outlaws had been moving eastward to rob the train even as Matt was tracking them to the west. That would mean Matt wouldn't have run into any trouble with them.

Was he home yet? she wondered. She was sure he would leave for St. Louis the minute he found her note. Would that be today—tomorrow, perhaps? She was sure that once Matt arrived in St. Louis and received her messages from Vida, he would come tracking them immediately. With luck, Matt might even catch up with Lacy before he left for Texas.

And what of her father? Would he arrive in St. Louis soon, as well, and travel on to Steelville to see her and Hannah?

Amy still felt stunned by the news that her father was planning to return to his family after all these years. She was most anxious to see him, but she had still held some anger toward him, too. She knew her mother was a monster to live with. But why couldn't her father have come to rescue her and her sister earlier on, when they so desperately needed him? She felt she understood many of his reasons for leaving; yet his desertion had always remained difficult to accept . . . .

"Amy, are we ever going to stop?"

Hannah's fretful voice now cut into Amy's thoughts. Amy realized that they had, indeed, been pushing long enough without food or a break. Spotting a shady stream up ahead, nestled between rolling hills, Amy nudged Lacy and said, "Lacy, don't you think it's time for us to eat that lunch Mrs. Peterson packed? We're long overdue a break, and the horse really looks winded."

Lacy grudgingly grunted his assent, stopping the buggy beneath a lush flowering dogwood tree. As he unhitched the little black horse, Amy bit her lip, remembering that for all practical purposes, they were traveling with a stolen horse and buggy. Amy had begged Lacy to purchase the horse and conveyance from the stable where he'd rented them for the night back in the city, but her pleas had fallen on deaf ears. Horse thieves were not dealt with lightly in this state! At the moment, the possibility of being arrested for horse thievery was probably the least of Lacy's worries, she thought grimly.

The recklessness of their flight so far today bothered her. Amy knew Lacy must be on the run from the law, but now she had to acknowledge that he was behaving like a scared man. And a scared man could easily turn desperate or even dangerous, she reflected uneasily . . . .

Moments later, the three were sitting on a cloth beneath the shade of the sycamore and sweet gum trees that lined the sparkling stream, eating ham sandwiches and apples and sipping cool, delicious spring water. Amy's senses were soothed somewhat by the scent of cedar and blossoms on the air, the lulling rustle of thick, verdant foliage, and the buzz of black dragonflies diving at the stream. She glanced at Lacy, wolfing down his sandwich. "You girls hurry up, now!" he mumbled, his mouth full of food.

"Lacy, why do we have to rush so?" Amy asked, disappointed that she might lose this opportunity to ferret information from him. Forcing a smile, she added, "Tell me, where is it you're bound to in Texas?"

"Dunno," came the grumbled reply.

"You mean you're heading down there without any clear destination in mind?" she asked dubiously.

He shrugged, then gritted, "You're wasting time with this gab, woman. Eat your sandwich."

"Can't we at least enjoy our meal without inviting indigestion?" she asked in exasperation.

Next to Amy, Lacy shifted uncomfortably. "Actually, Amy, I've been meaning to tell you that we'll be meeting some friends of mine down near the Meramec River, later on today."

"Friends?" Amy's voice rose shrilly, and the skin at the back of her neck prickled. "What sort of friends?"

Lacy didn't immediately answer, taking a long sip of water from his tin cup, while Hannah whispered shyly at Amy's side, "Amy, may I be excused to walk through the trees yonder?"

"Of course, dear," Amy responded. "Just don't venture far away." Amy and Lacy waited tensely until Hannah's blue skirts disappeared through the lush spring greenery. Then Amy again demanded, "What sort of friends, Lacy?"

He sighed fiercely, unable to meet her eye. "Just some fellers I'm going to Texas with," he muttered. While Amy smothered a gasp at this alarming revelation, Lacy stood, brushing off his dark trousers. "I'd best hitch the horse back up. Eat your grub, girl. We got a lot of territory to cover before sundown."

Before he could depart, Amy sprang to her feet and grabbed his arm. "You're still going to take us to Steelville, aren't you?" she demanded.

"Sure—tomorrow," came Lacy's gruff reply as he disengaged Amy's fingers from his arm and walked off.

Amy and Lacy spoke little during the afternoon ride, but Amy fretted a lot about the "friends" up on ahead. She didn't like the dire possibilities her mind kept suggesting. Amy began to regret her hasty decision to leave with Lacy this morning. It had never occurred to her that he might not take her and Hannah straight on to Steelville. Amy was steadily losing control of the situation, she realized a little too late.

Amy's thoughts became increasingly distressed and fragmented as the three continued at their breakneck pace, bouncing over rocks and banging into ruts. Lacy turned a deaf ear to Amy's pleas that he show more mercy to the winded, straining little horse. Finally, toward sunset, Lacy did ease off on the reins a bit, letting the snorting, lathered beast catch his breath. When Amy glanced at Lacy quizzically, he loosened his cravat and announced nervously, "We'll be there soon."

"Will we?" she answered ungraciously, brushing a strand of hair from her eyes. She wondered why he was slowing down now that they were finally nearing the meeting place he'd been driving for, hell-for-leather, all day. It wasn't concern for the exhausted horse, she knew that much!

Yet as they started up a rocky rise, Lacy slowed the animal down even more, holding the coughing, faltering little gelding in very tight rein. From the other side of the rise, Amy could hear the sound of rushing water. She assumed they were approaching the Meramec River, which Lacy had mentioned earlier. As he halted their conveyance near the crest of the hillock, Amy turned to him and asked, "What's over the rise, Lacy?"

He glanced at her guiltily. "Amy, I want you to reconsider. I want you to promise me you'll come with me to Texas."

"Texas?" Hannah cried with dismay from Amy's side.

Lacy tilted his wide-brimmed hat back on his head and turned to the child, speaking with surprising patience. "Yes, Texas. I'm going there to homestead, just like I told your sister. You can come, too, if you want to, honey, or I'll take you on to Steelville. In any event, your sister belongs with me."

Before Amy could open her mouth to protest this arrogant assertion, Hannah retorted stoutly, "Amy does not belong to you! She's married to Matt!"

"The marriage is not working out," Lacy stated flatly. "And besides," he added with self-importance, "Amy was mine first."

"I was never yours," Amy snapped back.

At her words, Lacy cursed under his breath and yanked the brim of his hat downward to shutter angrily sparkling eyes. He made no further comment as he slapped the reins across the back of the quivering, sweaty horse, and yelled savagely, "Hee-ah!" The horse snorted, then stumbled forward; they crested the rise and started down the tricky, sandy grade of a riverbank. Amy tensed in her seat as she glimpsed the valley below them, where the Meramec cut a curving swath through the golden, dappled landscape. An encampment was sprawled beneath fluttering cottonwood trees along the riverbank, consisting of half a dozen horses, a large, rock-encircled campfire, and three military-style tents. Six scruffy-looking men milled about—one was stoking the fire, another cleaning rabbits, another brushing his horse, while the remaining three were out in the river bathing, their chests naked above the rushing water.

"Who are those men down there?" Hannah gasped from Amy's side.

"Are those the friends you spoke of meeting?" Amy in turn questioned Lacy.

He nodded but made no comment. "Hey, down there! Howdy!" he called down into the hollow.

Lacy's greeting was not graciously received. In fact, to Amy's horror, one of the men instantly sprang out of the river, stark naked, and grabbed his gun from a nearby tree stump. Pointing the long-barreled pistol threateningly at the newcomers, the man barked out, "Hold it right there, mister. Who air ya?"

By now, the horrified sisters were holding on to each other for dear life. Amy shielded Hannah's innocent eyes from the vulgar, frightening scene below them, afraid to look herself, yet afraid not to. Down in the hollow, the two men near the fire had abandoned their tasks and had joined the naked man, their own six-shooters pointing menacingly toward the buggy!

Meanwhile, Lacy had turned sheet white, pulling the horse to a halt as he called down tensely, "Charlie, please, keep your hat on! It's me—Garrett—and, er, I've womenfolk here, for Chrissakes!''

At this the naked man laughed, and all three men lowered their pistols. ''Well, bring 'em on down, Garrett—we sure as hell don't shy away from womenfolk!'' one of the men called up, hand cupped about his mouth as he added a bawdy-sounding hoot.

Amy's heart was thundering now, and she would just as soon have descended into a nest of hornets. Next to her, Hannah was holding on for dear life, digging holes in Amy's arm with her fingernails. ''Lacy, who *are* those men?'' Amy demanded of Lacy, but he merely ignored her question, clucking to the horse.

Thankfully, by the time they had descended to the encampment on the riverbank, the tall, black-haired man who had greeted them in the nude had stepped behind a rock to don his britches. Lacy stopped the buggy on the embankment and helped the two girls to the ground. They found themselves face to face with the three fearsome-looking characters who had greeted them a minute earlier at gunpoint, all of whom stared back implacably from fierce, jaded eyes in whiskered faces. Finally, the one who had been naked before, and now stood before them with furry chest and dark head dripping, asked Lacy, ''All right, Garrett, who are the women?''

Lacy wrapped an arm about Amy, and she was too frightened, especially for Hannah, to offer any resistance. As her heart pumped wildly and she fought dizziness, she thought unaccountably that the bare-chested man looked very familiar. Lacy had called him ''Charlie.'' Where had she heard that name before? she asked herself frantically.

In the meantime, Lacy chuckled to his friends and answered Charlie's question. ''Why this is my sweetheart—Amy. You know, the one I told you about,'' Lacy informed the men with a conspiratorial smile. He nodded toward Hannah. ''That there's baby sister.''

''Well—I guess it's all right, then,'' the man called Charlie replied, sweeping damp hair from his brow. ''They comin' with us to Texas?''

Amy opened her mouth to answer, but Lacy pinched her middle in warning and replied, "Yes."

While Hannah cast Amy an amazed glance at this statement, the tall, damp man smiled, obviously relieved. Amy fought a shudder as she noted how wickedly dark the man's eyes were. "Well—ain't that fine, then," he muttered to Lacy. Turning to nod at Amy, he added, "Sorry, ma'am, about greeting you folks in the altogether, but me and the boys have had a few close calls lately and I guess we're a bit quick on the trigger these days. Hope you'll accept my apology—and welcome to our camp."

"Thank you," Amy muttered frozenly. Who on earth was she talking to? she added to herself wildly. She inquired in as steady a voice as possible, "May I ask who I'm addressing?"

"Oh, sorry, ma'am," their self-appointed host replied with a crooked grin. "I'm Charlie Pitts and that there''—he nodded at a thin man with a squarish head and a mustache—"is my friend Bob Younger and this here''—he motioned at a dark-haired man on the other side of him—"is Mr. Frank James."

No wonder Charlie Pitts had looked so familiar—he was the very same desperado who had passed them up during the train robbery two days earlier!

Amy was terrified, and could have killed Lacy for subjecting her and Hannah to such peril. But she knew she'd best watch her every move in front of these characters. Before she could really even contemplate the full horrors of their situation, Charlie Pitts confirmed Amy's thoughts by remarking with a lopsided grin, "Actually, little lady, you and I already met up, I reckon. It was Jim and Bob and me that robbed the passenger car the other day, while the James brothers and Coleman Younger blew the safe."

Amy felt herself breaking out in a cold sweat at this bland assertion. She noted that Hannah, who was clinging to her other side, was staring at the strange men agog. She prayed her sister wouldn't blurt out something damning.

Meanwhile, Frank James moved closer to the two women. Amy noted that he was a clean-shaven man in his thirties with a wide, bluntly chiseled face, deeply set blue eyes, and overlarge ears. James smiled at the two girls, then reached out, took Amy's hand and bent over and kissed it. Amy restrained a shudder as the man said, "I must compliment Garrett on his excellent fortune in finding you, miss. 'All grace be in one woman,'" he finished, quoting eloquently.

Amy smiled frozenly at James, remembering with a rising sense of hysteria that she had read somewhere that Frank James was a Shakespearean scholar. Meanwhile, the other three members of the group sauntered up. One, who limped slightly, was a stout, thirtyish-looking man with a tobacco-stained goatee, the second an average-looking, slim man with a mustache, the third a more delicately boned man who seemed to have an eye affliction that made him continuously blink. Bob Younger casually informed Amy that those who had just joined them were Cole and Jim Younger and Jesse James.

At the mention of the name "Jesse James," Hannah gasped, her eyes growing huge. The child threw a hand over her young mouth as she stepped away from her sister to suspiciously study the motley crew assembled about them in a circle. "Are you Jesse James?" she demanded of the rapidly blinking man.

The younger James brother grinned engagingly. "Yes, little missy," he informed Hannah.

Hannah stoutly put her hands on her hips. "Well, you're in a heap of trouble, mister," the little girl scolded in an irate tone. "My daddy—"

"Gentlemen, would you excuse us, please?" Amy interrupted shrilly, grabbing the child's hand. "Hannah and I must make a trip into the woods."

At Amy's ill-bred announcement, the six men laughed uproariously. Meanwhile, Hannah glowered at her older sister, the little girl's face burning with mortification. Amy realized she had doubtless humiliated Hannah with her immodest outburst, but she simply had to get the girl off alone. Not waiting for permission from the men, Amy muttered to the child, "Come on, now," and started off briskly for the woods with Hannah in tow.

"Wait a minute, ladies."

Amy's spine crawled as she turned with Hannah to face Jesse James again. He was smiling, but with his eyelids fluttering so rapidly, it was hard to gauge his true feelings. "What did your daddy say about me?" James asked Hannah.

Hannah's young mouth was poised to reply, when Amy blurted out with a short laugh, "Oh, fiddle, Mr. James! Hannah was simply referring to the fact that our father has followed all of your exploits in the newspapers. We've all found your life so interesting and—er—entertaining," she finished, throwing James a cheerful, admiring smile.

Amy's bravado paid off, as the half-dozen men again succumbed to hearty laughter. "Feisty little piece you've got there, Garrett," she heard one of the Youngers compliment Lacy as he elbowed the peddler.

Amy left the men to rib Lacy and dragged Hannah into the woods. Once the two girls were securely sequestered in the center of a stand of shagbark hickories, Hannah cried, "Amy, what do you think you're doing? Lying to those men—shaming me in front of them and dragging me off—"

"Hannah, hush and listen to me!" Amy ordered in a hoarse whisper, grasping the child by the shoulders and staring down at her sternly. "I don't know what in blazes Lacy is up to, but he has exposed us to deadly danger."

The unflappable Hannah shook her head. "I'm not afraid of those bushwhackers. Daddy will come and—"

"Hannah, please!" Amy pleaded. "We mustn't depend on Daddy to rescue us—we don't even have any idea when he'll arrive in St. Louis. And above all, you must remember to mention nothing to these men about Daddy being a Pinkerton man. Do you understand? Nothing!"

"Oh, all right," the child said grudgingly, crossing her arms akimbo. "If you insist, Amy."

"I do. And another thing—we must pretend we're going to go with Lacy and the others to Texas."

"No!" Hannah cried, shaking off her sister's grasp.

"Honey, we must," Amy scolded. "Those men are not going to let us go on to Steelville, not now that they know we can identify them."

"But I don't want to go to Texas!" Hannah cried, her lower lip trembling and tears threatening to spill from her bright young eyes.

Amy hugged her sister to her bosom, straightening the brim of Hannah's calico sunbonnet. She spoke comfortingly. "I know, darling, and I promise we'll find a way to escape these outlaws—maybe tonight while they're sleeping, maybe in the morning. But in the meantime, you must promise me you'll play along just like I've asked—and say as little to the men as possible."

"All right, I promise," Hannah said in a quavering voice.

"Good girl. Now, let's get back before they come hunting for us."

"Don't know if we should give you a cut or not, Garrett, seein's how we did all the dirty work the other day," Jesse James said.

"I tipped you off about the gold shipment, didn't I?" Lacy protested. "Found out from the Rolla banker for you, and that should count for plenty."

The outlaws laughed and continued to divvy up their loot and pass the whiskey bottle around the fire. Amy, sitting across from Lacy near Frank James, was appalled at the scene before her, but kept her expression impassive. The group had finished dinner now—a simple meal of roasted rabbits, ash cake and hot coffee. Amy was thankful that Hannah had retired early to the tent the outlaws had generously assigned their guests. Watching three of the men grab at watches, chains and rings as two others divided the gold spilling out from white bags, she was fiercely grateful her naive young sister could not witness this scene. Amy would have retired early, too, but she wanted to find out as much about these men as possible and determine the best time for an escape for herself and Hannah.

Bob and Jim Younger were now arguing over a particularly stunning ruby brooch, and their brother Coleman laughingly suggested the two of them settle their dispute through a game of chance he'd heard of called Russian Roulette. As the balding Coleman explained to the others the intricacies of the life-and-death gamble, Amy cried out, "Oh, no, gentlemen, please don't! A shot would awaken my little sister." By the time Amy had realized what she'd said and threw a hand over her mouth in horror, the men had erupted into new gales of laughter.

At last, Frank James, whom Amy had come to recognize as the mediator of the group, settled the dispute over the piece of jewelry by flipping a coin. "As for Russian Roulette," he scolded the two Youngers, "how can you boys even consider parlaying so frivolously, when mere weeks ago you lost brother John following that skirmish with the Pinkertons near Monegaw Springs? 'A fool's bolt is soon shot,' " he finished wisely.

The others waved the ruminating Frank James off and hooted guffaws as Jim Younger eagerly pocketed the brooch he'd won. As the outlaws continued laughing and parceling out the loot, Amy turned to the elder James brother, who was reclining against a hickory log on the other side of her, nursing his own bottle of whiskey and showing little interest in the accounting procedures. She realized this might be her only chance to find out as much as she could about Lacy's actual role with the gang. "Mr. James?" she ventured.

"Yes?" He favored her with the mellow, rather crooked grin of a man who has imbibed heavily, and this gave Amy new courage. Frank James seemed the most approachable of the six desperadoes, and the fact that he was drinking tonight might mean he would let his guard slip somewhat, she mused.

After a moment, she asked him thoughtfully, "Would you mind telling me what you and the others are doing in this part of the state? And why you're all bound for Texas?"

"It's the Youngers who are bound for Texas," Frank corrected. "Coleman has a woman down there, Belle Starr, who's waitin' for him. But you're right—we all usually operate much closer to the Kansas border. That is, we did till a few weeks ago, when the Pinkerton men started smoking us out of the border towns."

Amy absorbed this information, grateful that James, half sotted and blithely assuming she was Lacy's woman, evidently trusted her with details of the gang's movements. She was also quite interested in the activities of the Pinkertons, especially after Hannah had told her that their father was now a member of the famous detective force. "So John Younger—the one you mentioned earlier—recently died following a skirmish with these Pinkerton men you keep referring to?" she questioned James.

"Yes, ma'am, but not before Coleman and Jim did in a couple of those slimy weasels."

Amy restrained a shudder at this new proof of the gang's violence, and she was assaulted by fears for her father's safety, as well—if indeed Abel Harris came tracking them from St. Louis. She pushed her anxieties to the back of her mind in order to continue her interrogation of James. "Then I take it you all have moved to this part of the state until things cool down out west?"

"That's about the size of it, ma'am," Frank drawled. "And the Youngers—all of us—need to garner a stake so we can lie low for a while."

"Then Lacy will be in with the Youngers when we settle in Texas?"

James looked perplexed, setting down his whiskey bottle and turning toward Amy with a frown. "Hasn't he told you about it?"

Amy immediately realized her error. "Yes, of course we've discussed our plans—but as for his work there . . . You know how reluctant men can be to talk about their work," she finished coyly.

James grinned, wondering to himself why Lacy didn't tell her. "Yes, ma'am, I understand." He nodded toward Lacy, who was scooping up his share of the currency, his greedy features silhouetted by the snappy flicker of the fire. "Garrett's been right good about supplying us with information—especially for the train robbery the other day; and he helped out mightily in Jeff City and the bank job in Rolla, too."

Amy flashed James a white-faced smile, and with a shrug the outlaw turned to throw another log on the fire.

Amy resisted asking James further questions. She sat quietly by the fire for a while and listened intently. She learned much about the dynamics of the outlaw group. She heard of their guerrilla beginnings back during the war—their anger at the "Free Staters," Kansas Jayhawkers who opposed slavery, and their rage at Ewing's Order No. 11, which left hundreds of pro-slavery families homeless in western Missouri. Jesse James spoke with pride of the 1864 raid on Centralia, Missouri, in which he and several other gang members had participated—in less than twenty-four hours, Anderson's guerrillas had killed upward of two hundred Union soldiers and had also robbed a train of three thousand dollars. The gang's exploits following the war went on and on—the bank robbed at Liberty, Missouri, the fair hit at Kansas City, the train stopped at Gads Hill. As the men spoke of additional recent skirmishes with Pinkerton agents in western Missouri, it became understandable to Amy why the gang members had long since worn out their welcome in the border communities. Now, the Youngers were going to Texas, and the James brothers were planning to join them there later after they sneaked back home to court women they hoped to marry. Jesse seemed particularly smitten with a cousin named Zee Mimms. Both James men knew that their courting must be carried out with the greatest care and secrecy, and that neither could risk pulling any jobs in western Missouri for the time being. As Frank articulately teased Jesse, "Caution is the order of the day, brother. 'Many a good hanging prevents a bad marriage.'"

After a while the talk grew increasingly bawdy, cigars were lit and the cards were pulled out for a few hands of poker. Amy excused herself, asking Lacy to escort her back to her tent. She could no longer contain the urge to confront him that had been building over the last several hours. Once they were out of earshot, beneath a tree in the moonlight, she turned to him and hissed, "Lacy, how could you do this to Hannah and me? You promised me you'd see my sister to safety!"

"I ain't endangered the girl," he asserted arrogantly. "Hell, she's safer here than she was with your ma."

"Why, you scoundrel! How dare you claim to be the least bit concerned for Hannah's safety after bringing her here!

And to think you accused Matt of all those terrible things, when all the time you were acting as informant for those outlaws and joining them in their robberies!''

Lacy's features were suddenly cold and implacable in the moonlight above her. He put his hand on Amy's shoulder and wavered toward her, his expression dark and brooding. She could tell he was tipsy. ''Amy, please, just come with me to Texas—you and Hannah—and I'll explain everything later.''

''You can go straight to hell!'' she hissed, shaking off his grasp.

''All right! Think what you will,'' he replied nastily. ''But you'd better not tell any of those men that you want to go to Steelville, or I won't be able to account for the consequences.''

''Aren't you even going to take us there?'' she cried.

''No,'' he said flatly. ''We're heading straight for the southern border tomorrow, away from dear Cousin Josie.''

''Why, you—''

''Think, Amy!'' Lacy ordered, gripping her shoulders again. ''I'm sure your father will be heading toward Steelville—tracking us—and so will your husband, once he talks to Mrs. Peterson. We can't take the risk of heading in that direction.''

Amy's mouth dropped open, and she seethed at this positive proof of Lacy's self-centeredness and betrayal. ''Good night, Lacy!'' she snapped, not trusting herself to say another word to him. Whirling and stamping off in the darkness, she found the flap to the tent and ducked inside, grateful when he didn't try to follow her. She heard him turn on his heel and go back toward the fire.

Amy checked on Hannah, noting that the child was sound asleep, then lay down herself, extremely distressed. To make matters worse, the tent was drafty and cold and the ground miserably hard, their only bedding a couple of tarps the outlaws had lent them. Amy hoped that Lacy would bed down with the other men tonight and not try to join her. He might try it, she realized grimly, rather than risk losing face to his bushwhacker friends. Well, if he was foolhardy enough to try to share her bed in this tent tonight, she'd claw his eyes out, that was for sure! Damn him! And damn her own stupidity for ever leaving St. Louis with him!

She supposed it had simply never occurred to her that Lacy would go so far as to put their lives in danger this way. Obviously nothing was sacred to that scoundrel, not even the welfare of an innocent child!

What a horrible fix Amy had gotten herself and Hannah in. She had wanted to help Matt, but she now realized her husband would doubtless want to horsewhip her when he learned she had recklessly waltzed right into a band of bushwhackers. How on earth could she get herself and Hannah to Steelville now, much less back to Matt? It seemed impossible, yet somehow, she had to get the two of them away from these desperadoes.

Amy realized that their only recourse would be to try to make a run for it in the buggy—though not while the men were still awake, of course. No, she'd best wait until first light—with all the drinking and caterwauling going on now, they would sleep heavily and late in the morning.

And she'd best rest now, too—if she could. She'd need her wits about her tomorrow.

On a hillside above the camp, three men whispered in the darkness, crouched behind the shelter of fragrant forsythia bushes. "Should we take 'em now?" Jack Adams asked Abel, nodding toward the camp in the hollow below. "Your daughters are in bed."

"Nope," Abel Harris said, "the men are too liquored up and wild—no telling what they'd do. We'll have to wait till first light, when they're still sleeping it off. Agreed, Mathew?"

"Agreed," came a third muffled voice.

"One more thing," Abel went on sternly to Adams. "Remember what I told you on the trail, man, what Kendall here has told you, too. My daughters are totally innocent of any involvement with these bushwhackers. One hair on their heads harmed tomorrow, and mister"—Harris paused to whistle low under his breath—"I'd rue to be in your britches."

The governor's agent laughed softly. "Don't worry, Harris, I've no desire to harm the child. As for your other daughter"— he glanced askance at Matt—"we'll see that she's safely returned to her loving husband's arms."

Matt glowered back at Adams, clutching the stock of his rifle in the darkness. He'd had a lot of time to think during the hard ride today. He now understood why Amy had to go to St. Louis in the first place, and that she'd later fled the city with Hannah's welfare in mind. She had even wanted to help clear his name. Yet he was frightened and furious that she had exposed herself and Hannah to such danger. And she was with Garrett! How could she have left St. Louis with that snake, knowing how fully determined the peddler was to break up their marriage? Were Amy's motives truly noble, or did she still secretly harbor some feelings for her fancy man? Fears of what that conniving bastard have tried to do with his wife since they left Rolla on the train were driving him insane!

The hellish question was, was it in him to understand, to forgive? First, of course, he must bring Garrett and the others to justice, and make damn sure that his wife and Hannah didn't get killed tomorrow. . . .

Thirty-four

⋈

Before first light the next morning, Amy awakened, still fully dressed, her stomach gripped by nausea. Her malaise was so intense that she could do no more than glance at Hannah to make sure the girl was all right before she stiffly stumbled out of the tent seeking the privacy of nearby shrubs to purge her queasiness. Amy felt weak, if somewhat relieved, afterward, as she again took refuge in the small tent she shared with Hannah. Sitting motionless on the unyielding ground, hoping to quiet her still-rumbling stomach, she wondered why she had become ill. It could have been the supper last night, she thought, which she was sure the outlaws had prepared under careless, impure conditions. Or, it could be ... With a sense of wonder, she realized that her monthly time was overdue. Could she be carrying Matt's child?

The idea filled her with a fierce joy. No matter what problems she and Matt had, the thought of carrying his child was awe-inspiring. To think that they could actually create a new life together! Somehow, she must get back to her husband, so that together they could resolve their problems.

With renewed determination she turned her thoughts to the immediate problem at hand. When the spasms of her stomach subsided at last, Amy attended her coiffure as best she could in the cramped quarters, looked at her rumpled dress with dismay, then again left the tent, this time to assess the situation in the outlaw encampment.

Outside, the landscape was still and lackluster, a gray mist hanging about the river beyond her to the west. The quiet was accentuated only by the melancholy cooing of a mourning dove. The uncharacteristic drabness of the morning seemed an ill portent to Amy and filled her with a sense of dread that was difficult to shake. Cautiously, she walked toward the campfire, which still glowed with the embers of last night's fire. Four men—Jesse James and the three Younger brothers—were sprawled about the circle of rocks, snoring contentedly, a sack of the now-divided loot near each man. Amy assumed that Lacy, Frank James and Charlie Pitts must be sleeping in the other two tents. Lacy had been wise enough not to try to join her last night, she mused bitterly.

Relieved that no one was yet stirring, Amy tiptoed toward the circle of cottonwood trees where the horses were tethered, whispering soothingly to the animals as they nickered at her approach. She untied the small black gelding and led the animal to Lacy's buggy nearby. Amy was quite unfamiliar with tack, but she had watched Matt hitch their buggy enough times that she was finally able to get the accommodating little animal harnessed to the conveyance. When she finished, she was dripping with sweat; and it was the dampness of fear rather than exertion. Nonetheless, she was driven by a single thought, that of getting herself, Hannah and perhaps a wondrous new life she might be carrying, to safety. To Steelville—and then to Matt.

Amy hurried back to the tent and shook Hannah awake. The child had also slept in her dress, since Amy had wisely left their bag in the buggy last night. "What is it, sister?" the little girl murmured, sitting up and wiping sand from her eyes.

"Get your shoes on, honey—we're leaving," Amy explained in a low, tense tone.

"Just the two of us?" Hannah asked hopefully.

"Just the two of us. Now, hurry!"

"Are we going to Matt?"

"Yes."

"Yippee! I can't wait!" the child cried.

"Shhhh!" Amy scolded, pressing her index finger over her sister's lips. She unwittingly smiled at Hannah's lusty exuberance. "Get ready, now, and pray, hush. We mustn't risk awakening anyone." She added ruefully, "I don't want to be denied the satisfaction of going to the nearest sheriff and turning in this pack of scoundrels!"

Moments later, the two girls cautiously ducked under the exterior canvas flap and ventured outdoors. Amy noted with relief that there were still no signs of life in the encampment, then quickly led Hannah toward the waiting conveyance. She was helping the child up into the buggy when she felt her arm being grabbed from behind—

Amy gasped and whirled to see Lacy Garrett standing next to her. He looked bleary-eyed, unshaven and angry, and was wearing only trousers, boots and suspenders. His pistol was tucked into his waist. "Amy, where the hell do you think you're going?" he demanded, his jaw quivering with fury.

"To Steelville," she snapped back, trying to shake away from his unwelcome grasp.

"The hell you are!" he raged.

She finally managed to fling off his determined fingers. Teeth clenched and eyes snapping, she challenged, "What are you going to do to stop us? Shoot us both?"

"Damn it, Amy!" Lacy glanced helplessly from Amy to Hannah, who had now scurried up onto the buggy seat and glowered down at him with a menace to match her older sister's. He groaned, gesturing in exasperated defeat to both girls. "All right, if it means so damn much to you, I'll take the two of you to Steelville. But we'd best get the hell out of here before the others awaken. Let me fetch my—"

All at once Lacy paused in midsentence, whirling to the east with eyes wild, only to gasp, "Jesus Christ!"

Three men with guns blazing were charging down the hillside toward them.

Earlier that morning, while Amy slept, Matt Kendall and his two companions were already awake up on their rise overlooking the encampment, closely scrutinizing the scene below. Unable to risk starting a campfire, the three men had breakfasted on jerky and biscuits. The matter of the girls, the possibility of exposing them to danger, still deeply troubled Matt and Abel. Matt's hopes surged when he saw Amy stirring before sunrise, readying the buggy before anyone else was up. "Looks like she and Hannah are going to try to make a break for it," he whispered to Harris with great relief. "Let's wait till they're out of range before we attack."

"Agreed," Abel answered.

"Maybe I should try to sneak down there and give them a hand," Matt added worriedly, watching Amy go back to her tent to fetch Hannah.

"Not worth the risk, Kendall," Jack Adams interjected tersely from Matt's other side as he checked his Winchester rifle for munitions, then snapped the stock shut with an ominous click. "You could waken the others down there and get both them girls killed."

The frustration of knowing Amy and Hannah had been in the midst of that nest of outlaws all night had been eating Matt alive. But Jack Adams was right. Only the fact that the girls had gone to bed alone had kept him from charging down there in a blind rage. Now, he drew a steadier breath as he watched his wife and Hannah leave the tent and head for the small clearing where the horse and buggy stood awaiting them.

Then, disastrously, the appearance of a third character in the drama seized Matt's attention. "Damn! Garrett's up, and—son of a bitch—now he's talking to Amy! Looks like maybe they're planning to leave together," Matt added through clenched teeth.

"Looks to me more like they're arguing," Jack Adams put in shrewdly, watching the faraway girl shake off Garrett's grasp. "I'm betting Garrett's caught your wife trying to hightail it, and now he'll waken the others."

"What are we going to do?" Matt asked his two companions, fists clenched with desperation.

"Time to ride, boys," Abel Harris decided hoarsely, his lined face ravaged with emotion.

"But Abel," Matt protested, "Amy's still down there—and Hannah, too."

Abel restrained the younger man with a firm hand on his shoulder. "Mathew, all we can do is make sure we don't fire at Amy, or at Hannah. But Adams here is right. Garrett may waken the others. And if that happens, your wife—my daughters—are up the creek, and you know it, son."

Matt nodded quickly and grimly. Then the three men scurried for their mounts . . . .

Seconds later, the sun was breaking on the eastern horizon as the three men on horseback charged down toward the outlaw encampment. The bandits responded with astonishing agility. Although Jim Younger was immediately hit by a bullet in the leg, the other three bolted to their feet and hurried for the cover of nearby trees, dragging the wounded man along. As the outlaws returned the fire of Matt and the two detectives, Frank James and Charlie Pitts ducked out of nearby tents, adding their fire to the exchange as they dashed over to join their cronies in the stand of hickories.

The three men charging down into the hollow at once halted their advance, dismounting and taking cover behind two large oak trees that stood about halfway down the hillside. They resolutely blasted away at the bandits. Matt noted that Amy and Hannah had taken refuge behind a cottonwood tree near the horses. Next to the girls, Lacy Garrett, also shielded behind a tree, was returning their fire. Matt hoarsely warned Harris and Adams not to fire in Garrett's direction and risk hurting the girls. The three concentrated their aim on the group of outlaws bunched together.

Several minutes of fiercely exchanged gunfire followed. Then Matt noted that one of the gang members was dashing through outlying trees and foliage, making for the area where the girls stood—the circle of trees where the horses were tethered. Once in the tree-shielded clearing, the balding man frantically began throwing blankets and saddles on the mounts.

On the hillside, Matt reloaded his Colt .45 and cursed to his companions, "Damn, they're going to make a run for it! There's no way I can pick off the one saddling the horses, and the others are sure to follow him!"

Cole Younger had already saddled two mounts and was frantically working on a third. "Garrett—come help me!" he barked to Lacy, who stood behind the next tree, firing back at Matt and the others.

Lacy scowled in indecision, then finally hunkered down, crouching as he navigated across the clearing to help Coleman saddle the horses. Meanwhile, Amy and Hannah still huddled behind a nearby tree. "It's Matt out there! I saw him, I did!" Hannah whispered to Amy excitedly. "He's come to rescue us! And one of the other men must be Daddy!"

"I'm sure he is," Amy replied, grimacing at the continual blast of gunfire that assaulted her ears. She tried to absorb the fact that her husband had indeed come after them. She had recognized Matt charging down the hillside, although the two men riding behind him had been obscure figures in the scant light. She prayed that Matt had not been harmed so far in the savage exchange, and that the outlaws would let her and Hannah remain behind, if and when the gang made a run for it.

The expected moment came all too soon. With all six horses saddled, Cole Younger whistled to the other gang members to join him. Frank James and Charlie Pitts came first, dragging along the wounded Jim Younger, while the remaining three outlaws covered the fleeing men by firing rapidly at their attackers. Once the first three had gotten to safety, the remaining trio of men made a break for the horses, firing shots over their shoulders as they ducked away. Noting this, Matt and his two companions immediately remounted and again charged down toward the hollow. "Don't shoot until the girls are out of range!" Matt yelled ferociously to the other two men as he whipped down the trail.

Meanwhile, near the cottonwoods, the six members of the

James gang had sprung into their saddles with lightning finesse. "Come on, Garrett!" Jesse James called down to Lacy, who still hung behind.

Lacy turned to Amy. "Come on. You and Hannah get in the buggy and let's go."

Amy shook her head adamantly. "Take the buggy and go, Lacy. We're staying."

"Amy, damn it, this is no time to argue—"

"We're staying!"

By now, five of the six outlaws had thundered off down the riverbank on their mounts, heading for a crossing downstream, and only Coleman Younger remained behind on his nervously stamping bay stallion. Rapidly firing his pistol to slow the advance of Matt and the others, Cole shouted impatiently to Lacy. "Come on, Garrett—leave the women." He extended his free hand. "You can ride behind me."

Lacy gave Amy an anguished, desperately pleading look. When she again shook her head firmly, he turned to Younger resignedly. "Go on, Cole. I'm staying with the girls."

Catching sight of the three attackers swiftly closing in, Coleman Younger shrugged, then spurred his horse and galloped off. Meanwhile, Amy was incredulous that Lacy had chosen to stay behind. "Lacy, don't be a fool!" she snapped to him. "Take the buggy and go!"

"Amy, I—"

Amy heard a loud pop; then Lacy's face turned curiously white. He dropped his gun and fell to the ground at her feet . . . .

For a moment, there was a deathly silence. In horror, Amy studied Lacy on the ground, a red stain spreading quickly across his white shirt. Barely restraining a horrified scream, she fell to her knees beside him. "Lacy! God, you're hit! Why did you do this? Why did you stay behind?"

She heard two men thud past her on horseback, then the blaze of their guns as they pursued the fleeing bandits down the riverbank. Yet she was oblivious to the hard crack of weapons. She hurriedly ripped a strip of linen from her petticoat and tried to staunch the flow of blood from Lacy's side. He was conscious, but ashen-faced, wearing the blank-ly staring expression of a man in shock.

Amy bit her lip as she studied the wounded man. He had almost gotten killed on her account, when he could just as easily have fled with the others. "You'll be all right," she told him with a conviction she wished she felt, grimacing as the blood from his wound seeped through the makeshift linen bandage. "It doesn't look like a bad wound," she added with bravado.

The next event that occurred was so sudden and unex-pected that Amy could barely absorb it. She heard a snap of a twig and Lacy glanced up sharply. He abruptly flung Amy aside, rolling away from her with a violent strength that she would have sworn he could not possess. Lacy grabbed his pistol from the ground nearby and was frantically cocking it when Matt Kendall suddenly flew into the small clearing. He landed squarely on Garrett, pinning the wounded man to the ground by his hand and pressing his pistol against Garrett's forehead.

Amy took a frantic half-second to assess the situation. Lacy was helplessly trapped by her husband. Never had Amy seen Matt in such a cold rage as he held Lacy powerless beneath him.

"Matt, no, don't kill him!" Amy screamed, scrambling toward the two men on bruised knees. Yet her husband seemed possessed of a demon, his eyes blinking rapidly, his features savagely etched in stone. He did not even seem to hear her words or sense her approach.

Frantically, Amy moved closer, grabbing the pistol from Lacy's weakened fingers. "Look, Matt! I've taken his pistol away from him, and he can't hurt you now!" she cried, hysteria lacing her voice as she beseeched her husband with wildly frightened eyes. "Matt, he's badly wounded! You can't just kill him like this!"

Still, Matt ignored his wife's pleas, staring murder at Lacy. Amy sobbed, wretchedly watching Matt's finger tighten on the trigger. Lacy looked up at Matt with the appalled expression of a man who knows he's about to die. Hannah, who had been watching the scene in horror from a nearby tree, mercifully rushed up. "Matt, please!" the child begged in a frantic, tear-filled voice, her trembling young hand on Matt's shoulder. "Don't hurt Lacy. He stayed behind to help us. Please, Matt!"

At that, finally, something broke in Matt's expression and he relented. He glanced up at the child, his face stark with emotion. He finally released his hold on Lacy, removing his gun from his enemy's forehead. As Lacy rolled away, gasping for his breath, Matt stood, staring at Hannah. Then that same impassive mask again gripped his features. He snatched Lacy's gun from Amy's fingers and moved away.

Amy watched Matt with her heart in her eyes. Her husband looked totally unreachable as he sat down on a nearby log, Lacy's pistol tucked in his waist, his own gun still in hand as he glowered at his wife and kept a fierce eye on Lacy. She realized Matt was much angrier than she had feared. He hadn't even asked if she and Hannah were all right. Her plea for Lacy's life was obviously more than his pride could endure. Yet didn't he realize that if he had killed Lacy under these circumstances, it would have been no better than murder?

Lacy moaned, and Amy returned her attention to the wounded man, realizing she would have to deal with Matt later. She took a moment to reassure Hannah, who was clinging to her side, teary-eyed, then sent the child off to fetch Lacy a drink of water, hoping the chore would distract the little girl. Moments later, as Amy finally got Lacy's bleeding stopped, and managed to get some water down him, Matt's two companions rode back into the encampment. "Damned if those varmints didn't give us the slip," she heard one of the men say in a strange voice Amy didn't recognize.

Amy stood and stared at the second man, a familiar stranger who stood off to the side, silhouetted by the rising sun. "Pa?" she ventured.

Abel Harris doffed his hat and hesitantly stepped forward. The tall, graying man stared at his eldest daughter with tears in his eyes, a muscle in his haggard cheek twitching with emotion. Amy began to move closer, and Hannah joined her, looking awed. "Pa, I'm Amy," the older girl began rather stiffly. "And this is your other daughter, Hannah—"

But the awkward moment ended as the little girl burst forward, flinging herself into Abel's arms. "Daddy! Daddy!"

Amy joined the two in a trembling embrace, and the reunited family huddled together, weeping.

Thirty-five

✦✦

Abel Harris and his two daughters stood embraced for what seemed like a long time, quietly communicating their feelings in the stillness. Finally, Abel drew back a bit and studied the girls with concern. In the rushed tension of arising earlier that morning, Hannah had never donned her bonnet. Harris poignantly observed the child's wispy, cropped-off hair. He swallowed hard, reaching out tentatively, seeking to touch the tender golden curls on his child's head. Then his trembling hand fell back to his side and he hoarsely asked, "Are you girls all right?"

"Yes, Pa," Amy replied, powerful emotions welling up inside her, too. "Hannah here has been dying to meet you," she added with a brave smile.

Hannah, who had been studying her father with awe, abruptly grinned and asked, "Are we going to help you track the outlaws, Daddy?"

Abel Harris chuckled but didn't comment. Then he somberly announced, "I'm afraid I've some bad news for you girls. Yesterday when I arrived in St. Louis, your ma—well, she took ill rather sudden like, and—I'm afraid she passed away."

A wave of conflicting emotions rushed Amy and Hannah. No sooner had they begun to absorb this information than a black-clothed stranger sauntered up, grinning, a sack of loot in each hand. "Girls, this is Jack Adams," Abel explained to his daughters as the gunslinger approached in a jingle of spurs and gold coins. "Mr. Adams is an agent of Governor Woodson. He's tracking the James and Younger brothers." Nodding at Adams, Abel inquired, "What you got there, Jack?"

The bounty hunter grinned, holding up the heavy bags. "Looks like them bushwhackers left behind the take from at least their last two robberies." Setting the loot against a nearby tree, Adams went on to Harris more seriously, "Abel, I hate to cut short your reunion with your girls, but we've got a prisoner over there to attend to—not to mention this here money to turn in."

At Adams's words, Amy quickly glanced at Lacy, who was propped against a tree stump beyond them, still being guarded by a glowering Matt. Jack Adams stepped closer to Abel, gesturing toward the wounded man. "The nearest sheriff would be over to Steelville. You want to come with me to turn that varmint in?"

Amy swallowed hard as Adams spoke, feeling sympathetic toward Lacy. Despite his many faults, in the end, she found the thought of him hanging brought no joy. She watched her father shake his head gravely, and Abel Harris replied, "Nope, I figure it's time for me to head back to St. Louis, Jack, make a home for my child here." He affectionately slipped an arm about Hannah's shoulders. "I'll write Mr. Pinkerton and tell him what's happened, but after that, I'm resigning."

"Hate to see you do that, Abel. You're a good tracker," Adams commented, rocking on his bootheels.

"A good tracker, but a poor father—something I intend to remedy," Abel said, looking down at his children with loving wonder.

Adams shrugged, then sauntered over to where Matt was sitting. "How 'bout you, Kendall? Want to help me escort Garrett here to the authorities?"

"I do," Matt replied stiffly. He stood, holstering his Colt

.45 as he faced the gunslinger coolly. "But first, you and me got a score to settle, Adams."

"Oh?" The bounty hunter's stance was typically insolent, and he looked quite unperturbed as Matt approached him wearing a menacing scowl.

The next thing Jack Adams knew, several minutes later, he was flat on his back on the ground, staring up at a pale sky and wincing as he stroked a very sore jaw. The gunslinger glared up at Matt. "What the hell was that for, Kendall?" he barked, sitting up and gasping for breath. He started to reach for his holstered gun, then thought better of the idea as he watched Matt's fingers move with deadly speed to his own pistol. Adams wisely drew his hand back and sourly repeated his query to Matt. "Mind telling me why you just busted my jaw, mister?"

Matt shook a fist at the bounty hunter. "That was for shooting at Garrett when I told you not to, you shit-brained idiot! You could have hit my wife or her sister!"

Surprisingly, the gunslinger smiled sheepishly as he struggled to his feet and dusted himself off. The smile brought in its wake a painful grimace, and again Adams stroked his jaw. "Damned if you don't pack a punch, Kendall!" he muttered, the words carrying a hint of admiration. "Hell—you're right—I apologize for my zeal. To your missus and the girl, too," he added with a lame glance toward Amy. Inclining his head toward Lacy, the hired gun again questioned Matt. "Now—you wanna come with me to turn him in or not?"

"It will be my pleasure," Matt gritted, turning away.

Adams strode over toward Lacy, who was still propped against the tree stump. "Well, Garrett, tell the authorities what you know about the James gang, and maybe you'll escape the hangman's noose," the agent advised. Then Adams glanced meaningfully at Amy and her sister. "I'm betting maybe these girls can give us a juicy morsel or two, too."

But the man's words were lost on Amy. She had eyes only for Matt as he strode over to his horse and pulled a length of rope from one of his saddlebags. She assumed he was planning to use the rope to tie Lacy's hands during the trip to Steelville. She realized that this might be her only chance to talk with her husband alone. Squaring her shoulders, she started toward him, her courage spurred somewhat by the fact that he had exploded at the gunslinger for putting her and Hannah in peril. She arrived at his side and addressed his tense, muscular back. "Matt, I've so much to explain—"

But he whirled on her then, his fiercely angry words cutting her off. "What the hell do you think you're doing out here, woman, almost getting your fool head blown off and dragging Hannah along!"

"Matt, I just wanted to—"

"I think you'd better go back to St. Louis with your daddy, Amy, and grow up!"

"You don't even want to listen to me!" she accused, hands on hips.

"Right," he snapped.

Shouldering past her coldly, giving her no further opportunity to respond, Matt stalked off toward Lacy, carrying the length of rope. Amy was enraged. She followed him, grabbing his arm. "If you think the worst of me already, I'll have a word with Lacy before you tie him up," she informed her husband spitefully.

Matt's features clenched in a terrible war of emotion. Then finally he snarled, "Be my guest."

Ignoring Matt as he stood glowering nearby, Amy knelt beside the wounded man. She sighed as he glanced up at her and attempted a sheepish smile. "Lacy, why did you stay behind with us just now?"

He shrugged, and the weak smile became a self-deprecating grin. "Guess I don't know how to give up—not when it comes to you, Amy."

She shook her head. "I—I have to thank you for—for trying to help us, Lacy," she finally managed. She added in an urgent whisper, "And now—please do what Jack Adams suggests. Tell the authorities what you know about the outlaws and save yourself."

But Lacy shook his head adamantly. "I'm not a squealer,

Amy. The James and Younger boys know that. They know they can depend on me." He smiled ruefully. "I have an idea my friends will bust me loose before the authorities manage to slip the noose around my neck."

Amy glanced at him, startled. "Honor among thieves?"

"Right."

The two lapsed into silence, Amy finding the whole situation ironic. Lacy's lies had done their damage in her marriage to Matt. She felt consumed by mixed feelings toward her former fiancé—her outrage at everything he'd done mingled with the knowledge that, at one time, he had been her only friend in this world. "Good-bye, Lacy," she finally told him, biting her lip. On her feet, she turned and saw Matt staring at her, his fists clenched at his sides. She gritted her teeth and said to her husband simply, "Please see that he gets to a doctor."

Not waiting for Matt's response, Amy tilted her head proudly and returned to where Hannah and her father were standing, even as Matt stalked over to tie Lacy's hands. Observing Matt's actions through the corner of her eye, Amy managed to tell her father stiffly, "If you don't mind, Pa, I'd like to go back with you and Hannah to St. Louis for—for now."

"Of course, daughter," Abel Harris replied. He cast Amy a half-dubious, half-sympathetic glance, but did not question her motives.

Harris and Adams decided that Lacy should be taken to Steelville on Abel Harris's horse, while Abel took his daughters to St. Louis in the horse-drawn buggy, which, Amy explained, had to be returned to the stable there. As everyone prepared to leave, Jack Adams approached Amy. "Miss, did the outlaws say anything to you about where they're heading?"

Amy sighed, glancing at Lacy, now in the distance mounted on a dappled gray horse, his hands tied in front of him. Matt was standing nearby, still guarding his prisoner. Amy wished Lacy were willing to supply the requested information to Adams, to further his own cause. Yet she knew Garrett would stubbornly keep his peace. To the agent, Amy finally said, "The ones called the Youngers are heading for Texas, I believe. Frank and Jesse James spoke of sneaking back home to Kearney to do some courting. Of course, they may all change their plans, after what just happened."

"That's possible, ma'am, but thanks for the information anyhow," Adams replied, tipping his black hat.

As Adams walked off, Amy noted that Matt and her father were now engaged in a conversation, both men standing near Lacy. When Adams mounted his horse, Matt shook hands with Amy's father, then turned to mount his own palomino. From the saddle, he stared at Amy for a moment, his face still an unyielding mask; then he grabbed the leads to Lacy's horse and rode off with Adams. Amy was barely able to contain her tears as she got into the buggy with her father and Hannah.

The small family headed north for St. Louis, following the rocky road Lacy and Amy had taken southward the previous day. Hannah was full of questions—asking her father where he'd been, what he'd done, during the last eleven years. He answered the little girl's questions as best he could until the exhausted child fell happily asleep, her head in Amy's lap.

At first, it was hard for Amy to know what to say to this virtual stranger who was her father. She was dying to know what he and Matt had been discussing a few minutes earlier, but she was afraid to brave that question just yet. Finally, she ventured, "It seems so strange to have you here, after all these years."

"Amy," he began, clearing his throat, "I've been wanting to explain—"

"Yes? You mean, you want to tell me why you left, why you never came back for me—or Hannah?" Amy couldn't contain the bitterness that crept into her tone.

Abel Harris nodded as he clucked to the horse. "I was wrong, girl, and I'm sorry. I shouldn't have run from my responsibilities that way. The guilt has haunted me ever since."

"Then why did you go?"

Abel cleared his throat noisily. "Amy, your ma had some peculiar notions about what was proper between a man and his wife." Awkwardly, Harris went on, "Being a married lady yourself now, I'm sure you understand about the—er—duties involved in a lawful marriage."

"Yes," Amy murmured demurely, staring at her lap.

"Well, your ma was—er—she denied . . ." Wretchedly, Harris cleared his throat again, then said forcefully, "There's only so much a man can stand, Amy, and that time when I came home on leave from the war, I guess you could say I reached my breaking point. I did some things that . . . I've regretted to this day. Afterward, I felt I had to leave." He turned to her with stark emotion in his deep-set brown eyes. "I couldn't take it no more—the taunts, the coldness, the out-and-out hatred . . . ."

"I see," Amy replied, and she did see much more than her father would ever know. She remembered the frightening night many years before when her parents had fought so bitterly, when Abel had ultimately carried Esther off to assert his husbandly rights by force. Being married herself now, Amy could much better understand the natural needs of a man—and her father's resulting, terrible frustration.

"One thing I've learned, though," Abel now went on, "is that violence solves nothing in life."

With an instinctive motion, Abel loosened his collar, and Amy noted a thin white scar near the base of his neck. A vivid image of a bloody knife in the kitchen sink leapt into her memory, and she realized with horror that Esther Harris had, indeed, tried to kill her husband with the butcher knife that fateful night when he came home on leave! Amy felt tears stinging her eyes as she understood at last why her father had fled their home eleven years before. He had surely feared for his life—and his sanity!

After a moment, Harris sadly informed his daughter, "Amy, I want you to know, as God is my witness, that I had no idea how sick Esther became after I left, the things she subjected you girls to over the years. As you may know, for some time I sent your mother money. But I never, all this time, received an answer to my letters." Swallowing hard, he glanced at Hannah with a father's adoration mingled with terrible guilt. "I didn't even know . . . about Hannah. And then when I came back to the house yesterday and saw Esther . . ." Harris's voice cracked, and he continued in a tortured tone, "I couldn't believe my eyes, Amy Louise. It was like staring at a wild animal. Your ma shrieked crazy, hurtful things to me . . . . Then she lunged at me, bloodlust in her eyes, and the next thing I knew, she was dead at my feet. To think I drove her to that! To think of all the hurt I've caused!" Harris shuddered, wiping tears with one hand.

Amy patted her father's heaving shoulders. "Pa, you must remember that Ma did it to herself."

The two lapsed into a thoughtful, poignant silence. The sun had now burned off all the fog of the early morning, and the road curved through a wide valley ablaze with wildflowers and alive with the humming of bees and the chirping of birds. The two watched a spotted fawn and its mother sprint away from a sparkling stream up ahead, where they had been drinking. After a moment, Abel remarked to Amy, "Now, young lady, tell me what's been going on between you and that husband of yours."

She sighed. "I don't know where to begin, Pa."

"We've all day, dear. It's a long drive back to St. Louis."

"You really want to know?"

"Yes, dear. If you're willing to tell me."

"Of course I am." Amy went back to the beginning, telling her father of Lacy's standing her up back in St. Louis, of meeting Matt and later marrying him, of moving to his farm. "We were starting to adjust, and things were going quite well for us until Lacy made his appearance in Rolla," she told her father. She explained how Lacy had come to the community and begun cruelly telling lies, stirring up trouble between her and Matt. "Matt has been acting strange, irrationally jealous, ever since—not that I can blame him, especially now that I know what Lacy was really up to."

Abel shook his head grimly. "It's no wonder Mathew's

been riled, considering what Garrett did to him during the war.''

Amy's eyes grew bright with realization. "That's right! You were there, too! Oh, Pa, you must tell me what happened between Lacy and Matt during the war! You see, Matt will tell me nothing.''

"A man has his pride, and I'm sure the pain is very deep for Mathew,'' Abel maintained in defense of Amy's absent husband. He added quickly, "But mind you, I'm not saying I approve of what he did this morning, riding off in a huff instead of settling things with you. Oh, no. I just want you to understand that sometimes a man has his reasons for keeping his peace on things.''

"I know that, Pa—but please, tell me whatever you remember,'' Amy begged. "This may be my only chance to understand my husband.''

"Certainly, then.'' Gathering his thoughts, Abel gazed off at the distant horizon, where dozing purple hills melded into a misty blue sky. "When I first knew your husband, he was a very angry young man. Mathew's pa and uncle had been killed by abolitionists, and his ma soon afterward died of a broken heart. Poor Matt was consumed by bloodlust—and just seventeen years old, he was. Anyhow, soon after Maizy Kendall died, Matt and I enlisted in the Confederate cause, along with Lacy Garrett. Later, all three of us hooked up with William Quantrill.''

"Yes! That's what I want to know about,'' Amy urged.

A muscle quivered in Abel's clenched jaw as he clucked to the small horse. "Well, Amy, I think it took all of us a while to realize that Quantrill was no more than a savage outlaw. The raid on Lawrence, Kansas, opened my eyes at last.'' Cautiously, Abel asked, "Are you sure you want to hear all of this?''

"Yes!''

He sighed heavily. "As you may know, during the raid at Lawrence, Quantrill's men killed over a hundred and fifty people, many of them civilians. That time, both Matt and I realized that the guerrillas were going too far. They were carrying out orders from Quantrill to kill all the males in town, including children.'' Harris took a raspy breath and continued brokenly. ''Then Matt saw one of the guerrillas with his gun against the head of a Kansas lady. Bless Mathew's heart, he charged in, trying to prevent a murder. I would have gone to his aid, but I was busy trying to help a small boy who was bleeding profusely from a bullet wound in his thigh. Anyway, the next thing I knew, I looked up and saw Lacy Garrett coldcock Matt with his pistol, so the murderer would not be thwarted. Then there was a gunshot, and the woman slipped to the ground, dead—right next to where Mathew lay, unconscious. Garrett and the other man''—Abel shook his head and added with eyes bitterly gleaming—''they just laughed.''

''Oh, my God!'' Amy gasped. ''How horrible!''

''Aye,'' her father concurred. ''Even Quantrill himself, barbarian that he was, didn't hold with killing women.''

''But—but Lacy told me he was the one who tried to stop the murder and rescue that woman, that Matt was the one who hit him over the head!''

Harris shook his head grimly. ''He lied to you, dear.''

''I agree—damn him!'' Amy concurred fiercely, her fists balled at her sides, all her earlier sympathetic feelings towards Lacy evaporating. ''But why would Lacy tell such vicious lies about Matt?''

Harris shook his head. ''I think Garrett was always jealous of Mathew, for having the strength of character he lacked. Can you imagine his outrage when he discovered his old rival had married his sweetheart?''

''Yes,'' Amy replied, a hard glint in her brown eyes. ''I think Lacy came to Rolla more to torment Matt than to gain revenge against me.''

''I agree,'' her father put in.

''Then Lacy was tied in with the outlaws all along?''

''Yes. During the war, he remained with Quantrill to the end, I'm assuming—though I can't say that with a certainty since Matt and I left the band right after the massacre at Lawrence.''

''Thank God for that!''

''Aye. Lawrence gave me my fill of violence. And I think

after all the things we saw that day, the taste of revenge became like bile in young Matt's mouth.''

Amy nodded, feeling new empathy for both her father and Matt. "Oh, Pa, all this time, I just never understood Matt, the pain he must have gone through. Then, when Lacy told his lies . . . I was such a fool. For a time, I even wondered whether Matt might indeed be somehow connected to the outlaws active in our area." Briefly, she related to her father how Matt had on several occasions refused to defend himself against Lacy's charges. She told of her terror at the town meeting. "Even then, when I realized Lacy must be lying, Matt stood there and refused to say one word in his own defense.''

Abel nodded grimly when Amy finished her account. 'There's no doubt your husband has been prideful, but I hope you can understand. After a man's been through what poor Matt has suffered . . . well, it's right hard to trust people again.''

Amy nodded, then took a deep breath and ventured, "Pa, what were you and Matt discussing before we left camp this morning?''

Harris sighed. "I've been meaning to tell you about that, but I feared it might make you angry.''

"Please tell me!" Amy urged.

"Well, Mathew told me he'll be coming on to St. Louis in a few days to fetch you home. He wanted to be sure you'd be cared for in the meantime." With a rueful smile, Harris added, "I wasn't sure you'd take kindly to that, seein's he gave you the cold shoulder this morning. I'm sure the boy seems brash to you at times, but his heart's in the right place. He just knows he needs time to cool down right now.''

"I understand—and I'm not angry," Amy replied, feeling relieved that Matt hadn't rejected her entirely. "When I think of what Matt must have felt when I begged him for Lacy's life this morning! Not that I regret what I did—I know I did right, and I'd do it again. But still, it must have galled him.''

Abel nodded solemnly, leaning over to place a callused

hand over his daughter's smooth one. "It may not seem entirely fair, daughter, but I think it would be good if you made the first move."

Amy nodded. "That's just what I was thinking, Pa, and don't care whether it's fair or not." Earnestly, she told her father, "Please, you must take me to Matt. How could ever have doubted him? He must be suffering so! There are so many things I must tell him—not the least of which is that I love him."

Abel smiled. "Aye, I was hoping you would say that girl. We'll turn west at once. We can't make Rolla tonight but we'll get there by midmorning tomorrow, I'm thinking."

Wisely, Harris added, "And I'm betting Mathew will coo off soon after he delivers Garrett to the authorities."

Abel uttered guttural commands to the horse and maneuvered the conveyance about to the west. Amy smiled serenely feeling totally at peace with her decision to return to Matt. If he didn't want her back just yet . . . well, she'd see about that! As she had just told her father, she could understand now, so very well, Matt's feelings of anger and betrayal even his storming off this morning. She would just have to tell him she understood now, tell him she loved him, and hope for the best.

Amy and her father spent the rest of the day catching up on the years they had been apart. Abel told Amy of the jobs he'd held with various railroads since the war, the near-continuous travel that had been required, and she began to realize how difficult it would have been for him to be a father to her and Hannah during those years. After a while Hannah awakened and joined in with a thousand new questions. Late in the day, they stopped to make camp in the vicinity of Meramec Ironworks, near a sparkling, tree-lined stream. Abel erected a lean-to for his girls, using a tarp stakes and rocks, while Amy gathered wild strawberries to augment a simple supper of beans and biscuits. Hannah flitted about happily, chasing butterflies and picking wildflowers. Everywhere, the sun gilded the landscape, dappling the bubbling waters and sending riotous light showers through the fluttering trees.

Toward sunset, after the three had shared a brief supper along the breezy bank of the stream and Hannah had fallen asleep, Amy noticed that her father was missing.

She found Abel downstream a bit, sitting on a large rock, weeping in the golden light of the fading day. "Pa, are you all right?" she asked.

He turned at his daughter's approach, his face ravaged with emotion as he held up a bouquet of wildflowers. "The dear child picked them for me," he choked. As Amy sat down beside her father on the rock and held his free hand, he gripped her fingers tightly and added disconsolately, "Oh, Amy Louise, if only I'd come a few weeks sooner. I never even knew—after I came home on leave that time—that there would be a child later on . . ."

"Oh, Pa." Amy lovingly embraced the man who was her father, and her own voice was ragged with emotion as she replied, "Hush, now. It's all right. No matter what happened, something very good came of it."

Thirty-six

⧉

*I*t was midmorning the next day when the buggy bearing Abel Harris and his two daughters at last approached the Kendall farm west of Rolla. As the small conveyance crested the rise overlooking the hollow where the farmhouse stood, Amy's pulses quickened. She straightened the brim on her gold silk bonnet with its elegant lace inner ruching, then looked with approval at the crisp yellow dimity frock she had worn, with its full skirt, fitted waist and eyelet-trimmed bodice and sleeves.

Amy had gone to extra pains to please Matt with her appearance today. At sunrise this morning, she and Hannah bathed in a bubbling spring near their camp, and her golden locks now cascaded from her bonnet to fall in lovely waves about her neck and shoulders. She had even located a pair of crocheted gloves in her portmanteau, and these she had festively tied to the drawstring of her small knitted reticule.

Across from Amy, sitting next to Abel, Hannah also looked lovely, wearing a fresh skirt and lace-trimmed white blouse, along with a colorful gingham bonnet. Abel wore his suit of clothes from yesterday—a dark jacket with matching trousers, white shirt with black string cravat, and brown rancher-style hat. Amy now caught her father's warm smile as they started down the slightly rutted road into the small valley. The house beyond them looked picturesque, the wind creaking the porch swing to and fro in unspoken welcome. The landscape was sun-dappled, dewy, the air heavy with the nectar of spring and alive with the sounds of chickens and cows. Everything looked much the same in the lush, enchanted hollow, Amy reflected. Yet what if Matt wasn't back from Steelville yet? she wondered uneasily. What if he was still angry and wouldn't let her stay?

Mercifully, Abel Harris had no sooner pulled the buggy up before the house than Matt came out on the porch, wearing denim trousers and a long-sleeved checked shirt. The instant Amy saw the anguish in her husband's dark eyes, her doubts and fears fled and she knew everything was going to be all right.

Awkwardly, Matt came down the steps and approached the conveyance, staring as if mesmerized at his splendidly attired wife, who was sitting on the side of the buggy facing him. "Good morning," he whispered to her, giving Amy a shy smile as he studied her in the lovely outfit.

"Good morning," she murmured back, daring to glance at him but afraid to return his smile as yet.

Matt awkwardly cleared his throat and addressed Amy's father. "Won't you folks come in?"

Abel Harris shook his head. "No, thanks, son. We're only here to drop Amy Louise off. Hannah and I must return to St. Louis at once."

At Harris's words, "drop Amy Louise off," Matt's glance became riveted to Amy, and their gazes became locked for a long, emotional moment. Matt's eyes were glazed, and he was reaching tentatively for his wife's hand, when young Hannah interjected fretfully, "Aren't we going to stay here at all, Daddy?"

"What if I promise to bring you here for a visit very soon?" Abel asked his younger daughter, giving the child a cajoling smile.

"Fine!" Hannah agreed.

Meanwhile, Matt helped Amy to the ground, and she felt

his fingers tremble as they gripped her slender waist. Having him touch her so intimately left her pulses surging, but as soon as her feet were firmly planted on the ground, he backed off stiffly.

As Matt went to pull Amy's bag from the boot of the buggy, Abel cleared his throat and announced, "Well, folks, Hannah and I will be on our way, then."

Matt set Amy's portmanteau down and turned back to address his old friend. "Won't you and Hannah come in for a glass of tea—anything?"

"Nossir, we all just had a late breakfast at the Grant Hotel back in Rolla," Harris informed Matt, smiling as he patted his stomach. "But before I go, tell me, son, did you and Adams get Garrett to the authorities all right yesterday?"

Matt nodded, avoiding Amy's gaze as he shifted from boot to boot. "Yes, sir. Garrett's in the jail at Steelville now. Jack Adams headed back for Jefferson City to notify the governor as soon as we took care of . . . our prisoner."

"Mighty good. Well, so long, son." Abel extended his hand to Matt.

Matt immediately and warmly accepted the handshake. "Thanks, sir—for everything you've done for me. And Amy and I want you two to come for a visit soon," he added, smiling at Hannah.

"You can count on it, Mathew," Abel replied. Gripping the reins, the older man regarded the young husband sternly for a moment, then nodded toward Amy. "You treat her right, son."

"Yes, sir," Matt replied soberly, swallowing hard.

Amy rushed forward, quickly kissing her sister and embracing her father. Then the conveyance rattled off with Hannah waving to the couple through her tears. After the small buggy had crested the rise, Amy and Matt stood staring at each other for a terrible, tortured moment. Then both of them spoke at once, each saying the other's name. They laughed at the awkwardness, then Amy urged, "Please—you first."

Matt moved a step closer, but did not touch his wife. She

could smell the fresh scent of him, she could see the dark torment in his face, and the tension of their apartness seemed unendurable to her. The wind ruffled his thick blond hair, and she longed to step forward and smooth down his errant locks—soothe away all his pain, too. But she didn't dare make a move, knowing so much had to be said between them first.

After a moment, Matt drew a ragged breath and blurted, "Amy, I'm sorry."

"Me, too," she replied.

"I'm so glad you've come!" he added in a burst.

"This is my home. You're my husband. Where else would I want to be?" she asked simply.

He took another step toward her and said earnestly, "Amy, I was going to come get you just as soon as I cooled down—honest I was. I was an idiot to say what I said yesterday morning. I was just so angry that you had exposed yourself and Hannah to such danger. And when I saw you with Garrett, I lost control, and I couldn't even trust myself around you."

"I didn't intend to run off with him, Matt," Amy told her husband, meeting his gaze steadily. "Not ever."

He swallowed hard. "I know that, love." A sheepish smile tugged at the corners of his handsome mouth. "In fact, on the way to Steelville yesterday, Garrett himself did a right good job of telling me what a jackass I've been—how you've gone to great lengths to set him straight about things being over between the two of you."

Amy nodded, and now she did step forward and touch her husband's sleeve. "Matt, I want you to know that when I tried to stop you from killing Lacy yesterday, it was because I knew what it would do to you."

"I know that, too, now." Spontaneously, they moved even closer together, both finding breathing rather difficult. "Let's go inside," Matt said huskily, picking up his wife's bag and slipping his free hand into hers.

They climbed the steps hand in hand and entered the house. While Amy hung her bonnet and reticule on a wall peg, Matt set down her portmanteau. Then together they went into the parlor. He stopped by a wing chair, politely waiting for her to choose a seat. Disappointed, she went to the settee. "Aren't you going to sit by me?"

He shook his head, his eyes reflecting the fierce turmoil within. "Amy, if I start touching you, I won't be able to stop."

She felt herself blushing from head to toe and caught a quick breath. "Would that be so terrible?" she whispered, her feelings stark in her eyes.

"We need to talk first," he replied in a none too steady voice.

"You're right," she agreed, lowering her eyes as they both sat down.

She heard Matt shift uneasily in his chair. Then he said abruptly, "It hurt that you went off with Garrett."

Amy glanced up quickly at her husband, stunned that Matt would reveal his inner feelings to her this way. "Matt, surely you know that I didn't leave Rolla with Lacy—at least, not willingly?"

"Yes. Mrs. Peterson told me how Garrett forced his presence on you on the train."

She nodded, then explained, "The morning after you left, Lacy brought out the letter from Mrs. Peterson telling me that Hannah was in danger. I knew I had to leave then—I had to think of Hannah, and I had no idea when you'd be back. Lacy offered to escort me to St. Louis, but I refused. Then later, he joined me on the train and I just couldn't shake him off. Anyway, I had to get to my sister."

Matt nodded soberly. "I know that, Amy. Don't you know I kicked myself a thousand times after I came home and found you gone? God, how I wished I hadn't been so stubborn and closemouthed all those months! And I should have been here to take you to St. Louis, too, instead of going off in a huff like I did." He gave her an anguished look. "Still, it was hard. Finding out you were with him...."

She glanced at him tentatively. "Are you still angry at me?"

"No," he said. "I understand now." With a menacing

scowl, he added, "Though I'm still not too happy that you took off to Steelville with Garrett. By then you knew he was probably hooked up with the outlaws."

"I know. But Matt, I had to get Hannah away from my mother, and I wanted to help you by finding out more about Lacy's activities—"

Matt cut in sternly, "You could have helped yourself and Hannah straight into the next life, woman, and I know you scared me half there!"

Amy fought a smile at her husband's endearingly irate countenance. "I'm sorry I scared you," she told him sincerely. "I guess I just didn't have time to think everything through back in St. Louis, with Mother running off to the police and all."

He frowned at her a moment, then said magnanimously, "Well, in that case, maybe I'll forgive you."

"You'd better!" she laughed.

A silence settled between them, then Amy ventured more seriously, "Matt, Daddy told me what happened between you and Lacy during the war. Why didn't you tell me before?"

He shook his head. "Too hurt and too proud, I reckon," he replied. He continued in an anguished tone, "You must understand, love. Those were the worst days of my life. Back when the war began, when I lost my uncle and my parents—well, something died inside me, too. I seemed to lose everything, even the faith of my childhood." He glanced at her searchingly and the hurt gripping his features touched her deeply. "Do you know that the preacher man came to our home and told me it was God's will that I lost my folks and my uncle?"

"How terrible!" Amy gasped. "How old were you then, Matt?"

"Seventeen. And I knocked that sanctimonious prig on his heels, too," he added through clenched teeth.

"Oh, Matt!" Amy conjured an image of a bitterly vengeful seventeen-year-old boy, a young man who had lost almost everything in the world that he held dear. And then to have a pious clergyman blandly assure him that it was all God's will . . . ! "No wonder you've always resented the reverend so much," she murmured, thinking out loud.

He laughed shortly and cast her an amazed glance. "I never thought of it that way, love, but I'm sure you're right."

"So after your folks died, you enlisted in the Confederate cause?" she pursued.

"Yes. All I wanted to do was to kill the Unionists who were responsible for the deaths of my loved ones."

"Then later, you, Lacy and my father joined up with Quantrill's Raiders?"

His nod was a half-shudder. "It seemed to help for a time, the violence I committed with the guerrillas—burning homesteads, raiding border communities. But then Quantrill took bloodlust too far." Matt looked at his wife, a world of turbulent feeling in his eyes. "Sometimes, Amy, the memories of those days still haunt me. I never murdered anyone in cold blood like some did, but I did some things that shame me even now."

"But you left the guerrilla band when you realized what they were really about," she pointed out. "My father told me all about it."

"Yes, Abel and I both left Quantrill after Lawrence, Kansas. Thank God your father was there to help bring me to my senses before I went beyond redemption."

Amy leaned forward on the settee, daring at last to broach a very sensitive subject. "It must have killed you, what Lacy did, knocking you out during the massacre at Lawrence and assisting in a murder. Then later on, when he came to Rolla, when you thought that he and I . . ."

Matt nodded mutely, and another silence stretched between them. "It was hell," he finally conceded, the words ragged with his pain.

"Then you must have known all along that Lacy was still hooked up with the outlaws!" she cried.

"Yes, I did."

Amy shook her head incredulously. "Why didn't you tell the authorities?"

He shrugged. "I had no real proof of Garrett's involvement. And besides, why would the authorities have believed me? You see, I did move most of my money to a St. Louis bank, because I was sure sooner or later the gang would hit Rolla. But I never realized my actions would make it look like I was involved, too. So what could I say to anyone? Lacy was liked in town—I wasn't."

"That's only because you wouldn't let people get to know you," Amy pointed out. "You wouldn't even let *me* get to know you."

"I guess I wanted you to trust me, no questions asked."

"Matt, I did want to trust you! But you made it so hard sometimes, when you wouldn't talk to me, when you were so angry, so locked up in yourself . . ."

He nodded. "I know. I'm sorry." Contritely, he added, "I was just so jealous—so scared I was going to lose you, especially after Garrett showed up."

Again his honesty warmed her. She looked at him with love in her eyes, and all at once none of it seemed to matter. "Matt, you had no reason to be jealous. And—I'm never going to leave you."

He smiled, and she could tell he was quite moved by her words. Then a shadow crossed his dark eyes. "There's something I must know."

"Yes?"

He gave her a stark look, and his voice was hoarse as he asked, "Did you love him?"

Amy took a long, steadying breath and considered her next words very carefully. "At one time I thought I did," she finally admitted. Watching his jaw tighten, she quickly added, "But love is—well, it's more than candy and flowers. It's really caring, it's being there for someone else." She shook her head. "Lacy was like a tumbleweed. He never was really there for me. I guess I thought I loved him once because I just didn't know any better." She cleared her throat and went on in an emotional voice, "But as soon as I met you, Matt, I realized you had all the strengths I wanted in a man, all the qualities Lacy lacked. I knew then that what I'd felt for Lacy was only a childish emotion. It didn't take me long after I met you to realize that—that I loved you." She looked at him through her tears. "And I still love you, Matt. I always will."

His eyes lit with incredulous joy. "You can say that after all I've put you through?"

"I think I could have said it almost from the first moment I met you."

"Oh, Amy." He was half out of his chair. "I've loved you, too, from that moment on . . . ."

Simultaneously, they were both on their feet and hurrying across the room. The distance between them was closed at last, and they embraced, in tears. Matt gripped Amy almost violently in his strong arms, kissing her as if he'd never taste enough of her, and she returned his kiss with equal feeling. When at last their lips parted, he wiped her tears with his fingertips and breathed, "Oh, darling, I've missed you so."

"Me, too," she whispered.

He clamped his mouth on hers ravenously now, his tongue penetrating, hot and searching, into her mouth, his powerful body trembling with the force of his need. His hand reached for her breast, caressing the supple flesh through the fabric of her dress and chemise. He groaned deep in his throat, his impatient fingers slipping inside her boat-shaped bodice. She gasped with wonder and desire as his fingertips kneaded a taut, aching nipple. Amy could feel his manhood grow hard against the front of her, and it produced an answering ache deep within the womanly core of her.

They were at once consumed with hunger for each other. At first, Amy thought Matt would take her right there in the parlor, his desire was so urgent and intense. Then he said gruffly, "No, you're my wife, you belong in my bed. I'm going to welcome you home good and proper, Mrs. Kendall. It's been much too long."

"I know. For me, too," she whispered.

Matt lifted her up into his strong arms and carried her up the stairs, his eyes never leaving her flushed, passionate face. Upstairs in his bedroom, they undressed each other impatiently, both unashamed, both feverish with need. At last they stood naked together in the golden light spilling through the curtains, Amy's body taut and burning, Matt's desire proudly displayed. Matt took a long moment to peruse Amy's beautiful womanly curves with passion-darkened eyes, and she thought she would die if he didn't embrace her, take her. At last he drew her down with him on the soft bed, tenderly kneading a painfully taut nipple with his fingertips. Kissing her, he pressed his rigid manhood insistently between her thighs and said huskily, "I want to have a baby with you."

She blushed, his words reminding her of her nausea the previous morning. "Matt, I think . . . I mean, yesterday, I awakened with the queerest feeling. Perhaps I'm already, I mean—"

He chuckled deep in his throat. "Splendid, love." He drew back slightly, caressing her face with his strong, rough hand. "But we'll want to keep trying—just to make sure, now won't we?"

"Oh, yes," she breathed, hooking an arm around his neck and pulling his lips down to hers.

For long, sensual moments, they kissed, their tongues mingling freely. Then Matt turned his attention to Amy's breasts, his mouth sucking and pulling on the nipples, his teeth cutting just enough to drive her insane, until she beat on his back with frustrated desire. He smiled down at her triumphantly, more determined than ever to torment her, his lips sliding inexorably down her warm, soft stomach, trailing hot fire. When his mouth found the bud of her passion, his tongue teased her endlessly, until the entire realm of her femininity throbbed with unendurable longing and she begged him to take her, tears in her voice. Yet still he continued the sweet torture. Finally, desperately, she pushed him away and reached for his manhood, stroking it in wanton welcome. His response was immediate and violent. He pulled her beneath him and parted her thighs, wrapping her long legs securely about his waist. By now, he was totally engorged with desire, and his deep, ravishing plunge left her breathlessly crying out. He stiffened momentarily, and she quickly reassured him. "It's all right. Please, love me just as you will . . . ."

"Oh, Amy!" Above her, Matt wanted to be gentle, but her words of encouragement had driven him wild. He withdrew and surged into her powerfully again, and this time she gasped with delight and arched upward to receive him. Her warmth felt wonderful about him, tight yet liquid and yielding, and he wanted to dive all the way inside her, never to be found again. He slipped his hands beneath her and tilted her into his powerful possession, and she met him fully, without holding back. He rode her freely and fiercely, all the while feeling her move with him, grip him, urge him even deeper. Their movements reached a fever pitch. Then he felt the convulsive beginnings of her climax, as she tossed her head from side to side, biting her lip to keep from moaning aloud. "Cry out, Amy," he urged. "I want to hear—feel—everything you're feeling . . ."

She clutched him to her and moaned her ecstasy, even as he, too, lost control, pounding out a tumultuous climax and coming to rest deeply inside her.

Afterward, both were left trembling and panting, covered with a fine sheen of sweat. Matt slowly withdrew from Amy's flesh and sat up against the headboard, drawing her into his lap. For a long, soul-shattering moment he simply kissed her, his tongue rotating in slow, sensuous circles inside her mouth. She kissed him back, tears of exquisite release falling freely down her face. She throbbed with the wonderful memory of his total possession; she felt bathed with his love, satiated.

"Are you all right?" he asked raggedly after a moment.

She looked up at him with eyes shining with devotion. "Matt, I want to feel everything you're feeling—until I drive all those demons from your mind forever."

"And then?" Now his eyes gleamed strangely, too.

"I'll want even more."

His arms clenched possessively about her and he rained her face with soft kisses. "From this moment on, darling, all my memories will be of you. And I know there must be a good Lord smiling up in the heavens now, watching over us, or I never would have been granted the miracle of your healing love.''

And they worshiped that miracle until the sun was low in the sky.

About the Author

Eugenia Riley is also the author of LAUREL'S LOVE, published by Warner Books. A native Texan, she lives in Houston with her husband and two daughters.

The author welcomes mail from her readers. Please write to Eugenia Riley, P.O. Box 840526, Houston, Texas 77284-0526.